Praise for the Novels of Avalon

Marion Zimmer Bradley's Ravens of Avalon

"Marion Zimmer Bradley would be proud of this. . . . The story line smoothly combines ancient history with fantasy elements to please fans. . . . Readers of the delightful Avalon series will appreciate learning what occurred that led to the formation of the Society of the Ravens."
—*Midwest Book Review*

"Based on the wishes of the late author of *The Mists of Avalon*, fantasy veteran Diana L. Paxson's latest addition to the Avalon story cycle brings to life the tale of the legendary queen who defied the greatest power in the ancient world. Solid storytelling and memorable characters add to the appeal of this smooth blend of ancient history, fable, and magic."
—*Library Journal*

"This stirring prequel to *The Forest House* . . . is sure to please fans of the late author of *The Mists of Avalon*."
—*Publishers Weekly*

Marion Zimmer Bradley's Ancestors of Avalon

"Magical. . . . [*The Mists of Avalon*] devotees won't feel let down by *Ancestors*. . . . Provides plenty of pleasurable reading hours."
—*Fort Worth Star-Telegram*

"An elegant stylist, Paxson captures the awe, tragedy, and resounding mystery of ancient Britain and mist-enshrouded Atlantis."
—*Publishers Weekly*

continued . . .

"Paxson fashions an entirely new entry in the Avalon saga. . . . [Her] storytelling features the requisite veins of mysticism, but, like Bradley, she excels at bringing the vast sweep of imagined history to an accessible level. . . . A rich and respectful homage that will dazzle readers longing to revisit Bradley's sacred, storied isle."   —*Booklist*

"Once again, Diana L. Paxson has beautifully elaborated on Marion Zimmer Bradley's beloved Avalon saga with this dramatic new installment . . . an extraordinary journey."
—*SFRevu*

"Paxson is an excellent choice as successor to Bradley for this series. Her style and the details of the plot retain the sense of the mysterious past and the feminist awareness that was an underlying theme in the originals."
—*Chronicle*

"*Ancestors of Avalon* may be the best of the Avalon tales. The story line stands alone due to the strength of the characterizations . . . yet also interconnects the myriad plots from the previously published books."
—*Midwest Book Review*

Priestess of Avalon

"[*Priestess of Avalon*] is a strange and wondrous story that no fan of the previous Avalon books should be without."
—*SF Site*

"*Priestess of Avalon* does a stunning job of recapturing the legendary power of the original. . . . [It] brings rich imagery to its prophetic scenes."   —*The Green Man Review*

"The story flourishes and comes to life. . . . [Bradley's] fans will not want to miss it."   —*VOYA*

"The message that all religions call on the same higher power should go over well with fans of *Mists [of Avalon]*. Paxson's own skill at bringing historical characters and places to vivid life enriches Helena's story."
—*Publishers Weekly*

"Stunning . . . this rich and moving novel merits its place beside Bradley's fantasy classic." —*Booklist*

"A guilty pleasure for history buffs, and a sure hit for the goddess crowd." —*Kirkus Reviews*

"Bradley creates a powerful tale of magic and faith that enlarges upon pagan and Christian traditions to express a deeper truth." —*Library Journal*

Lady of Avalon
The National Bestseller

"Combines romance, rich historical detail, magical dazzlements, grand adventure, and feminist sentiments into the kind of novel her fans have been yearning for." —*Publishers Weekly* (starred review)

"Compelling, powerful." —*San Francisco Chronicle*

"The prose is as smooth as those sacred stones on which so many interesting things take place." —*Kirkus Reviews*

"Bradley's women are, as usual, strong and vibrant, but never before has she so effectively depicted the heroic male. . . . An immensely popular saga." —*Booklist*

The Forest House

"The setting evokes a fascinating time of change. . . . The mythic elements grow to hint satisfactorily at the Arthurian wonder to come. . . . The stuff of legend." —*Locus*

"A seamless weave of history and myth." —*Library Journal*

"The sure touch of one at ease in sketching out mystic travels." —*Kirkus Reviews*

Other books in this series

Marion Zimmer Bradley's Ancestors of Avalon
Priestess of Avalon
Lady of Avalon
The Forest House
The Mists of Avalon

MARION ZIMMER BRADLEY'S

RAVENS OF
AVALON

Diana L. Paxson

A ROC BOOK

ROC
Published by New American Library, a division of
Penguin Group (USA) Inc., 375 Hudson Street,
New York, New York 10014, USA
Penguin Group (Canada), 90 Eglinton Avenue East, Suite 700, Toronto,
Ontario M4P 2Y3, Canada (a division of Pearson Penguin Canada Inc.)
Penguin Books Ltd., 80 Strand, London WC2R 0RL, England
Penguin Ireland, 25 St. Stephen's Green, Dublin 2,
Ireland (a division of Penguin Books Ltd.)
Penguin Group (Australia), 250 Camberwell Road, Camberwell, Victoria 3124,
Australia (a division of Pearson Australia Group Pty. Ltd.)
Penguin Books India Pvt. Ltd., 11 Community Centre, Panchsheel Park,
New Delhi - 110 017, India
Penguin Group (NZ), 67 Apollo Drive, Rosedale, North Shore 0632,
New Zealand (a division of Pearson New Zealand Ltd.)
Penguin Books (South Africa) (Pty.) Ltd., 24 Sturdee Avenue,
Rosebank, Johannesburg 2196, South Africa

Penguin Books Ltd., Registered Offices:
80 Strand, London WC2R 0RL, England

Published by Roc, an imprint of New American Library, a division of Penguin
Group (USA) Inc. Previously published in Viking hardcover and Roc trade
paperback editions.

First Roc Mass Market Printing, September 2009
10 9 8 7 6 5 4 3 2 1

To Sarah Rachel,
who fought long and hard . . .

NAMES IN THE STORY

CAPITALS = major character

+ = historical figure

(   ) = dead before story begins

[   ] = ALTERNATE OR LATER FORM OF NAME

PEOPLE

BRITONS

(Note: Most of these names are attested from written documents of the period; however, I have left the British nominative ending "os" on some but not on others to provide variety and lessen confusion for the reader.)

+Adminios—middle son of Cunobelin, exiled king of the Cantiaci

Anaveistl—mother of Boudica

Antebrogios—Durotrige chieftain defending the Hill of Stones

+Antedios—High King of the Iceni

Argantilla—Boudica's younger daughter

Aurodil—an Iceni maiden

Beric—son of Segovax, a young warrior in the rebellion

Bethoc—an old woman from a fishing village on Mona

Bituitos—bodyguard to Prasutagos

+Bodovoc—king of the Northern Dobunni, subject to Togodumnos

+BOUDICA—daughter of Dubrac, later wife of Prasutagos and queen of the Iceni

Bracios [Braci]—Boudica's youngest brother

Brocagnos—an Iceni farmer

Calgac—a warrior in Boudica's service

+CARATAC [Caratacus]—third son of Cunobelin, king of the Cantiaci and leader of the fight against Rome

+Cartimandua—queen of the Brigantes

Carvilios—a warrior in the rebellion

Caw—a freedman in the service of Boudica's daughters

Cingetor—king of the Silures

+Cogidubnos—grandson of Verica, later, king of the Atrebates and Regni

+Corio—king of the Southern Dobunni

Crispus—a Gaulish freedman in Boudica's service

(+Cunobelin [Cunobelinos])—king of the Trinovantes and Catuvellauni, overlord of southeast Britannia)

Drostac of Ash Hill—a chieftain of the Iceni

Dubnocoveros—eldest son of Dubrac and brother of Boudica

Dubrac—father of Boudica, a prince of the Southern Iceni

Eoc Mor—bodyguard to Prasutagos

Epilios—youngest son of Cunobelin, foster brother of Braci

+Esico—goldsmith minting coins for Prasutagos

Kitto—the son of a farmer near Manduessedum

Leucu—an Iceni warrior in the service of Dubrac

Maglorios—overking of the Belgae

Mandos—an Iceni warrior

Morigenos—an Iceni clan chieftain

Nessa—an old servant in Boudica's family

Palos—owner of the farm near the Horse Shrine, husband of Shanda

+PRASUTAGOS—son of Domarotagos, High King of the Iceni, Boudica's husband

Rigana—Boudica's older daughter

Rosic—a farmer near Eponadunon, father of Temella

Segovax—an Iceni clan leader

Shanda—wife of Palos, of the farm near the Horse Shrine

Tabanus—a Trinovante slave in Colonia

Tancoric—king of the Durotriges

Tascio—son of Segovax, a young warrior in the rebellion

Taximagulos—an Iceni farmer

Temella—Boudica's maid

Tingetorix—a war leader in the rebellion

+Togodumnos—son of Cunobelin, king of the Trinovantes and Catuvellauni

+Venutios—king of the Brigantes

+Veric [Verica]—king of the Atrebates expelled by Caratac

DRUIDS

Albi—a boy in training with the Druids

Ambios—Druid attached to the household of King Caratac

ARDANOS—a Druid priest

Belina—a niece of Cunobelin and a priestess

Bendeigid—a Cornovian boy in training with the Druids, later husband of Rheis

Brangenos—a Druid bard from Gallia

Brenna—a Brigante girl in training with the Druids

Brigomaglos—a Durotrige Druid

Caillean—an Irish girl fostered by Lhiannon

(Catuera—a legendary priestess)

Cloto [Lucius Cloto]—an Atrebate boy in training with the Druids

Coventa—a Brigante girl in training with the Druids, later a priestess

Cunitor—a Druid priest

Elin—an old priestess

Divitiac—chief Druid of the Durotrige tribe

Helve—a senior priestess, later High Priestess

Kea—a girl in training with the Druids

LHIANNON—a young priestess

Lugovalos—Arch-Druid at Lys Deru

Mandua—an Atrebate girl in training with the Druids

Mearan—High Priestess when Boudica arrives on Mona

Nan—an old priestess living at Avalon

Nodona—a young priestess, Helve's second protegée

Rheis—daughter of Ardanos, later wife of Bendeigid

Rianor—a Trinovante boy in training with the Druids, later a priest

Sciovana—wife of Ardanos

Senora—a girl in training with the Druids

Romans

Calvus [Junius Antonius Calvus]—a Roman lawyer

+Catus [Decianus Catus]—Roman procurator in charge of collecting debts

+Claudius [Tiberius Claudius Caesar Augustus Germanicus]—emperor 41 CE to 54 CE

Crispus—a Gallo-Roman freedman in the household of Boudica

+(Gaius Julius Caesar, imperator and leader of a successful campaign in Britannia in 54 BCE)

+Gaius Nero "Caligula"—emperor 54 CE to 68 CE

+Gallus [Aulus Didius Gallus]—governor of Britannia 52 CE to 57 CE

+Narcissus—a freedman and secretary of state to Claudius

+Nero [Nero Claudius Caesar]—emperor 54 CE to 68 CE

+Paulinus [Gaius Suetonius Paulinus]—governor of Britannia 58 CE to 61 CE

+Petilius Cerialis—commander of Legio IX in 60 CE

+Plautius [Aulus Plautius]—commander of the invasion force, military governor of Britannia 43 CE to 47 CE

+Poenius Postumus—commander of Legio II Augusta, the legion that failed to come to Paulinus's aid

Pollio [Lucius Junius Pollio]—a tax collector in Britannia

+Scapuola [Publius Ostorius Scapuola]—governor of Britannia 48 CE to 52 CE

+Seneca [Lucius Annaeus Seneca]—senator and playwright, one of the regents for the emperor Nero

+Silanus [Lucius Junius Silanus Torquatus]—senator, son-in-law of Claudius

+Vespasian [Titus Flavius Vespasianus]—legionary legate in command of Legio II Augusta during the invasion (emperor, 69 CE to 79 CE)

ANIMALS

Bogle—pack leader of Boudica's white, red-eared hounds

Branwen—Boudica's white mare

Roud—Boudica's red mare

DEITIES

Andraste—battle goddess of the Iceni

Argantorota [Arianrhod]—Lady of the Silver Wheel

Arimanes [Arawn]—ruler of the Underworld (or Arihausnos)

Belutacadros, Cocidios, Coroticos, Lenos, Olloudios, Teutates—war gods

Brigantia—goddess of inspiration, smithcraft, and healing, also territorial goddess of the Brigantes

Cathubodva—"Battle Raven," see Morrigan

Dagdevos [the Dagda]—the Good God, a god of fertility, mate of the Morrigan

Epona—the Horse Goddess, patroness of the Iceni

Lugos [Lugh]—the many-skilled, honored at the harvest

Morrigan—"Great Queen," a title for the battle goddess, also called Cathubodva ("Battle Raven") and Nantosuelta ("Winding-One")

Sucellos—"the Striker," a Gaulish equivalent to Dagdevos, mate of the Morrigan

Taranis—god of thunder

PLACES

An-Dubnion [Annwyn]—the Underworld

Briga/the Brigante lands—Yorkshire and Lancashire

River Brigant—the Braint, in Anglesey

River Brue—near Glastonbury

Camadunon [Cadbury Castle]—a hillfort at the edge of Somerset that in the sixth century was to be refortified as King Arthur's Camelot.

Camulodunon [Camulodunum, Colonia Victricensis, Colchester]—chief dun of the Trinovante territories, capital for Cunobelin, and later administrative center for Britannia Superiore

Carn Ava [Avebury]—a stone circle north of Stonehenge

Danatobrigos, the Hill of the Sheep [Sedgeford, Norfolk]—Boudica's farm

Deva [Chester]—home fort for Legio XX and IV

Dun Garo [Venta Icenorum, Caistor St. Edmunds, Norfolk]—Iceni capital, just south of present-day Norwich

Dun of Stones [Hod Hill, Dorset]—hillfort defended by the Durotriges

Durovernon [Durovernum Cantiacorum, Canterbury]—dun of Caratac, the Cantiaci capital

Durovigutum [Godmanchester]—a Roman fort at the edge of the Iceni country

Earth-ring—Arminghall Henge, south of Norwich

Eponadunon [Warham Camp, Norfolk]—King Prasutagos's dun

Eriu [Ireland]

Garo—river Yare, Norfolk

Gesoriacum [Boulogne]—Roman port in Gallia

Great Road [Watling Street]—an early Roman road bisecting Britannia from London to Wroxeter

Horse Shrine [Sedgeford, Norfolk]—local offering place near Danatobrigos

House of the Hare (near Teutodunon)—home of Boudica's parents

Isca Road [Fosse Way]—Roman road from Exeter to Lincoln

Isle of Vectis [Isle of Wight]

Laigin [Leinster, Ireland]

Lake of Little Stones—Llyn Cerrig Bach, Anglesey

Lead Hills [Mendip Hills, Somerset]

Letocetum [Wall]—a Roman fort on Watling Street in the Midlands

Limes—the border between the pacified and unpacified lands, running roughly from present-day York to Usk in Wales

Londinium [London]—administrative center and trading town on the Tamesa

Lys Deru (Oakhalls) [near Brynsiencyn, Anglesey]—the Druid community on Mona

Lys Udra [near Aldborough, Yorkshire]—Queen Cartimandua's home

Medu [the Medway]—in Kent

Mona [Anglesey]—an island off the northwest tip of Wales, the Druid sanctuary

Manduessedum [Mancetter, near Nuneaton]—site of Boudica's last battle

Narrow Sea [English Channel]

Noviomagus—Chichester, Sussex

Rigodunon—Venutios's hillfort at Stanwix, near Carlisle

Sabrina [Severn River]

Sacred Spring—Holy Well at Walsingham, Norfolk

Salmaes Firth [the Solway]

Tamesa [River Thames]

Teutodunon [Thetford, Gallows Hill]—dun of the Iceni clan of the Hare, home of Boudica's family and site of Prasutagos's great hall

Verlamion [Verulamium, St. Albans]—Catuvellauni capital

Vernemeton, the Forest House (near Chester)—sanctuary to which the surviving Druid priestesses are moved after the fall of Mona

Tribal Territories
(Borders Approximate and Shifting)

Atrebates—Hampshire, Berkshire

Belgae—Wiltshire, Hampshire

Brigantes—York, Lancaster

Cantiaci—Kent

Catuvellauni—Oxfordshire, Hertshire

Deceangli—Flintshire (north coast of Wales)

Demetae—Pembrokeshire (southwest Wales)

Dobunni—Gloucestershire

Durotriges—Dorset, Somerset

Iceni—Norfolk

Ordovices—western Wales to Anglesey

Regni—Sussex, Surrey

Silures—Glamorgan and Monmouthshire (southern Wales)

Trinovantes—Essex, Suffolk

PROLOGUE

Lhiannon Speaks

At Samhain, we open our doors to the spirits of those who are gone. These days I find it easier to remember the dead than the living. I recall the most insignificant details of dress and habits of the women who were priestesses when I was young, and forget the names of the girls who serve me now. Even at this season of chill winds and falling leaves the house they have made for me beneath the trees of Vernemeton is comfortable, but when I remember our sanctuary on the Isle of Mona, it is all one golden afternoon, for Lys Deru was a place of magic.

These girls have grown up in the shadow of Rome. How can I show them the glory of that world in which we lived before the Legions came? I suppose it was no more perfect than any other society of humans, but it was our own. The Druids of Lys Deru preserved a noble tradition that we can practice only in pale imitation here.

Ardanos says that to survive we must bow our heads, conceal our powers, compromise. I do not gainsay him—what use would it be? But sometimes I wish that we could make these young ones understand why we fought to stay free. They say that the Society of Ravens is rising again. Will they call upon the Lady of Ravens to lead them? Boudica did, and nearly brought Rome to her knees.

In those days we loved deeply and dared greatly. Now all we can do is endure. It is the turn of Ardanos's granddaughter Eilan to serve me. Perhaps this evening, when we wait for the procession of spirits to come to my door, I will try to tell her the tale . . .

ONE

They had come to the Druids' Isle just before sunset, Boudica sitting very straight in the saddle so that no one would know she was afraid. She blinked back memories of blue waters hazed with magic and conical thatched roofs against a fading sky, a crowd of bearded men in white robes and veiled women with eyes full of secrets, and the little shock as they passed between the carved and painted gateposts that warded Lys Deru—the court of the oaks.

They had taken her to the House of Maidens. Eight girls of varying ages, from nine or ten to fourteen, her own age, stared back at her.

"Is it always cold here?" Boudica asked. She did not know whether she was shivering from exhaustion or from magic.

"Cold?" answered a dark-haired girl who had been introduced as Brenna. "In the winter surely, but now it is spring!" She was dressed in the simple sleeveless tunica of undyed linen that all the girls wore, pinned at the shoulders with bronze fibulae and girded with green.

"You will learn how to keep your inner fire burning so that you are not cold," Brenna went on. "But for now, let us see if we can make it warmer in here . . ." She frowned in concentration, then gestured, and the sticks on the central hearth burst suddenly into flame. From Brenna's smile, Boudica thought that she had only lately learned this skill herself. She smiled back, trying not to show how much the feat had impressed her. She might be a novice to magic, but she came of royal kin and had been fostered in the household of the great king Cunobelin.

Boudica was very aware of having lived in the woolen tunica and breeches she wore beneath it for the past month of journeying, but the simple garments the other girls were wearing seemed a poor alternative. And as for a wash—the Druids probably bathed in the chill waters of the stream. She straightened and stroked the fox fur edging of her cloak, which was so near in color to her hair. Better they should think her vain than weak. She had wept the first few nights of this journey across Britannia, huddled in cloak and blankets upon the hard ground, but she would not do so now.

"You are from the Iceni country, are you not? Let me introduce you to the rest of our company. This is Coventa—" Brenna put her arm around a small fair-haired girl. "She comes from the Brigante lands, like me. And that's Mandua, of the Atrebates—" She pointed to an older girl with a discontented face. As the names flowed by, Boudica saw curiosity and judgment in their eyes.

Clad, as they were, all alike, she could not tell which ones were the daughters of chieftains and which were the daughters of farmers. That was probably the intention. It was customary to give the children of good families a season or two among the Druids so that they might have a grounding in the deeper philosophy behind the superstitions of the common folk. But the peasant children chosen by the priests for their talent might well look down on those whose birth was their only qualification for being here. Boudica had already sworn they would have no cause to look down on *her*.

"But the Isle of Mona belongs to no tribe," Brenna finished. "That is why the School of the Mysteries was established here at Lys Deru."

"Truly?" asked Mandua. "I thought we settled out here at the end of the world to stay beyond the reach of Rome."

Boudica sat down on the bed, remembering the sheer mass and might of the mountains they had passed. And yet the road, however difficult, had brought her here. In Camulodunon it had seemed that nothing was beyond Rome's reach. But here, so far from everything she had ever known, she was not so sure. She summoned up a bright smile for the other girls.

"I bless the hour of our meeting. I am sure you will all have many things to tell me . . ."

"It is Lhiannon you have to listen to," said little Coventa with a laugh. "Helve has the title of Mistress of the House of Maidens, but Lhiannon does the work—" She broke off at Brenna's frown. "Well, it's *true*, and is not truth what we are seeking here?"

Boudica lifted an eyebrow. "If it is, then the Druids are different from any other group of people I ever knew," she said dryly.

"Do you think you know so much more because you were fostered in a king's dun?" objected Brenna. "Here we serve the gods!"

"But you are not yet gods yourselves." Boudica shrugged. "The Druids who served King Cunobelin were as avid for power as any of his chieftains."

Coventa frowned. "Perhaps living in the world corrupted them."

"Well, we must not quarrel about it on your first night here," Brenna said peaceably. "What was it like in Camulodunon? Does Cunobelin's dun really have golden thatching and marble walls?"

Boudica laughed. "Only the gold of wheatstraw, but it is cut in layered patterns, and the outer walls are whitewashed and painted in spirals of color."

"It sounds like a dwelling of the gods," sighed Brenna.

"It was . . ." said Boudica, eyes prickling with a sudden surge of longing for the place that had been her home since she was seven years old. But the great king was dead, his household dispersed, and her father had sent her here to the end of the world.

"We are not gods here, but we will not let you starve—" came a voice from the doorway.

Looking up, Boudica saw a slim young woman in the blue robe of a full priestess whose fair hair fell halfway down her back beneath a dark veil. As she came into the roundhouse, the other girls straightened and bowed.

Boudica cast her a swift look, wondering how much she had heard. If the woman was a power in this place, she would have to treat her carefully. She looked again and found her glance held by eyes of a blue so light they seemed luminous. The blue crescent of the Goddess was tattooed between pale brows.

"My name is Lhiannon," the woman said then. As she smiled her lashes veiled that blue gaze, and Boudica was able to look away. "I will be your teacher."

*T*he current in the stream was running fast and strong. Overhead, three ravens called as they danced on the wind.

Boudica had been glad for a break from lessons, but fighting the water was not her idea of fun. She waded carefully toward the middle of the stream, where brown waters were frothing around a tangle of branches. The stream was said to be sacred to the goddess Brigantia, but if so, she was an angry goddess now.

The priests had set all the young ones to clearing the course of the creek that flowed behind Lys Déru, swollen now with water from the spring rains. The flood had brought down quantities of debris that choked the watercourse and threatened to flood the roundhouses, and the ditch that kept cattle from wandering into the village was not deep enough to carry the overflow. As Lhiannon pointed out, they always needed firewood. It would have been ungrateful to waste the bounty.

The young priest Ardanos, who the girls said was courting Lhiannon, had told them that clearing the stream would be a service to the spirit who lived there. Boudica hoped so. She got a good grip on the nearest branch and began to pull, swore as her fingers slipped on the wet bark, and pulled again. Something gave way, then snagged. A twig had hooked under another branch and was holding it there. Clearly, this task needed more hands. She turned, eyes narrowing as she looked for the others. More clouds were piling up overhead. The rocky coast that fronted the sea of Eriu would take the worst of any storm, but the rain would sweep across the island.

"Mandua!" she called, recognizing the girl's brown braid. "Mandua—lift that branch for me so I can get this one free!" The other girl turned in surprise, then tossed the stick she held toward the bank and began to splash downstream.

It had been a good idea, Boudica thought as the wood

came free. A branch this size would keep a fire going for hours. And the pile was full of more just like it. It seemed a pity to waste time hauling the branch she had all the way back to the bank. She glanced at the other muddy forms.

"Senora! Coventa! Come here. We can pull this wood in ever so much faster if we pass it hand to hand! The boys won't get nearly so much." As they looked at her doubtfully she pointed downstream, where the lads were working. "They promised that those who made the biggest pile of firewood would get honeycakes tonight."

In a few minutes she had Brenna and Kea tackling the next log pile, with the smaller girls helping them. Boudica hauled at the wet wood, lips pulled back in a fierce grin. It no longer mattered that this was no fit labor for a royal woman of the Iceni. So many of the Druid ways were strange to her, it was a relief to tackle something that she could really *do*!

Lost in the rhythm of the work, she had no attention for anything but the tangles of wood before her. It was only when there were no hands ready to take the next log that she focused once more on her surroundings.

"I can't hold it, Boudica—my hands are numb!" Senora held them up.

"Trade places with Coventa and put your hands in your armpits while you wait for her to hand you the next one," she ordered. "Come, Coventa—no, it's not too deep. Here, take this end of the stick and pass it along."

Coventa looked almost as pale as Senora, but she obeyed. Now the others were whining as well. Boudica was cold and wet, too, but that must not be allowed to matter. They were making good progress. The brown water ran swiftly where they had cleared the channel, and the pile of branches on the bank was higher than Coventa.

"Haven't we done enough?" asked Mandua, shouting above the rush of the stream. "I can't feel my feet anymore!"

"Not until we *are* done," called Boudica. "Look, there is only this last pile and our part of the stream will be clear."

The light was fading, but she could see where to grip the next piece of wood. She inched her way toward it, brac-

ing herself against the current, which had grown stronger
as the obstructions were taken away. As she touched the
bark she heard a scream.

"Coventa! Coventa fell!" Senora was waving wildly,
pointing downstream.

Boudica caught sight of a pale bubble of cloth bobbing
past and launched herself in a low dive. Her hands, colder
than she had allowed herself to realize, tried to close on
the cloth and failed. She went down, got her feet under
her, lunged, and caught the other girl by one arm. Coventa's cold flesh was slippery, but Boudica held on. Now
both went under. Was it a waterlogged branch that was
tangling in her tunica or cold hands that sought to drag
her down? Once more she struggled upright, grabbing
Coventa around the body. Brenna splashed toward her
with the others behind her. Hand to hand they passed the
girl to the shore, and then Brenna was helping Boudica
up the bank, where she sat, teeth chattering as much with
shock as with cold.

Presently Ardanos lifted her to her feet and she was hustled back to the House of Maidens. Coventa had been taken
to the healers, but no one seemed to care that Boudica,
too, was wet and chilled to the bone. She rubbed herself
dry as best she could and pulled on a wool tunica and her
fur-trimmed cloak, then sat by the little fire with only the
stone head of the house spirit in its niche by the threshold
for company.

Were they going to send her home? Boudica did not
know whether to hope or to fear. To go home in defeat
would gall her soul. She would rather stay the year, and
when the tribesmen came with next year's offerings she
could choose to leave with them.

Her hair had dried from wet auburn to its usual curling red-gold when the hide that covered the door rustled.
Boudica looked up and recognized Lhiannon's slender silhouette in the gloom.

"Why are you sitting here? Dinner is ready and I saw
you were not there. Aren't you hungry?"

Boudica nodded. "No one came. I thought I was being
punished."

"Ah . . ." Lhiannon poked at the coals and a spurt of flame

gleamed on her fair hair. With a sigh she sat down on the other side of the fire. "Do you think that you should be?"

"No!" the answer burst out. "It was an accident! The river was running fast—anyone could have fallen! And . . . I think the stream spirit wants an offering."

"That has been attended to," Lhiannon replied. She waited, holding Boudica in that calm blue gaze until the girl had gotten her breathing under control once more.

"Is Coventa all right?" Boudica swallowed, remembering how limp the other girl had been in her arms.

"Well," said Lhiannon, "if that was not the first thing you said, at least you asked . . . We think Coventa knocked her head on a stone when she went down. But she is awake now, and asking for food. The healers will keep her for a time to make sure the water she swallowed has done her no harm, but she should recover well."

"I am glad," Boudica whispered. She sat back, relief at the release of a fear she had not known she felt sending a flush of heat through her veins.

"You should be. So I will ask again—do you think we should punish you?"

The girl shrugged. "People always look for someone to blame when something goes wrong." She had seen that all too often in King Cunobelin's hall.

"Let us look at it another way," Lhiannon said. "If Coventa had died, would you owe compensation for her loss?"

Boudica looked up at her, understanding that this was a different question. "Do you mean that what happened was my responsibility?"

Lhiannon looked at her, the pale eyes gleaming faintly. "Why was Coventa in the stream?"

"Because you ordered us to clear out the wood that blocked it!" snapped Boudica.

"Indeed, and it should not surprise you to hear that the High Priestess and I have already had the same conversation that you and I are having now. That you were there at all was my fault, and I should have stayed to supervise you."

"But we were doing very well . . ."

"It was a good plan," Lhiannon agreed, "but even

the greatest warrior cannot fight well with a weakened sword."

Boudica frowned, seeing in her mind's eye the small form of the younger girl. "She was too little . . ." she said at last.

"She was not up to the job you had given her, and all of you had worked too hard and too long. It is my guess that you have not spent much time with other children—is that not so?" As Boudica nodded she went on. "You come of the Belgic race, who are a tall and vigorous people, and you yourself are strong beyond most girls your age. You must learn to see others as they are, not as you would wish them to be. You made yourself their leader, and so they were your responsibility."

"King Cunobelin had a gift for that," said Boudica. "Even when men tried to betray him they served his purposes, because he put them in positions where their natural inclination would further his goals. But I am only a girl. I never thought—"

"Do you think that because you are a woman you have no power? They say that among the Romans it is otherwise, but we Druids know that the Goddess is the source of sovereignty, and it is through the queens and priestesses that it is bestowed upon men. And you are the child of generations of chieftains. I am not surprised that the other girls obeyed."

The girl bristled at the tone. What did this woman know about the ways of kings? But she had a point—Boudica had always been subject to someone. It had never occurred to her that she, too, might have power.

"I understand," she said slowly.

"Well, if you do, then something useful has come out of this day!" Lhiannon said briskly. "Come with me now and get something hot in your belly, and then, if you like, we can pay a visit to Coventa and you can assure yourself that she is well."

In the week after Coventa's near-drowning, a last rainstorm sent waters laughing through the cleared bed of the stream. Then the weather turned warm, as if the spirit of the stream, having been propitiated, had brought the spring. It was not until the night of the new moon that Lhiannon had a chance to speak with Ardanos.

As they passed through the woods toward the grove he had slowed his usual swift step to match hers. He was barely taller than she, and wiry in build rather than muscular, but he had a natural authority and other men respected him. He was whistling softly. She blushed as she realized it was a song he had written for her—

> *"My love is a girl with hair like golden flax,*
> *With eyes like the summer sky,*
> *The reeds bow down in envy at her walk,*
> *The swaying willows sigh . . ."*

Seeing her response, he laughed. "And how is our Iceni princess settling in?" he asked.

"Rather too aware that she *is* a princess, I fear," answered Lhiannon. She lowered her voice as a group of younger priests moved past them, their robes a pale blur in the dusk. "But she is a natural leader. She might make a priestess, if she can learn humility."

"Ah well, she wouldn't be the first to have that problem . . ." Ardanos replied.

He meant Helve. Lhiannon followed his gaze. Long ago this part of the forest had been planted with a triple circle of oaks whose dagged leaves rustled softly in the evening wind. The moon glimmered like a curved river pearl caught in a net of branches. The cloaks of the priestesses made a dark blot beneath the trees. She gave his hand a squeeze of agreement before she crossed the grass to join them.

"Lhiannon, your presence honors us," said Helve. She was a senior priestess, and almost as talented as she thought she was. Lhiannon could not quite tell if she spoke in mockery. "Were the girls difficult to settle for the night?"

If you had been there, she thought, *you would not need to ask.*

"That new one, the Iceni girl, will bear watching—perhaps I should take her for special training," Helve went on.

"You are the Mistress of the House of Maidens," Lhiannon said quietly, but she was thinking, *if you want to teach Boudica, I suggest you begin by learning her name!*

She was not sure whether to hope Helve took the girl off her hands or to fear it. Boudica was just as proud as the priestess, and might be even more stubborn. The girl might rebel, or worse still, Helve might encourage her in arrogance rather than teach her humility.

A shimmer of bells sounded from across the circle. Escorted by her handmaidens, the High Priestess was emerging from among the trees. Moving with the pace of ritual, Mearan's stout figure had a balanced grace. Though all the community worshipped together, the moon rites belonged to the priestesses, as the priests took charge of the solar rituals, and this was the Lady's hour.

"Behold, O my children, how the Maiden Moon shines above us." The voice of the High Priestess rang across the circle. "She is early to rise and early to seek her bed—young and full of promise, like the children who have come to study here. From us they will learn our ancient tradition. But what will we learn from them? This evening we ask the Goddess to open our hearts and our minds. For though the wisdom of the old ones endures, the world is ever changing, and the meaning of that wisdom changes as well. It will profit us nothing to stay safe on our island if we grow so apart from the people we are here to serve that they cannot understand our words."

The circle was silent. In the oak grove, a dove called once, and then was still. Focusing on her link to the earth, Lhiannon tried to let her tensions drain away. The hush deepened as the others did the same, and the circle's silence became charged with energy.

The High Priestess approached the standing stone in its center. "To you, beloved Lady, we bring these offerings." One by one her handmaidens laid the spring flowers they carried upon the stone, and Lhiannon and the other priestesses moved inward to surround them.

"Holy Goddess, holy Goddess..." Women's voices soared, invoking the sacred name in woven harmonies.

"Upon these holy ancient trees
Now cast thy lovely silver light;
Uncloud thy face that we may see
Unveiled, its shining in the night—"

Mearan stood before the altar, hands lifted in adoration. As the song continued, the moonlight seemed to focus around her, as sweetly and gently the Goddess entered in. Her stout figure was growing taller, her face radiant; she shone with power. Forgotten now was the face of wrath the Goddess showed when men called her as Raven of Battle. It was the sweet Lady of the Silver Wheel who had come to them here.

"Holy Goddess, holy Goddess . . ." the men were chanting, as if the solid earth had found a voice to reply.

"Shine forth upon the fertile earth,
Shine bright upon the sounding sea;
Send down thy tender light to bless
All living things that pray to thee."

The Goddess turned, hands opening in benediction. In Her deep gaze they found forgiveness, understanding, love.

Lhiannon sighed, releasing the last of her resentment. And as if that had been the offering awaited, she felt her soul filling with white peace. *Ah, Boudica, this is what we have to offer you*—a stray thought came to her. *I hope that one day you will understand . . .* Then that, too, was gone and there was only the light.

 It was not until autumn that Boudica's turn to serve Lady Mearan came. The High Priestess occupied a large roundhouse at the edge of the Sacred Grove. Each moon two maidens and one of the younger priestesses would join her there.

Boudica told herself there was no reason to be nervous. She had served in the dun of a great king. But kings only wielded physical power. Life among the Druids was not full of signs and wonders, but in the six months since she arrived she had glimpsed enough strangeness to know that the power was there. And yet in daily life the High Priestess seemed little different from any other woman of her years. She slid her arms into the sleeves of her tunica one at a time, and got tangled if her attendants had folded the garment wrong. But when the High Priestess was looking at her, Boudica could always feel her gaze.

In the house of the High Priestess, the sweet scent of drying herbs mingled with the smoke of the hearthfire, and there was always a copper kettle of water for tea hanging over the coals. The only sounds were the murmur of women's voices, the crackle of the fire, and the whisper of falling rain. On one such evening, when the dusk had drawn in early, Boudica found herself alone with the High Priestess while the others fetched food for the evening meal. She tensed as the older woman motioned her to sit nearby.

"So, have you been happy with us here?" Mearan asked.

The girl ventured a quick glance at the priestess. Age had loosened the flesh that covered the strong bones, but the woman's dark eyes were like a deep pool into which excuses or prevarications would simply disappear.

"I like Lys Deru," Boudica said abruptly. "But I have no talent for the things you do, and I don't like being treated like a baby because I can't do them . . ."

"To see what must be done and lead others to do it is a gift as well," said the priestess. "Do not be so certain you know all that you can and cannot do . . ."

Boudica was trying to find the words to ask what she meant when she heard voices at the door. Mandua shouldered through, followed by Lhiannon and Coventa, all laden with food. They were followed by a gust of stinging rain.

"This looks splendid," said the High Priestess. "And the water in my kettle is near the boil, so we shall have tea soon."

"And bannocks?" asked Coventa hopefully.

"As soon as the stone is hot," answered Boudica, pouring a little fat into the bowl of ground oats. It was pleasant to listen to the rain lashing the trees outside while sitting with friends beside a good fire. She dribbled sour milk into the mixture, working it into a paste, sprinkled oatmeal onto a flat board, and turned the mixture onto it, coating her fingers with more meal before she began to knead. The ruddy light colored the long folds of the robes that hung from the house posts and touched the shapes of less identifiable bags and boxes with magic. Probably, she thought, they *were* magic—herbs and stones and bits of this and that, the things a Druid needed for her spells.

Coventa flicked a drop of tea onto the flat slab of slate they had placed on the coals. As it sizzled, Boudica patted the dough into a circle and swiftly quartered it. A splash of fat upon the stone and it was ready for the bannock. In moments, the warm smell of baking oatcake began to mingle with the other scents in the room.

"Listen to the wind!" said Mandua, shivering.

"It whispers stories of all the places it has been," Coventa agreed.

"Or shouts them," corrected Boudica, listening to the framework of branches that supported the conical thatched roof flex as a new gust hit.

Lhiannon smiled. "On such a night I always think of those who braved the storms to reach this island. They say that the first wise folk to dwell on Avalon came there from a great island that was overwhelmed by the sea."

"But how did the Druids get here?" asked Coventa, scooping the toasted bannocks from the stone into a basket.

"It seems an appropriate night for the story . . ." Lady Mearan drizzled a little honey on her bannock and took a bite with a satisfied sigh. "Those first Oak priests must have found the ocean frightening when they came here, following the first Celtic war leaders to see this land. Their people had grown great, and their clans spiraled outward in every direction. Some fared north to settle Gallia, and from there they ventured to these isles."

"The Atrebates are of the Belgic tribes, which were the last to come here, and so are the princes who rule the Iceni lands," added Lhiannon. "Though there is older blood in the people they rule." She turned back to the

High Priestess. "Who was the first of our Order to come to Avalon?"

"The first?" Mearan smiled. "There is a tradition that it was not a priest who came first to Avalon, but a priestess, fleeing the destruction of her dun in one of the early wars. Her name was Catuera. The winter storms had been fierce, so that Avalon was indeed an island. In such weather, when the mists lie close upon the marshlands, it is easy to lose your way. Catuera blundered through the mists, soaked and shivering, until she came . . ." Mearan paused for a sip of tea.

"To Avalon?" Coventa said eagerly.

The priestess shook her head. "She came to a place with neither sun nor moon, where the trees are always in fruit and in flower. And the queen of its people, who have been here longer than any human folk on these isles, took her in. For a time out of time she stayed there, and when she was healed, she passed through the mists once more. That was how she came to Avalon."

"Were priestesses living there?" asked Boudica.

"Priestesses and priests," Mearan replied. "Descended from the mingling of the first people in these islands and the masters of high magic who had come from the Drowned Lands. But there was this difference—while among those early Druids the priestesses were present only to serve the priests in the rituals, on Avalon priest and priestess worked together, and it was the Lady of Avalon who wielded the greater power."

"And that is still the difference between our Order here and the way it is, or was, in Gallia," added Lhiannon.

"The wisewomen of Avalon taught Catuera, and sent her back to make peace between her people and the men of the old race, and though wars and raids continued, they were never so evil as they had been, and in the end we became one people as we are today."

"And all men honor our priestesses . . ." added Coventa in satisfaction.

"Let us take care to deserve that reverence," said Lhiannon.

TWO

"$\mathcal{O}$ne is for the Source, the Divine Origin, nameless, unknowable, beyond perception," chanted the boys and girls who sat beneath the ash tree.

For the first time in weeks the clouds had let through a little sunshine, and the teachers had brought their charges out to enjoy it. Ardanos had sent the bardic students to practice beyond the grove. Even their mistakes sounded sweet in the spring air.

Truth may be forever One, thought Lhiannon, *but its manifestations in the world are always changing.* The thought made her shiver.

"Two is for the God and the Goddess, male and female, light and darkness, all opposites that meet and part and join once more." She spoke the words unthinking, then paused.

Spring was giving way to summer. In another week they would light the Beltane fires. At the festivals when man and woman lay down together to bring the power of the Lord and the Lady into the world, only those priestesses who had vowed virginity for the sake of the higher magics stayed apart. She cast a quick glance at Ardanos, who sat on the other side of the circle, and felt the hot blood heat her cheeks.

Even from across the circle she could feel his desire for her. When winter chilled all fires it was easy to deny the body's demands, but when the sun kindled new life in every leaf and blade of grass, she remembered that she was young, and in love.

"Three is for the Divine Child that is born of their union, and three the faces of the Goddess who gives life to the world." The spring sun filtered down through the new leaves, crowning the students with light. Coventa's fair hair shimmered silver-gilt, and behind her she glimpsed a bent head like a blazing fire that could only be Boudica.

Were these the only children Lhiannon would ever have? Once more she glanced at Ardanos. She might dream of bearing him a child, but she had never cared much for babies. Let others create bodies—here at Mona, she and Ardanos formed minds and souls.

She wanted to sit in the seat of prophecy and soar through the heavens, but she also desired the wiry strength of his arms around her. The senior Druids taught that one must choose between the body and the soul. Lhiannon's lips continued to move as the chant droned on, but her mind was far away.

As the young people trooped back toward Lys Deru, Lhiannon could hear them speculating on what they had heard. Boudica in particular seemed thoughtful. It was about time. After a little more than a year the girl still sometimes acted like—a Roman visiting barbarians. But Boudica was forgotten as Lhiannon felt a warmth at her side and turned to find Ardanos there. Her whole body flushed with response as he took her hand.

"When I read the heavens, they tell me that Beltane is near . . ." he said softly. "Will you dance with me when they light the festal fire?"

Will you lie with me? He did not need to say the words aloud.

The priests said that the flow of energy in the body was altered when a woman lay with a man, blocking the channels through which power flowed in prophecy. But what hope did Lhiannon have of sitting on the Oracle's stool as long as Helve was the priests' darling? The energy that flowed between man and woman raised another kind of power. Was she a fool to refuse that ecstasy for the sake of an opportunity that might never come?

She could not speak, but her grip tightened on his hand and she knew that her body had replied.

*B*ut girls don't play hurley! Boudica, they'll never let you on the field!" cried Coventa, grabbing for her sleeve. From the field came a shout as one of the players caught the leather-covered wooden ball on his cumman stick and lofted it back over the goal.

Boudica resisted an impulse to stride on, dragging the smaller girl behind her. At fifteen, she had nearly reached her full height.

"It's a game to train warriors," Coventa said when she had caught her breath. "In the old days it was not a little ball they hurled with that stick, but the head of an enemy."

"I know that!" retorted Boudica. "They play it in my tribe as well. But Druids do not fight, so why are they playing? Anyway, in Eriu, the women still go to war."

Coventa blinked, trying to sort out the logic, and Boudica started forward once more. The Druids recognized that a healthy mind functioned best in a healthy body, and a large meadow near Lys Deru had been made into a playing field. When thirty youngsters pursued the ball with knees, elbows, and three-foot ash staves, the game could be almost as dangerous as a battlefield. It was only a matter of time before someone was taken out of play.

"Oh, very well." Coventa sat down on the grass. "You always do what you want anyway."

A shout from Ardanos had separated the combatants, who regrouped into their teams, facing their own goals across the center line. The young priest threw the ball into the air and dashed backward as the two sides closed once more.

Beyond the strait, the great humped shapes of the mountains stood like a wall upon the horizon. Were they a protective barrier or a prison wall? To be given to a husband would be to go from one captivity to another. But did Boudica want to stay here as a teacher or go to some chieftain's clanhold or perhaps to the marshes of the Summer Country to serve the Goddess upon the Isle of Avalon? How could she decide?

She flinched as the ball spun toward them from the center of the heaving mass of boys and sticks. Ardanos's student, Bendeigid, smacked the ball toward a dark-haired Trinovante boy called Rianor, who pelted after it, stick whirling as he leaped forward. The first swing missed, but the second sent the ball hurtling toward the two holly trees that flanked the goal.

It is a good thing the ball doesn't fight back, thought Boudica. *If that was an enemy with a sword, he would be dead before he could strike a second blow.*

She tried to discern the pattern of the play, but if either team had a plan it was not apparent. In that, also, it was like the way her people made war. The game grew more and more desperate. She heard someone scream and Ardanos calling a halt. Panting, the players surrounded the writhing figure on the ground.

The player struggled to sit, face white beneath his freckles, supporting his leg with his hands. His name was Beli, and he had been on Rianor's team.

"Take him to the healers," said Ardanos with a sigh. "And unless you have reinforcements hidden somewhere, this will end the game."

There was a babble of protest from the boys and a groan of disappointment from the crowd. Games usually ran until one team had scored ten goals or the sun went down. Nine colored scarves fluttered from the other team's goal tree and nine from Rianor's. Boudica stood up, heart pounding in her breast.

"I'll take his place," she said in a clear voice. She kilted up her skirts and strode onto the field. Silence fell. Now everyone was staring at *her.*

"But you're a girl," Rianor said at last.

Someone giggled and was hushed. Boudica shrugged. "I'm bigger than most of your boys. Of course if you want to play it safe, you can blame your loss on the accident. But if you have the courage, try me!" She held his dark gaze with her own, and saw the battle-light suddenly kindle in his eyes.

"Why not?" He grinned with a lift of the hand as if he were throwing dice.

Ardanos looked at Cloto, a sturdy lad who was the leader of the opposing team.

"Fine with me," he sneered. "Now I *know* we'll win!"

"That's settled, then," said Ardanos, frowning down Rianor's hot reply. With a last glare for Cloto, the boy shut his mouth and handed the cumman stick to Ardanos, who offered it to Boudica. "Do you swear that you bring no charm or device of magic to this field, and will play honestly and truly, with no aid but your own body's power?"

It was a necessary question in a school where some of the students could make the ball move by will alone, thought Boudica as she gripped the stick and swore the oath.

"Beli's position was there—" Rianor pointed to a spot halfway down one side of the field.

She took her place, noting the locations of the other players. It had been a long time since she had played, but she remembered the few guidelines that passed for rules. She saw Ardanos approach the middle with the ball and hefted her stick. It had never occurred to her before, but the widened tip made it look more like one of the big wooden spoons the cooks used to stir stew in a cauldron than a sword. She grinned suddenly. Why shouldn't a girl play this game? They were using a woman's weapon, after all!

The ball flew upward and someone on the other side swung and sent it angling toward her own team's goal. Stick poised, Boudica ran to intercept it, dodging the knot of boys racing forward with the same thing in mind. She heard the smack of wood against leather as someone whacked the ball, and the crowd of players surged after it in a confused mass, spinning off boys to either side. She glimpsed Cloto hurtling past, saw him turn and leap toward her instead, deliberately ramming the point of his shoulder into her breast. As she went sprawling she heard his laughter. Outraged, she opened her mouth to curse him—hurley was a rough sport, and the shoulder block a legal move, but only to stop an opponent from getting the ball—but pain robbed her of breath.

I'll kick his balls up between his ears! For a moment she could only lie curled around the agony as rage spread black wings across her vision, screaming for prey. When Boudica staggered to her feet, still hunched over, she saw Ardanos running toward her and waved him away. The scrimmage was dangerously close to her own team's goal. Beyond it she glimpsed white robes and blue gowns among the spectators, but she no longer cared if the Druids were watching. One hand cupping her bruised breast, she scanned the heaving mass, trying to find Cloto, but what she saw was the ball hurtling toward her.

The pressure behind her eyes eased. Winning would be an even better revenge.

She darted sideways and swung, whacking the small sphere toward the enemy goal. Someone shouted behind her, but she was already in motion, her braid thumping her back as she galloped down the field. The opposing backfield had seen the danger. One of them scooped up the ball and sent it whizzing past Bendeigid, who managed to smack it sideways with his left hand, was spun around by the impact, and sat down hard on the grass. One of Cloto's boys swung down his stick to stop it and the hurtling ball rebounded toward Boudica.

For a moment, then, it seemed that she had all the time in the world to watch the ball spinning toward her. She set her feet, gripping the cumman stick two-handed like a sword, shoulders flexing as she swung, lips drawn back to release her rage in the Iceni war cry.

The impact as stick and ball connected shocked through her body, and abruptly she was part of the world once more, still spinning with the follow-through of her blow as the ball soared over the heads of the backfielders and goalkeeper alike.

All eyes fixed on the ball's flight. Dust puffed as it hit the earth between the holly trees. And in the moment of amazement as they realized that the game was over, Coventa screamed.

Boudica ran toward her friend, who was sitting bolt upright with staring eyes. As she reached her side, Coventa seized her arms.

"The Red Queen! Blood on the fields and cities burning, blood flowing everywhere . . ." Coventa gasped and hiccupped. Her grip slackened and Boudica caught her. For a moment her wavering gaze focused on Boudica's face. "It was you! You were swinging a sword . . ."

"It was only a hurley stick," Boudica protested, but Coventa's eyes had rolled back in her head.

"Let her go, girl. I will take her now—"

Boudica looked up and recognized Helve, her dark hair

bound around her head in precise coils. "I can lift her—" she began, but the priestess shouldered her aside, feeling for Coventa's pulse and then signing to one of the priests to take the girl in his arms. Only then did she turn to Boudica.

"Does she have these fits often?"

Boudica shrugged. "She has nightmares, but this is the first time when she was awake. She hasn't been strong since she had the fever after her . . . accident . . . last year." She flushed with shame.

But if Helve remembered Boudica's part in that accident, she did not seem to care. She watched as the young Druid carried Coventa away, speculation in her gaze.

"She touched the Otherworld. That is all that is needed sometimes. We shall see what some training can do . . ."

But what if Coventa does not want *to become an oracle?* Boudica opened her mouth, but Helve had not been speaking to her. The girl sat back on her heels, staring, as the priestess stalked away.

*F*or months, the heavens had alternated between storm clouds and watery sunshine, like a coy maiden unable to decide whether to encourage a suitor or turn him away. *Like me,* thought Lhiannon, closing her eyes and turning her face to a sun that was blazing in a blue sky. But now everything—the white blooms of the hawthorn in the hedges and the creamy primroses beneath them, the upright green blades of the growing grass and the tender curls of the new oak leaves—seemed lit from within. *Tonight the Beltane fires will burn brightly, and so will I.*

She had been to the herb-sellers to purchase more poppy seed for the potion the priestess drank before the ritual. The open fields around Lys Deru had filled up with traders' booths and tents and wagons and stock pens. All the farmers who were oathed to serve the Druid community were here, along with a scattering of families from the mainland. Lhiannon was not the only one who dreamed of meeting a lover at the Beltane fires. Young people from villages where they had known everyone of their age since babyhood came here to seek new faces and new blood for their clans. After this night there would be handfastings in plenty, and weddings to follow.

But before Lhiannon went to the fires, she must assist at the ritual of the Oracle. When they sang the sacred song, she would know if its summons was stronger than the one her body was sending her now.

As she approached the enclosure she heard Helve, in her usual autocratic mood. It was with shock that Lhiannon realized that the other woman's instructions were not for Mearan's comfort, but for her own. Lhiannon twitched aside the curtain that hung before the doorway.

"Where is the High Priestess?" she whispered to Belina, one of the senior priestesses. Helve stood naked before the fire, stretching out her white limbs so that the others could bathe them with spring water infused with herbs.

"She is not well," the other woman replied, lifting one eyebrow. "Helve will sit in the high seat this Beltane eve."

"May the Lady grant her inspiration," Lhiannon said dryly, and Belina sighed. Lhiannon went to the corner where old Elin was grinding herbs in a wooden mortar and handed her the poppy seeds. As she turned back, she saw Coventa coming into the room. Her smile died as she realized that the girl was swathed in the same midnight blue as the priestesses, her brows bound like theirs with a garland of spring flowers and sweet herbs.

"Helve, what is this?" she exclaimed. "The child is untrained. You cannot mean her to attend you in the ceremony!"

Helve's pale eyes flashed with annoyance, but her voice, as always, was sweet and low. "Without her the number of attendants escorting me will be uneven, and I have been training her." She smiled at Coventa. "Have I not, my little one? You will do very well."

She will look like a child dressed in her mother's robes, thought Lhiannon, but Coventa was radiant with delight. She looked at the other priestesses for support, but they were carefullly avoiding her gaze. For a few moments the only sounds were the trickle of water as the priestesses dipped the cloths into the herbal bath and the rasp as Elin ground up the poppy seeds.

Lhiannon sighed and took off her veil. If Helve was nervous, she had some reason. This would not be her first time in the high seat, but she had not served as Oracle often, and if Mearan's indisposition was sudden, she would not have had much time to prepare. For the first time it occurred to her that Helve's natural talent for autocracy must make it especially difficult to surrender her will even to the gentle direction of Lugovalos.

It would be easier for me, she thought bitterly. *I cannot even assert myself enough to stand up for Coventa.* But she could at least keep an eye on the child during the ritual.

Above the hearth a small cauldron was bubbling. Elin cast in a pinch of ground poppy seed to simmer with the mistletoe berries and mushrooms and other herbs, then stood stirring the mixture, chanting softly. Helve continued to chatter as they dressed her in the flowing robes of the Oracle. When Lhiannon approached with the garland of columbine twined with spring flowers, she saw triumph in the other woman's pale eyes.

Helve will never allow me to sit as Oracle. Why have I denied myself so long? Lhiannon wondered then. Mastering a surge of hatred, she set the garland upon Helve's brow, and the other woman fell silent at last. Elin ladled some of the potion into the ancient jet bowl and set it to cool. Presently the door curtain rustled and the Arch-Druid entered, leaning on his staff. His silver beard glistened against the creamy wool of his robe.

"It is time, my daughter," Lugovalos said softly, and Elin set the jet bowl in Helve's hands. She took a deep breath and drank, shuddered once, and swallowed it down. Elin and Belina took her elbows and escorted her to the litter that was waiting outside. As Lhiannon fell in behind them she could feel the vibration of the drums through the soles of her feet, as if the earth's heart were beating out the rhythm of the festival.

In the west, the sky was a translucent blue, deepening overhead to the same midnight shade the priestesses wore. A great crowd had assembled before the sacred grove. Helve swayed when she was seated upon the three-legged stool, and for a moment Lhiannon feared she would fall, but before anyone could touch her she straightened, seeming to grow taller. Lhiannon felt a breath of warm wind, scented with flowers no mortal garden could boast, and knew that the Goddess was here.

Relieved, she drew Coventa back to stand with the others and relaxed as they settled into the familiar rhythms of the ritual. She had to admit that Helve was a powerful seeress. From her place behind the high seat she could feel the woman's aura expand as she sank deeper into trance, and brought up her own barriers to shield against it.

The first question came from Lugovalos, and was, as expected, about the prospects for a good harvest. There was a murmur of satisfaction as the seeress spoke of sunny skies and fields golden with ripe grain. Now the air around her was beginning to glow. Lhiannon smiled. Mona was one of the breadbaskets of Britannia—it would take an evil fate indeed to threaten that harvest. Coventa swayed beside her, humming softly, and Lhiannon gave her hand a sharp squeeze.

"Fasten yourself to the earth, child," she whispered sharply. "Only the seeress is supposed to go through the gate of prophecy." Coventa hiccupped and then grew still, but she remained unsteady as Lugovalos spoke once more.

"In Gallia, the Legions of Rome have placed an iron yoke upon our people, and now their emperor has banished the Druid Order from their lands. Say then, seeress, what the future holds for us here in Britannia?"

There was a silence, as if not only the Arch-Druid but all Britannia was waiting to hear.

The blossoms in Helve's garland began to tremble, and Lhiannon felt Coventa shake as if in sympathy. Once more she damned Helve's pride. The child was being caught up in the vision and had no defense against it.

"I see oars that lift and dip like wings on the water . . ." muttered Helve. "As the geese flock north in the spring they come—three great flocks of winged vessels stroking across the sea . . ."

"When will they come, wise one?" Lugovalos asked urgently. "And where?"

"Where the white cliffs rise and the white sands gleam," came the answer. "When the hawthorn is in white bloom."

Time was notoriously difficult to fix in prophecy, thought Lhiannon as a murmur of unease swept through the crowd. But at the earliest, it could not be until next year. To collect so great an army would take time, and though the Druids might be banned from Gallia, the Order had agents in plenty on the other side of the sea. Surely when an invasion was planned they would know. She put her arm around Coventa, holding her close and praying that Helve would finish soon. But the Arch-Druid wanted more.

"And what then? Where are our armies?" he demanded.

"The Red Crests march westward and none oppose them. I see a river . . ." Helve's moan was echoed faintly by Coventa. The glow around her deepened to a fiery hue. Lhiannon shook her head as vision teased at her awareness, armies locked in combat and corpses floating downstream.

"The river runs red . . . red . . . it becomes a river of blood that covers the land!" Coventa's thin scream joined Helve's shriek in eerie harmony. Focused on Helve, the priests did not appear to notice, but the other priestesses turned in alarm.

"Get her out of here!" hissed Belina in Lhiannon's ear.

Coventa's limbs were twitching now. With the strength of desperation Lhiannon lifted the girl and stumbled backward into the trees. Behind her she could hear Helve's wail and the murmur as Lugovalos strove to stem the torrent of visions. The Druids would have more questions about the Romans, but Lhiannon did not need to be in trance to predict they would not be asking them at a public festival.

Panting, she leaned against a tree. She tensed as a shadow appeared beside her and then relaxed, recognizing Boudica. Coventa had gone limp, still muttering. Together they carried her through the trees and back to the House of the Healers.

*W*ill she be all right?" Boudica looked from her friend's still face to the strained features of the priestess, alternately lit and shadowed by the flickering of the little fire. Coventa had quieted as soon as they got her away from the grove, and now she lay as one in a deep sleep. She leaned forward, wondering in what dream Coventa wandered now. "Should we try to wake her up?"

"Best not," answered Lhiannon. "People often fear being lost in trance, but if one cannot return consciously, it is better to simply pass into normal sleep. Coventa's mind will reorder itself before waking again. All we can do is to guard her. If she wakes too suddenly some part of her spirit may be dream-lost, and it will be difficult to fetch it back again."

"But you would do it, wouldn't you." It was not quite a question. "Would Helve?" The sound of the festival was like distant waves on the shore—they might have been alone in the world.

Lhiannon looked at her in surprise, and Boudica held her gaze. Except for Coventa, for a year she had refused all offers of friendship, especially Lhiannon's, suspecting condescension, or worse still, pity. Lhiannon was so beautiful, what use could she have for a gawky, head-blind girl? But tonight they were united by a common need and a common fear. Boudica was the one who had noticed that Coventa was in trouble. Tonight she could face her teacher as an equal and dare to wonder what lay behind the serene face the priestess showed the world.

"Oh yes. You must not underestimate her skills. It is likely that she will be High Priestess after Mearan." From outside they heard the joyful shout that hailed the lighting of the Beltane fire.

"I find it hard to like her," said Boudica. Lhiannon said nothing, but her lips tightened, and Boudica understood what the priestess was too loyal to say. "She flirts with every male she sees, but she gives her love to none."

"She must keep pure to serve as Oracle," Lhiannon said evenly. "When Mearan fell ill it was a good thing we had another priestess who was qualified."

"You could do it," Boudica said warmly, and noted the betraying color that reddened Lhiannon's cheekbones. "Is that why you are here instead of dancing around the fire?"

She had seen how Lhiannon and Ardanos looked at each other when they thought no one could see.

"I am here because Coventa needs me!" snapped the priestess, and this time, her response was sharp enough to warn Boudica off.

"I do not understand all this emphasis on virginity," the girl said at last.

"To tell you the truth," Lhiannon said wryly, "at this moment, neither do I!"

Boudica smiled, finding it surprisingly sweet to know herself forgiven. "I do not like the idea of being at the beck and call of a husband, but I would like children. Mearan has always seemed like a mother to this community. I am surprised that she has none."

"In the past the High Priestess often bore children, and another woman served as Oracle," Lhiannon replied.

"But is it so important?" asked Boudica. "How do they manage in Rome?"

"The Romans have no seers of their own," Lhiannon answered, obviously relieved to move the conversation to more neutral ground. "They visit the oracles of Hellas, but when the Sibyl of Cumae offered the books of prophecy to their last king, he refused twice, and she burned six of them before the tribal elders insisted he buy the last three—for the same price she had originally asked for all nine!" Both women laughed. "Now they consult omens or pore over the verses that remain, or make pilgrimage to oracles in other lands."

"I have heard there is an oracle in Delphi. Is she a virgin?"

"That is what they say. The pythia is an untried maiden, though in other times they chose older women who had already raised their families."

"But no one who has a husband or a lover . . ." observed Boudica.

Lhiannon sighed. "There are other kinds of divination a married woman can do. To read omens does not require the same level of trance. Or even to prophesy on the fingers' ends or in answer to a sudden question, as they do in Eriu. But the rite of the bull-sleep in which the Druid divines the name of the rightful king requires the priest to prepare with prayer and fasting, and to sit on the tripod involves an even deeper surrender, for which all the channels must be clear." She sighed.

"And you want to do that," Boudica said.

"Yes. The visions call me as they called Coventa, but I know I must resist them."

Above the crackling of the fire they could hear the skirling of pipes and a sudden shout as some lucky pair leaped over the flames. Lhiannon turned, her eyes shimmering with unshed tears.

"I must resist them," she said. "Helve is the priests' darling, and I will never sit in the high seat while she is here."

"Then go after what you *can* have," Boudica told her. "Coventa needs only a guardian. If someone is waiting for you," she said tactfully, "go to the fires—I can keep watch here."

"There was someone, but I don't suppose he is still waiting now," the priestess said softly, head bowed so that her face was hidden by the shining fall of pale hair. "Once I thought that the Goddess had called me to serve as an oracle, but now the way seems blocked. I am halted, whichever way I turn!"

Boudica stared, shaken to find that even a sworn priestess could be as tormented by doubt as she herself had been.

"How do you know the Lady's will?" she exclaimed. "Does She speak to you?"

Lhiannon looked up at her with a shuddering sigh. "Sometimes . . . though I am usually too fixed on my own pain to listen at those times when I most want to hear."

Such as now . . . thought Boudica.

"Sometimes She speaks to me through the lips of others," Lhiannon managed a wry smile, "as I think She is speaking through you now. Once or twice She has spoken to me aloud, when she occupied Lady Mearan's body during a ritual, and sometimes I have heard Her speaking in the stillness of my soul. But sometimes we know what our choices were only after we have made them. I thought that to gain love I would have to relinquish power, but instead I appear to have traded love for duty."

"Or perhaps for friendship?" asked Boudica, only now, when she found herself letting down the barriers that had kept her solitary here, realizing how lonely she had been.

"Yes, little sister—perhaps that is what I have done." Lhiannon managed a smile.

THREE

*O*n a hot afternoon just before the feast of Lugos, the blare of the bronze carynx horn echoed across the fields. After the Beltane Oracle the Arch-Druid had summoned the kings to take counsel for the fate of Britannia, and they were coming at last. Boudica ran for the House of Maidens to change her clothing. For more than a year her world had been limited to the community here on the isle. What could she say to them? Would any of those she had met at Camulodunon remember her?

Her second summer at the Druids' Isle had been as bountiful as Helve had promised. By midsummer the barley hung heavy on the stalk and the lambs grew fat on the rich grass. But for those who had heard the Oracle's predictions, the blessings of the season were an evil omen, for if Helve was right about the harvest, she might be right about the Roman invasion as well.

Swiftly Boudica pulled the white gown over her head and jerked the comb through her thick hair. Brenna and Morfad were already settling wreaths of summer asters on their heads. She snatched up her own wreath and hurried after the others down the road that led from Lys Deru to the shore.

The chorus of youths and maidens formed behind the senior Druids and priestesses. At the narrowest part of the strait the cliffs were steep on both sides of the water. Boats made their landing farther down, where between the cliffs and the sandbanks there was a narrow beach. A barge was angling toward them across the blue waves. There was a haze upon the water, and all Boudica could make out within were the bright blurs of clothing and a glitter of gold. Another craft followed; she glimpsed the shapes of horses. No doubt the rest of their retinue had been left to camp upon the far shore.

The Arch-Druid had sent out his summons to all the southern tribes. No one at Lys Deru seemed to doubt they would obey, but if Cunobelin, with all his devious skill, had only been able to bring the Trinovantes and the Catuvellauni under his yoke, would even Lugovalos be able to impose unity on tribes that had been enemies since their fathers came into this land?

As the barge reached the midpoint of the strait it seemed to lose way. Boudica remembered that moment from her own arrival, when even untrained and exhausted as she was then, she had felt the pressure of the invisible wall that protected Mona.

"Who approaches the holy isle?" Lugovalos's voice rang out across the water.

"Kings of Britannia, come to take counsel with the Wise," came the answer, blurred by something more than distance.

"Pass, then, by the will of the mighty gods," cried the Arch-Druid, and the priests and priestesses behind him began to sing. There had been no chorus of Druids to welcome the pack-train that brought Boudica, only two priests and a priestess. But she had felt an odd tingle when their voices joined in the spell. There were twelve here now, and the thirteenth was the Arch-Druid standing before them. Their chanting vibrated through her bones.

The Druids were reshaping the relationship between sky and sea. For a moment that vibration matched her own; Boudica saw each particle shimmering and understood what her teachers meant by the harmony of all things. When she could focus again, she saw the two barges and their passengers clearly. But the far shore behind them was still veiled by a golden haze. Their guests had passed the barrier.

Boudica recognized Cunobelin's two sons immediately; wiry, red-haired Caratac, who had taken over the Cantiaci kingdom, and Togodumnos, grown more portly already as he settled into his father's dignities. With them were two more whom she did not know. Behind Togodumnos she glimpsed another man, tall with fair hair and a mustache.

She raised one eyebrow as she realized it was Prasutagos, brother of the Northern Iceni king.

As the barge approached the shore, the youths and maidens began to sing:

> "It is to the land of gifted men that you have come,
> It is to the land of wise women that you have come,
> It is to the land of fair harvests that you have come,
> And to the land of song.
> You who sit in the seat of the hero,
> You who sit in the seat of the king,
> You who give ear to good counsel,
> Be you welcome here . . ."

If both Helve and Lady Mearan have foreseen a Roman victory, why have you called us here?" said King Togodumnos. Unusual among the younger men, he wore a short beard. "Are you counseling us to bare our throats to the Roman wolf without a fight?"

There was a growl from the other leaders, and Boudica, who was refilling the golden drinking bowl, stopped with it in her hand. The kings had spent half a day already debating whether the visions should be believed. At this rate, deciding what to do about them might take till the next full moon.

"I am willing to go down fighting," added Caratac, "but I would rather not know that I am doomed before I begin!" As he leaned forward the firelight kindled a new flame in his russet hair. He was not so kingly a figure as his older brother, but though he always spoke to and of Togodumnos with respect, Boudica judged that of the two he had, if not the greater intelligence, certainly more energy.

To house their guests the Druids had repaired the huts in the meadow where they held the festivals and removed the wicker sides from the long feasting hall to admit air and light for their deliberations. In the central trench a fire was kept burning, providing light and warmth and a witness to oaths as well. Several stave buckets bound in bronze and filled with ale served to lubricate the deliberations. Boudica, who had lived in a royal household, was an obvious choice to bear around the drinking bowl. She was not sure whether or not to consider it a privilege, but at least her duties were clear.

"If doom was certain do you think I would have called you here?" the Arch-Druid replied. "What we foresee is what might be if matters continue as they have begun. But fate is like a river, constantly changing. The addition of a new stream can turn it to a flood; a pebble—or six"—he surveyed the men before him with a wry smile—"can alter the flow. We are not foredoomed, but forewarned."

"The easiest way to avoid bloodshed would be to welcome the Romans when they come," observed Tancoric of the Durotriges. His lands, Boudica recalled, included the Summer Country and the Isle of Avalon.

"If we make treaties," he went on, "they will not need to conquer us. Let the emperor call us client-kings. He will be in Rome and we will be here, enjoying the benefits of Roman trade."

"And paying Roman taxes, and sending our warriors to the ends of the earth to fight his wars," snapped Caratac.

"Roman trade may be as great a danger as Roman armies," King Togodumnos said slowly. "My father kept his freedom, but by the time he died he was more Roman than Catuvellauni. I, too, have grown accustomed to their luxuries, but I am beginning to fear them. If we continue to trade with them we will still change, but slowly. If they rule us, the next generation of Britons will be speaking Latin and making their offerings to the Roman gods."

And the Druids and their wisdom will be gone from this land . . . thought Boudica.

"If we do choose to fight, do you truly think that we can win?" King Maglorios of the Belgae said then. He was an older man, going bald now but still strong, whose lands lay between those of the Durotriges and the Atrebates. He gestured and Boudica came forward to offer him the drinking bowl with the elegance she had learned in Cunobelin's hall. He gave her an appreciative look, and she dodged a more-than-appreciative pat as she took the bowl back to fill it again.

"If you join together," answered the High Priestess, "I believe you can make them retreat, just as Caesar, despite his boasts of conquest, did a hundred years ago." She looked tired. Boudica had heard that when the Druids had performed a second, private ritual, Mearan had seen even more bloodshed than Helve.

"I will gladly clasp hands with all those who are here," said Tancoric, "but what about those who are not? I notice that the Regni refused your invitation."

"There may be more than one reason for that," said Mearan.

"Perhaps they heard that the sons of Cunobelin were going to be here," said Maglorios, and the others laughed. The Regni lands were bordered on the north by the territory ruled by Togodumnos and on the east by the Cantiaci country, where Caratac was now king.

"And perhaps the Atrebates heard that *you* would be here!" retorted Togodumnos. "They are your neighbors, after all."

The Arch-Druid shook his head. "I did not invite them. King Veric has a treaty with the Romans. He sent his grandson Cogidumnus to be fostered by the emperor, and would not dare to turn against them even if he desired."

"The Isle of Vectis has a tempting harbor. The Romans could march straight up the middle of Britannia through the Atrebate lands. We will have to do something about Veric . . ." Caratac said slowly. He looked at his brother and Boudica shivered. Cunobelin's sons had inherited his ambition to unite Britannia. The threat of Roman conquest might be what they needed in order to succeed.

"And will the men of art fight with us?" came a new voice. The others turned as Prince Prasutagos leaned forward. He had not spoken often in this council, but when he did, men listened to his words.

"Indeed," said the Arch-Druid with a wintry smile. "The Romans will not give *us* the option of surrender. Our magic is perhaps not all that legend makes it, but we have some power over wind and weather, and the reading of omens. We shall send our most talented priests and priestesses to march with you when the time for battle comes."

The prince nodded, and Boudica came forward to offer him the drinking bowl. When he looked up to take it, there was sadness behind his smile. The servants said that the prince had recently lost his wife in childbirth. It was too bad. He had a good face, and she thought he would have made a kindly father to little ones.

"Then I hope your seers can tell us when the invasion will come. It will be hard to gather an army, and even harder to keep it together," said King Maglorios.

Boudica carried the drinking bowl around the circle, and the discussion of warriors and supplies and strategies went on.

*M*uch as Lhiannon loved Lys Deru, at times its atmosphere of focused dedication could become constricting, especially now, when the presence of the royal strangers reminded them so forcibly that there was another world beyond the Druids' Isle. She had been honored to accompany the kings to make their offerings at the Lake of Little Stones, although she was still not certain whether Mearan wantèd her assistance as a priestess or as a chaperone for Boudica, who was striding along ahead of her.

They had started that morning, passing through patches of woodland and shorn fields where crows seeking fallen grains amid the stubble flew up in raucous alarm. It had been a bounteous harvest indeed, and in coming seasons the grain that filled the storage pits might be needed to feed people whose fields were trampled by war.

But Mona's fields, though rich, did not cover the whole island. A few miles inland, the fertile ground on the eastern side gave way to a swath of marshland that ran from the southern shore halfway across the island. As Lhiannon took a deep breath of air rich with the scent of vegetation and a hint of the sea, the swoop of a gull drew her gaze across the marshes. Something was moving among the reedbeds. She recognized the stately stalk of a heron, gray feathers sheened with blue in the sun. A flotilla of ducks and terns moved into view on the open water that gleamed beyond, feathered rumps pointing skyward as they dove. Humans were not the only ones to find a good harvest here. The wind tugged at her veil and she unpinned it, letting her fine hair fly free as Boudica's. Tonight both would

have a mass of tangles, but they could help each other with
the snarls.

From ahead came the deep rumbling of male laughter
where the kings marched together. After them came the
Arch-Druid, flanked by Ardanos and Cunitor, with young
Bendeigid leading the gentle mare that carried Mearan.
The High Priestess was the only one of them who was rid-
ing. These days the pain in her hip made walking difficult.
Lhiannon suspected other ills that the older woman hid,
but none of them dared to question her.

As Lhiannon watched, Ardanos dropped back to speak
to Mearan. She shook her head and he looked up with a
worried frown that wrenched Lhiannon's heart. *Oh my
dear, of course she is in pain, but she will never admit it
to you . . .* But she loved him for trying. Since the aborted
tryst at the Beltane fires there had been a constraint between them. He said he understood why she had not come,
but she saw the hurt in his eyes and did not dare try to heal
it until she was certain she understood what the Goddess
wanted of her.

From behind she could hear an irregular clop of hooves
and a jingling of harness from the ponies that carried the
offerings. The island had few roads fit for wagons, and
there were places where even laden horses could not go. It
was a roundabout way that would take them to the sacrificial pool, but on such a fine, sunny day, Lhiannon found
it hard to care.

Just past noon they crossed the stream that fed the
marsh and turned westward. Thick woodlands shrank to
tangles of gorse that clung to scattered outcrops of gray
stone, and reed-edged rivulets drained the land. As the
day drew on, Lhiannon began to wish that she had spent
more time in physical activity and less in meditation. She
glared at Boudica, envying the girl's limber, easy stride.
Her back ached and her feet were sore.

They halted at last in a hollow where a standing stone
marked a narrow path turning off from the road. The sun
was disappearing behind the gray mass of the holy mountain ahead of them, but to their left the ground fell away
toward the sea. Nearer still a small lake reflected a translucent sky.

"Sit, child," said Lhiannon, waving at Boudica, who had climbed the outcrop to get a better view. "It makes me tired to watch you." Lhiannon eased back against a boulder and stretched out her legs with a sigh as the girl slid down again.

"Is that the sacred pool?" she asked, pointing down the hill.

"That is the pool we call the Mother," answered Lhiannon. "The Daughter lies farther along, protected from casual view. We will seek her fasting, at dawn."

"But we'll eat tonight, won't we?" asked Bendeigid, who had wandered over to join them. Ardanos and Cunitor were helping Mearan off the horse and leading her to a seat covered with folded cloaks. Though she smiled in thanks, she looked pale.

"If it were up to Lugovalos, we would not," Lhiannon answered, "but even the Arch-Druid will not require such self-denial of kings. Console yourself with the thought of the meat we'll feast on tomorrow. If we are to get any dinner at all this evening we had best get busy now." She levered herself to her feet and hobbled over to the fire pit.

Some of the men had already set up tall fire-dogs of wrought iron to suspend the riveted bronze cauldron and gotten a fire going beneath it. Lhiannon stood over the cauldron, waiting for curls of steam to rise from the water. When she saw them, she dropped in the bag of barley. Boudica balanced a board across two stones and began to chop greens.

The long summer day was fading to twilight in ever more delicate shades of rose and gold. The bubbling of the cauldron blended into an evening hush that muted even the voices of the men. Three ravens came flying from the direction of the holy island, their elegant shapes sharply defined against the luminous sky.

"Sorry, brothers—we've nothing for you this time," called King Tancoric. "Come back tomorrow and we'll feed you well."

"And when the Romans come, we'll make you a truly worthy offering," added Caratac. A burst of laughter echoed his words.

The ravens circled the campsite as if they were listening. Lhiannon shivered as with a last harsh cry they sped away.

"Are you cold? I could fetch a cloak," said Boudica.

The priestess shook her head and gave another stir to the cauldron. "It was the birds," she explained. "We call the gods for blessings, but they can be terrible, especially Cathubodva the Battle Raven, whose birds those are . . ."

"What did he mean by a worthy offering?" asked Bendi.

"He means corpses," said Ardanos, joining them. "After a battle, the wolves and the ravens feast on the dead. You know what the oakwood looks like in the fall when acorns cover the ground? The acorns are the mast that the pigs eat, but they say that on a battlefield the severed heads of the fallen lie like acorns, and they call them the 'mast of the Morrigan,' the Great Queen whom we also call Cathubodva . . ."

He turned to Lhiannon. "The High Priestess is chilled. Is there anything I can give her?"

"Hand me that cup—the barley is not yet tender, but enough of its essence has gone into the water to do her some good." Lhiannon ladled broth into the cup and dropped in a pinch of salt. "Here, Bendi." She turned to the boy. "You are learning to be a healer. Sometimes food is medicine, too. Take that to the Lady, and when she has finished it, ask if she wants more."

"Does the Morrigan *enjoy* the bloodshed?" asked Boudica when he had gone.

"She weeps . . ." Lhiannon said softly. "The night before a battle she walks the field and shrieks in despair. She waits at the ford and washes the bloody clothing of the doomed. She begs them to turn back, but they never do."

"And then, when battle is joined," Ardanos added grimly, "she grants the madness that gives the warriors the strength of heroes, and allows them to do deeds that no man could face in cold blood. And so kings sacrifice to her for victory."

"Is she good or evil?" asked Boudica.

"Both," Lhiannon said with an attempt at a smile. "When she makes love with the Good God at the river she brings life to the land. He balances her destruction and makes her smile once more."

"Look at it this way," said Ardanos. "Is a storm good or ill?"

"I suppose it is good when it brings the rain we need and bad when a flood washes away our homes."

"We do not always know why the rain falls," added Ardanos, "or why the gods do what they do. Folk call the Druids wise, but you must realize by now that we should be called the people who seek wisdom. We study the visible world around us and we reach out to the invisible world within. When we truly understand them we become like the gods, able to command their powers because we move within their harmony."

This is what I love in him, thought Lhiannon, *not only the touch of his hand but the touch of his soul.*

And as if he had felt her thought, Ardanos looked back at her, and the breach between them was healed.

*I*t was the gray hour just before the dawning. They rose in silence, the white robes of the Druids ghostly in the gloom. Even the kings moved quietly as they loaded the offerings onto the horses. Boudica rubbed sleep from her eyes and wrapped her cloak more tightly around her shoulders, wincing as the movement jarred muscles she had not known were sore. Then, with the others, she followed the Arch-Druid down the path. In the dim light, the shape of his goosefeather headdress and the stiff folds of his horsehide cape loomed as contorted as the stone outcrops that crouched like monstrous guardians against the brightening sky. A torch flamed in his hand.

Behind him came the High Priestess, supported by Ardanos and Lhiannon, her frail form swathed in dark draperies from which an occasional glint of silver gleamed. With each movement came a faint shimmer of sound from the silver bells tied to the branch in her hand.

As they left the campsite, a harsh call split the silence. The ravens were back again, wheeling above like shards of night.

They remember the feast the kings promised them, thought Boudica. Suddenly the shapes of rock and tree seemed insubstantial, as if they were only a veil that at any moment might be drawn aside to reveal some more luminous reality, and she understood why the sacrifice had to take place at this liminal hour between night and day.

Halfway down the slope the ground leveled. She could not see what lay beyond it. The kings unloaded the horses, then took them back up the hill, except for the last one, a white stallion that had borne no burden but his own gleaming hide. Him, they tethered to the thorn tree that grew at the edge of the overhang. In the gloom she could just make out three dark shapes among the branches. The ravens. Waiting . . .

The High Priestess and Lhiannon stepped forward to face the Arch-Druid at the edge of the cliff. Below it, the waters gleamed black and so still that the surface was etched with smooth spirals by the passage of the gulls that floated there.

"By heaven that gives us life and breath," sang Mearan. "By the waters in whose movement all things grow and change; by the solid earth on which we stand . . . O spirits who dwell in this place, we ask your blessing."

"By the fire of life that illuminates the spirit; by the pool from which we draw power; by the tree that links earth and heaven . . ."— Lugovalos held his torch high— "we call the Shining Ones to witness."

Lhiannon moved forward. "By all the hopes borne on the wind; by all the memories that lie within the pool; by present knowledge in the fields we know; we call on the wisdom of our fathers and mothers who have gone before."

"Hear us! Bless us! Be with us now!" they cried as one. The stallion pulled nervously at his tether and the startled gulls burst yammering into the air.

The sky had brightened to a translucent pale blue. The sun was still hidden behind the mountains on the mainland, but its coming was proclaimed by a growing radiance. Togodumnos picked up a long sword and the light gleamed on its blade. The Druids taught that there were two kinds of sacrifice: those that were shared to bind men and gods in one community, and those that were broken and put beyond use by humankind. It was the second they meant to offer now.

"These weapons we won from our foes in battles between the tribes. As I destroy this blade"—he set his heel upon the point of the sword and leaned, and the metal groaned and gave—"I end the enmity that was between us. Gods of our people, accept this sacrifice!" The sword wheeled outward as he released it, the distorted curve carving the pale sky, and disappeared with a splash into the dark waters below.

Caratac snapped the shaft of a spear, then broke off the tip against a stone. "Never more shall this spear drink Celtic blood! May the Lady of Ravens accept the sacrifice!"

If only, thought Boudica, *the hatreds between the tribes could be drowned so easily!* But perhaps the Roman threat would frighten them into setting old enmities aside. One by one the kings came forward with swords and spears, shields with bosses of bronze sculpted in graceful triple spirals, pieces of horse harness, and fittings for the wicker chariots that were the tribes' most terrifying weapon in war. These were works of art as well as use, a treasure that could have bought support from followers, but there might be no followers if they did not have the favor of the gods. As the pile dwindled, Boudica fingered her dagger, wondering if she ought to throw it in. But though she was of the blood of kings, she herself had neither position nor power. What business did she have bothering the gods, especially at this ritual?

Holy Ones, she thought then, *if you will tell me what would please you, I will do my best to make the sacrifice.* She had a sudden sense of vertigo as if the earth had shifted beneath her. For a moment she found it hard to breathe. Boudica had always *believed* that the gods were listening, but suddenly she *knew* that she had been heard, and shivered, wondering if it had been wise to make so unconstrained an offering.

And now the ripples from the last dented shield had stilled. A breath of wind brought the scent of the fire that Bendeigid was tending. The sky was bright now, and the jagged edges of the eastern horizon edged in gold. Ardanos and Cunitor stripped off their white robes and laid them aside, then went to the thorn tree and untied the stallion's halter.

The Iceni were great lovers of horses. Boudica had

missed not being around them. This was a fine animal, whose shining coat and bright eyes proclaimed its good condition. But as she looked at the horse she sensed something more. She had seen beasts in plenty slain for the table or as offerings, but at this moment everything—the animal, the humans, the dark waters beneath the cliff, seemed suddenly more *real. No,* she thought then, *the sacrifice makes everything more* holy . . .

The beast skittered nervously as one of the ravens gave a hoarse cry. This time no one made a joke about it. They could all feel that not only the birds but the gods themselves were eager for the offering.

As the two younger Druids held the horse, Mearan paced slowly around him, shaping the air around his body with the branch of silver bells. The stallion's ears flicked nervously, following the sound.

"The head of this horse is the dawn! His eye is the sun and his breath is the wind," Lugovalos sang. "His back is as broad as the bowl of the sky. The sun rises in his forehead and sets in the crease between his quarters."

The deep rumble of the Arch-Druid's voice seemed to vibrate in the very earth. Was it his words or the blessing of the bells that made the air around him glow? It was a song of transformation, the part becoming the whole, the world of the flesh offered to the world of the spirit.

The stallion jerked as a breath of wind made the torch flare. "This horse is the earth and the stars of heaven. This horse is the steed that journeys between the worlds. This horse is the offering."

Bendeigid offered Ardanos the sacrificial blade. Steel caught the light as he reached to draw it across the animal's throat and the stallion neighed and surged upward, striking at the air. A flailing forefoot caught Ardanos in the ribs and the knife flew glittering from his hand and splashed into the pool. Lhiannon cried out and ran to Ardanos as he fell.

The kings leaped aside as the horse dragged Cunitor across the ground, but Prasutagos dodged the hooves and leaped forward, grabbing the halter and using his greater weight to hold the animal still.

"He's had the wind knocked out of him," said Lhiannon as Ardanos gasped. She began to probe his torso with gentle fingers, but when she felt down his ribs he screamed. "And broken some ribs," she added. "Be still, my dear. We must bind you up before you try to move."

The stallion ceased to struggle as Prasutagos spoke to him, his voice a gentle unceasing murmur like the wind. Only then, looking at the others, did Boudica realize what a disastrous omen this must be.

She drew her knife and ripped at the bottom of her tunica, gritting her teeth until the strong linen gave way and she could tear a strip from the hem. "Use this," she said, offering it to Lhiannon.

"Cunitor, bring the horse back," said Lugovalos. "We must complete the ritual."

"I will bring him," said Prasutagos. "He senses your Druid's fear."

Well, that was no wonder, thought Boudica, seeing what had happened to Ardanos. But she could not help feeling a spurt of pride. The Iceni were known for the training as well as the breeding of horses, and Prasutagos was clearly a master.

The prince led the animal back to the edge. He stroked the satiny neck, whispering into the pricked ear until the noble head drooped and the horse grew still. Still whispering, he leaned on the strong neck and touched the animal's knees until the horse knelt and rocked and lay down.

Lugovalos took off the feathered headdress and rustling hide cloak and laid them aside.

"Take my dagger." Caratac held out a shining blade. "It is newly sharpened."

"This horse is the offering . . ." the Arch-Druid said in a low voice. Moving slowly, he came up on the animal's other side and crouched, holding the knife at his side until the last moment, and then, in a swift, smooth motion, drawing it across the throat.

Blood gushed out in a shining stream. For a moment the horse did not seem to realize what had happened. Then he jerked, but Prasutagos had his weight on the animal's neck, still murmuring, and presently the great head drooped and the prince lowered it gently to the ground.

In the sudden light of the risen sun the world seemed

turned to scarlet as blood pooled beneath the white body and flowed in a red river toward the edge of the cliff. Boudica blinked, seeing the shimmer of energy that had surrounded the stallion move with it into the pool. But it seemed to take a long time until the life force left entirely and there was only a carcass lying there.

In silence Cunitor and the other men butchered the animal, taking the heart and liver and carving off great chunks of flesh from the hindquarters. Boudica helped to work pieces of meat onto iron skewers and suspend them above the fire. The head and legs were left attached to the hide, which was dragged down to the waterside and suspended from a post that had clearly been used for that purpose before. When they were done, the guts were heaped beside the thorn tree and the rest of the carcass tipped into the pool.

The morning stillness was shattered by the triumphant cawing of the ravens as they descended on their share of the feast. The hem of the Arch-Druid's gown was bloody and the front of Prasutagos's tunic crimson where he had cradled the head of the horse as it died. Nausea warred with hunger as the scent of roasting horsemeat filled the air.

Everything is food for something . . . thought Boudica. *May my death be as worthy when the time comes for me.* But she was acutely aware that all those who shared the feast not only offered, but were part of the sacrifice.

FOUR

"Velve did not want me to sit with you," said Coventa. The folds of Boudica's fur-lined cloak were still sufficient to wrap both of them as they waited for the midwinter feast to arrive. "But I don't mind if she blisters my ears tomorrow if this evening you will keep me warm!"

When the kings left Mona they had taken the summer with them, and the winter that followed was turning out to be colder and wetter than any since Boudica had come here, or perhaps it only seemed that way because for every tribe that had agreed to join the alliance there was one that refused the Arch-Druid's call.

A ripple of music brought Boudica's head around. At the end of the fire pit, screens of laced hides kept drafts from the dining couches and side tables where the senior Druids reigned. That new man, Brangenos, had come in and was adjusting the strings on his crescent-shaped harp. A bard of the Druid Order from Gallia, he had only recently reached the haven of the isle. He was tall, and thin almost to the point of emaciation, with a streak of white through his black hair. He was also a much better harper than Ardanos, who had been the chief of their bards until now. But even when he smiled, one could see sorrow in his eyes.

As he finished tuning, there was a stir at the door. The Arch-Druid was entering. In honor of the festival, over his white robe he wore a thick fringed mantle woven of seven colors. After him came the senior Druids, followed by Ardanos and Cunitor and the other younger priests. Where, she wondered as they took their places at the head of the fire pit, were the priestesses?

At a nod from Lugovalos, Brangenos rose, the harp cradled in the crook of his arm, and began to sing:

*"The people cheered for the leader of war-bands
The king of the marching men called the tribes to war
Now all the shouting is silent and the wind plays a harp
of bone."*

The harp gave forth a shimmer of sound as the Druid
drew his fingers across the strings. *He comes from the land
of Vercingetorix,* remembered Boudica. *At least the only
Gaul who bested Caesar in battle is remembered there.*

Everywhere in the Celtic lands they knew the story of
how Vercingetorix had united the Gaulish tribes, using
the hillforts and the hills themselves as bases from which
to attack Caesar's legions. But in the end the Roman imperator penned him up in Alesia and starved him out.

*"The high king came to the lord of the eagles
Laid down his arms to save his warriors
Nameless is his grave, and the wind plays a harp of bone."*

Once more sound sighed from the strings. Then the
harp was still. The Gaulish king had been dragged through
the streets of Rome in Caesar's triumph and imprisoned
for years in a hole in the ground before the Romans killed
him. This was certainly no very cheerful music for the
solstice. Why was it always the defeated who got the best
songs?

While the bard was playing, Mearan had appeared. For
a moment Boudica was disappointed to have missed her
entrance, for the High Priestess usually took her meals in
her own house, and her appearance at the high festivals
was attended by some ceremony. But even the ruddy firelight could not disguise the fact that she was pale. Perhaps
she had taken advantage of the distraction to keep them
from noticing that she had to be assisted into her chair.

Helve, on the other hand, was blooming. The priestess
had always been pleasant to Boudica, but that was more
because she knew that Boudica was highborn than from
any personal feeling. The girl had seen that look on sons
of kings who were eager to inherit their fathers' honors.
And she had seen them afterward, sometimes, when the
choice of the chieftains fell upon another man of the royal

kin. She did not think that Helve would deal well with disappointment, but she wondered how the rest of them were going to deal with Helve if her expectations were fulfilled.

The hides that covered the doorway were drawn aside once more and the marvelous scent of roast boar filled the hall. Crowned with ivy in honor of the season, old Elin led the procession. There were bowls of porridge with dried fruit, platters of root vegetables, and baskets of sausages and cheese. Two of the older boys bore between them a plank from which chunks of pork sent white curls of steam into the air. Mouths watered as the Arch-Druid lifted his hands and began to intone a blessing over the food.

$\mathcal{B}$oudica drained her wooden ale cup and sat back with a sigh. "That was good. This is the first time in days I have felt warm inside and out."

"Your cheeks are flushed from the ale," observed Coventa. "Or is it because Rianor is staring at you?"

"He is not—" Boudica looked up and saw that the boy had taken her glance as an invitation and was coming toward them with two of his friends.

"I think he likes you . . ." Coventa grinned, and squealed as Boudica pinched her.

Rianor was no longer a boy, she realized suddenly. He had shot up during the past months, and his chin bore a trace of dark beard. It was just that compared to warriors such as those who had visited them last summer he still seemed a child.

"Move over, maidens," he grinned. "Or did you eat so much there's no room on the bench? It's not fair that you should block all the heat of that fire."

"Are you saying I've grown fat?" protested Boudica, but she was already sliding over so that Rianor could squeeze in. She flushed a little as he put his arm around her shoulders. His friend Albi tried to do the same and missed, landing in the straw at their feet, where he was joined by the other boys, playfully cuffing each other like her father's hunting dogs used to scuffle before they stretched out before the fire.

In the pack there was an order—in the boy pack, too. Rianor was a leader. So was Cloto, but since the visit of the kings many of his former followers were avoiding him.

"What did you think of our new bard?" Rianor asked.

"He has such sad eyes," observed Coventa with a sigh.

"Well, his song was sad enough," Albi agreed.

"Then we should learn from it," Cloto said harshly. "You can't fight Rome. Vercingetorix tried, and died, and all those proud kings who came here will die, too."

"Caesar conquered Vercingetorix and Caesar is dead," objected Rianor. "This emperor they have now is not a warrior."

"He does not have to be," Cloto said grimly. "He has generals who will do the work for him."

"And so you think we should just lie down and let them?" exclaimed Albi. As they grew louder, others began to turn. Boudica made a hushing motion and for a moment everyone was still. When Cloto spoke again his voice was intense, but low.

"We should welcome them, make treaties. They will have to treat us fairly if we are protected by their law."

"Like Veric," said Boudica. Cloto shrugged. Everyone knew he was a cousin of the Atrebate king. Of course he would agree with him.

"And when we are all as tame as the tribes of Gallia, what then?" whispered Rianor. "Our children will grow up speaking Latin and forget our gods."

"I don't think that is quite fair," Albi said slowly. "I've heard that all the peoples of the Empire are free to worship their own gods so long as they also honor the gods of Rome."

"All except the Druids . . ." Coventa said suddenly. Her eyes had gone unfocused and she was trembling. "The Druids of Gallia who did not flee were killed."

Boudica gripped her arms and gave her a little shake, willing her to focus on the here and now. If she went into one of her fits they would have the priests down on them for sure. For a moment the younger girl sat rigid beneath her hands, then she relaxed with a sigh.

"It's true," Rianor said then. "We Druids don't have a choice. If the Romans rule Britannia, the people may survive, but they will no longer be Atrebates or Brigantes or Regni." His voice rose. "By the gods, we of the tribes love our freedom so much we will not even join together as Britons beneath one king! How can you think it would be better to be swallowed up by Rome?" He glared at Cloto and the other boy leaped to his feet, fists balled and ready.

As Rianor surged upright to face him Ardanos appeared suddenly behind them, gripping each boy's shoulder in a strong hand.

"What are you thinking?" he hissed, his ginger hair appearing to stand on end. "Your quarrel profanes the festival! Thank the Goddess, the High Priestess and the Arch-Druid have departed already."

They gaped at him. How much had Ardanos overheard? Boudica knew that the Druids were having the same arguments as the young people they trained. But not, she had to admit, in front of the whole community at a festival.

Ardanos let the boys go. "If you can fight, you can work! The feast is over. Get busy cleaning up the hall."

*A*re the gods many, or are there only two, or one?" Lugovalos leaned forward, his white beard glistening in the light of the spring day. Boudica rubbed her eyes and tried to pay attention. She had recently passed her sixteenth birthday, and her long limbs were finding a new harmony. She would so much rather have been chasing sheep or gathering spring greens for the pot, or any kind of labor if it let her *move*.

"Lhiannon teaches us that all of those are true," said Brenna with a grin for their mentor. "All the goddesses, all that we see as womanly and divine, we call the Goddess. But when we pray, She wears one face or another—Maiden or Mother or Wisewoman, or Brigantia or Cathubodva."

And none of them, thought Boudica, *seem to want to talk to me.*

"All that is divine and male we call the God. We call on them as Lord and Lady at Beltane . . ." Brenna blushed. She had just returned from her womanhood ceremonies on the Isle of Avalon and was making sure everyone knew that she planned to seek a lover at the Beltane fires.

"Your teacher has taught you well," said the Arch-Druid. Lhiannon bowed her head, but she did not look as if the praise had made her very happy. Or perhaps it was the reference to Beltane. Would she go to meet Ardanos this year?

"So," said Lugovalos, "you understand that the gods are both one and many. We honor the One, but there are few indeed who can bear the touch of that power." For a moment he paused, his upturned face illuminated, and Boudica was abruptly certain that he was one who had been in the presence of the Source of All. Then he smiled and turned to them again.

"Perhaps we know more while we are between lives, but as long as we are in human bodies with human senses, it is to the many that we make our prayers and our offerings."

Rianor raised his hand. "My lord, which god should we be praying to now, when we face war?"

"How do you name that power in your own land?"

"The Trinovantes offer to Camulos," came the proud answer. "Camulodunon is the war god's dun."

Boudica nodded, remembering the stately circle of oaks in the meadow to the north of the dun. It housed a slab of stone where the god had been carved standing between two trees, wearing an oak-leaf crown.

Other students were offering additional names—red Cocidios in the north, Teutates among the Catuvellauni, and Lenos of the Silures. The Belgae sacrificed to Olloudios and the Brigantes to Belutacadros. Among her own people, Coroticos was the name they called when they went to war, but like many among the tribes, it was a goddess, Andraste, to whom they prayed for the battle fervor that would bring victory.

"When the tribes join together, which god or goddess should lead them?" Bendeigid asked.

"I will ask you a question," the Arch-Druid replied. "What is the difference between an army and a warrior?"

"A warrior is one man and an army is many," the boy replied. He was not the only one to look confused.

"But the army is more than a collection of fighters. When you say 'a Druid,' you could mean me, or Cunitor, or Mearan. But when you say 'the Druids,' you are talking about a greater entity that includes all of our powers and our traditions."

"People are like that, too," said Coventa suddenly. "A woman can be a daughter, and a mother, and a priestess, but people talk to you as only one of those things at a time."

The Arch-Druid nodded. "An army is also more than the sum of its warriors. It has a spirit, a mind of its own. And so it is with the gods. When the fighters in an army call the war god by different names they call into being a greater power that includes them all."

"Not all of them . . ." someone said quietly. Ardanos was standing at the edge of the circle, looking grave. "The god of the Atrebates will not fight with us. Caratac has driven Veric from his land."

For a moment silence held them all. The news was not unexpected, but to hear it suddenly, and in this context, was startling, as if by talking about the god of war they had summoned him. In the faces around her Boudica could see the shock of that awareness.

"Curse you all!" Cloto jumped to his feet, glaring around him. "And you most of all!" He spat at the Arch-Druid's feet. "The Catuvellauni have always lusted after our lands, but without your support they would not have dared to take them!"

Cunitor laid a hand on the boy's arm. "Come, Cloto, here we are no longer Atrebate or Trinovante, but Druids. Lugovalos has done what he thought best for the whole of Britannia."

"He has brought doom on our people!" Cloto wrenched his arm from Cunitor's grasp and stood with clenched fists, defying them all. Lugovalos could have immobilized him with a word, but the Arch-Druid only gazed at the boy, sorrow in his eyes.

"You think you are so wise!" Cloto spat. "Do you not see that you will bring upon us the very thing you fear? Caratac has driven Veric into the arms of the Romans. Their treaty requires them to help him, and this will be all the excuse they need!"

"But Helve *saw* them invading," said Coventa, holding out her hands in appeal. "Don't you understand that to unite against them is our only chance to survive?"

For a moment they stared with locked gaze, the furious boy and the fey girl. Who had the right of it? Was fate fixed, as it had been in the stories Cunobelin's old Greek slave used to tell?

"Curse you! I curse you all!" Cloto screamed. "When this island runs with blood you will remember, and wish you had lis—"

And now, at last, Lugovalos lifted his hand, and though the boy's lips continued to move, no sound came. In the sudden silence someone giggled nervously, then gulped and was still.

"Enough," the Arch-Druid said. "If you will not stand with us, you are no longer one of our company. You will gather your things and go to the landing. A boat will be waiting for you there."

Speechless, they watched Cloto stalk away. Lugovalos had silenced him, but even the Arch-Druid could not wipe those words from everyone's memory. What if Cloto was right? Was it better to fight for the right reason, even if you failed, or to surrender for the sake of safety? The Druids had no choice. And if they were doomed, at least the bards could sing about how valiantly they had tried.

*T*hat summer brought rumors of war on every wind. Some said that King Veric had been killed, others, that he had fled across the sea to hold the emperor to their treaty and would return with a Roman army to win back his land. If so, thought Lhiannon grimly, Lugovalos's efforts to create a defensive alliance were creating an excuse for the attack the Britons feared. But as spring gave way to summer, she found it hard to care, for Lady Mearan was dying.

As Lhiannon came up the path to the roundhouse where the High Priestess lived she saw Boudica push through the cloth that hung across the door, a wooden basin in her arms.

"How is she?"

"The Lady has kept nothing down today," Boudica exclaimed. "She has grown so thin, Lhiannon! I think that only the strength of her spirit is keeping her alive!"

"She always had courage," murmured the priestess.

"I saw King Cunobelin die. He drifted between sleep and waking until finally he woke no more. But Mearan is awake. Is there nothing you can do for her, Lhiannon?"

"If she cannot take the infusions, we cannot help her with medicines, but I may be able to help her detach her mind from the body's pain."

Boudica nodded and carried the bowl off to empty it. Lhiannon took a last breath of the hay-scented air and went inside. As she noted the waxy pallor of Mearan's skin, she had a sinking feeling that the battle being waged here was one that they were going to lose.

"My lady, how fare you? Are you in pain?" she asked softly, kneeling beside Coventa at Mearan's side.

Slowly the bruised eyelids opened. "Not now. I feel . . . light . . ."

And well she might, thought Lhiannon. It seemed to her that the strong bones of the older woman's face poked through the skin even more sharply than they had the day before.

"I think that soon I will float away." Mearan paused, then drew breath again. "It is not by my will that I leave you, but some good may come from this. Between the worlds, I can *see* . . ."

"You must not tire yourself." Lhiannon heard herself say the denying words even as she realized that Mearan was right. It was said that the final vision of an adept had great power.

"*You* must not delude yourself . . ." the High Priestess echoed wryly. "I know that I am dying."

Lhiannon sat back on her heels as Boudica came in with the emptied bowl and a pitcher.

"My lady, here is cool water from the sacred spring," said the girl. "It will ease you." Lhiannon helped the sick woman to sit upright so that she could drink and then laid her back upon the pillows once more.

"Thank you . . ." Mearan closed her eyes. For a few moments her labored breathing was the only sound. "Hear me. This morning I lay in a waking dream . . ." she said. Lhiannon straightened, attention narrowing to the focus in which all she heard would be remembered, as she had been trained to do.

"I saw you, Lhiannon—only you were old. Older, I think, than I will ever be."

"Is that who it was!" exclaimed Coventa. She flushed as she caught Lhiannon's disapproving glare. "I know I should not, mistress, but truly I could not help it. I was half asleep, and sitting right beside her, so I saw . . ."

Lhiannon sighed. If the child picked up the visions of a seeress in the chair, it was no surprise that she should share Mearan's visions now. For her own good, Coventa should be given other duties, but if Lhiannon suggested it, Helve would no doubt disagree.

"Never mind, child," she murmured. "Lady—what else did you see?"

"You were in a house surrounded by forest, some place I have never been. You wore the ornaments of a high priestess." Eyes still closed, she smiled.

Lhiannon stiffened in shock, looking at the two girls to see if they had heard. "Mearan," she whispered, "what do you mean? Am I to be High Priestess after you?" It was the privilege of the High Priestess to choose her successor, though the Druids could decide whether to accept that choice. And Helve had been so sure . . .

"High Priestess . . ." The sick woman's voice strengthened. "Yes . . . that you will be, but not now, my daughter. And not here . . ." She coughed. "Between that time and this there is a void. There is something there—fire—blood . . ." Her head rolled fretfully on the pillow. "I cannot see . . ." she moaned. "I have to see!" The words were cut off as she retched into the bowl that Boudica held.

"Mearan! Drink this! Don't try to talk, dear—I don't need to know!"

"To know . . ." The sick woman gasped. For a few moments her labored breathing was the only sound in the room. "Not here . . ." she whispered at last. "Take me to the Sacred Grove. There . . . I will see." Lhiannon eased the priestess back on the pillow where she lay with eyes closed, breathing carefully. She did not speak again.

*M*earan died just after the Feast of Lughnasa, having delivered with her dying breath a prophecy whose details only the senior priesthood knew. But when her body was released to the fire, it was Helve who presided as High Priestess, not Lhiannon. Boudica recalled only too clearly Mearan's hoarse whisper when she spoke of *seeing* Lhiannon with the ornaments of the High Priestess on her brow. None of the students had been present at Mearan's final ritual, but through the autumn and winter that followed, the school had been full of wild rumors about what the dying woman had said. Had she changed her mind, or had the senior Druids refused her selection for some reason of their own?

Tonight those questions seemed trivial. Winter had given way to a stormy spring, and across the narrow sea Roman armies were gathering. Caratac and the Cantiaci were preparing to resist their landing, but Helve had sworn that they should not come at all and summoned Druids and students alike to join their powers in ritual.

As darkness fell the wind that whipped the flames of the torches felt as if had come directly from the peaks of the mountains across the strait, where snow clung still. Helve stood as High Priestess before the altar, dark robes falling away like black wings as she lifted her arms. On her wrists golden bracelets gleamed in the torchlight; a golden torque weighted her neck. Had those ornaments belonged to Mearan? Boudica could not remember if she had seen the old High Priestess wear them. When Mearan led the rites you remembered what she *was*, not what she wore . . .

The new High Priestess had settled into her role with less disturbance than some might have expected, or perhaps it was only that she spent much of her time with the senior Druids in conference and they saw little of her. But she was like a high-bred mare that Boudica's father had once owned, strong and beautiful and as likely to bite as to bear you.

Lhiannon had been given the title of Mistress of the House of Maidens, and now, as if even that much recognition was a threat to her, Helve had assigned her rival to go with Ardanos and the other Druids who were being sent to Durovernon to support Caratac with battle-magic if this ritual should fail.

Boudica jerked back to attention as the murmur of invocation ceased, a shiver of mingled anticipation and apprehension chilling her spine. At the equinox the world hung balanced between the old season and the new. What was done at this moment would push the luck of the new season in one direction or another. But did they really want to involve the gods? It was one thing to discuss the Lady of Ravens in a teaching circle at noon, and something else entirely to call on her as darkness swept across the land.

The Arch-Druid touched one of the torches to the seasoned wood laid ready on the altar and it exploded into flame.

"Raven of Battle . . ." the High Priestess cried, and like a sigh the priestesses echoed her. "Hear us!"

> *"Virgin, hag, and lover—*
> *Lady of the twisted mouth—*
> *Lady of the open thighs—*
> *Bone-witch, bride of shadow—*
> *Truth-teller, Nightmare rider—*
> *Great queen who gives victory—*
> *Great queen who gives death—"*

"Cathubodva! Great Queen! Hear us!" The response grew ever louder, male and female choruses clashing as they drove each other to greater intensity. "Your meat is death, your drink, life's blood! Here is food for your ravens, Lady—receive our offering!"

Two of the younger Druids came forward, carrying some small furred creature that jerked and struggled in their hands—a hare. Boudica suppressed a pulse of superstitious terror. The hare that rose reborn from beneath the scythe was sacred. It was never eaten—this sacrifice would not be shared, but taken to some lonely spot and given to the Goddess entire.

One man grasped the creature by its long ears, holding it stretched. Steel flashed red in the firelight as Helve slashed the hare's throat. A deeper crimson stained her hands as its blood spurted sizzling into the fire. The air above the flames shimmered—with smoke, or was she seeing the life energy of the animal? Boudica's nostrils flared at the burnt meat smell as the emptied carcass was set aside.

"You shall take from our foes the blood of their hearts

and the kidneys of their valor!" More pungent clouds billowed upward as the High Priestess cast a handful of herbs onto the fire. "Upon our foes you shall cast the shadow of fear and loathing, the shadow in the ocean, the shadow in the forest, the shadow in the spirit . . . When they turn toward Britannia, every night terror, every noonday fear their hearts hold shall rise up to haunt them!"

Helve turned, arms outstretched, but no one moved. It was not their bodies she was calling, but their souls. From two dozen throats came a cry, bearing with it the power of those who shouted, and the priestess bound it into the roil of energy above the fire.

Above the circle the smoke was forming itself into a shape alternately seductive and monstrous. One of the priestesses had fainted, and Boudica saw a white huddle where a priest clutched the grass in fear, but the others, pale as she knew that she herself must be, continued to sing. Helve's eyes were white-rimmed, teeth drawn back over lips in an ecstatic smile.

"It is I, Helve, who conjure you, I who command you! Hearken to my will!"

Should she be saying that? Surely the place of a mortal was to entreat, not to command . . . For a moment Boudica felt a different kind of fear.

"Cry out upon the Romans that they shall not come against us! Crush their courage! They shall not come!"

Once more her arms swept upward, and she screamed. Boudica cowered beneath the gaze of eyes black as a night without stars.

I am fury . . . said a voice in her soul. *I am fear . . . Which will you choose?* An oak tree split asunder as power descended, and sleeping birds exploded in screeching flocks from the grove. *With blood you have called me, and blood will flow until I am satisfied!*

Boudica screamed—they were all screaming as the shadow swept over them and was borne south and east upon a wave of sound.

*A*cross Britannia it blew, a nightmare wind that set dogs to barking and babies to crying as it galloped through men's dreams, over Britannia, and across the heaving gray waves of the narrow sea to a place called Gesoriacum on the coast of Gallia. It struck the close-ranked leather tents like a thousand furies, snapping guy ropes and flinging poles through the air. And the men of the legions woke gibbering with fear.

And in the morning they looked upon the sea and saw in each wave a face of terror, and they turned in their ranks to face their officers and said, "We will not go . . ."

FIVE

Lhiannon twitched as the smith's hammer clanged on the glowing bar. After a month in Durovernon she should have grown accustomed to the clamor, but each stroke jarred all the way up her spine. She looked at the piles of iron swords and spear points, bronze harness fittings and helms and shield bosses and remembered the offerings the princes had given to the sacred pool. How many of the weapons the smiths were beating out now would end up in the water, and who would throw them there?

Since the equinox three weeks had passed. The Romans had not come, but clearly the narrow sea that had once made Caesar's landings so hazardous was kinder to the traders who fared back and forth between the Celtic tribes of Gallia and Britannia, for through the gate of the dun a wagon driven by a swarthy Greek was creaking, full of southern luxuries. As the trader began to unload, men gathered around him. Lhiannon drew closer, followed by the other Druids, with Bendeigid close behind. A few moments later they were joined by Caratac and some of his chieftains.

"You warriors go home now." White teeth gleamed in a black beard as the trader grinned. "Those Romans, they all afraid! They call the Middle Sea 'Our Sea,' but these waves"—he gestured eastward—"that's *Ocean*—full of monsters to eat 'em if they go that way. And here"—he waved vaguely around him—"this be the end of the world."

"They mutinied?" snapped Caratac.

"That they did—just after the equinox!" the trader grinned again. "All of 'em woke up screaming. When the officers lined 'em up, they say Britannia no place for civilized men an' they won't go!"

There was a whoop of triumph from one of the men, and another went dashing off to spread the news.

"The Turning of Spring..." echoed Ardanos. "They did it, then—the Calling..." Before he and Lhiannon and the others left Mona, there had been a great deal of discussion regarding what role Druid magic might play in the struggle to come and what form of magic might best serve their cause. The glance he exchanged with Lhiannon communicated what he could not in this company say aloud—*So Helve is good for something after all*...

"But we knew that already," Lhiannon said softly. "The night of the equinox we felt the power pass."

"And now we know it worked!" said Cunitor. "May it work according to our will!"

Caratac raised one eyebrow. "That night of terror was the work of the Druids? I wish you had told us at the time."

Cunitor had the grace to look ashamed, but in truth it had not occurred to any of them to share what they knew with those who were not Druid oathed and trained.

"That was the Lady of Ravens who screamed through our dreams," explained Ardanos.

And she is a force that once invoked may be hard to banish, thought Lhiannon, but that was not something that Caratac needed to know.

Belina bent to murmur in Lhiannon's ear, "Did you really think Helve would choose any lesser working when she could call on so spectacular a power?" Lhiannon nodded, but said nothing. Belina, who had never been in the running for High Priestess, could afford to express herself without being suspected of jealousy.

"Well, whatever you accomplished, my warriors seem to be convinced you worked a miracle. Good for your reputation, not so good if I want to keep an army." Caratac pointed toward the encampment that had sprung up outside the dun, buzzing now like an overturned hive. Already some were packing up their gear.

Bendeigid watched them wistfully. In the last year he had grown gangly with the approach of manhood. Since they arrived at Durovernon he had spent most of his time badgering the warriors to teach him sword and shield. There had been times when the hardships of the journey had made Lhiannon painfully aware of just how easy her life at Lys Deru had been. But bruised feet and aching muscles were a small price to pay to be with Ardanos instead of wondering how he fared.

"How many do you think will stay?" Ardanos was asking now.

"Half of Britannia already believes that this gathering is a ploy to make Togodumnos High King over all the tribes," Caratac said bitterly. "And those who did answer my call will be wanting to get home to sow their fields."

The Druids nodded. All men knew that the time for fighting was summer, between planting and harvest. It was only the Romans who had made war a way of life and could field an army at any time of the year.

"The question is whether the Romans are truly discouraged, or only waiting," observed Cunitor. "They will not have forgotten how Caesar's ships were savaged by our storms. Surely they will not board ship before summer, if indeed they come."

"I would just as soon they came now, while I still have an army," muttered Caratac. Frowning, he turned to Lhiannon. "I know that some among your order are trained as oracles. Lady, if you are such a one, will you seek to see what is going on? Surely you understand why I wish to know!"

"So do we all . . ." murmured Lhiannon.

"She will try, but not until the eve of Beltane." Ardanos's words cut across her own. "In three weeks, the energies will be stronger, and she must have time to prepare."

There was an edge to his words that only Lhiannon could understand. Helve's accession as High Priestess had changed many things about Lhiannon's relationship to the community at Mona. It was not yet clear whether her relationship to Ardanos had been among them. At night, on their journey here, she had been acutely aware that he was sleeping on the other side of the fire. What would it be like to sleep *beside* him, with the length of his body curled against hers, the little snorting sounds he made as he slept tickling her ear? Sometimes he would wake, and she would feel his gaze like a touch upon her soul, and know that he was wondering, too.

But their journey, which might have offered so many opportunities, had been quite lacking in the privacy to take advantage of them. And if she was needed to serve Caratac as a seeress, there was a reason to preserve her virginity after all. Helve would probably prefer that she be the only one to serve as Oracle, but was not this one of the Druidic skills that they had been sent to Caratac to provide?

Now Ardanos was looking at her, and she understood both the pain and the resolve in his eyes. *He knows that this means that he will not lie with me this Beltane ... and we would make the same decision again.* She felt an odd pain somewhere near her heart as she realized that they would always choose duty above their desires.

*I*n the days that followed Beltane, it occurred to Lhiannon that when most people thought about oracles, they had it the wrong way around. Seeing visions was easy. The hard part was understanding what you had seen. They had gone to one of the mounds the ancient ones had raised for their dead for the ritual. She had seen an eagle fight with a raven, and a white narcissus blossom that towered over all. And the eagle had become three flocks that flew toward Britannia.

But they were not left long to wonder what the vision might mean. Before a week had passed, a light craft came skimming over the waves from Gallia with news. The mutiny was over. One of the emperor's secretaries, a freedman named Narcissus, had halted it, haranguing the soldiers from the general's podium, and after the first shock, appealing to a sense of humor one would not have suspected the legionaries had. And now the fleet that had waited for so long was being loaded with supplies and men. Three fleets there were, as Lhiannon had seen—one to return Veric to his country and the two others to seek Caesar's route to the Cantiaci lands.

The Druids joined their energies to send out a psychic warning to any who could hear. Those of their order who served as priests in the villages would alert their warriors—if anyone believed them. And Caratac had sent

runners to summon those who had so recently returned
to their homes and who were now in the midst of work in
the fields. They came, but slowly, and the king had gathered scarcely half his force by the time the Roman general
Aulus Plautius beached his prows on Britannic soil.

The Romans had made their landing on the coast to
the east of Durovernon where the river flowed into the
sea. Black ships in the hundreds lay in rows on the shelving
sands like some unseasonable migration of waterfowl. The
scouts Caratac had sent to observe them reported that they
had marched a short way inland and raised some simple
defenses on a low hill. They must have wondered why no
one was there to meet them, but the king's orders had sent
even the farmers fleeing from their path.

Soon the Roman horde was marching westward, har-
ried by anyone who could throw a spear or shoot a bow.
And still Caratac waited, as in ones and twos and tens the
men of the Cantiaci and Trinovante warriors from across
the Tamesa came in, until in the final days of Beltane
month the Romans neared Durovernon, and Caratac must
choose whether to surrender his dun or make a stand.

*F*eel the earth tremble," said Cunitor. "I felt such a
quake once in the mountains when I was a boy."

Lhiannon set her palm to the soil. From the wood at
the top of the hill where the Druids had been stationed
they could see little, but a faint, regular tremor vibrated
beneath her hand. To create such a rhythm how many feet
must be striking the earth, and what kind of discipline kept
them in such unison? For the first time she had a sense of
the magnitude of the force that had come against them.

"It's a drumbeat, not a quake," said Belina quietly. "The
drum of war." A flicker of sunlight gleamed on new threads
of silver in her brown hair.

"Are they coming?" asked Ambios. He was Caratac's
Druid, an older man grown portly with soft living, and
until now, undecided whether to welcome or to resent the
reinforcements who had come from the Druids' Isle. With
the enemy approaching, he seemed relieved to have their
company.

Lhiannon got to her feet and lifted a branch to see. The slope fell away in a tangle of wood and meadow until it reached the river's meandering blue gleam. Upriver at the ford, the thatched roofs of the dun shone in the sun. Below, Caratac's forces were a patchwork of plaid, highlighted by a gleam of iron and bronze and gold. But to the east a dust cloud was rising, broken by the vicious sparkle of steel. She felt a warmth that was as much of the spirit as the flesh as Ardanos rose to stand beside her.

"They are coming . . ." she whispered. Instinctively she reached out and he took her hand.

As they watched, the dust began to resolve into four divisions of marching men divided into dozens of smaller squares, following the same route Caesar's legions had found. Mounted officers moved among them and cavalry trotted to either side.

Now the other Druids were on their feet, peering through the leaves. She looked up as a shadow flickered between her and the sun. A raven's wing flared white as it caught the light, then black again as it circled and then settled onto a branch. It called, and others answered.

You can afford to be patient, Lhiannon thought bitterly. *Whoever wins this battle, you will have your reward.* For the first time she wondered whether the Lady of Ravens herself cared which side won.

Ardanos nodded to Bendeigid, who lifted the horn he carried and blew one long call. A ripple of motion passed through the Britons gathered below as their boar-headed trumpets blatted defiance and the Roman trumpets responded with a brazen blare.

"Wait for them," muttered Ardanos. "Caratac, you have the advantage of the ground—let them come to you!"

Onward came the legions, inexorable as the tide, hobnailed sandals crushing the young grain. The dun had been emptied, but the enemy passed as if a barbarian capital were no temptation. Nor was the river, at this point both broad and shallow, any barrier. But now the precise formation was breaking up at last—no, it was shifting, in a movement as disciplined as a dance, one legion moving forward as the others spread out to support it, a spearhead aimed at the multicolored array of Celts on the hill.

From the Celtic line first one naked warrior, then another, would dash forward, shouting insults at the foe, but Caratac still had his men in hand. Behind the champions waited the chariots, and behind them the mass of shouting warriors. The air boomed hollowly as long swords clashed against their shields.

Lhiannon trembled at the sight of that deadly beauty, but the time for contemplation was past. The others were joining hands, setting feet firmly in the loamy soil and drawing breath for their own part in this fray.

"Oh mighty dead, I summon you!" Ardanos cried. "Ye who fought the fathers of this foe, hear us now. Arise to aid us, ye whose lifeblood fed these fields when Caesar led the legions here, for the old enemy assails us once more. Rise up in wrath, rise up in fury, rise up and send the Roman horde screaming back across the sea!"

From below came an answering clamor as the Celtic warriors, released at last, swirled forward in a shrieking mob. "*Boud! Boud!*" they shouted. "*Victory!*"

The chariots sped toward the foe, seated drivers reining the nimble-footed ponies around obstacles, the warriors who stood behind them by some miracle maintaining their balance as they hefted their javelins. Closer they sped; they turned, Romans fell as javelins arced through the air.

But the heavy Roman pilum, though it had a shorter range, was just as deadly. As one chariot came too close Lhiannon saw a missile embed itself in the body of the cart. The weight of the shaft bent the long neck of the spear until it tangled in the wheels and in another moment the light frame was smashed. Spearman and driver leaped free as the ponies galloped wildly away, spreading panic among friend and foe.

On the hill a shiver that did not come from the wind stirred the leaves. The prickle that pebbled Lhiannon's skin was not caused by cold. She did not know whether it was Ardanos's invocation or the Celtic war cries that had awakened them, but the spirits were here.

With doubled vision she saw the struggling masses of the living on the field below and their ghostly counterparts above, locked in mortal combat as they had been almost a century before. Beyond them, she glimpsed other figures, so huge that she could only catch glimpses of a plumed helm or a spear that struck like lightning, a cloak of raven wings whose wearer fought someone with the head of an eagle that tore with wicked beak at his foe.

She felt her throat open in a cry, doubled, quadrupled as the others joined her in a screech of fury that resounded through both worlds. It was not the scream of the Morrigan, but it was enough to make the first rank of legionaries waver. For a moment the Druids savored triumph, then the Roman trumpets blared once more, and the enemy surged forward with renewed energy.

Lhiannon's fists clenched with fury. If only she could be out there, striking the foe! From the tree above her a raven called, but what Lhiannon heard were words: *"You can, you can, fly free on my wings, fly free . . ."*

Vision blurred; dizzied, she swayed. She heard someone swear as she fell, but that made no sense—she was rising, abandoning the weak flesh to soar above the battlefield.

In a moment she sensed another raven flying with her and in that part of her mind that still possessed memory recognized Belina. But her focus was on the men who struggled below, the flash of swords and the splash of blood as flesh met steel. Where she swooped low, screaming, men faltered and fell, but there were always more. Consciousness whirled away on a red tide.

*T*he ground was shaking, each jolt a hammer that stabbed through her skull. Lhiannon whimpered and felt a strong arm lifting her, water touched her lips and she swallowed, then swallowed again. The pain eased a little and she struggled to see. Now it was the trees that were moving. She closed her eyes once more.

"Lhiannon—can you hear me?"

That was Ardanos's voice. No one was screaming. Instead she heard the creak of wood and the clop of hooves. Slowly it came to her that she was in a wagon, lurching along a rutted road somewhere that was not a battlefield.

"Ardanos . . ." she whispered. Her reaching fingers found his hand.

"Thank the gods!" The pain as he squeezed her fingers was a distraction from the ache in her head.

"Roman sandals . . ." she said, "are marching through my skull . . ."

"No surprise there," he growled. "They've chased us the length of the Cantiaci lands."

"We lost." It was not a question.

"We're still alive," Ardanos answered with an attempt at cheer. "Everything considered, I count that a victory. But we left half our warriors on the field. They fought bravely, but the Romans had the numbers . . . and the discipline," he added bitterly. "We are in retreat. We would not have gotten even this far if their general Plautus had not stopped to loot and burn Durovernon and put up some kind of fortification there. Caratac lost half his army, but more have joined us since then. He means to make a stand beyond the Medu River. Please the gods, we're almost there, and thanks be that you are awake. I wasn't looking forward to carrying you across the river slung over my shoulder like a sack of meal."

"How long have I been unconscious?"

"You have lain there moaning for three eternal days! Damn it, woman, what possessed you to fly off like that? I was afraid . . ." Ardanos swallowed, and added so softly she could hardly hear him, "I didn't know if you were going to come back to me . . ."

Lhiannon managed to get her eyes open and felt her heart lurch at what she saw in his. In the next moment he looked away, but she felt a warmth within that went far to ease her pain.

"Possessed . . . yes. I was a raven . . . I hated them so much—it was the only thing I could do."

"Well, don't do it again," he growled. "I'm sure you scared the wits out of some of the enemy, but against such numbers?" He shook his head. "You can do more good in your right mind."

"I will try not to," she agreed. "I don't think I like ravens much anymore."

Ardanos sighed and cradled her more comfortably against his chest. "The ravens are the real victors. They don't care on whose flesh they feed."

*   *   *

*P*ull back! The Batavians have crossed the river—pull back!"

Above the general clamor Lhiannon could scarcely hear the cry. She stared at the broad gray flow of the Tamesa, trying to see.

"Damn them! Not again!" Cunitor swore.

Two weeks before, the Romans' Batavian auxiliaries—men from the delta of the Rhenus who were as water-wise as frogs—had forded the Medu, taking Caratac by surprise. They could only hope that the Durotriges and Belgae under Tancoric and Maglorios had fared better against the force the Romans had landed in Veric's lands.

But the Medu had been a small river. The Tamesa was as wide as a pastureland, a slowly winding pewter ribbon beneath a sky of gray. No one had thought the Batavians could swim so far. It was like one of those nightmares that repeat without end.

"Get the supplies back into the wagon!" snapped Ardanos. "They will be bringing the wounded to the rear, wherever that may be!"

The strategy that had failed Caratac on the Medu ought to have worked for him and Togodumnos at the Tamesa. To cross the river the Romans must use great slow rafts and barges, easy to attack as they wallowed toward the shore. As Lhiannon grabbed the piles of bandages they had laid ready she could see the barges beginning to put out now, shrunk by distance to the size of trenchers, glittering with armed men.

But the combined force of Trinovantes and Catuvellauni and the surviving Cantiaci could not attack them if their flank had already been turned by the Germans, fierce fighters whose tribes were close cousins to the Belgae. Though that should have been no surprise—these days native Italians were a minority in the Roman army. Most of the men on those boats were the children of conquered peoples. If the Britons were defeated, one day their own children might wear that hated uniform.

Lhiannon threw the sack of bandages into the wagon and scooped the pots of salves into another, glad that they had at least persuaded Bendeigid to stay back with the supplies. Around her the tribes and clans were becoming a great confused mass as they tried to regroup to face the foe. The first of the Roman barges was coming into range. Arrows thrummed overhead, shot by the archers Togodumnos had placed where the ground began to rise. A legionary toppled over the side of one of the barges and was pulled under by the weight of his armor. His red shield, painted in gold with paired wings to either side of the boss and wavy arrows extending up and down, bobbed downstream.

The pony's ears flicked nervously as the tumult grew louder. Belina grabbed the halter and got the animal moving, murmuring in some language horses knew. Grabbing the last bag, Lhiannon hurried after.

The clamor swelled to a roar as the Batavians plowed into their flank. The slingers had time for one volley, the fire-hardened clay pellets snicking past like maddened bees, before friend and foe melded into a confused mass. To watch a battle from above had been a horror; to be in the midst of it was a terror that only a lifetime of mental discipline enabled her to endure.

The faces of the men who ran past her were set in a rictus of rage. Lhiannon could feel the Lady of Ravens taking shape above the battlefield, summoned by the fury that beat like black wings in her own soul. But her promise to Ardanos kept it at bay. Armoring her spirit, she grabbed for the side of the wagon and clung as it lumbered up the hill.

To the west, the southern Dobunni were locked in the struggle with the Batavians. Their northern clans should have been fighting beside them, but King Bodovoc had turned traitor, allying himself to the Romans before the battle at the Medu. Now the first barges were sliding up the slick mud at the river's edge. A volley of pilums pierced Celtic flesh and stuck in shields, buying space for the first rank of Romans to leap to the shore, where they locked their own shields to form a line behind which their fellows could disembark.

More boats drew in behind them, disgorging ever more legionaries to strengthen that line of steel. Moment by moment it extended and thickened, pushing forward like a moving rampart against which the long spears and slashing blades of the tribesmen beat in vain. But a more orderly movement was emerging on the hill as the distinctive growling blare of the king's trumpeters rallied his houseguard.

Men began to draw aside as the swirl of movement resolved into rank upon rank of warriors. Above, the clouds were parting as if to flee from the clamor below. Sunlight blazed suddenly on golden torques and bracelets, on manes of stiffened hair bleached brighter than its normal red or gold, on the milky skin of sleekly muscled bodies that were bared only to make love or war.

Heedless of the turmoil around her, Lhiannon stared. Surely this was how the war band of the gods must have looked when they marched out with Lugos of the shining spear to confront the armies of darkness. Above their heads she could see the king himself, balancing easily on the tenuous wicker platform of his war chariot with his driver squatting at his feet, heels braced against the curving sides.

As the champions spread out to either side Togodumnos came fully into view. The cloak that flowed from his shoulders was woven in the Catuvellauni's favorite blues and greens. Golden plates glittered from his belt and the leather corselet that covered his broad torso, his neck was circled by a torque of twisted gold cords as thick as a spear shaft, and his thinning hair covered by a helm of gilded and enameled bronze surmounted by the image of a bird with hinged wings.

Caratac came close behind him, his battered gear an ominous contrast to his brother's majesty. But any deficiencies in his outfit were more than compensated by the fury that shimmered around him. Other chariots followed, and if none bore so much splendor, still the eye was dazzled by cloaks striped and checkered in red and purple and green and gold.

More warriors thronged to either side, stripped down for ease in movement to their trews or no clothing at all, woad-painted sigils spiraling across the fair skin of torso and back. By tribe and clan the warriors of the Trinovantes and the Catuvellauni, with the surviving Cantiaci scattered among them, hurried past on their way to death or glory. The Iceni contingent trotted by with Prasutagos's older brother Cunomaglos in the lead. Like a spear to the heart came the certainty that win or lose, the world Lhiannon had known was changing. They would never see such a riding again.

Like a herd of wild ponies stampeding toward the water the warriors swept past; she heard the roar as they met the Roman line. Now all she could see was a confusion of tossing spears. Presently the chariots forced their way back to the rear. It would be foot fighting now in the mud and the blood by the waterside. Sound beat against her hearing as the emotions of the fighters buffeted her spirit; the clangor of blade on blade beat out a rhythm for the dreadful music of battle cries and screams.

Now the wounded began to come to them, carried by their comrades or leaning on broken spears. The Druids were kept busy sewing and binding wounds. Some stayed only long enough to drink a little water, and then limped back into the fray. Some they laid in the wagon or sent off the field. For others, the most they could do was to numb the pain as lifeblood soaked the soil.

Lhiannon had promised to keep her spirit tethered, but nothing could prevent her from drawing power from the earth and projecting it outward to support the fighting men. Presently she realized that the shape of the battle was changing, the eye of the sword-storm moving gradually up the hill. Stamping feet churned the drier ground to billowing clouds of dust through which flocks of screaming ravens flew. She wondered if Togodumnos had been wrong to catch the Romans between his army and the water. She had heard an old warrior say it was a mistake to leave an enemy nowhere to run to. Once disembarked, the Romans had no choice but to fight their way through their foe.

She was just turning to ask Ardanos if perhaps they ought to move the healers' wagon when suddenly a knot of struggling men surged toward them. A javelin hurtled past and stuck quivering in the side of the wagon. Ardanos snatched up a handful of dust and cast it outward with a muttered spell. Suddenly the air was dark around them, the roar of the battle like the growling of a distant storm.

One man only crashed through the barrier. As the Roman rolled to his feet, sword waving, Lhiannon grabbed the javelin and batted wildly, knocking him off balance. One of the wounded whom she had thought on the point of death grabbed his ankle, and plunged a knife into his throat as he fell. The Roman gurgled horribly as blood spurted from the jugular, his eyes bulging with the same disbelief she had seen in the faces of their own as they died. The stink as his sphincter released mingled with the iron tang of blood. The Celt who had killed him was dead as well, but his lips were drawn back in a snarling smile.

"Leave them!" snapped Belina. "We've got to get out of here!"

Mute, she nodded, sweeping the supplies into her veil. They would be out of bandages soon. As Cunitor and Ardanos guarded the rear, Belina took the pony's head and they creaked toward what they hoped was the new edge of the killing field. Men with horses and chariots cantered past them, ready in victory or defeat to carry their masters away.

Before them the ground fell away in a long slope to the east, where pastureland was broken by thickets, around which the battle swirled as floodwaters divided around snags in a stream. The healers set up their new station in the shade, and soon they were hard at work once more. They ran out of water, and when the local people who had come out to help came back with more, they said that the Roman boats lined the shore for a mile. A swath of piled and scattered bodies showed where the battle had rolled on. There were more Celts than Romans, they said. Lhiannon hugged her arms, feeling suddenly very cold.

The setting sun was beginning to cast long shadows across the field, and the Druids had lit a torch so that the wounded could find them, when the mass of struggling figures surged toward them once more. In another moment they realized that all the warriors coming toward them were Britons.

"They're not fighting . . ." whispered Cunitor unbelievingly. "This is a rout. We've lost . . ." His face was smudged with dust and blood, his fair hair standing on end.

It can't be true, she thought numbly. *We tried so hard.*

We cannot lose now! She started as Ardanos gripped her arm. Were the Romans coming? A chariot lurched toward them across the field with as much speed as its driver could coax from the tired horses. In another moment she recognized the gilded harness and the black ponies, though without them she would not have known the half-dozen weary men who stumbled along beside it for the splendid warriors who had followed their king into battle only a few hours ago.

Lhiannon recognized the driver—she had seen Caratac in this state two weeks before. Only now the emotion that contorted his features was not fury but despair.

"Caratac," said Ardanos, "are you—?" The question died on his lips as Caratac pulled himself upright and they saw the body of Togodumnos sprawled beside him. Ardanos felt for a pulse at the king's neck, then passed his hands over the body, seeking to sense the energy there. Slowly he straightened, hands dropping in defeat. "My lord," he said more formally, "the High King is dead."

One of the warriors fell to his knees. Belina tried to hush him as he began to wail.

"Let him be," said Caratac tiredly. "No enemy will hear him. We gave them a good savaging, but the Romans hold the field. Why should they risk more men chasing us around in unfamiliar country in the dark?"

More men were gathering around them. One by one they began to kneel. "You are the oldest of Cunobelin's sons now living," said one of them. "We are your men now."

"Where shall we bury him?"

"Will you make a stand at Camulodunon?" came another question from the dark.

"Take him home . . ." Caratac answered at last. "Build a mound for him where our father lies."

"Do not mourn. Togodumnos feasts now with his fathers in the Blessed Isles," said Ardanos, but his voice was thin with strain.

For a moment Caratac simply looked at him. "Did you think I was weeping for my brother?" he said grimly. "Today, the dead are the lucky ones. I weep for the living, for all of us who must still fight this war!"

He bent and kissed his brother's brow, then gripped the heavy golden torque, twisted it, and eased it off the dead man's neck. The torchlight flickered on the king's face, and cutting through the blood and the dust Lhiannon saw the glistening track of tears.

"Camulodunon cannot be defended," he said harshly. "Not from such as these."

"You must go west," Lhiannon heard herself saying, fatigue and sorrow leaving her suddenly vulnerable to vision. "In the land of the Durotriges there are fortified hills where you can take refuge. So long as the tribes fight the Romans one by one they will fall. Build an alliance. If we unite against them, the Romans cannot hold what they have won."

Caratac nodded. He bent his head as if the heavy gold already weighed him down and settled the torque he had taken from the neck of Togodumnos around his own.

SIX

"Boudica, thank the gods you are back!" cried Brenna. "Coventa's had another of her spells and we can't wake her!"

Boudica dropped the bag of herbs she had gathered and ducked through the door of the House of Maidens. Coventa was writhing on her bed as Kea tried to hold her down.

"Coventa!" Boudica knelt by the bed and gripped the thin shoulders, feeling the fine bones flex like those of a captive bird beneath her hands. "Coventa, come back, my dear. It's me, Boudica! I need you, Coventa, talk to me!" Lhiannon could have fared into the spirit world to find her; Boudica could only try to persuade her back to the world of humankind.

Coventa drew a shuddering breath. "Blood . . ." she whispered. "There's so much blood . . ."

"Never mind that—it's not yours." Boudica tried to remember the words Lhiannon used to bring someone out of a trance. She took Coventa's hand and rubbed it against the blanket. "Feel the bed beneath you, feel the rough wool. That's reality!" She felt a spurt of hope as the girl's fingers moved. What else might serve? Lhiannon said that smell was the oldest and deepest of the senses. She took a deep breath, seeking to identify the scents in the air.

"Now breathe, Coventa. Smell the woodsmoke from our fire. In the fields the hay is almost ready to cut. Breathe in . . . and out . . ." She pitched her voice low. "Smell the ripe grass, still warm from the sun. You're here on Mona, you're safe here with me!" she added as the girl's breathing steadied. She could feel the tense muscles beginning to relax beneath her hands.

"And with me . . ." another voice cut in smoothly. Boudica looked up, eyes narrowing as she saw Helve's tall figure in the doorway, silhouetted against the fading sky. One of her braids was still unpinned. The strands wreathed down her neck in serpentine coils, like the lady with snakes for hair in the tales told by Cunobelin's Greek slave.

"You may go," the priestess said in a lower voice. "I'll take care of her now . . ."

"I've almost got her calmed down—" Boudica began, but the authority in Helve's gesture had her on her feet before she could think of resisting it. She moved back as Helve knelt by the bed and laid a white hand on the girl's brow.

"Coventa, daughter of Vindomor, I call you!"

Boudica took a step even though the priestess had not been speaking to her.

The girl on the bed took a shuddering breath. "Lady, I hear . . ."

"You hear my voice, you hear my words, you will go as I bid you and see as I say."

"I hear and I obey," came the faint answer.

Boudica stiffened. Was this how Helve had been training her acolyte?

"Seek to the west, where the Romans march. What do you see?"

What was she doing? Was she going to force Coventa to endure the horror all over again? Boudica bit her lip, gaining focus from the pain.

"Blood and fire!" Coventa's breath caught. "Bodies—"

"Let her go!" Boudica broke in. "Can't you see how she suffers? She—"

"Be still!" It was the same blast of power Lugovalos had used to silence Cloto, and like him, when she tried to protest, Boudica found her powers of speech locked tight.

"I have noticed, Boudica, that you have a strong instinct to protect your friends. That is no bad thing, but you need to choose your fights wisely. There are some powers you cannot oppose, and you will only end up hurting yourself if you try. I am one of them."

Helve glanced back at Coventa, rather, thought Boudica, as a farmer might consider a prize ewe.

"You must not meddle with what you cannot understand. When the vision is allowed to run its course it passes and leaves the seer in peace. But if you try to suppress it, the horror will remain in her soul and return to haunt her. The child will take no harm." Helve lifted one exquisitely arched brow. "Indeed, has she ever complained to you about her work with me?"

Boudica shook her head. Now that she thought about it, she realized that when they were together, Coventa scarcely spoke of her teacher at all, but whether that was from respect, aversion, or because Helve had suppressed her memories, she could not tell.

Helve's lips twitched in scorn. Then, so sure of her power that she did not even call to have Boudica removed, she turned to Coventa once more.

"Coventa, child, rise above the battlefield. You are a bird, soaring above a scene that has nothing to do with you. Fly higher, my dear one, and tell me what the bird sees . . ."

The girl on the bed gave a long, shuddering sigh. "Night falls. Women wander the field, looking for those they love. Men drag logs to build pyres and the ravens feast on the slain."

To Boudica, it was as if those black birds were caged somewhere deep within. Dark wings beat at her awareness.

"Then the kings have lost the battle," Helve said grimly. "Now you must seek for Ardanos and his companions."

"I see the Druids. They are moving northward from the great river. In the wagon they follow lies the body of a man with a beard and brown hair."

"Togodumnos . . ." Helve sighed.

Held by the spell, Boudica shook where she stood. Denied physical release, her rage exploded inward. In a moment it would break the barrier that protected her identity. But it was no longer simply an emotion—she could feel it taking a shape, coalescing into a being that could laugh at the priestess's spell. *I am fury . . .* it whispered. *I am power. Let me fly free!*

"And what of the Romans?" asked Helve.

"They are building a bridge . . ." whispered Coventa. "They have built a camp with a square palisade and there they stay. I see no more." Coventa shifted position with a sigh, the relaxation of sleep replacing the intensity of trance.

The priestess sat back, frowning. In the small part of her mind that remained her own, Boudica saw her arm lifting, and knew that in a moment she would strike the woman down. Now her own terror warred with that Other who had been born of her rage—or had She always been there, waiting only for the moment of stress that would break the barriers that kept Her locked within? Her lips opened on a strangled gasp, and Helve turned.

For a moment her eyes widened. Then she straightened, eyeing Boudica as if she were a warrior confronting a foe. But then no one had ever doubted the woman's courage.

"Speak!" It was the same note that had bound Boudica's tongue. "Who are you? I did not call you here!"

The response was laughter. A woman's laughter, laced with mockery, that to Boudica's relief began to transmute the rage.

"Did you not? Have you forgotten already the rite by which you called Me at the Turning of Spring?"

The look of appalled recognition on Helve's face went far to reconcile Boudica to this invasion of her spirit.

"Great Queen," she murmured, with a dip of the head that might have been intended as a bow.

"This is a strong mare you have bridled for Me," said the Other—Cathubodva, thought Boudica, as appalled as Helve as she realized Who ruled her body now. The Goddess rose a little on Boudica's toes and stretched out Her arms as if trying to expand the girl's body enough to fit comfortably inside.

"But I can see that was not your intent. Indeed, very little you Druids have done this past year has had the results you expected. Is that not so?"

Boudica had seen Mearan speak with the Voice of the Goddess at festivals, but carrying the gods was only done by the most senior Druids, and then only within the strict boundaries of ritual. And even for them it was not clear whether this should be considered a burden or a privilege.

"You speak true," said Helve.

"Always," replied the Goddess, "when I am asked. But you did not ask, did you? You did not seek My wisdom. You invoked My wrath, which explodes like a wildfire and burns all in its way."

"But it worked! You terrified the Romans into mutiny!"

"Until they found their courage once more," Cathubodva agreed. "All the stronger because it lay on the other side of their fear."

Boudica felt her body relaxing as the Goddess settled into it and moved to a bench that stood against the wall to sit, one leg bent and the other outstretched.

"But what else could we have done? What else can we do now?" Helve wailed.

"What you cannot do is to keep things as they have been. All things alter, one transforming into another until the world itself is changed. Bend or break—it's up to you." Once more, Cathubodva laughed.

From the corner where awareness lurked, Boudica listened in fascination. Was this truly the Goddess speaking, or her own suppressed desires? It was true that some of these thoughts had crossed her mind, but she did not think she could have expressed them, or at least not with such assurance and power.

"Very well," said Helve sullenly. "I am listening."

"Such obedience! Such awe!" the Goddess laughed. "You do not bend your neck easily, priestess, and these days there are few to make you. This child whose body I have taken is more like you than either of you would care to admit. Even the years allotted you are the same."

"Then I will spend them fighting to preserve our learning and our lore," Helve replied.

"And not your own position and power?"

The priestess grew very still. "The prestige of the High Priestess serves our cause. Is it so wrong to enjoy it?"

"If you remember that it is the High Priestess, not Helve, to whom the honor belongs," Cathubodva replied, more gently than she had spoken before.

"It will not matter whether I do or not if the Romans destroy us all."

"Do you think you are the first to pray to the gods for help when an invader set foot on these shores?" She was not laughing now. "Once it was your people who were the enemy. One day the Romans will face an enemy they cannot overcome. That is the way of the world."

"And you will be forgotten!" Helve said spitefully. "If you will not help us for our sakes, will you not do so for yours?"

"Forgotten?" The Goddess shook Her head. "Names change, but so long as warriors hate and women weep, I will be here." Her voice deepened. "Do you not yet understand? In the face of danger life burns most brightly, and the tomb is the womb of life that springs anew. I am the Good God's Cauldron. The only true death is to stand still."

Helve paled, and in that place that was not a place Boudica went as still as a mouse that knows itself to lie beneath the falcon's eye. For a few moments Coventa's regular breathing was the only sound.

Then someone called Helve's name from outside. The priestess blinked, her face smoothing into its accustomed proud calm, and rose.

"Great Queen, I thank you for your counsel, but the time has come for you to return to the Otherworld."

The Morrigan lifted an eyebrow and the sense of something too huge for human comprehension dimmed. "Will you not even offer Me a drink?" She said wryly. "I came uninvited, but I am sure you would not wish Me to report you lax in hospitality . . ."

With one eye still on her guest, Helve went to the door of the hut and spoke, and presently brought back an earthenware beaker filled with the foaming dark beer that was old Elin's special brew. Boudica felt Cathubodva's appreciation of the nutty, full-flavored fizz as in one long swallow it went down. She had a moment to wonder that an immortal could enjoy such a simple pleasure, but whatever the delights of the Otherworld, she supposed that even the gods were dependent on human senses to enjoy the taste of beer.

Then the mug slipped from a suddenly nerveless hand. Boudica collapsed like an emptied wineskin as the Goddess flowed out of her, consciousness following in a dark rush as she crumpled to the floor.

*   *   *

*B*oudica came to herself, gasping. Helve stood over her, a dripping water bucket in her hands. Coventa was sitting up on the bed, staring at her with wide eyes.

"Boudica, what happened to you?"

Boudica swallowed, tasting beer, and flinched at the cold calculation in Helve's eyes. "Did I faint?" she asked weakly. "Why am I sitting up?" Coventa never seemed to remember what went on in her trances. Whether Boudica was meant to recall what had passed she was not sure, but it was clear that she would be better off if Helve did not realize what she knew.

*B*oudica sped across the ripening summer grass, swinging the cumman stick to keep the ball in play. But no crowd cheered her, no opponent tried to stop her. In the past weeks so many of the students had left the school to return to their tribes that there were no longer enough students to make up two hurley teams. But the activity eased some of the restlessness that for the past several days had made sleep well nigh impossible, even though she played alone.

It helped to imagine it was a Roman head she sent hurtling across the grass. She understood why the boys who left had gone. She even understood why Helve had insisted on making Coventa speak all her vision. How else could they know what was going on, stuck here at the edge of the world? Lhiannon was out there somewhere. She and Ardanos were in danger—Helve had probably sent them to help Caratac *because* of the danger. Certainly, the new High Priestess had been happy to get rid of the two who were most likely to dispute her will while the Arch-Druid was also away, attempting to persuade wavering chieftains that the Romans could be opposed.

No doubt Helve would like to see the last of me as well, she thought, aiming a vicious kick at the ball. *Or maybe not. She watches me as if she's not sure whether she hopes the Morrigan will pay another visit, or fears She will* . . . Boudica had spent most of her recent meditations armoring her spirit against another such violation, but she rather enjoyed keeping Helve wondering.

As she sent the ball hurtling past the goal she heard Coventa calling her name.

"Boudica, you must come!" The girl stopped to catch her breath. "Lady Helve wants you. There's a messenger!"

Lhiannon's been hurt! she thought, but news of the priestess would go first to the senior Druids. Had something happened to her father? Had he been in the battles? But she was already running, leaving Coventa to pant after her.

The day was warm, and Boudica found Helve sitting beneath the oak tree whose branches embraced the conical roof of her dwelling. She slid to a halt and straightened, waiting.

"A messenger has come—a man called Leucu. Do you know him?"

Boudica nodded. "He has served my father since before I was born." Her heart had been pounding from exercise; now it raced with anxiety. But she refused to give Helve the satisfaction of seeing her beg for news.

"Your father bids you return home."

Boudica nodded, giving nothing away. She supposed Leucu was the perfect escort—familiar with the whole island and too old to threaten a princess's virtue. *Too old to stand with the warriors,* she thought grimly, holding Helve's pale glance with her own. Surprisingly, it was the priestess who spoke first.

"He tells me that the Romans are marching on Camulodunon. It would appear that Coventa . . . saw true," the priestess said tightly. "The Iceni have decided to make submission."

"Surely he does not need me for that!" Boudica burst out in spite of her resolution. Unless there was someone he wished her to marry. She took a deep breath. "Do I have a choice in this?"

Helve sighed. "You do," she responded a little reluctantly. "You would have had to decide soon in any case whether you wished to stay with us or return to your home. I will tell you now that I do not see in you the potential to make a priestess, but you have some talents that might be useful," she added obliquely, and Boudica suppressed a smile. "If you wish to stay, we will welcome you."

"How long do I have to decide?"

"You may decide to go home with Leucu now, but I have also another message," Helve added reluctantly, "from Lhiannon."

She was safe! Boudica tried not to show her joy at that realization.

"As you know, it is the custom to send our maidens on retreat to Avalon before they take their place as women in our community. Lhiannon asks that you go to meet her in the Summer Country. Ordinarily you would be sent with a group of priestesses, but in these times I can spare no one. Lhiannon will know what must be done."

I will not complain—of you all Lhiannon is the one whom I would choose, Boudica thought then.

"Afterward you will go to Camulodunon. When you have seen both, with the eyes of the woman instead of a child, you shall decide where your path lies."

As Helve spoke, her voice had grown more resonant— for a moment she sounded almost like Lady Mearan—and by that Boudica understood that Helve was speaking as High Priestess in truth, despite what she might personally feel. And it was to the priestess, not the woman, that she bowed.

"Lady, I thank you. I will go to Avalon."

*I*nstead of the tedious journey by horseback that Boudica had expected, the Druids found a trading ship heading south whose captain was willing to take her and Leucu down the west coast of Britannia to the wide estuary where the Sabrina met the sea. Still, her physical misery muted the sorrow of leaving the place that for four years had been her home, and by the time she was accustomed to the boat's motion, the places they were passing were all new and strange.

Now the boat turned eastward along the coast, where the mountains protected them from northern gales. From there it was two days' sail across the channel of the Sabrina to a coast of reeds and mudflats through which placid brown waters wound toward the sea.

Boudica drew a sharp breath as the land wind brought her the rank, fecund scent of the marshes beyond.

"Aye, it does stink, mistress," said the captain, misinterpreting her reaction. "I'll be glad to turn back to the clean breezes from the sea."

Boudica laughed. "I don't mind," she said. "I come from the Iceni country. It reminds me of the fens near my home."

"That's as well, as you must journey that way to reach the holy isle." He pointed vaguely eastward. Between the marshland and the sea she saw a cluster of huts on poles. Mist hazed whatever lay beyond the tangled trees. "We'll find you a boatman in yon village. They're an odd folk hereabouts, little dark people who have been here since this land was made, but they know their way through the marshes, and they're loyal to the holy ones of Avalon."

Boudica continued to watch as they eased slowly shoreward, trying to decide whether the pointed shape she thought she saw was really the Tor about which she had heard so much, and wondering what she would find there.

SEVEN

The child has grown! thought Lhiannon, watching Boudica make her way up the path, pausing to stare at the pointed cone of the Tor. At her back, reed and thicket laced the shining expanses of the fen, islanded with green hills and fading away to the silver shimmer of the sea.

Or perhaps she had simply forgotten just how impressive Boudica's long-limbed stride and flaming hair could be. She moved like a young goddess as she climbed the hill. The girl was a welcome sight after all the horrors Lhiannon had seen. She had hoped that the two weeks she had spent on the Tor would bring healing, but her nerves still twitched at any sudden sound. Maybe Boudica's robust cheerfulness would be a medicine.

Lhiannon stepped from the shade of the wild apple trees that made a natural orchard on the hillside. A wide smile brightened Boudica's face, newly freckled from the sea voyage, as she saw the priestess waiting there.

Lhiannon gave her a swift hug. "Come, after two days in the marshes you must be hungry—I hope the boatman fed you something better than pond-lily bulbs and smoked eel."

"We ate smoked *something*," answered Boudica. "Just what, I didn't really care to ask . . . ."

The priestess laughed. "Has the boatman taken your father's man to the Lake Village? He will be their guest until we are finished, although I can't answer for what they will feed him. We have greens and barley cakes and some roasted duck for *your* dinner. The huts where we sleep are simple, but in this weather we need little more."

"Lhiannon, you are babbling," said Boudica, peering down at her. "And you don't look well . . . I know you were at the battles. Did you take some wound?"

"Only to my spirit . . ." Lhiannon felt her mouth twist with grief, started to turn away, then looked back again. How could she teach Boudica self-knowledge if she hid her own pain?

But it was not until after they had eaten that the time seemed right for talking. Lhiannon cooked their simple meal over a fire outside the cluster of houses near the sacred spring where the priestesses stayed when they visited Avalon. A gentle hill partially hid the Tor beyond, but one was always aware of its presence. The only permanent residents were a few old Druid priests who spent their time in contemplation in scattered huts on the northern side of the isle.

Lulled by the chuckle of the water that welled continually from the Blood Spring, they sat and watched the evening deepen around them. Mist was rising on the marshlands, lapping the lower vale in mystery, but the sky above the Tor blazed with stars. As the fire dimmed, Lhiannon began to speak, and in reliving the blood and anguish, she found that she could release it at last.

"So King Togodumnos is dead?" said Boudica when she had done.

Lhiannon nodded. "It was a hero's death. Now he feasts in the Blessed Isles. The flower of the Trinovantes dwell there with him, and far too many of the Catuvellauni and Cantiaci as well. Caratac means to seek out King Tancoric in the west country and try to build an alliance there."

"Did you and Ardanos bury the king at Camulodunon?" Boudica asked softly after a while.

Lhiannon nodded. "Eventually. That first night was a terror, running and hiding and running again, wondering when the Roman scouts would find us. It was not until the third day that we dared halt long enough to burn the body. We carried the ashes to the gravefields just outside the dikes of Camulodunon and buried them near those of his father. It was a poor funeral, with no grave goods, but we left him his spear and his shield." She looked up with a sigh. "How did you know?"

"Coventa saw you—" Boudica stopped short, as if there were more that she would not say. Somewhere an owl gave three hoots and then was still.

"That poor child . . . Helve will use her without mercy,

as I suppose I should myself, if the choice had fallen on me." She leaned forward to stir the fire. "In the days to come we will need every advantage."

"And what are the Romans doing now?"

"Waiting." Lhiannon gave a mirthless laugh. "The Roman general has built a bridge across the Tamesa, and they say he is waiting for his emperor to cross it and complete our conquest."

"Can he do so?" A stray gleam of firelight blazed in Boudica's hair.

"My dear, in the southeast there is no one left to oppose him. Whether we will *stay* conquered is the question."

Julius Caesar, after all, had come, proclaimed himself a conqueror, and gone away, and Britannia had been left alone for a century thereafter. Wind whispered through the treetops, but if it was trying to answer her, she could not understand the words.

"It's getting late." Lhiannon stood up suddenly and started toward the roundhouse. "We should get some sleep. Tomorrow I will show you the isle, and when the moon is new on the day after, we will do your initiation at the Blood Spring."

*I*n the gray hour before dawn the air held a chill that reached the bone. Boudica supposed she ought to have expected that, having become accustomed to sunrise ceremonies on the Druids' Isle, but somehow she had assumed that being farther south, Avalon would not be so cold. In the afternoon sunlight the holy isle had seemed a place of beauty and power. But as she followed Lhiannon's cloaked shape toward the fold between the orchard hill and the Tor where the Blood Spring emerged, the dim shapes of tree and rock shifted around her with a protean ambiguity, and she could not tell whether their new forms would be wondrous or terrible.

I suppose that is the first lesson . . . she thought as she picked her way along the path. *We all have the potential for both good and evil, and knowing that, we must choose . . .*

They came to a halt before a yew hedge. In the dim

light she could make out a gap at its base. She turned to ask if this was the entrance, but the other woman had disappeared.

"Boudica, daughter of Anaveistl, why have you come here?" came a voice from the other side of the hedge. Boudica blinked. Always before, she had been known as the child of her father, but they were concerned with women's business here. For the first time, she wondered how her mother had felt about becoming a woman. She would not have had *this* ceremony, but the passage into womanhood was always honored in the tribes.

"I have been a child—I would be a woman. I have been ignorant—I would seek wisdom."

"Remove your garments. Naked you came into the world. Naked you must make the passage to be reborn . . ."

Boudica knew the speaker must be Lhiannon, but she sounded . . . strange.

"Come!"

Shivering, Boudica let her cloak fall. Stones cut her knees and the pointed needles of the yew scored her back as she crawled through the gap. She crouched lower to avoid being flayed.

The sun was still hidden behind the hill, but as she emerged, she found that she could see. The hedge extended on either side to join the orchard hill. The sacred spring flowed from somewhere above them, trickling down to fill a wide pool, edged and lined with stone dyed rusty red by the iron in the water.

On the other side stood the cloaked figure that she knew—she hoped—must be Lhiannon. She wondered what this rite was like when it was done by a full complement of priestesses, and could not decide whether to feel disappointed or glad that she would receive this initiation only from Lhiannon, who was the one she most trusted of them all.

"You have come into the temple of the Great Goddess, who though she wears many shapes is formless and nameless though she is called by many names. She is Maiden, forever untouched and pure. She is Mother, the Source of All. She is the Lady of Wisdom that endures beyond the grave. And She answers to all the names She is given in all the tribes of humankind. The Goddess is in all women and all women are faces of the Goddess. All that She is, you shall be. Creating and destroying, She births all transformations. Are you willing to accept Her in every guise?"

Boudica cleared her throat. "I am . . ."

"Behold the Cauldron of the Mighty Ones." The priestess gestured toward the pool. "Whosoever enters it unworthy shall die; the dead that are put into it shall live. Will you dare the Mystery?"

The sky was brighter now. Boudica wondered if the faintly gleaming water it showed her was as cold as it looked, but her voice was steady as she answered. "I will . . ."

"Then descend into the pool."

At the first step, the water's icy touch shocked through her. She shook with the effort it took not to leap out screaming. But though Helve might scorn her abilities, Boudica had mastered some of the Druid disciplines. She took a deep breath, seeking the fire within. She could feel it beneath her breastbone, pulsing like a tiny sun. With another breath she willed it outward into each limb.

She stepped downward without hesitation, skin tingling as the ice without met the fire within, and looking up saw another figure descending the steps on the other side, its movements mirroring her own. It was Lhiannon, she told herself, but against the glowing sky she saw only a silhouette. In the posture she recognized something of Mearan, in the grace, her own mother, and the turn of the head was one she had seen in herself when she bent over a reflecting pool.

Ripples broke their images into myriad reflections as they sank breast-high into the water. Red and fair, leanly muscled and slender, they moved toward one another through the pool.

"By water that is the Lady's blood may you be cleansed," whispered that Other who both was and was not Lhiannon. "From this womb may you be reborn . . ." Their breasts brushed as Lhiannon moved closer, then she set her hands on Boudica's shoulders and pressed her down.

As the water closed over her, the wounds where the hedge had scratched Boudica's back stung fiercely, then began to tingle with a sensation that spread across her entire body, as if she were indeed being created anew. She could feel the hands of all those who had been initiated in this pool blessing her. The pulse of blood in her ears was like the beating of mighty wings; she bathed in light and did not know whether it came from without or within.

"Beloved daughter . . ." From the depths of her awareness came a voice. At first she thought it was the Morrigan's, but this was far greater—it resonated in her bones. *"In blood and in spirit you are My own true child. I give you to the world, and the world to you. Whatever may befall I shall never be far from you, if only you will look within. Go forth and live!"*

Then strong hands drew her upward. Skin slid smoothly across skin as she emerged into the circle of Lhiannon's arms. From the water light flared and glanced around them, a multitude of bright spirits rejoicing. During those moments when she lay in the water the sun had risen, and they stood in a lake of fire.

*W*as the womanhood rite like this for you?"

At Boudica's diffident question Lhiannon finished tying the strings of her shoe and looked up. Two days had passed since the initiation. Last night had been cloudy, but the mists were clearing from the marshes, and beyond the apple trees the Tor rose smooth and green against a smiling sky.

"It is always the same, and always different," she said smiling. "The structure of the ritual has not altered much, I suppose, since the People of Wisdom first initiated their daughters in this pool. But the power it invokes, the internal transformation, must be different for each maiden it blesses."

She remembered her own initiation as a slow unfolding of awareness, level upon level, like the opening of a flower, until at the end she had glimpsed the core of light. An entire lifetime, she thought, might be too short to comprehend what she had touched as she stood in the pool.

She did not think that what Boudica had experienced was the same, but clearly something had happened to the girl. And as always in ritual, the giver was as blessed as the one who received. Lhiannon still bore grief for Britannia's slaughtered warriors, but she had been reminded that the Great Mother who weeps for her children also gives birth to them anew.

"I am still trying to digest all the wise words you gave me afterward, when we broke our fast beside the pool," Boudica said.

Lhiannon frowned. In the euphoria that followed the blessing, their bare bodies still warmed by the sacred fire, she had found herself telling Boudica things she had scarcely admitted to herself. Not even when she walked with Ardanos could she share so deeply. Their souls had been as naked as their bodies, no longer teacher and student, but two women together in an intimacy of the spirit that would have been impossible if they had not been alone. Now she was beginning to suspect that a bond had been forged between them that she had not anticipated.

There is potential in this girl that in four years we never suspected, she thought wistfully. *Yet that missed chance is not what will give me sorrow if she decides to go back to her people, but the loss of the first soul I have found who might be a true friend.*

"If you understood everything already, that would have been no true initiation," Lhiannon answered, trying to hide her emotion. "This is a beginning. You will have the rest of your life to learn what it means."

"I suppose so . . . Do I have to decide about staying with the Druids today?"

Lhiannon took a deep breath. *No, thank the gods . . .* Aloud she said, "We have some days yet before you must choose. Allow each day its lesson. Today, I propose that we climb the Tor." She picked up her staff.

She could see Boudica biting back another question, and smiled. They could talk more later. They still had time.

Their way led around the base of the orchard hill and past the yew hedge that hid the sacred pool. Beyond it the waters of the Milk Spring seeped slowly down to join the overflow, leaving their own pale film on the stones. Red and white, blood and milk, they nourished the land. Here the women stopped to fill their flasks. After the iron tang of the Blood Spring, the waters of the Milk Spring tasted of stone.

Around the base of the Tor, trees clustered thickly, but in some previous age they had been cleared from the slopes, and sheep had kept the hill free of them thereafter. As the women emerged from beneath the branches the long spine of the Tor rose up before them.

"Are we going to climb straight up?" asked Boudica. From here the first steep slope hid the more gentle incline that followed it, and the stone circle at the summit could not be seen.

"We could—or we could circle around to the back and take a way that is shorter and steeper still, if all we wanted was to reach the top and enjoy the view . . ."

She waited, watching as Boudica considered the undulating expanse of turf above her. The base of the Tor was roughly oval, lying on a northeast-southwest axis. From afar, it appeared as a perfect cone, but its summit was at the northern end. From a distance it also seemed smooth, but here one could see clearly that it was ringed by terraced paths.

"Those are not natural, are they?" Boudica pointed. "Is this one of the Druid mysteries?"

Lhiannon shook her head. "The paths were here when our people first came to these isles. The People of Wisdom made them. They are not rings, but a maze. One walks in silence, as a meditation, to reach the crown."

Boudica looked at the path before them, its beginning marked by an ancient stone. "And when one has threaded the maze," she asked carefully, "where will one arrive?"

Unexpectedly, Lhiannon laughed. "At the top of the Tor—usually. But sometimes, they say, the path leads inward to the Otherworld."

Beneath the broad straw hat Boudica's face lit with an answering smile. "I think that you are more likely to find that path than I. But take care that you remember the way back again."

"We'll arrive nowhere if we don't begin." Lhiannon stepped past the stone and started around the hill.

For the first circuit, she was very much aware of Boudica following her. The path led along the middle of the northern side of the Tor and sunwise around on the south until they neared the stone, then dipped downward and turned back widdershins all the way around, looped down once more, and skirted the base of the Tor. Here the going was easy. Lhiannon strode along, enjoying the sun on her back and the way the wind fluttered the skirts of her gown. She had been this way before, and the exercise was welcome on such a beautiful summer day.

Only when the path neared the entrance again did it lead up the spine of the hill and around in a long widdershins loop, reversing halfway up the slope to angle upward toward the standing stones. That was when Lhiannon began to suspect that this time might be different. The light seemed paler, though no cloud covered the sun. Each step seemed more deliberate. She did not feel heavier, but rather as if some force were pulling her toward the Tor.

Lhiannon looked back along the path. She could see Boudica halfway down the slope below her, moving slowly, pausing sometimes to gaze toward the range of hills to the north and the distant sea. The vale of Avalon lay between two such ranges, a sheltered land with the Tor at its secret heart. The girl—no, the younger woman—would come to no harm. With a sigh of release Lhiannon returned to the path.

She could see the sacred stones above her now. The air overhead was shimmering. She circled behind them, started forward once more, so close she could almost touch them, but by now she did not need to see the path. A current of power bore her past as if she walked in a flowing stream. The path turned back upon itself and downward, made a wide loop back and a longer one forward, taking her farther from the peak. But now the sun had disappeared. She walked through a luminous twilight as she swept back and around and up again at last to the point of power within the circle of stones. The land fell away to every side as it had before, but now every tree was radiant and every reed shone, and the hillock-islands were glowing points that marked the flow of power.

Lhiannon stood, skin tingling as it had in the sacred pool. Every Druid priest and priestess had made this ascent, and scarcely one in a hundred found the way between the worlds. How many had never noticed the moment of potential transformation? How many had sensed it, and drawn back in fear? She wondered why she had been given this gift, and wished that she could have shared it with Boudica.

"Only when the soul is ready can it find the way."

It took a moment to realize that this was not her own spirit speaking. Heart pounding, she turned.

At first she thought she saw Lady Mearan standing there, but even as she flushed with joy she realized that this woman was as small as one of the folk of the Lake Village, clad in a deerskin wrap and crowned with summer flowers. And yet the joy remained, for the wisdom and power she read in the woman's face were the same. Instinctively she bent as she would have bowed to a high priestess of her own kind, for surely the queen of the faerie folk was of equal degree. And she was far older.

"The Oak priests have trained you well," the woman said, smiling. "But your people do not come to visit me so often as in times past. Have you come here for refuge, now that your people are at war?"

"It is true that an alien people have invaded us, but most of our wise ones are safe on the isle of Mona. I cannot think they will ever come there," Lhiannon answered with a spurt of pride.

"Time runs differently here, and I have seen many peoples come and go in this land. But you, at least, may stay in safety." The faerie woman gestured, and Lhiannon saw that a cloth had been spread upon the grass within the circle, and food and drink laid there. Her stomach gurgled as she looked at the fair white breads and roasted waterfowl and the bowls of berries and nuts of every kind. It had been a long time since the morning meal.

At the thought she had a sudden memory of Boudica stirring the porridge with the early light kindling her bright hair. Lhiannon had known the younger woman faced a choice, but she had not expected to be offered one, too.

"Lady, I would not insult your hospitality, but I cannot leave my friend."

The woman looked at her thoughtfully. "Friendship is one of the great virtues of your kind. But she is not yet ready to understand. If your friendship endures, perhaps a time will come when together you may return to me . . ."

"Can you see the future, then?" Lhiannon asked eagerly. "Will we expel these Romans from Britannia?"

For a moment the woman simply looked at her. "I forget how young you are . . . Your human life is a river, and you are all part of it, like the streams and the clouds and the rain, each thing moving according to its own nature, one current flowing strongly, then giving way to another in its turn. The Romans are very strong, but it is only here that I can tell you the future, for only my realm is without change."

"Does that mean it's useless to resist the Romans?" Lhiannon fixed on the only part of this she could understand.

"Useless? No deed of a brave heart is lost. If your kings fail you, look to your queens. Your love and your courage will be a mighty current in that stream. But you will know pain, and one day you will die."

"But I will grow," said Lhiannon slowly, "and here I could become no greater than I am at this hour."

"Perhaps you are not a child after all," the faerie woman said then. "Go now with my blessing. Daylight will be fading in the world of men."

"Thank you," said Lhiannon, but both the woman and the faerie food were gone. Still wondering, she took the first step, and found herself once more in the world of humankind.

Though the skies above the vale were clear, out to sea a storm was building. The setting sun kindled the distant clouds to banners of flame. Boudica drank the last of the water in her skin and thought about going down the hill. It was very still. Even the raven that soared above the vale did so silently.

No doubt Lhiannon was already back at the roundhouse, getting dinner ready and wondering when Boudica would get there. The other woman had not passed her going down, but she must have done so, perhaps when Boudica was on the long loop on the other side of the hill. When she reached the top she had looked in every direction, and Lhiannon was nowhere to be seen. She was a little surprised—no, in truth, she was a little hurt—that her companion had not troubled to let her know she was leaving. They had seemed so close, after that morning in the pool. But Lhiannon had said this climb was supposed to be a solitary meditation. Perhaps she had left Boudica alone so that she could make up her mind.

"I don't want to decide!" she observed rebelliously.

"What *do* you want?"

Boudica stared. A moment ago she had been looking across the circle at the stones, and now Lhiannon was in front of her. If it *was* Lhiannon. The priestess had always been fair, but now her face shone.

"Where have you been?" Boudica found herself on her feet without quite knowing how she got there.

"I found the other road . . . I found the way within," the priestess said exultantly. "I found the way to Faerie . . ." She looked around her with mingled disappointment and wonder and Boudica believed her. "About halfway through the maze it began to change. Did you see nothing? I hoped that you would follow me . . ."

"I saw nothing but the green earth and the sky above."

In Lhiannon's eyes the light of the Otherworld still glowed. Boudica realized the gulf between them. *Lhiannon is half a spirit herself—no wonder she found the way to their world,* she realized. *If I had gone it would only have been because she was there. She longs for the Unseen—but the sunset that gilds the green grass on this hill is magic enough for me.* With mingled relief and regret she realized that her decision had been made.

"I am not a priestess. This world is enough for me."

Their eyes met, and in Lhiannon's she saw sorrow that faded gradually to acceptance, and something else that she could only identify as love.

"Then I am glad that I am still in it . . ." said the priestess, and smiled.

Boudica's heart lifted. If she was not to be a priestess, she must marry, but whatever the future might hold, the link between her and Lhiannon would remain.

EIGHT

*I*n the name of all the powers of earth, sky, and sea, what is *that*?"

Boudica turned at Lhiannon's exclamation, eyes widening as she glimpsed what appeared to be a haystack on four stumpy gray legs, moving slowly across the field. As they watched, a snakelike appendage reached up and plucked some of the hay.

"I think . . . it's some kind of animal." She shaded her eyes with one hand.

As the wind shifted, their ponies began to snort and plunge. "Definitely an animal," Lhiannon agreed in a shaken voice. "This must be one of those strange creatures we heard about last night—the *elephanti* the Romans brought with them across the sea."

They judged the animal to stand at least twice the height of a tall man. The brass caps on its ivory tusks glinted in the afternoon sunlight. Her mind boggled at the idea that such a thing could be carried on any kind of oceangoing craft. No doubt the emperor had brought the beasts to terrify the natives—it was certainly spooking the horses, but the sheer unlikeliness of the creature made Boudica want to laugh.

"It's no concern of ours," Leucu growled. "If we are to reach your father's tent before the evening meal we must move on."

He wrenched his horse's head around and booted it forward along the track that led to what had once been Cunobelin's dun. The Romans had burned the buildings in which the old king had taken so much pride—after first looting them, of course. The tribal leaders who had come to make peace with the emperor were camped in Camulodunon's fields.

No doubt Leucu would be glad to relinquish responsibility for his chieftain's daughter. He had spent much of their three-week journey across Britannia in a state of nerves that shortened both his sleep and his temper. But it was only in the previous days that they had encountered Roman patrols, the last of them at the gap in the dikes that had not, in the end, protected Camulodunon. Two women and an old man seemed unlikely to threaten the legions that surrounded the emperor, and they had been allowed to pass.

"I still don't like this," said Boudica as they rode across the pasture.

"What, are you afraid of the elephants?" asked Lhiannon.

Boudica snorted. "No—it's just that I thought I was going home!" As they journeyed across Britannia and her limbs remembered the joy of riding, she had begun to dream of the rolling pastures where the Iceni bred their horses. "But it is an evil homecoming when I arrive just in time to see my father submit to Rome!"

The Roman troops in Camulodunon were a spear aimed at the heart of all the lands that had once been under Cunobelin's sway. But would the conquerors be content with submission, or would she soon find herself in chains on a ship bound for Rome? However constricting life with the Druids had been, at least it was free. She had tried to convince the priestess to leave them, but Lhiannon seemed serenely confident. Or perhaps she was so determined to go to Camulodunon because Ardanos was still there.

They crossed the pasture and turned onto the droveway that led between the fields. The growing wheat lay trampled, with only a few clumps left to be harvested by the birds. The cattle, too, were gone. No doubt they had served the soldiers for a feast to celebrate their victory.

Another ditch, its rim crowned with hawthorn, surrounded the compound, but the roundhouses whose pointed roofs should have showed above the hedge were gone. It had been a month since the Romans burned them, but the acrid reek of smoke still hung in the air. And yet the pasture beyond the compound bore a bright harvest of tents, as if this were a belated Lugos festival. The chieftains who had not marched in time to defend Camulodunon had come to make submission to their conquerors.

After listening for four years to Druid diatribes, Boudica found it unsettling to see her own people baring their throats to the foe. She had known she would be returning to the bondage of marriage. Indeed, she and Lhiannon had spent much of the journey speculating on who her husband would be. She fought down anger as she realized that her tribe was to be bound as well.

As they rode into the camp, people emerged from tents to see who had arrived. Abruptly Boudica was aware of how she must look to them—a leggy, freckled young woman with a tangle of red-gold hair, dressed in an undyed linen tunica grimed by weeks of travel and grown ragged at the hem. Looking like a slattern had been a good guise for a traveler, but it was less so here, where men read who you were in what you wore.

The clusters of tents were marked by poles with standards. She peered upward, looking for the russet banner with the leaping white hare of her own clan. *Perhaps my parents will not recognize me,* she thought glumly. *Then I will have no choice but to return to Mona with Lhiannon . . .* Surrounded by so many brightly clad people, she had to stifle an impulse to turn around and ride back down the road.

Lhiannon saw her putting her hands over her ears and shook her head. "You cannot go through life like that, child—think for yourself a veil that only those sounds you want to hear can get through."

Boudica shut her eyes for a moment and was rewarded when the sound level dimmed. When she opened them, she realized it was because her father had come out to meet her, with her mother scurrying to catch up as usual. He looked even more dour than she remembered, and there was entirely too much gray in his hair. Her mother, too, was silver-headed now. When had her parents become so *old*?

"So you are here at last. You appear to have taken your time . . ." He looked his daughter up and down, but his expression did not change.

Boudica bit her lip. Surely whatever time they had lost

at Avalon they had saved by making part of the journey by sea. But Leucu was mumbling something about delays to avoid the Romans, and she relaxed again.

"Never mind, man," Dubrac said at last. "Go take some rest. I'm sure you've earned it. At least you got her here . . ." He turned to his wife. "Get her cleaned up, Ana. She must be fit to show to the princes by the evening meal." He turned away.

"Is it a feast or a cattle market I'm going to?" Boudica muttered as she swung a leg over the pony's back and slid down. She sent a beseeching glance to Lhiannon, but the priestess only smiled.

Then her mother was hugging her, stepping back to look up into her face, and embracing her again.

"Oh, my darling, how you've grown! But you're as brown as a berry, child, or is that dirt from the road? Never mind, never mind—oh how I've missed you! I have dreamed of this day."

I haven't, Boudica realized with a stab of guilt. But it was curiously comforting to be clucked over as if she were eight, not eighteen years old, and for all her questions, her mother did not seem to expect much in the way of a reply.

"And to you, my lady, all my gratitude for your care." Ana turned as Lhiannon also dismounted, ducking her head in a sort of truncated obeisance.

The priestess's blue robes were a little dusty, but she appeared otherwise untouched by the stains of travel. *As if,* thought Boudica with a familiar exasperated wonder, *she used some Druid magic that directed all the dirt to me!*

"My women have prepared a place for you." Ana gestured vaguely toward the other tents as a serving girl came forward. "Whatever you need for your comfort, you have only to ask . . ."

Boudica had scarcely the time for a nod of farewell before her mother drew her into one of the tents, a roomy affair made by stretching a cover of oiled wool above wickerwork walls. Sighing, she allowed Ana to feed her oatcakes and mint tea, to cluck over her hair and her skin and discuss what she should wear. It had been like this, she remembered, when she was a little girl. As her husband took over the training of each son, all Ana's motherly instincts had focused on this one surviving daughter, who in turn only wanted to prove herself a better boy than any of her brothers. But Boudica realized that among other things, her time with the Druids had shown her that there was more than one way to be a woman, and more ways than one to be a woman of power.

Rhiannon, having left Boudica to her fate, set out to find Ardanos. A few discreet inquiries brought her presently to a group of tents over which the boar banner of the Southern Iceni flew.

She found him sitting cross-legged, carving a piece of wood, and paused to taste the pleasure of simply seeing him there, alive and well. He had enjoyed carving when he was a boy. Was it a sign of contentment that he should do it now, or was he so frustrated by the situation that he could think of nothing else to do? Frustration, probably, she thought as she moved closer. He was carving birds.

"And when you have made them, where will they fly?" she asked softly.

For a moment he was utterly still, but she saw his knuckles whiten on the handle of the knife. Very carefully, he loosened his fingers and set down the blade. Only then did he look up at her.

What, my beloved, did you not want me to see in your eyes? she wondered. They glimmered with water he was too proud to wipe away. She knelt beside him and picked up one of the birds.

"King Antedios has a little daughter," he said, almost steadily. "They are water birds, and she will set them in the stream . . ."

"And from the stream to the river, and then they will float to the sea, and from there they may come at last to the Blessed Isles. I understand."

"All went well?" Ardanos reached up to pluck a leaf that had attached itself to her veil; the touch became a caress that brushed a strand of hair back from her brow and lingered there.

"Very well, both for Boudica and for me, even though—maybe because—we were alone. Ardanos, this time when I climbed the Tor, I went inward! I have to tell you—"

"Not here!" he said harshly. "It would profane the memory. When we are on the road. Now that you have come, we can get out of here."

"Ardanos!" she exclaimed, torn between annoyance and laughter. "I have been riding for three weeks. Boudica was born on a horse, I think, and has recovered all her old skill, but I was not, and not even for you will I sit on a saddle again until the bruises on my backside have healed. Besides, I must wait until Boudica—"

"Damn Boudica! I want to get you safely out of here!" He shook his head. "At least wear a band across your brow to hide that blue crescent while you are here!"

Lhiannon frowned. "That mark is borne only by those of our Order who have been initiated on Avalon. The Romans will not know what it means."

"Unless someone tells them . . ." His face was grim. "There are far too many here who would curry favor with those who bestow the luxuries of Rome. Wear a headband or a veil."

"And what about you?" she said wryly. "It is certain they will know you for a Druid if they see that shaven brow."

"Everyone already knows who I am." He shrugged. "When there are Romans about I have a cap that I can wear."

"See that you wear it, then." She eased down beside him. "And since we must stay here for a time, suppose you tell me who has come to this disaster, and what you think will happen now."

The festival of Lugos had always included a cattle fair, where folk sold off superfluous animals and bought beasts whose breeding might improve their own herds. To Boudica, standing in the middle of her parents' tent while her mother directed a covey of clucking maids to scrub, oil, comb, and adorn her, the comparison seemed uncomfortably appropriate. All that kept her from bolting was the knowledge that if she should decide for Mona, Lhiannon and Ardanos were quite capable of spiriting her away.

"There now, my darling." Her mother stood back, inspecting her. "Now you look like a woman of the royal kindred." She held out her bronze mirror, its back incised with graceful whorls and tendrils, so that Boudica could see.

Admittedly the closest thing to a mirror on Mona was a still pool, but the face that looked back at her belonged to no one she knew. They had braided her hair back from her temples with scarlet ribands and allowed the rest of the mane to flow down her back in waves of copper and gold. An artful application of Roman cosmetics reddened her lips and defined her brows.

Her tunica was of thin linen that followed the lines of her body and fell in graceful folds, pinned at the shoulders with fibulae of gilded bronze and girdled with gold, and dyed as deep a red as the root of the madder would allow. Golden earrings and a necklet of twisted gold completed the ensemble, with a mantle woven in the reds and tans and yellows of her tribe.

"It will be too warm for this," she said, and tried to hand back the wool.

"You can sit on it when you are not bearing around the pitcher of wine," her mother replied tartly.

"I am honored," Boudica said dryly, remembering the last time she had served kings. Of the rulers who had come to plot the defense of Britannia in answer to the Arch-Druid's call, Togodumnos was dead and Caratac in hiding, and the kings of the Durotriges and Belgae were waiting to see where the Roman eagle would strike next. Of those whose cups she would fill tonight, only Prasutagos, whose brother's death had made him king of the Northern Iceni, would remember.

"Well, you should be," her mother said briskly. "Most of them have queens already, of course, but they have sons and brothers. I have no doubt we shall place you well."

Boudica took a deep breath, grateful for Druid lessons in self-control. "And what if I choose not to marry? When you packed me off to Mona, wasn't it the understanding that I might decide to stay?"

"But . . . you came back . . ."

Seeing her mother's face crumple, Boudica put out a consoling hand. Two of her brothers had followed Togodumnos to the Tamesa, and died, leaving only Dubnocoveros, the brother next to her in age, and little Bracios. Her mother was still mourning, and did not need more grief from her daughter now.

"I promise you I will give it a chance. I will not disgrace you at the feast this evening, and I will listen to whatever offers may come."

"We called you 'filly' when you were a little one, you were so wild." Her mother shook her head with a sigh. "I hoped you might have changed. But at least you *look* as a royal woman should."

With this qualified approval both of them must be content. In silence, Boudica followed her mother toward the fire circle where stretched cloths shaded an outdoor feasting hall.

*B*oudica was not the only royal woman to come late to the gathering. That afternoon the Brigante delegation had arrived, and Lhiannon, finding herself superfluous among the Iceni, made her way through the welter of tents and wagons to the one where the black horse standard flew. By rights, the banner ought to have shown a herd of horses, for the Brigantes were not so much a tribe as a federation of clans. The marriage of Cartimandua and Venutios had more or less united them. But Lhiannon had known the Brigante queen when they were both girls in the House of Maidens on Mona. She wondered if Cartimandua had changed.

Apparently not, for as she approached she could hear a crisp, rather high voice giving a flurry of orders. A maidservant popped through the door as if shot from a bow and dashed off, and in the moment of silence that followed, Lhiannon ducked inside.

"Welcome to Camulodunon, my lady," she said softly.

Cartimandua whirled, her shining black hair swinging like the tail of the sleek pony that was the meaning of her name. Small and elegantly curved, she owed her royal blood to the tribes that had ruled this land when the Belgic princes first came over from Gallia.

"Lhiannon, by all that's holy! You always did find out everything the great ones were doing. I ought to have known you would be here."

Lhiannon found herself enveloped in a scented embrace, then held away as the women conducted a mutual inspection.

"You've kept your figure, I see," said the queen. "Is it any use to you, or are you still fighting Helve for the right to sit in the Oracle's chair?"

Lhiannon felt herself blushing in spite of herself. Clearly Cartimandua's speech had grown no less frank since she had become a queen.

"Lady Mearan died earlier this summer. Helve is High Priestess now."

"Oh ho—and I'll wager she loves it! Do you remember the summer we plagued her with frogs? Frogs in her bed and frogs in her shoes and everywhere. I don't think she ever did figure out which of us holy maidens was responsible. So she rules now, and you and Ardanos are in exile, eh?"

"We were sent to assist Caratac," Lhiannon said, a little stiffly.

"Ah, that was a bad business." Cartimandua's mood shifted and she sighed. "So many beautiful men lost. But it does no good to fight the tide. The Romans are too strong, and we must make the best peace we can."

"So you and Venutios mean to surrender?"

"To become a client-kingdom, if we can," the queen corrected. "We'll pay for it, but we will keep some freedom. And there will be favors from the Romans as well." She laughed suddenly. "I can live with such a bargain. It's the same I made with Venutios, after all!"

Lhiannon blinked. "Does your husband love you?"

Cartimandua lifted a dark eyebrow. "*Love* is not a word often used between princes. He is brisk in bed, when the situation requires. The rest of the time ... he respects me."

She has lovers, thought Lhiannon. But surely that was no surprise. At Lys Deru, Cartimandua had taken any lad who pleased her to her bed even before she was officially of an age to go to the Beltane fires. It had been something of a scandal at the time, but everyone knew that the Brigantes had their own ways, and some of their clans still counted royal descent through their queens. She suspected that Cartimandua would have been a law unto herself in any land.

"And what are you doing here? Do you have Caratac tucked away somewhere disguised as a groom? Not that I wouldn't like to see him again, but I don't think the Romans would welcome him."

A sudden caution stopped Lhiannon from telling Cartimandua where the Cantiaci king was now. Instead she began to talk about Boudica and their journey from Avalon.

"No doubt I will see her at the feasting," said the queen. "Poor child. With two sons killed, Dubrac will use her to buy an alliance somewhere. Prasutagos's wife died three years ago. My guess is that they will marry him to Boudica to unite the northern and southern royal lines."

I am seeing the last riding of free Britannia, thought Boudica as her father led his little cavalcade out to join those of the other kings. Until now the reality of their situation had not truly touched her. Fighting a surge of panic, she gripped the side of the wagon as it jolted along the road.

The Romans had built their camp between the old protecting dike and a new triple ditch and bank extending straight as a spear to the river, making no concession to the lay of the land. For the first time she began to understand the sheer size of an empire that could permanently dedicate so many men to such a purpose. And this was only one of Rome's armies.

Only a few poles with standards could be seen above the dikes, but she could hear the noise of the Roman camp, like the humming of an enormous hive. And then they came to the gate in its center, lined with legionaries whose armor blazed in the summer sun. They watched the Britons with narrowed eyes. From the goat-fish painted on their battered shields she knew them for the legion led by general Vespasian, who at the battle on the Medu had been responsible for the victory.

Be easy, she thought grimly. *We have not come to fight you, but to pass beneath the yoke of Rome.*

Boudica turned away as her father and brother unbelted their swords and gave them to a bemedaled centurion. Then, teeth drawn, each group of native princes was escorted within. This camp held thirty thousand men. Only now, seeing the precise ranks of leather tents stretching away to either side, did she begin to comprehend what that number must mean. If they could ever be gathered, the Britons would have more warriors, but she could not imagine a Celtic army ever achieving such discipline. Her own response to a challenge had always been to fight, but this enemy was overwhelming. *The Romans cannot be defeated,* she thought with a sinking heart. *Each tribe must seek the best terms of surrender it can.*

They were being marched straight down the main avenue toward a pavilion as large as Cunobelin's feasting hall, of sturdy fabric dyed a deep purple and trimmed with glittering gold. The area before it was fenced with tall soldiers whose armor was ornamented with gold, and whose expressions showed less hatred but greater pride. These dark blue shields had never seen battle. The gold thunderbolts extending from the silver wings above and below the boss and the silver stars and moons in their corners were unmarred.

"The Praetorian Guard . . ." murmured her brother Dubnocoveros. "They murdered Claudius's predecessor, Caligula. They are the only ones allowed to kill an emperor, it would seem . . ."

A glare from one of the officers silenced him, whether because the man spoke Celtic or because no speech was allowed. The former was possible, she supposed—the man looked like a Gaul.

One by one the little groups of royalty were led in to make their submission to the emperor. Queen Cartimandua, resplendent in an embroidered green gown that made Boudica feel underdressed, marched in with her husband, heavily jowled and dour, by her side. Did the Romans understand that the Brigante rulers could speak only for the clans of that vast northern region that in the shifting web of Brigante alliances were for the moment on their side? Or was Cartimandua depending on Roman help to tip the balance of power and bring them all under her rule?

Bodovoc of the Northern Dobunni stood apart from the others, smugly aware of his advantage in having submitted to the Romans *before* they conquered. He would have to keep peace with his southern cousin Corio now. The other early collaborator, King Veric, had already been presented. He and his toga-clad heir, Cogidubnos, had the privilege of standing with the senators and watching the humiliation of their fellow kings. No one waited here to make submission for the Cantiaci, the Trinovantes, or the Catuvellauni. They were conquered peoples, and their lands would be administered directly by the Roman governor.

And then it was the turn of the Iceni. The high king Antedios, graying at the temples and gaunt from recent anxiety, stepped forward, followed by Dubrac, who was now his closest male relation, and Prasutagos, whose brother's death had left him lord of the Northern Iceni clans.

My possible future husband . . . she thought, considering him with new eyes. Although in theory she had the right to refuse, her father had made his preference clear. At least she had met Prasutagos already, and supposed him to be kind. She remembered him as a man of few words. Just now he was so quiet he seemed hardly present at all. As they passed into the Imperial tent their eyes met, and Boudica knew he must be remembering all their proud boasts on Mona.

Yet here we both are, and you will not tell them I was trained by the Druids, and I will not say that you were Caratac's ally. Perhaps they ought to marry to ensure each other's silence. But first they had to survive the next hour.

A dim illumination, purple as a winter dusk, filtered through the heavy cloth. As her eyes adjusted, she began to pick out the grim, weathered profiles of the guards, the clean-shaven faces of the senators, calculating or bored, and the emperor, Tiberius Claudius Caesar Augustus Germanicus himself, draped in an embroidered silk garment the same purple as the tent, so that his face seemed to float above it like the apparition of a god.

He was a tense, tired god, she thought, with a lined face and ears that stood out from a head that seemed too big for its neck. The physical infirmities of which she had heard were hidden by the flowing robe. But his eyes seemed unexpectedly kind. How comforting, she thought, to know that whatever he ordered done to them would not be out of spite, but from policy.

She knelt with the others, grateful for the rich carpet that covered the floor. If they must abase themselves, at least it would be in luxury.

One of the emperor's servants began to declaim something in which she recognized the Iceni names, translated into Celtic, phrase by phrase by the interpreter.

"You are here to submit to the Senate and People of Rome, to offer yourselves and your families, your tribesmen, and your servants as willing and obedient subjects of the Empire. Do you agree to this bond?"

Antedios, Dubrac, and Prasutagos set the palms of their hands upon the floor. "May the earth open to swallow us, may the sea wash over us, may the sky fall upon us, if we fail to keep faith with the High King of the Roman tribes."

The translator spoke again. "This is Lucius Junius Pollio." One of the Romans, draped in a toga but without the purple stripe of a senator, stepped forward. Lean and dark-featured, he looked military, despite his flowing garb. "He will collect your taxes under the procurator, but you will keep your own laws and govern your people as our clients, so long as those laws and governance are not in violation of the laws of Rome. Our allies will be your allies, and your enemies our enemies."

The emperor bent to whisper something to one of his advisors, who spoke to the translator in turn.

"The emperor asks whether you have heirs."

"King Prasutagos is newly come to lordship and has neither wife nor child," came the answer. "King Antedios is his overking, and his next heir is Dubrac, whose son Dubnocoveros kneels at his side."

Boudica saw her brother stiffen as the emperor spoke again.

"Your people cannot become good subjects of the Empire until they understand Rome. It is therefore our policy to educate royal heirs in our own court, as we did Prince Cogidubnos. Dubnocoveros filius Dubraci will go with us along with the other young men of good family when we return."

Dubi's convulsive twitch was stilled by his father's hand. This had not been discussed, but taking hostages was Roman policy. She saw now why the kings had been instructed to bring their families. The governor's man, Pollio, was staring at her as if he wished *she* had been the hostage. She willed herself to invisibility, grateful the decision was not in his hands.

"Rise, allies of Rome!"

First Antedios and then Prasutagos received a golden chain with a medallion showing the face of the emperor. One by one they were allowed to kiss the imperial hand. And then they were being ushered out into a day that seemed robbed of warmth, as if the Romans had taken the sunlight along with their freedom.

*T*hey have even stolen the stars," said Boudica.

Lhiannon looked up, startled by the bitterness in the younger woman's tone. No need to ask who *they* might be. Above the Roman camp the sky was red with the light of a thousand fires. She knew the clouds were reflecting the light, but there was something unnerving about that bloody glow. They had walked out into the fields beyond the Iceni encampment to talk, but there was no peace here.

"Beyond the clouds the stars still shine," she said bracingly. "And we will see them again one day."

"Is that some Druid prophecy? Your foretellings have proven true enough—you should have listened to them." Boudica's voice shook with pain.

"The situation looks grim, but the Romans only hold one corner of Britannia. If Caratac can rally the other tribes—"

"He will fight with greater hope if you don't let him hear the Oracle's predictions," Boudica replied. "You haven't seen the Roman camp, row upon row of metal-clad men. How can anyone stand against them?"

Lhiannon winced, remembering how beautiful the Trinovante warriors had looked as they ran forward to dash their naked bodies against the Roman steel.

"Come back with me to Mona. You will be safe on the Druids' Isle." The path led them alongside a thorn hedge. As they passed, a hare leaped out from its shadows and went bounding across the grass.

"Do you really believe that? We both heard Lady Mearan's words. The Romans know that until they eliminate the Druids, their hold on Britannia will never be secure. They will find Mona. It is only a matter of time."

Lhiannon moved a little away, instinctively raising mental shields against the younger woman's despair. "I have to believe there is hope," she said in a low voice. "Even if I am wrong. I cannot betray the men I saw die at the Tamesa by giving up now."

"Ah, I am sorry! I did not mean to hurt you!" Boudica reached out to hug her. "When I first got here I despised my father for surrendering so easily. But now I think that he is right. To cooperate is the only way we can retain any independence at all!"

"And so you will stay and marry Prasutagos, as you tell me your father desires?"

"With Dubi a hostage, our family needs a firm alliance with the other Iceni royal line. At Mona, I would never be more than a minor priestess. I may be able to help our people as a queen."

They walked on in silence, and found that their steps had brought them onto the droveway that led to Camulodunon. The friendly darkness hid the worst of the destruction, but even at night the dun had never been so utterly still.

"And will he love you?" Lhiannon asked softly after a time.

"Does that matter?" Boudica snapped back. "Ardanos loves *you*, but it has not made either of you happier, that I can see!"

Lhiannon stopped, desolation tightening her throat as she admitted that what Boudica had said was true. She stumbled forward and sat down on a broken wagon.

"Ah, now I have hurt you again!" There were tears in Boudica's voice as well. "But you have to understand—the last time I stood here, this was a great king's home. I don't want this to happen to my father's dun!"

When Lhiannon said nothing, she eased down beside her. "I trust Prasutagos to work for our people. I am making an alliance. But it will be easier if I know that you still love me . . ."

"I will pray to the Goddess that you find joy in your duty," whispered Lhiannon. *Even though She has given me little enough in mine . . .*

She could feel Boudica nodding as they wept in each other's arms.

NINE

Living in the closed community of Lys Deru, Boudica had forgotten what it was like to gallop across the open heath beneath an endless sky. Just now she needed the escape as never before. Even Helve at her worst had not been as annoying as Anaveistl's endless nattering about the astonishing array of goods and gear Boudica was expected to take with her to her new home. Tomorrow they would journey to Dun Garo on the River of Eels. King Antedios had claimed the honor of hosting the marriage between his most important subking and the daughter of his heir.

Will Prasutagos let his wife gallop over the hills? His clan-hold was in the north near the sea. Going there would be like being a newcomer at the Druids' Isle all over again, but this move would be lifelong.

Boudica's lips twisted wryly as she realized what was really bothering her. Her people bred horses, and she knew, more or less, what human breeding involved. A few exploratory fumblings with Rianor had even shown her why one might enjoy it. She realized then that it was not so much the act that she feared as the idea of submitting to a stranger.

Her old dun pony tossed its head and juttered to a stop as a gray hare, startled from its form in the heather, dashed across the moor. Boudica caught her breath and made a sign of reverence as it disappeared.

For generations the Clan of the Hare had grazed sheep and horses on this undulating land where the sandy soil retained only enough water for grasses to fill in the spaces between the clumps of gorse and heather, though more recently her father had taken advantage of their position where the ancient trackway forded two rivers to set up a weavers' center where the thread the women spun could be made into cloth.

As the season of harvest drew to a close the heathlands glowed with the purple of heather and the gorse's rich gold. The trees that flourished along the rivers that drained westward into the fen country shaded from green to all the autumn colors. There lay the sacred grove that sheltered the shrine of Andraste, who had been honored here since before the Belgic princes came from across the sea.

Boudica kneed her mount into motion again and they trotted down the path that wandered amid the old barrows. She slid down and tied the rein to a blackthorn bush where the horse could nose at the dry grass.

The Turning of Autumn was just past. On one of the mounds a dessicated bouquet of heather and asters lay. That would be old Nessa's doing—she was the one who knew all the old tales. Boudica began to walk the pattern around the barrows as the old woman had taught her, finishing at the mound in the middle—the only one it was permissable to climb.

Four miles to the northwest she could see the roundhouses of Teutodunon, overlooking the ford where the river was crossed by the ancient track. Her mother's garden lay behind the chieftain's house, the pens for sheep and horses and the weaving shed beyond. It looked deceptively peaceful from here.

Tomorrow they would set out for Antedios's dun and her wedding, and when would she see her home again? She had agreed to the marriage, but just now she felt like the sacrificial hare that had struggled in Helve's hands.

She found a piece of oatcake in her bag and placed it in a crevice between two stones on top of the mound.

"Old one, your earth and water built my blood and bones. Accept this offering. Guard this place as you have done for so many years, and though I must leave you, remember me . . ."

Gradually, her panic eased. Coventa, she thought wistfully, would have heard an answer. For Boudica there was only a sense of peace, until the light began to fade and she knew it was time to go home.

*　*　*

The mare shook her head, a shrill neigh expressing her disdain for the lad who clung to her leadrope. Her coat shone richly chestnut as the sun broke through the clouds, a shade deeper than Boudica's hair. The boy set his heels to hold her, but it had rained that morning, and he was pulled through the mud instead.

"I don't think that filly wants to be saddled," said one of King Antedios's warriors.

"Take a good man to ride her," answered his companion.

"Prasutagos has good hands for a horse, they say . . ."

Boudica flushed as the men glanced at her and laughed. But it was indeed a beautiful horse, and it was hers, a wedding gift from her prospective husband.

Her mother tugged at her elbow, and she allowed herself to be led toward the roundhouse. Draped and jeweled in the red gown and plaid cloak she had worn at Camulodunon, she moved carefully, afraid of disturbing the elaborate braids in which her mother's maids had done her hair. A wreath of golden gorse and wheat heads crowned the arrangement over a gauzy crimson veil.

Since waking she had been in a strange, suspended state, allowing the women to dress and adorn her as if she were the image of a god. And that, she thought distantly, was almost true. Today she was the Bride, not Boudica. This ceremony would celebrate the union of two royal kindreds that strengthened the tribe, the union of male and female that renewed the world. The symbolism was there in any wedding, but kings and queens carried the luck of the tribe. She had been caught up in the surge of emotion that flowed from people to the king when her father performed the rites at planting and harvest. The Druids had given her the background to understand what was happening. But now it was she who must carry that power. It felt different from inside.

A twitter of women's voices from ahead told her that the women's procession was forming. Boudica was surprised to see the Brigante queen Cartimandua among them. She wished that Lhiannon and Coventa could have been there.

Her mother chivvied the others into some kind of order as a harper began to strike rhythmic chords. Anaveistl set a sheaf of grain in Boudica's arms and pushed her into place behind the chattering girls with their baskets of herbs and late flowers. The rest fell into place behind them as they started along the path through the fields.

Somewhere a drum was beating, a deep vibration that she felt as much as heard. Or perhaps it was her own heartbeat. Harp and drum fell silent as the men's procession approached from the woods to the northeast, led by boys carrying green branches and a youth with a burning torch. They circled an ancient earthen ring about the height of a man and defined by shallow ditches to meet the bride's party at the entrance.

As her mother led Boudica forward, the boys began to sing—

> *"You are the moon among the stars,*
> *You are the foam upon the wave,*
> *You are the lily among the flowers,*
> *You are the spark that starts the flame,*
> *You are the beloved."*

Prasutagos, dressed in a splendid fringed cloak checkered in seven colors over a blue tunic and braes striped in blue and red, emerged from the crowd of men to stand beside her as the maidens who had escorted Boudica replied—

> *"You are the sun above the clouds,*
> *You are the wave that strikes the shore,*
> *You are the oak within the wood,*
> *You are the torch that lights the hall,*
> *You are the beloved."*

Inside the ring King Antedios and his queen, his Druid, and Boudica's father were waiting. As she passed through the gap Boudica had the odd sense that the earth had shifted. Prasutagos steadied her as she stumbled and she took a deep breath, staring around her. Here were no ancient stones to bear witness to the past, but earth was older still. For how many lives of men had this earthen embankment defined sacred ground?

Among the Druids she had thought herself head-blind, but moving around the fire that burned in the circle's center, she knew that her time on the isle had changed her. She had sensed nothing different about this place when she had visited as a child, but now, when she looked through the gap that framed the pointed roofs of the dun and a low hill across the river beyond, she could feel the current of power that linked them. Everything outside the embankment seemed blurred, as if seen through the heated air above a fire. She wondered if this was how Lhiannon had felt when she was in the Faerie world. For a moment she had a sense that all times were simultaneous, as if by simply shifting her focus she could *see*.

Did Prasutagos feel it, she wondered as they halted before the fire. His usually pleasant features looked stern, his gaze a little inward. Or perhaps he was remembering his first wife and mourning the necessity that required him to marry Boudica.

The Druid, robed in more colors than even Prasutagos wore, turned to the others. His white beard flowed down his chest like carded wool, stirring a little in the wind.

"Of what blood do this man and this woman come?"

"I stand for Prasutagos, since his father is no longer living," said Antedios. "Of the People of the Ram he is chieftain. Let him be married to this woman with the blessing of his kin."

"I stand for Boudica of the People of the Hare," her father spoke then. "I release my daughter from clan-bond and clan-right that she may become part of her husband's family. Let her be married to this man with the blessing of her kin."

The Druid moved around the fire, a length of braid in his hand. He was a small man, a little bent with age, but there was a light in his eye that reminded her of Lugovalos. "Prasutagos and Boudica, you have come here with the blessing of your families to be joined before the people, the ancestors, and the gods. In flesh and in spirit you shall be mated. Do you both consent to this binding?"

What would happen if I said no? she thought wildly.

She heard the man's murmured assent joining her own as the priest draped the cord around their wrists. But she had committed herself already when she told Lhiannon she would not return to the Druids' Isle.

"By what vows will you be bound?"

Prasutagos looked at her fully for the first time since they had entered the circle. His eyes were gray, but around the iris she saw flecks of gold. *In time,* she thought, *I will know everything about this man,* and then, with a tremor, *and he will know everything about me . . .*

"I, Prasutagos, do pledge you, Boudica, to live as your husband."

She took a deep breath and replied, "I, Boudica, do pledge you, Prasutagos, to live as your wife."

Together they continued the vows.

"Your hearth shall be my hearth, your bed shall be my bed. For your loyalty I shall return love, and for your love grant you my loyalty. Upon the circle of life I swear it, by earth and fire, by wind and water, and before the holy gods."

"I am your staff and your sword," said Prasutagos.

And Boudica replied, "I am your shield and your cauldron."

The queen held out a loaf made from grain that had been grown at the House of the Hare mixed with some from Prasutagos's lands.

"From the earth that bore you this bread was made," the Druid proclaimed, "many seeds ground together to become one loaf. May your union be fruitful; and may that bounty extend to field and forest, to plowland and pasture, and all the land you rule." Despite his age, his voice was full and strong.

Boudica broke off a corner, dropped a few crumbs on the ground and into the fire, and fed the rest to Prasutagos.

"As I break this bread, so I offer my life to nourish you," she said.

"As I take it, my body shall become one with yours," he replied.

The bread was given to Prasutagos, who did the same. As Boudica swallowed the coarse grains she found herself suddenly aware of his physical presence.

The Druid took the rest of the cake and crumbled it

over their heads. It seemed to her that she could feel each grain.

The king came forward with a bowl of carved jet filled with water.

"This water is the blood of the earth, drawn from two sacred springs," the Druid said then. "As these waters have become one, may your spirits blend, and may the springs that water your land run ever pure and clear."

The king offered the bowl to Prasutagos, who spilled a little on the earth and flicked a drop into the fire. Like the grain, it was a blending from both their homes.

"As this water is poured, I pour out my spirit for you."

"As I drink it, my spirit mingles with yours," she replied.

Prasutagos held it to Boudica's lips and she drank. Then the Druid handed the bowl to her. As she repeated the words, she found her eyes filling with tears and tried to quell the surge of emotion that came with them as she blinked them away.

When it was done, the Druid set the bowl aside and turned them to face each other. "The free air of heaven is the breath of the ancestors. Breathe deeply, let their spirit fill you, and give it back to each other again."

It was true, she thought as she drew the charged air into her lungs. If the earth was made from the dust of all that had lived, this air held their breath, generation after generation, changing, exchanging, inspiring, and expiring with each birth and death.

Among women, Boudica was tall, but Prasutagos stood a span taller. With his free hand he tipped up her chin. She controlled her involuntary flinch, felt the tickle of his mustache as he set his lips to hers. They were dry and cool, firmly demanding. *Soon enough he will have the right to take more than a kiss,* she told herself, forcing herself to let her lips open beneath his.

"By earth and water and air you have been joined together. Let heart-fire and hearth-fire witness your vows." The old Druid stepped back.

Still bound together, Prasutagos and Boudica circled the fire, once, twice, and a third time, to stand before the Druid once more. Had it grown hotter, or was it the heat of Prasutagos's body that was kindling her own?

"Now it is done. Now you are bound in the sight of earth and heaven. King and Queen, Priest and Priestess, Lord and Lady you shall be to each other and to your land." He turned them, and together they crossed the gap and left the earthen ring with the others falling in behind them. As they emerged, the boys and men began to sing—

> *"You are the breeze that cools the brow,*
> *You are the well of sweet water,*
> *You are the earth that cradles the seed,*
> *You are the oven that bakes the bread,*
> *You are the beloved."*

And once more the women replied—

> *"You are the wind that shakes the oak,*
> *You are the rain that fills the sea,*
> *You are the seed within the earth,*
> *You are the fire upon the hearth,*
> *You are the beloved."*

*D*id you think all this was in *your* honor?" Cartimandua turned to Boudica, gesturing toward the bonfire around which a circle of young men were dancing, their coordination only a little impaired by the quantities of heather ale they had drunk this evening. As a ruling queen, she had been given the place of honor next to the bride.

Food in plenty was set out on the long cloth spread before the royal guests—roasted venison and wild boar, beef from their pastures and salmon and eels from the river, bread and beans and barley, fruit dried and fresh, and pungent cheeses. If the purpose of the wedding feast was to imprint the event on people's minds, this marriage would be well remembered.

"The Romans have come," the queen continued. "And despite all those fine words at Camulodunon, no one really knows what will happen to Britannia now." For a moment her dark gaze rested on young Epilios, who had dragged Boudica's little brother, Braci, into the dance.

So far everyone had conspired to keep the Romans ignorant that another son of Cunobelin still lived. But now that they were Roman clients, he might not be safe in the Iceni lands, and he would make far too valuable a hostage for Caratac's good behavior. At the thought, Boudica remembered her other brother, now on his way to Rome. Her father was already beginning to groom little Braci as his heir. Dubnocoveros might never return, and if he did, he might be more Roman than Celt, like that priggish boy Cogidubnos whom Boudica had met in Camulodunon.

Cartimandua shrugged. "A wedding is a promise that life will go on, and getting drunk is a safe way to release the frustration of not being able to come to grips with your foe."

Boudica put down the piece of roasted boar she had been pretending to eat and took another sip from her silver cup. They had been served mead, fiery as the wedding torch and as sweet as love was supposed to be. A gabble of conversation rose around her in which from time to time she would catch a name—Morigenos . . . Tingetorix . . . Brocagnos—that she supposed she ought to know. These were the chief men of the Iceni kingdom, with whom she would have to deal as queen.

And what about my *frustration?* she wondered.

Prasutagos was talking to the king about breeding cattle. Indeed, since their vows in the earthen ring he and she had exchanged scarcely a word. And yet, though the braid no longer tied them together, she was acutely aware of the mass and heat of his body next to hers.

I am bound, she thought resentfully. *But is* he? She held out her cup to be refilled and drank again. Halfway up the sky a full moon was rising, sending shafts of silver light to challenge the glow of the fire.

"And how do they celebrate weddings in your land?" she asked the queen.

Cartimandua's glance flicked down the line of feasters to her husband and she laughed. "Not so tamely as you do here! There are vows and blessings, to be sure, but first the man must carry off his bride from among her kindred. They come to her home and she pretends to hide, or they attack the bridal procession, and she sets heels to her horse and he must run her down."

"Even at the wedding of a king and a queen?"

"Especially then." Cartimandua smiled reminiscently. "In my country we are very proud of our horses. The stallion is not allowed to breed unless he can catch the mare."

"The Iceni breed fine horses, too!" Boudica exclaimed.

"Indeed they do." Cartimandua gave her a speculative look. "I would wager that red filly your husband gifted you has a fine turn of speed ..."

The servants had at last ceased to bring out new dishes, but they were still replenishing the mead. The musicians fell silent, and the murmur of conversation stilled as King Antedios rose to his feet.

"Let us drink to this happy occasion—a toast to the bridal pair!" He raised his goblet. "The two branches of the Iceni are once more united! To seal the bargain, Dubrac gives his new son forty white ewes and six breeding mares."

"And the finest of them is that filly who sits at Prasutagos's side!" The comment was just loud enough to carry. There was a general rumble of masculine laughter, and Boudica felt her face heating. She had resented being ignored, but this was not the kind of attention she craved. She held out her cup to be refilled.

Where now were the noble vows they had exchanged in the circle? No matter how you dressed it up with ritual, the truth was that she had been married off to a man almost twice her age to cement an alliance, last if not least in the tally of livestock with which Prasutagos was being paid to take her on. In exchange, Dubrac would receive cattle, and several farmsteads up on the northern coast would be Boudica's own.

She blinked hazily as retainers carried in the gifts from the other wedding guests to be admired—rolls of wool and linen and a beautifully carved loom so that she could stay busy making more, a set of ruddy Samian ware dishes made in Gallia, several amphorae of Roman wine.

Very pretty, thought Boudica, *but were they worth our freedom?* At least the red mare, adorned with her rich harness and sidling nervously as she was led among the feasters, was home-grown. Boudica drank down the last of her mead.

The queen's women were forming up in front of the house that had been prepared for the bedding of the bride. "It is not day, nor yet day," they sang. "It is not day, nor yet morning: It is not day, nor yet day, for the moon is shining brightly . . ."

It was, too, thought Boudica, squinting as she tried to bring it into focus. There seemed to be two moons dancing up there, or maybe it was three. Plenty of light for the drunken fools who would bang on pots outside the door and shout ribald suggestions as to how Prasutagos should serve his new mare.

"Time to get you ready for your wedding night, my child," said Cartimandua, putting out a steadying hand as Boudica tried to rise. "And a pity it is to waste such a night beneath a roof. With the moon so full, 'tis nigh as bright as day."

Boudica gained her feet and swayed as the world spun around her.

"Oh dear," said the queen. "Well, it's only the husband who dares not risk being made incapable. If you're a virgin, you might even prefer to be drunk your first time . . ." Boudica's mother started toward them and Cartimandua waved her away.

"I need . . . the privy," Boudica said with as much dignity as she could muster.

"I'm sure you do, my child." Cartimandua set a hand beneath her elbow and steered her away from the fire.

To accommodate the numbers of guests they had dug new privies down by the horse lines. The red mare, still wearing her embroidered blanket, was tied to a fence post by her halter. She threw up her head and snorted as Boudica and her escort passed by.

The walk through the crisp air had cleared Boudica's head enough so that she could go behind the wicker screen alone, and by the time she had relieved herself of as much of the mead as possible, there was only one moon in the sky. A pity, she thought glumly. Cartimandua was right. She was about to be deflowered, practically in public, by a man for whom she was just another broodmare. It would all have been much easier through a haze of mead.

At last she stood, adjusting her skirts and pinning her

wool cloak more securely. Now that the alcohol was leaving her system, the air felt cold. Cartimandua was waiting. In silence they started up the path.

"Wait a moment," she said as they came to the place where the mare was tethered. "The horse is mine, and I've not yet given her a name." She moved quietly forward.

The mare bobbed her head and snuffled as Boudica reached up to rub the place behind her ear where the headstall pinched. She brought her hands down to cradle the horse's head and blew into her nostrils.

"Hey there, my lovely lass. Shall I call you Roud then, my red one? And have they left you bound?" She slid her hand along the shining neck, and the mare rubbed her head up and down her shoulder. "It seems a pity on such a night, when you should be running free over the hills . . ."

From somewhere near the fire, men were shouting, "Bring out the bride!" "Bring out the mare—the stallion is ready!" "Where is she, lads? Let's go find her! Show us the bride!"

"Do you know . . ." Boudica said over her shoulder to Cartimandua. "I do not care to be everyone's entertainment this evening. Your people are not the only ones who believe a queen ought to be respected." She sighed, remembering Lhiannon's counsels at Avalon. She ran her hand along the saddlecloth and found that the cinch was still tight.

"But I find what you've told me about Brigante customs quite appealing. King Prasutagos ought to earn his bride, don't you agree?" She reached under the mare's neck and gave a tug to the knot. As she had hoped, it was the sort that released quickly. The horse took a step forward as the rope loosened, moving between Boudica and the queen.

"Oh indeed," breathed Cartimandua, her voice shaken with consternation, or possibly laughter.

"Prasutagos did not court me," Boudica continued in the same even tone, easing the horse around, "nor did he buy me." She set her hands on the mare's withers and back. "Catching me is the least he can do." With a heave she got her belly across the smooth back, scrambling to get her leg up and over, the halter rope still in her hand.

And then she was seated, her long legs gripping the

mare's sides, and in the same moment the horse leaped forward. Boudica bent over the shining neck, not much caring where they went, so long as it was away from here. As they sped down the road, she heard the shouting begin behind her, and above it, the ringing peal of Cartimandua's laugh.

TEN

The mare's first wild dash carried them out of the dun and splashing across the ford of the Tas. As she came up the bank Boudica turned and saw the dun alight with moving torches. Prasutagos would have to follow or be forever shamed, but all the other horses were loose in the pasture, and by now most of the men would be too drunk to catch them. Several roads rayed out from the ford, white in the moonlight. Laughing, she gave the mare her head, wondering which way the horse would choose.

It was north. As the miles fell away behind them, it was clear that the mare was heading for the fields she knew. By the time Prasutagos found them they would be halfway home. From time to time she pulled the horse back to a walk, listening. But except for the occasional bark of a dog as they passed a farmstead, the land lay quiet beneath the moon.

The Druids had spells to confuse a pursuer or blind a trail, but Boudica had not learned them. And in any case, she did want Prasutagos to find her . . . just not . . . yet.

There were two more rivers to be crossed, the last one deep enough that the mare had to swim. By the time they reached shore, Boudica was shivering in the predawn cold. Still, she was warmer on the horse's back than she would have been on the ground, and her Druid training had taught her to ignore the body's discomfort. By now the mare was willing to go at a walking pace, and they continued until the autumn sun had steamed Boudica's clothing dry.

By the time she reined her mount off the road and into a wood where a spring offered water and grass grew thickly among the trees, they had covered nearly twenty miles. She rubbed down the horse and used her belt to fashion hobbles so that the animal could graze, then laid the saddle cloth on the ground for a bed and rolled up in her cloak to rest, wondering how long it would take Prasutagos to come.

When she woke, it was well past noon and she was regretting having eaten so little of the wedding feast. The mare, on the other hand, had made the most of the rich grass, and was very willing to be off once more.

The land here was gently rolling, a mixture of woodland and heath broken by scattered farmsteads surrounded by long rectangular fields. By this time Boudica no longer feared to leave a clue for anyone who followed, and ventured to stop at one of the farms and trade some of the ribands from her hair for a meal and a bed by the fire. She had dreaded having to find answers for their questions, but the folk here were slow-speaking and patient, keeping their own counsel and seemingly willing for her to keep her own. It was only later that she remembered the gestures of warding she had been too tired to notice at the time, and realized they must have thought her some creature strayed from Faerie.

Boudica was surprised to wake the next morning and see no sign of the king. At this rate, she thought in exasperation, she would reach his dun before he caught up with her and be waiting to welcome him—if they would admit her. To be captured in the wilderness might be romantic, to greet him as a beggar at his gate would be embarrassing.

She set out with enough apples and bannocks in the fold of her gown to last a day or more, letting the red mare go at her own pace along the road. This was a wider and more open land than the country around Antedios's dun, and to judge by the many stubbled fields, better drained and more bountiful. The anxieties and resentments that had plagued Boudica at the wedding seemed very far away. This was a new land, and as she had done on Mona, she would have to learn its ways.

Unless, of course, Prasutagos repudiated the marriage and sent her home to her father in disgrace. The thought was enough to plunge Boudica into glum contemplation for most of the afternoon. That evening she had no heart to seek shelter at another farmstead and lay once more in the woodland, gazing through a net of branches at the starry path across the heavens that seemed to be pointing the way.

She was awakened by the smell of roasting sausage. For a few moments she thought it was part of a dream, but now she could hear the crackling of a fire. She frowned and turned over, rubbing her eyes. Morning light turned the smoke to a golden haze in which she could make out only the shape of the man who knelt by the fire. But she knew his height and breadth of shoulder. A rush of emotion brought her to full awareness, composed equally of relief, exasperation, and dismay.

"Two days . . ." she said, sitting up. Her brothers had always told her that attack was the best defense. "You took your time, my lord."

"There was no hurry. The land is at peace, and I knew where the mare would go." Prasutagos turned the sausages and looked back at her. Hair and mustache were neatly combed, even the silver strands glinting gold in the morning sun. He was dressed in sturdy trews and a tunic of dull green, appropriate for the road. And he was clean.

"I should hope so." She picked a wisp of grass from her hair.

"You were not difficult to follow. The countryside is full of rumors of a red woman on a red horse, though report disagrees as to whether she is one of the goddesses or some refugee from the Roman wars, and whether this is a good omen or a portent of doom."

Boudica could feel the blush heating her skin beneath the dust and grime. She cleared her throat.

"And which view is yours?"

"I think she is an autumnal deity," he answered dryly. "I promised to find her, and assured them that the magic of the king was sufficient to counter any spell." He lifted the sausages from the fire and stuck the ends of the sticks on which they had been toasting into the soft ground.

"Excuse me," she said with what dignity she could muster. "I am going to the stream to wash."

"Excellent idea. In the pack by the willow tree you will find clean clothes," he said gravely. "Don't run from me again. I don't think my reputation could survive losing my bride a second time . . ."

* * *

*B*oudica followed her new husband through the golden autumn afternoon. In the pack he had brought for her she had found a sleeved tunic of a light wool the color of the harvested fields. She suspected it would be a long time before she dared to wear crimson again in Prasutagos's land. He had also brought the trews she wore for riding, very welcome to her chafed legs after two days with no protection but the folds of the linen gown.

The king's big bay had a longer pace than the mare's, and she found herself always a little behind him. She wondered how he had managed to escape from his household. But then, as a younger son he had never expected to inherit a war band, and perhaps he was accustomed to riding about this countryside alone. Certainly the folk at the steading where they paused for a rest and a drink of milk fresh from the cow did not seem surprised to see their king wandering the roads with his new bride.

Prasutagos was accustomed to being alone, she thought as the miles passed. Despite the morning's embarrassment, she had hoped that the constraint between them would disappear. But she suspected now that at the feast he had been quiet from habit, not from inhibition.

If Coventa had been here, she would have filled the emptiness with her chattering. Boudica had never needed to do that, and just now she hardly dared.

"Where will we spend the night?" she asked after an hour without a word had gone by. "Or do you mean to ride straight on to your dun?"

"The horses need rest," he said, reining in to answer her. "A little up the road there is a holy well where folk come to pray to the Goddess for healing and the granting of desires. I give the people at the farmstead some support so that they may feed travelers. We will stay there."

*T*hey came to the Lady's well just as the first stars were kindling in the sky. The water that flowed from the spring chuckled through a shallow valley between wooded hills. But the path was well marked, the area below the spring had been cleared, and the grass was still green. Thatched shelters used by earlier pilgrims stood among the trees. No one else was here so late in the year, but clearly this was a popular shrine.

Prasutagos left Boudica to arrange their bedding while he went up to the farm for food. She wondered if that division of labor had been tact, to allow her to choose whether or not to consummate their marriage now. If he had pressed her, she thought wryly, she might have resisted, but she had to face the fact that his remoteness was a challenge, and the binding that had been set upon them in the sacred circle demanded completion. She laid out both sets of blankets full width, one atop the other.

When her husband still had not returned by the time she was finished, she picked up their waterskins and one of her remaining ribands and took the path to the sacred spring. A pool had been dug out to catch the water that welled from the slope of a little hill. The fading light was just enough for her to see the fluttering bits of fabric tied to the hazel tree whose branches shaded it. At its base a piece of wood had been thrust into the ground, carved with staring eyes and the hollow of a woman's vulva below. Smiling, she tied her own ribbon to a twig with the rest and knelt at the edge.

"Lady," she whispered, "by whatever name you favor in this land I honor you. Help me to be a good wife to Prasutagos and bear him children . . ." And then, more softly, "Help me to win his love . . ." She scooped up water in her hands and drank, then set the waterskins at the edge to fill.

She sat back on her heels, sweeping the distracting thoughts from her mind one by one as she had been taught on the Druids' Isle, until presently there was only the sweet music of the spring. But from that simple melody came an awareness that remained in her memory as words.

"You may call me Holy Mother, for the milk from my breasts is always welling, always flowing, always poured out for my children in eternal love. Go in peace. In your joy and in your sorrow, I am here . . ."

Boudica dipped up more water and touched it to the hollow in the image, feeling an answering throb of anticipation between her own thighs.

In peace she rose and took the skins she had filled. When

she returned to the shelter Prasutagos had a fire going, and by the hearth there was fruit and new bread. Still entranced by the stillness of the spring, Boudica found herself at ease with his silence. When he excused himself after the meal she stripped off her clothes and slid between the blankets.

He was gone for what seemed a long time, and when he returned he brought with him the cool breath of the holy well. She wondered if they had both prayed for the same thing. But it was a condition of such miracles that they never be spoken aloud.

The fire had burned low, and once more she saw him as a dark shape outlined in gold. She tensed as he inserted himself into the blankets beside her. He raised himself on one elbow and with his other hand lifted a lock of her hair and he murmured something soothing that she could not quite make out.

She wanted to tell him she was not afraid, but he was still whispering, still stroking her hair, and she could not find the words. She remembered how he had gentled the white stallion at the offering pool. It was horse magic, she thought, to tame the red mare . . .

Prasutagos bent to kiss her, and this time his lips were warm. His hands moved across her body, caressing, commanding, until she lay open and accepting, her whole being flowing to enfold him, welcoming as the waters of the sacred spring.

*Boudica!" Nessa's voice came from across the yard. "Come now, lovey—your lord has said you must not lift anything so heavy—do come away!"

Boudica sighed and set down the armful of wood she had been about to bring into the roundhouse. Soon after she and Prasutagos reached Eponadunon, a caravan of wagons bearing all the gifts from the wedding had arrived and with them old Nessa, sent by her mother to be her servant in her new home. Or perhaps her guardian—by the beginning of the new year it was clear that Boudica was pregnant, and since then Nessa and Prasutagos had conspired to treat her as if she were made of Roman glass. That had been all very well during the winter, when freezing rain kept everyone inside the roundhouses, but the Turning of Spring was nigh, and the fair weather urged everyone outdoors. In retrospect, she supposed she ought to be grateful her mother had not sent the old woman with her to Mona, although the image of Nessa facing off against Lhiannon made her smile.

She *missed* Lhiannon, whose calm good sense would have been so helpful as she settled into her new home. Eponadunon lay in a bend of a small river half a day's ride from the sea, or rather the marshes, for the northern coast edged out gradually in bands of salt marsh and mudflat, with a narrow channel where boats might come in to shore. To the south, another half day of riding would take them to the sacred spring, though since she arrived she had been too busy to visit it again. She would have liked to show it to Lhiannon.

"Come in now, dearie, into the house." Nessa appeared at her elbow.

Boudica turned on her. "I am young, healthy, and I never felt better in my life! Nor will I melt in the spring sun!"

"One of the lads who watch the cattle has come in. He saw riders on the road—you had better change out of that old gown."

As Boudica sighed defeat and followed Nessa into the largest of the three roundhouses she was aware of a prickle of excitement. Eponadunon was nearly as remote as Mona, and Prasutagos did not have the Arch-Druid's network of informants to keep him apprised of the news, although now that the first shock of the Roman conquest was over, peddlers and tradesmen were beginning to reappear.

And from time to time there was gossip. When Claudius returned to Rome, it was boasted that he had received the submission of eleven kings. Of course they said that his Triumph had also portrayed the conquest of Camulodunon as the capture of a walled city. Closer to home, men said that the legion left to hold down the Trinovantes was building a fortress on the hill above the ruins of the dun.

But the newcomers were no tradesmen. As Boudica was pinning her tunica, one of the girls who had been washing clothes at the stream came rushing up to inform them that a party of Romans was coming up the road.

"The king rode off to the new dun on the shore this morning—we can send one of the lads to find him, but we'll have to entertain these people until he arrives," she told the girl. "Our bread is still baking. Girl, when you've sent the message run over to the nearest farmsteads to see what they have on hand. In the meantime our guests will have to be content with meat and cheese."

As the dun exploded into activity around her, she reached for her jewel box to add necklace and bracelets to her attire. The king lived simply here, and the dun would not impress their visitors, but at least she could look like a queen.

By the time the strangers rode through the wooden gate, the house had been swept and the worst of the clutter tidied away. Boudica stood waiting with a drinking horn filled with the last of the wine from the wedding in her hands. In times of peace Prasutagos kept no more than a half-dozen warriors at the dun. Calgac, a lanky young warrior who had been assigned her escort, stood with the three who had not gone with the king as the Romans rode in.

Automatically she counted them—a *contubernia* of ten soldiers, escorting three men in civilian tunics and knee-length riding breeches and one in checkered trews who must be their guide.

"*Salutatio.*" She offered the beaker to the best dressed of the riders, eyes widening as she recognized the big nose and dark eyes she had last seen in the purple shade of the emperor's pavilion. Surely the taxes they were supposed to pay the Romans were not already due! Her smile grew a little stiff as she continued. "Lucius Junius Pollio, *salve!*" That was all the Latin she remembered from her years at King Cunobelin's dun.

"Greetings," Pollio replied in her own language. "I drink to you, my queen . . ." He had an Atrebate accent.

Boudica lifted an eyebrow. She had not expected that the Romans would have the sense to send a man who spoke the British tongue.

The next few minutes were occupied with getting everyone dismounted and arranging where to put horses and men. She directed a quelling gaze at the younger of her warriors. Some of them were new to the king's service, replacements for men who had fallen at the Tamesa, and they glowered at the Roman legionaries. By the time she had everyone settled and fed, Prasutagos had still not returned. Rather than sit staring at Pollio across the fire, she suggested a tour around the dun.

Steps had been cut into the inside of the grass-covered earthen embankment that surrounded it. On the outside, the bank was faced by a palisade. "My husband's family has held this dun since his great-great-grandfather's days," she said as they gained the top, "but the clans here have been at peace for many years."

"Yet King Prasutagos is building a new place." It was not quite a question. "A new dun to guard the harbor where the ships that cross the Wash come to shore?"

"I think he likes to build things." She shrugged. She had ridden out once to view the massive rampart faced with blocks of chalk, but workmen's huts were the only lodging, and the king had been too focused on the work to notice whether she was there or not, so she had not stayed.

"He does indeed . . ." Pollio agreed. His gaze moved briefly to the swell of her belly and then away. "The bank gives you a fine vantage point."

She smiled a little, as she always did when she stood here and looked across the fields. At this season the country was richly green with new grass, broken by the corrugated brown of newly plowed and seeded fields. A flock of crows had settled on the nearest, pecking for grain. A child ran across the field shouting, followed by a barking dog, and the crows exploded upward in a yammering cloud.

Cathubodva, take your chickens away, she prayed. *There is neither meat nor mast for you here!* Although she would rather share with the goddess than with the Romans, she thought, glancing sidelong at the man beside her. Disconcertingly, he was looking at her, not at the fields.

"It is true that we have no steep hills on which to build our forts as they do in the Durotrige lands," she said blandly. Even out here they had heard that the Roman campaign in the southwest had slowed to a crawl as General Vespasian besieged each hillfort in turn.

If that had stung him, he gave no sign. "You grow barley here, and cattle?" His dark gaze flicked away.

"And spelt, and sheep on the heaths," she added, putting a little distance between them. "Our fields are not so rich as those in the Trinovante lands but we feed our people, most years. In a bad winter there are floods, and we are lucky to get a crop at all."

"I understand," he said smoothly. "But that is where you benefit from being part of the Empire. In such years we can make loans to tide you over, and when you have a surplus you can repay. Nor do you need to fear that some other tribe whose crops have failed will try to take yours. Our general Vespasian has already taken many hillforts," he went on. "Soon all the west will be conquered as well."

She would have liked to wipe away that smug smile, but unfortunately what he had said was true. *Goddess keep Lhiannon from harm!* she thought then. But surely they would keep the priestesses out of the war. She made her way along the bank and he followed her.

"You speak our language well," she commented as they reached the strong timbers that supported the gate.

"The emperor assigned me to be a companion to young Cogidubnos when he came to Rome and to learn his tongue as I taught him ours. Claudius, of course, knows the language from his youth in Gallia," he replied.

How long had the emperor been thinking about the conquest of Britannia? she wondered wildly. Had all their struggles to prevent the attack mattered at all? She took a deep breath. "To speak the language of the people around you is always a useful thing. Indeed, I have been thinking that it would be well to have someone here who could teach the Latin tongue."

"You are wise. If you are to become citizens of the Empire you will need to speak its language, although to be sure there are many who still hold that Greek is the only civilized speech."

Boudica resented the unconscious superiority she sensed beneath Pollio's words. But now she could see horsemen on the road. Even at such a distance there was something in the relaxed balance with which the first rider sat his mount that she recognized. *It is less than a year,* she thought in wonder. *Have I become so linked to him al-*

ready? Perhaps she ought to have expected it, even though he was for the most part as silent as ever. Perhaps it was because she was carrying his child.

She stretched and waved as Prasutagos cantered toward them, as grateful for rescue as if she had been besieged.

ELEVEN

Lhiannon faced Ardanos across the fire, their voices twining in the chant as the column of smoke twisted toward the sky. The earthen ramparts that protected the barrows of the ancient dead were covered by grass and eroded by the years. It was the hilltop across the valley to the south that would be Caratac's refuge. Even now, Durotrige tribesmen were toiling up the slopes with hods filled with earth and stone to reinforce defenses built by people whose names were lost from the land.

In the days of peace the Turning of Spring had been a time to work for a bountiful growing season. But this year the blood of men would fertilize the fields. Through the heat-haze she saw Ardanos's features exalted and intent as always during ritual. *He would look like that while making love . . .* She tried to banish the image, but these days they were so linked that he felt her thought, and when his eyes met hers her whole body flushed with desire. Her first instinct was to suppress it, but this, too, could be an offering.

As the circle began to move sunwise she allowed that energy to grow, flowing out through her left hand through the circle to the Druids and village priests who had joined them for the rite.

> *"Equality of day and night,*
> *Balance point of dark and light—*
> *This is the day, and this the hour,*
> *To choose the purpose, raise the power—"*

Since the submission of the tribes in the south and east the previous summer she and Ardanos had been moving steadily ahead of the Roman advance westward, always together, but never alone. King Veric had died shortly after the Roman emperor left Britannia. While General Vespasian was busy putting down the last of Caratac's supporters on the Isle of Vectis and establishing Cogidubnos in his grandfather's place, Lhiannon and Ardanos had gone to King Tancoric. The Durotrige lands were rich in hillforts built in ancient days and rebuilt during the west country's endless intertribal wars. Surely the Romans would not be able to capture them all . . .

Wind gusted across the hilltop and the fire flared suddenly, sparking along the juniper boughs that had been twined among the oak logs in sigils of flame. Now the pine branches caught with a crackle of resin, adding their spicy scent to the smoke that was being blown eastward by the ever-present wind. Eastward . . . toward the advancing enemy.

The fire flared and hissed as now one, and now another dancer would dart forward to throw an offering of oil or mead or blood on the flames. The smoke grew thicker, billowing above the hill. Lhiannon could feel power building within the circle as they danced.

> *"By our words and by our will,*
> *Here upon the holy hill,*
> *A blessing bid on all we see,*
> *A spell we cast for victory!"*

Wind gusted again, blowing the hair she had left unbound for the ritual across her face. She shook her head to dislodge the fine strands and her smile faded as she realized that the wind had changed. Ardanos pulled his side of the circle forward, arms lifting to release the power, and rather raggedly the others followed. The column of smoke that had flowed eastward to threaten their foes was now drifting north, toward the hill of stones.

Lhiannon sat down on the bench and drew up one foot, drying it with her cloak of heavy, oily wool. The skin was pale and waterlogged, the flesh cut and bruised from going barefoot in the mud. At least when your refuge was a hillfort, most of the rainwater that did not go into the cistern ran downhill. The folk of the fens around Avalon were said to have webbed feet. She wished that she did. She wished she were on the Isle of Avalon and not besieged on this hill. She peered upward, hoping that the fine mist that had begun to fall meant a possible break in the clouds, but all she could see was gray.

The omen at the equinox ritual had proved a true one— the Roman advance had caught up with Caratac's forces a week later and dug their own bank and ditch all around the base of the hill. With them came the rain. Lhiannon looked up as a dark-haired warrior scrambled down from the rampart and over to the pile of stones to scoop more ammunition for his sling into the bag hung from his belt, and she gave him what she hoped was a cheery smile. The defenders of the hillfort had laid in supplies enough for a lengthy siege, but construction had focused on strengthening the ramparts and deepening the ditch between, not the buildings within. Yet though comfort might be lacking, they had plenty of water, and plenty of stones.

Now, of course, they could not forage for thatching straw or whitewash to protect the wattle-and-daub walls. The circles of hastily erected roundhouses clustered on the muddy turf of the hilltop were less secure than the buildings in which folk kept their cows at home, and there were no withies with which to mend the fencing that kept the cattle they had brought here penned. The food had been moved to the best shelter, and even then, some of it had spoiled. Humans were expected to be more resilient. With a sigh she picked up her other foot, grimacing at the touch of cold mud when she put the first one back down.

The reason she had refused to stay with Boudica was standing on the rampart, peering between two of the pointed logs that formed the palisade. Ardanos's white robe was mud-colored now, but then so was Lhiannon's priestess-blue gown. What was needed here was a nice, neutral gray. But new clothing was another thing they were going to have to do without for a while.

Someone shouted and she squinted upward, following the flight of the incoming stone with wary gaze. The Roman catapults were quite powerful, but the area protected by the double rampart that surrounded an extended square atop the hill was extensive enough that apart from the wear and tear on everyone's nerves, they rarely did any harm. The boulders that struck the palisade were another matter, but they still had logs enough to replace by night what was smashed during the day, bolstered by the stones with which the enemy had gifted them.

Why was it that the epics the bards were so fond of reciting never mentioned the sheer misery of standing siege in the rain? She hoped the Romans were equally uncomfortable. She hoped that their iron breast- and backplates were rusting together, the laminated arms of their ballistas becoming unglued, their leather tents rotting away.

Lhiannon stood up with a sigh and pulled the cloak over her hair as the rain intensified once more.

*W*e have held this place longer than any of the others," said Caratac, coughing as a draft set the smoke from the hearthfire swirling around the roundhouse where the chieftains had gathered. Lhiannon shielded her face with her veil and dipped up more herb tea from the cauldron. The rain on the thatching made a dull patter beneath the whisper of the fire, so familiar that it was only at moments like this, when everyone fell silent, waiting for the smoke to clear, that she even noticed the sound.

"Nearly two moons . . ." said Antebrogios, the chieftain Tancoric had put in charge of the defenses. "But longer is not forever." He coughed, either from the smoke or from the catarrh that afflicted most of those here. "Our supplies are getting low and we have sickness among the men."

"So do the Romans," muttered one of the others. "At night you can hear them coughing in their tents. They curse the climate of Britannia, and they curse the emperor who sent them here."

"Then let them go home to sunny Italia," muttered someone. "If this rain keeps up much longer I'll be wishing I could go, too."

"If they run out of food or men they can ask for replacements," pointed out his chieftain. "We cannot."

"Are you saying we should give up?" challenged Caratac. He held out his beaker for Lhiannon to refill. Like the rest of them, he was gaunt and grimy, honed down by hardship to muscle and bone. *If he had foreseen this day at the council on Mona, would he have spoken so boldly?* she wondered as she handed the cup back to him. Would any of them?

Her gaze met that of Ardanos, sitting in the shadows near the door, and she thought he was wondering, too. He had grown thin in the past weeks, with hollow cheeks and haunted eyes. Always before he had had a wry comment or a cheerful word, but in the past weeks he had been uncharacteristically quiet. They had not been tempted to dance together at Beltane, for the defenders had not had wood enough for a bonfire. He no longer tried to persuade her to his bed, and that was the most disturbing sign of all. But she had grown silent, too.

She looked away. *If we speak, we are afraid we will have to admit that there is no hope of victory . . .*

"The Romans out there outnumber us," Caratac said with quiet intensity. "Their legions outnumber the Durotriges as they did the Trinovantes when we fought on the Tamesa. But they *do not* outnumber the Britons of Britannia! If we do not give up, if we make them bleed for every hillfort, every river crossing, every foot of ground, there will come a time when the gold and grain they can seize from us cease to be enough to pay for the lives of their men. *That* is why we must hold out as long as we can, and if we are driven from this stronghold we will retreat to another. We *can* outlast them. This is our land!"

Perhaps even Caratac would have quailed, a year ago, if he had known what was to come, but it was clear to Lhiannon that he could not do so now. The others might surrender, but he must continue. He had paid too much already to give in.

But what if the Romans felt the same way? What if every legionary who fed the Morrigan's ravens strengthened General Vespasian's resolve to destroy those who had brought him down?

Outside someone raised the alarm. Cursing, the chieftains snatched up their swords and crowded through the door. Slipping and sliding in the mud, one hand holding their shields up in a linked mass to repel missiles from above while the other gripped a sword, the Romans were assaulting the ramparts yet again.

*I*t was not until midsummer that the rain let up at last.

Great shining fortresses of cloud drifted slowly eastward, having surrendered all their store of rain, leaving the sun as victor on a field of blue. At the Dun of Stones, besieged and besiegers alike paused a moment in their labors, turning toward the light like flowers as the strengthening sun drew moisture from the soaked ground of the dun in curls of steam. The humid air lay heavy in Lhiannon's lungs, but it would dry, and the mud on the slopes of the dun would dry, and the Romans would attack again.

Overhead ravens were circling, dark and bright in turn as their glossy wings caught the light of the sun. *Be patient,* she thought. *Soon you will feed!*

She stripped down to her linen undertunic and draped her blue robe over the thatch of her roundhouse, then began to undo her braids.

"Your hair is like spun sunlight . . ."

She felt a touch and turned almost into Ardanos's arms.

"And you like a faerie child in your pale gown, with your white arms gleaming in the sun." Smiling a little, he began to work at the tangles with which she had been struggling.

"Mud-colored around the hem, though it is kind of you to say so . . ." she answered as steadily as she could. "But if death is coming, at least I will face it in dry clothes."

"Probably . . . almost certainly, I would say," he answered with an attempt at his old sardonic detachment. "When I looked over the palisade there seemed to be a lot of activity down the hill. The Romans are moving the ballistas into position for an assault, with no attempt to do so unobserved. And why should they? Whenever they choose to assault us we can only meet the attack with what we have. Which is not much. We have almost no arrows, and even the supply of slinging stones is getting low."

"And a fortress cannot run away," she agreed. *Nor can those trapped inside it.* But there was no need to say that aloud.

He finished working on the second braid, combing the strands out with his fingers so that they lay soft upon her shoulders, shining in the sun.

"How is it that lack of food only makes you more beautiful?" he said then. "You were almost too thin before, but now your spirit shines like a lamp through your skin . . ." For the last week the food ration, never ample, had been cut. The Romans might not have expected them to hold out for so long, but Antebrogios had never expected the Romans would have the patience for so long a siege.

Ardanos had grown gaunt as well. She saw now how he would look when he was old, if indeed either of them survived to see old age. At this moment it hardly mattered. To hear that gentle note in his voice, to see that light in his eye, was what she needed now. If he was fey, then so was she. It was not only hunger that made her lightheaded as she moved into the circle of his arms.

*T*he activity in the Roman camp continued all afternoon. In the dun, the evening meal was quiet, but the cooks served out the best of the food that remained. There was only water to drink, but the chieftains pledged each other as if it had been wine.

"If this night we are fated to fall, we should go rejoicing," said Ardanos as the horn came to him. "The Romans we kill may go down to gloomy Hades, but for us the Blessed Isles are waiting, until it is time to enter the Cauldron and be born anew."

The Isles of the Blessed, or the Otherworld the faerie woman showed me . . . thought Lhiannon. If that lady should open such a gateway here and now would she go through it? Not alone, she thought, looking at Ardanos. Never, if she had to take that road alone.

"By all the gods, you men of the Durotriges will surely feast among the heroes," exclaimed Caratac. "None ever fought more bravely, or endured so well."

"None ever had such noble chieftains to lead them," came the response from the men.

When the meal was over, Lhiannon and Ardanos wandered out past the empty livestock pens, looking up at the stars. The men who walked the ramparts were singing. When they paused, one could hear a murmur like distant thunder from below. But here on the pile of straw where Ardanos had spread his cloak, it seemed very still.

Lhiannon rested her head upon his shoulder. They were both still fully clothed, and he had made no move to change that. She could feel a regular quiver beneath her palm, as if she held his heart in her hand.

"I never thought it would be in such a time and place when I finally lay with you in my arms," Ardanos said at last. "Or that it would be enough to simply hold you, and know that this is where you chose to be."

The more ascetic among the Druids starved themselves to achieve a state in which the flesh would no longer hunger. Perhaps that was what had happened to her and Ardanos, or perhaps it was that in the place where they were now, beyond all the distractions of ordinary life, they could speak soul to soul.

"When they come," he whispered after a little time had passed. "When they break through, will you come with me to the Blessed Isles? They will know us for Druids, and they will drag us captive through the streets of Rome and give us to the beasts in the arena if they take us alive."

"Yes, my love. But not yet. There are brave men here, and it would be wrong to desert them too soon."

He laughed a little at that and kissed her forehead. "I never doubted your courage, Lhiannon."

The stars were growing pale as the full moon climbed the sky. On such a night it seemed impossible that soon men would die. The Romans called the moon a chaste goddess. Could they not see that to break the peace of this night with violence was a blasphemy?

Lhiannon sat up, lifting her hands to the skies. "Holy Goddess, holy Goddess," she sang:

"Upon the world of warring men
look down and make their hatred cease.
O holy Goddess, hear us now,
oh hear our prayer and give us peace . . ."

As if in answer, a ball of fire arced across the face of the moon. It landed on a thatched roof and began to burn.

"Goddess have mercy on us all. It has begun!"

More fireballs fell, some catching buildings, others sizzling on the ground. From the gate came shouting. As she and Ardanos started toward it, a warrior ran past them screaming, clothes streaming flame. She screamed herself as a bolt from a ballista whipped past and skewered another man to a wall.

Farther along the wall men were shouting. Fire billowed up where the logs of the palisade had caught and men scrambled back from the flames. *This is what the storms prevented,* Lhiannon thought numbly. *I am sorry I cursed the rain . . .*

Bands of men dashed here and there as the alarm was shouted from different parts of the wall. She and Ardanos separated to get the chests where they had kept their remaining bandages and surgical tools; when she emerged from her hut, she saw one of the chieftains grab Ardanos's arm. The man pointed toward the other end of the dun and he nodded, cast one desperate glance back at her, and started off at a run.

Now they were bringing wounded into the space before Antebrogios's house and laying them on blankets brought from those huts that were not yet in flames. Lhiannon hurried to the nearest, who had a ballista bolt through his thigh. The shaft was a stout piece of ash wood a little over two feet long, but all she could see protruding from his flesh were the three fins on the end. An arrow could have been broken off, but this shaft was too thick; she would have to pull it. There was not much blood; they could hope it had not severed an artery.

"Hold him," she said to the man beside him, whose leg would need splinting next. Grimacing, he nodded, and leaned his weight on his companion as she gripped the shaft beneath the fins and gave a sharp tug. Her patient

screamed and then went limp. Lhiannon gritted her teeth
and pulled again, using all her strength. She felt something
give, then the thing came loose, the evil quadrangular head
spattering blood across her skirts. More blood welled from
the hole. She grabbed a wad of wool and pressed down
hard, then bound it tightly in place.

The wound ought to be washed out with wine. The
man should be kept quiet and fed infusions of white willow for the pain. She could even do it, if he lived—if any
of them lived—through the next few hours. As it was, he
might live until morning and die of infection thereafter.
He might survive to live in slavery and wish he had died
today.

But they were setting a man before her with a splinter
from a smashed log through his shoulder, and here was another whose knee had been crushed by a catapulted stone.
Her awareness narrowed to the next decision, the next in-
cision, to red blood and firelight and pain. Men screamed
and bled beneath her hands, some fainted, and some of
them died. Once when she looked up she saw the moon
glowing red from the smoke in the air. No chaste goddess
she—this was the bloody shield of Cathubodva, the moon
of war.

The regular hollow boom that shook the earth beneath
her might have been her heartbeat. It was only when men
began to run past that she realized the Romans were attacking the gate. Despite all the missiles the defenders
could rain down upon them, the locked shields they called
the "tortoise" were protecting the men who swung the
ram.

She saw Caratac in all his battered splendor shouting a
group of warriors into position at the top of the steep slope
that ran down to the gate.

"Get out of the way!" One of Antebrogios's house-
guards yanked her to her feet and shoved her toward the
roundhouse. "Take cover! You can't help them now!"

Where was Ardanos? Lhiannon hesitated, staring
wildly at the confusion of moving men. There was a rending groan and the great bar across the gate cracked and
fell. The timbers shivered beneath another stroke; held
in place by the rocks piled behind them, they splintered

under the impact of a third great blow. The defenders reeled beneath a new shower of missiles as the first armored enemies squeezed through.

She edged back until she was huddling beneath the overhanging roof of the roundhouse, but she had to see! More Romans were pouring through the gap. Steel clashed as they drove against the Britons waiting there. She heard Caratac's war cry. A sword skittered across the ground to her feet and she picked it up, then dropped it again. She was a healer; her heart was torn by anguish, but even now there was nothing within her that answered to the Morrigan's rage.

The embattled knot of men were moving toward her. As she realized it, the defenders broke and ran. She saw Caratac rise up from the tumult, laying about him with great strokes of his long sword. Romans reeled back from the terror of that blade and for a moment the space around him was clear. He leaped forward, saw her cowering, and hauled her into the shadow behind the house.

"They shall not have me or you either, priestess! The palisade is down on the west side. Come with me!"

His arm was like iron around her waist. Half dragged, half running, she fled from house to house as the battle raged on. As they neared the palisade she thought she saw Ardanos's white robe in the midst of a group of running warriors. She tried to call out to him, but she had no breath. Then Caratac was thrusting her through the splintered gap in the logs; she tripped and rolled down the bank. He slid down after her, pulled her over the second bank, and together they skidded down it into the darkness beyond.

Lhiannon looked back. The sky above the hill was red; most of the houses must now be burning. A haze of heat and smoke obscured the sky. Or perhaps her vision was dimmed by tears.

As Caratac led his party up the lane, a turmoil of dogs, spotted and brindle and gray, came tumbling through the gate of the farmstead barking in a cacophony of keys. Roused as her pony shied, Lhiannon, startled into awareness for the first time in days. Ardanos would have had a Word of Power to calm them, she thought sadly. King Caratac, however, had the voice of authority. The dogs swirled back and then, as someone else called them, fell silent, tails wagging and heads down. Lhiannon's heart leaped as she glimpsed a white robe behind them. It was a Druid's robe, but the tall figure beneath it bore a boy's face above a young man's soft black beard.

"Lady Lhiannon! What are you doing here?" he exclaimed, and hearing his voice, she recognized Rianor, who had been a student with Boudica. He looked down the line of weary men and his face changed.

They were a tattered crew, many of them bandaged, warriors who had escaped after the fall of the Dun of Stones and been collected by Caratac in those first frantic days as they dodged Roman patrols. The king was no longer the pleasant young man who had visited them at Mona, no longer even the exhausted warrior who had wept over his brother's body at the Tamesa. Above the royal torque, Caratac's face was worn to a framework for eyes that blazed with purpose. The berserk energy that had gotten her out of the Dun of Stones was leashed and focused now to the service of their cause.

"Holy gods, you were at the dun—we all heard how bravely it was defended," said Rianor. "We were praying for you at the Isle. My mother was of the Belgae, so they sent me here . . ."

"As you see, we have wounded," said Caratac. "Some of them will recover well enough to fight again, and some should not travel farther."

"Are the Romans coming? Are you here to command the defense of Camadunon?" Rianor gestured toward the hill to the south of the farm.

In the long years since the hill was last needed as a place of refuge forest had grown up around it, but someone had already started cutting trees to rebuild the palisade. With a kind of numb despair Lhiannon found herself calculating where an enemy might try to scale the hill.

Caratac shook his head. "King Maglorios is sending men to hold it. I must fare to the country of the Silures. The tribes to the north and west will be our best defense if the south fails." He turned to Lhiannon. "Lady, I will be traveling fast and hard, so I must leave you. This dun guards the approaches to the Summer Country, and from here you can find escort to Mona or to Avalon."

"Thank you." It was all she could say, though there had been too many nights when she had cursed him in her heart for not leaving her to die with Ardanos.

Rianor helped her to dismount, and together they watched the king ride away with the three of his own tribesmen who had survived. She wondered if she would ever see him again.

"Ardanos is not with you?" ventured Rianor as he showed her where she would sleep until more huts were built in the dun.

"We were separated when the enemy broke through. I last saw Ardanos with some of Antebrogios's men. Caratac got me away, but we have had no word of the others. It is most likely"—with an effort she kept her voice calm—"that he is dead or captive." She had sought him on the spirit roads without success. In her current state of weakness that might mean nothing. Surely if he had been killed she would have felt his passing. But if he lived, why had he not reached out to her?

"Oh, my lady, I am so sorry!" exclaimed Rianor. "We all knew how much you loved him, and he you. Otherwise you would have been made High Priestess instead of Helve."

Lhiannon closed her eyes in pain. Did they all assume that she and Ardanos had been lovers? It seemed hard to have the reputation without having had any of the joy. And yet that was not entirely true, she thought, remembering how they had lain together beneath the moon. Soul to soul, they had been united with a completeness that few who had experienced only the body's sweaty couplings ever knew.

"My lady," he said then, "have you had any word of Boudica? I—we hoped that she would come back after your visit to Avalon."

"She chose to return to her tribe," Lhiannon said steadily. "A marriage was arranged for her with King Prasutagos, to unite the two branches of the Iceni. I suppose she will be as happy as any can be in these times. He seemed to be a good man."

"If he is good to her, that is enough for me!" Rianor said fiercely. "But it is strange to think of her married to one of those who bent the knee to Rome. At least she will be safe in the Iceni lands." He got to his feet. "I wish that we could say the same—if the Roman advance continues, they will come this way."

TWELVE

Routed from the west country, the rain clouds that had soaked the Durotrige country moved north and east to deluge the Iceni lands, and the season that should have brought sunshine saw a succession of storms. As water pooled in the fields, drowning the growing grain, there were times when Boudica wondered if her words to the Roman had been prophetic, for this year there would be little to no harvest. Nor could they hope for help from Dun Garo, where the land was even lower and the rivers bigger. All of the Iceni chieftains would be begging the Romans for the grain they needed to get their people through another year.

As the rains continued to fall, the roundhouse smelled perpetually of woodsmoke and dung and the woolen garments that had been hung from the beams to dry. The most valuable of the breeding stock had been brought to the higher ground of the dun and penned inside, but every day, it seemed, someone would come splashing up from one of the other farms, asking help to rescue marooned sheep or strengthen the dike that protected a house from a rising stream. And soon the coughing sickness began to stalk the countryside, and Nessa and Boudica were both kept busy brewing herbal teas and broth.

In the days that followed her arrival at Camadunon, Lhiannon realized that torment in the mind, unlike pain of the body, was best treated by activity. Work that required all one's attention was better than riding. She had no wish to spend more days as a passenger, staring at mental images of Ardanos in chains or dying, and in any case no man could be spared to escort her to Avalon. Here there were wounded men who needed her nursing, food to be cooked for the laborers, and when there was no other work, an extra pair of hands could always be used at the dun.

From time to time a shepherd or farm lad would trot into the steading with word of the Roman advance. Vespasian had left engineers to build Roman fortifications on the Dun of Stones and then continued his campaign. Rumor had them marching north or south or stopping entirely, but by the feast of Lugos it was known that they were on their way.

They had done all they could at Camadunon. The ditches between the four stone and timber ramparts that surrounded the hillfort had been dug deeper and the topmost bank was crowned with a new palisade. Stone faced the slots that led to the gates on the northeast and southwest sides. An ox had been offered to the gods at the new shrine and supplies had been laid in, and from the surrounding countryside came men.

Camadunon stood on the border between the farmlands and the Summer Country. If it fell, Avalon would have no defense but its fens. At night Lhiannon would lie sleepless, remembering the Dun of Stones. She began to realize that she could not endure the mounting despair of a siege and the terror of an assault again, but how could she desert the people who had come to depend on her?

*B*oudica came out of the herdsman's hut and wrapped the heavy wool of her cloak around her. Rosic was the chief of their shepherds, but he was better with sheep than with children, and had come begging her help when his wife fell ill. His daughter Temella had tried to nurse her siblings, but she had been close to panic when Boudica arrived.

At this season there should have been some hours of light left, but clouds from the afternoon's rainstorm still covered the sky, leaching color from the sodden fields. She rubbed the small of her back as the baby kicked sharply. When she was inside with the children she had not noticed the ache. At least her own child was warm and safe in the cradle of her womb, and Rosic's younger ones had kept down the soup she fed them. Temella could take care of them now.

Boudica squinted at the sky, too accustomed to the bastions of gray cloud covering the heavens to notice their beauty. A little yellow edged them in the west. The light should last long enough for her to get home. If not, she had been over this ground so often in the past few days she could hardly miss the way. She tucked the wooden bowl in which she had brought the soup under her arm and began to pick her way down the path.

It was slow work, for the puddles had grown deeper. A change in the wind sent a fine mist into her eyes and she swore, but in the past weeks she had grown accustomed to the damp. A little more would do her no harm. This would have been easier, she thought as she slipped in the mud, if she had brought a staff. But on the way over she had needed both hands for the bowl. The ache in her back was increasing, which surprised her, since usually it was eased by exercise.

Boudica blinked and pulled the cloak over her head as the rain got harder. Its oil-rich wool would repel most moisture, and even damp it was warm. Water sloshed around her ankles and she stumbled. The path here bordered what in normal times was a small stream. The water was edging across the pathway now. Perhaps she should have stayed in the cottage, but the ways back and forward were equally dangerous now.

A new gust rocked her, she took another step, felt the ground give way, and sat down hard. When she levered herself up, her skirts were sopping, and it was only gradually that she realized that the warm water soaking her shift was not from the rain. She stopped, wincing as her belly contracted with a sudden sharp pang. She was only seven months along—this was too soon!

Boudica took a few steps farther and stopped again. The rising water had obscured all trace of the path. Without light, she could easily be swept away by the stream. But higher ground loomed dimly ahead. She splashed toward it, halting when the pangs came, and clambered to the top on her hands and knees. As her heartbeat slowed she looked around her and realized where she was.

Long ago the people who built the dun had buried one of their chieftains here. Although his name was forgotten, the folk of Eponadunon brought him offerings on Samhain Eve. Surely the ancient spirit would not grudge her this refuge until Prasutagos came to rescue her. First babies always took a while—every old wife who had tried to frighten her with tales of bad birthings during her pregnancy had agreed. She still had time . . .

But as the birth pangs came more quickly Boudica remembered that the king had ridden out to one of the outlying farms that morning. In such weather he would no doubt stay the night where he was, and it was only too likely that Nessa and the rest would assume that she had done so as well. A moan burst through clenched teeth as she realized that nobody was going to come.

And the old wives were wrong about how long it would take, at least when a baby came too soon. And she had been wrong to think she could walk in all weathers with no escort. It was all going wrong! She crouched on hands and knees as the contractions racked her body, screaming out her outrage and pain.

I want Lhiannon, her spirit wailed, but each pain yanked her back into her body again. *If I had stayed on Mona, this would not be happening . . . If the Romans had not come . . .* She fought for focus. "If" would not help her. She would have to get through this alone.

When the pains gave her a moment of respite Boudica cut two strips from her shift with her dagger and laid them ready. When she felt the contractions begin to change she got the bulk of the cloak underneath her and squatted, weeping as her belly contorted again and again. She caught the red, wriggling thing that was expelled at last and managed to cut and tie the birth cord. It was a son, with hair as red as her own. At the touch of the cold air he let out a thin wail. Gasping, Boudica got the neck of her shift open enough to settle the babe between her breasts and tied her belt below to hold him there. Small as he was, he fit easily.

"Lie over my heart, little one, as you lay beneath it," she stuttered, tensing as her womb clenched once more and the bloody mess of the afterbirth slid free. Shivering, she curled her body around the burden at her breast, curving her palm over the fragile arch of the skull, and the infant stilled. He was so tiny a mite to be the beginnings of a man, tender as a sprout that might one day become a mighty oak tree that would shelter them all.

"When you are grown you will be a king and a warrior," she murmured, "storm-born and fiery as Lugos himself, eh?" She smiled as the babe mewed and nuzzled her breast. But now that the birthing was over she realized that she was cold.

*O*n the night of the full moon, Lhiannon stood on the rampart, gazing across the tangle of marsh and mere. For the first time in weeks, there was nothing left to be done. Tomorrow, said the scouts, the Romans would be here. The night was cool and clear, but to the west rain clouds were rolling in from the sea. How long, she wondered, before this moon also was stained red, this peace destroyed by the cries of dying men? She started at a touch on her shoulder and turned to find Rianor beside her.

"Look—" He pointed to the northwest, where a pointed hilltop stood clear against the sunset clouds. "You can see the Tor, and on a very clear day in the morning, the pyramid knoll on the coast. The earth power flows from them through this hill and onward. Can you feel it here?"

It was a measure of her preoccupation, or perhaps her desolation, thought Lhiannon, that it had not occurred to her to try. She closed her eyes, reaching out with senses too long unused, allowing awareness to sink to a depth that was not entirely physical until she felt a kind of vibration like the thrum of the current beneath the timbers of a boat on the sea, and with it came a vivid memory of the Otherworld into which she had fared on the Tor of Avalon. If she had stayed there, how much grief she could have forgone—*and how much joy . . .*

The faerie woman had told her that all the worlds were connected. Rianor had just reminded her that power flowed from Avalon to this dun. Could that power be used? Was it the faerie woman or the Goddess who was filling her mind with images now?

I am a priestess, she told herself, *and subject to no*

man's command. While I had Ardanos, I followed him, but I must make my own choices now.

"Rianor . . . for the past weeks you and I have labored till our backs cracked and our hands bled, doing no more than any laborer could do, and in my case at least, not half so well. We have forgotten who we are."

He blinked, and she knew that he had also been too focused on the next log and the next stone to think any further.

"If the Romans attack us here, in the end they will take this place as they took the Dun of Stones. Don't you think it would be better if they never came here at all?"

"It would be better, my lady, if they had never sailed across the Narrow Sea." He sobered as he saw she was not laughing. "What do you mean?"

"We have cloud." She pointed toward the billowing masses to the west. "Cloud and rain and the mist that so often covers the fens around Avalon. If we draw it down the line of power we can wrap it around this hill."

Now, she sensed, was the time to set the power in motion. With a dreamlike certainty she wrapped her cloak tightly around her and lay down next to the palisade, covering her face and closing her eyes to retain the image of the clouds she had seen.

"Guard me. Let no one disturb me until I come back to you. Lend me what power you can . . ."

It would have been easier if Ardanos had been beside her, balancing her energy with his own, but as Lhiannon sank deeper into trance she could feel Rianor's young strength supporting her. She slowed her breathing, calling on disciplines long-mastered to detach mind from body and let it wing free. For a moment, she touched someone's anguish. But the pain was unlocking her nightmares of the war. She thrust the awareness away, turning desperately to the untouched west.

And there, like a caress, she found another mind. "*So, my sister, you have returned . . . in your world, has it been long?*"

"*But I haven't! I am not on the Tor!*" With a sense deeper than sight she recognized the Lady she had spoken to when she was in the Faerie realm, but how could she be here?

"Nor am I," came the answer. *"We are between the worlds, where all worlds have their meeting and all powers join in the great dance. Sing the spell, sister, make the music that will serve your need . . ."*

Why had she never reached out to this power before? She had not been sufficiently desperate, she realized then, and she had believed in Ardanos's wisdom and depended on him for direction. *I must trust my own wisdom now . . .*

Mist and fog, cloud and rain . . . hear my calling, come again . . . Once more, it seemed to her that someone was calling, but she dared admit no distraction. In the world of men she was silent, but she made a mighty music within. With inner vision she could see the layers of warm and cool air thronging with spirits. *Heat and cold mix in the skies . . . where they meet, the mist will rise . . .* Laughing, she beckoned to the air sprites, drawing them into the dance.

In the far distant place where her flesh lay, it was growing dark and cold, but time had a different meaning where she was now. Her inner senses rejoiced when the cloud sprites began to release a light cool rain; she called to the warm air and the rain turned to fog before it could fall.

It was mist, not rain, that precipitated from the damp air, wraiths of mist that floated over hill and valley, thickening as night drew on. Fog covered Camadunon, jeweling the thick wool in which Lhiannon lay shrouded and beading on Rianor's curling beard. Mist shimmered around the torches that lit the Roman marching camp and condensed on armor and spears.

*S*ometime in the past hour it had stopped raining. The stream had begun to go down. A cold wind was whipping at the clouds, and a full moon struggled to break free. Its watery illumination showed Boudica the shape of the land. Her thighs were slick with blood. Too much? She could not tell. If she had been at home, she could rest now, her labor done, but it was not enough to bear her son alive.

If I die, you die . . . she told the child at her breast. *We must have shelter, and soon . . .*

For just a little longer Boudica lay where she was, but she was beginning to shiver now. With a final effort of will she got herself upright, wrapped the cloak around her, and clambered down from the mound.

Saplings grew at its base; as she grabbed for balance, one came loose in her hand. With the help of the stick she was able to feel her way forward and cross the stream. From there it was a little over a mile across the fields to the dun.

"Not far . . . not far . . ." she whispered. "When I am old, you shall carry me. Shall we surprise your father, sweet child? How pleased he will be . . ."

Murmuring, she staggered onward. If it had not been for the child, she would have collapsed halfway there and made no effort to rise. As it was, after each fall she found the dun a little nearer when she levered herself upright once more.

The gate, of course, was closed. Had the guard sought shelter inside as well? It would be a great irony, observed a small voice within, to expire at her own gate after having come so far. With her last strength, Boudica drew breath as the Druids had taught her and in a great voice cried to be let in. And then it was all a confusion of voices and firelight and blessed, blessed warmth.

"Take him," she murmured as they laid her on the bed. "Take care of my son . . ." Someone exclaimed, but she could not make out the words. There was only the heat and the comfort of the dark.

*A*t Camadunon, there was no sun to be seen at the next day's dawning, only the thick gray blanket of the fog. The Roman army, setting out in its usual precise array, took the road that seemed most open, and came at nightfall to a hill where an old barrow was surrounded by eroded ramparts half choked by trees. Here were no screaming Celtic savages, only the ghosts of ancient wars. The rumors, decided the general, must have been mistaken. The next morning he gave the order to march southwestward toward the Dumnoni lands, never suspecting the existence of the dun that waited in mist-shrouded silence barely five miles away.

*   *   *

*B*oudica lifted her hand, surprised at how hard it was to move. Her memory was a confusion of alternating nightmare and oblivion. Prasutagos was a part of those memories, his usually calm features racked by anguish. She could even remember the scalding touch of his tears. That must have been one of the times when she was cold.

I have been ill, she thought. *But I'm never sick. How odd . . .*

"She wakes!" said someone. She could hear all the familiar sounds of the dun—the complaint of a cow, someone whistling, clucking chickens at the door.

"Drink this, my lady." A strong arm went around her shoulders, raising her. Obediently she swallowed the liquid they held to her lips. It was warm milk, with an undertaste of white willow bark. She could vaguely remember having tasted it before.

At the thought of milk her breasts began to throb. Her flaccid belly was sore; all her limbs ached with the sensitivity that comes after a fever. Her eyes flew open as she realized what she had not heard. There had been no baby's cry.

She tried to speak, swallowed, and tried again. "Where is my son?"

The silence that followed lasted too long. Old Nessa's face wavered above her, cheeks furrowed with tears.

"He was too little, my darling, and too cold. He only lived one day."

"Praise be to Brigantia that you survived," one of the maids added brightly. "We thought we were going to lose you as well."

"Prasutagos?" she asked weakly.

"He named the child Cunomaglos after his brother. The babe lies in the grave-field with his kin."

"Where is the king now?" she managed.

This silence was not quite so long. "When we knew you would live, lady, he took two men and rode off to see who else needed help."

Leaving me in an even greater silence than usual,

thought Boudica. But it no longer mattered. What could they have to say to each other now?

*M*y lady—for you—"

Lhiannon turned in time to see a small hand offering a bunch of rather wilted asters. As she peered around the doorpost to smile at the bearer, the child blushed, dropped the bouquet, and darted away.

"Why will they never stay and let me thank them?" she sighed, looking around her for some vessel in which she could put the flowers.

"Let me!" Rianor plucked the bouquet from her hand, took yesterday's offering from the clay beaker, and settled the asters in their place. He was not meeting her eyes, either, she realized suddenly.

After the magical working that had saved Camadunon, she had roused only to eat before falling once more into a sleep without dreams. By the time she was able to take notice once more, weeks had passed. But every morning since then the offerings had appeared, and perhaps before then, for all she knew. Yesterday, it had been a spray of bronze and ocher leaves. While she lay in what the farmfolk clearly considered an enchanted sleep, the summer had passed away.

She herself diagnosed her collapse as the cumulative effect of the hunger and fear she had experienced at the Dun of Stones. And sorrow . . . she had not known that grief could become an illness that sapped strength from body and soul. The pain of losing Ardanos was still there, but if she was careful she could go for as much as half a day without tears.

"Tell the children that I am grateful." As she gained strength, she found herself focusing on simple pleasures—the taste of new milk, the colors of the turning leaves. "If they wish to visit me, they will be welcome."

"They respect you too greatly, lady . . ." he said softly. "To them, you are the white lady who turned herself into a cloud to save us from the Romans, and they are afraid."

"Well, you should reassure them," she said tartly. "We Druids are servants, not gods!"

"Of course, Lady Lhiannon," he replied, flushing as he met her eyes. In his, she caught the same look of awe with which they had regarded the High Priestess when she bore the power of the Goddess in ritual at Lys Deru.

Oh dear. She had assumed there would be rumors about the magical mist that had saved the dun, but she had not realized that her long recovery would allow them to become so well rooted here.

"The farmers hereabouts have come to me," he said then. "They wish to build you a house on the slopes of the dun, near Cama's spring. They would be honored if you would make your home here . . ."

As their local goddess and tutelary spirit, Lhiannon thought wryly, *with Rianor as chief priest of my cult!*

She shook her head. She needed peace, not worship. To stay here would be ludicrous. But even the thought of re-turning to Mona, where she would be reminded of Ardanos at every turning of the way, made her spirit bleed anew.

"I cannot stay here," she said gently. "We send those in need of healing to the Tor. I would like to spend the winter in retreat on Avalon, and then we shall see . . ."

"We will need to gather provisions. The house will need repair. But it is not so far." His face brightened. "I will ar-range it, lady, in your name."

*T*he days passed, and Boudica's strength returned to her, though her breasts continued to leak and her tears to fall. Had the mound-spirit stolen the life of her baby? Or had it simply been an evil chance? As everyone was so eager to remind her, in any family more children died than lived to bear children of their own. To be told that she was young and would have others hurt even more. She would rather have blamed someone, or something, than accept that the loss of her child had no meaning at all.

She thought of sending for Lhiannon, but somehow it seemed to her that she *had* called, and the priestess had failed her, and in any case, to call would have required her to abandon her lethargy. Her husband coped by staying at the dun he was building near the shore, as if, having lost his son, earthen banks would be his immortality.

Perhaps the child had been taken as a sacrifice, she thought grimly, for as the season progressed, it seemed as if the spirits of the sky had been appeased. The clouds moved onward and the muddy ground dried. On a few fortunate hilltops there was even a little grain. Boudica's spirits, however, did not improve, and Nessa began to suggest that she should pay a visit to the sacred spring.

Her first reaction was revulsion. To return as she was now to that place where her marriage had truly begun, where she had felt such hope and known such peace, would seem a sacrilege. But as she thought about it, she began to realize that the lady of the holy well had wronged her by promising her so much and betraying it all. She should go, she thought grimly. She had a few things to say to the spirit of the spring.

They rode south from the dun on a smiling day when the first hint of autumn touched the air. Boudica made no attempt to discourage attendants. These days other people appeared to her as ghosts and shadows. If such wished to follow her, she could not summon the energy to discourage them.

A half-day's journey brought them to the shrine. The place was full of pilgrims, some of whom were unceremoniously evicted from their shelters when the entourage of the queen of the Northern Iceni arrived. Boudica cared little where she slept, so long as it was not in the shelter she and Prasutagos had shared before. While the others arranged their bedding she walked among the trees. She ate the food they cooked for her, but it was not until the next morning that she went to the spring.

Morning was for hope, she thought as the path curved and she crossed the stepping stones through the marshy area below the spring. But to her the sunlight seemed thin and the gurgle of water a mockery. Bits of fabric, some old, some new, still fluttered from the branches of the hazel tree. She reached up and untied the riband she had put there almost a year before.

The cool breath of the water had not changed, and the water itself continued to well upward from unknown depths, sweet and clear.

"I would rather have come here to thank you for a safe

delivery," she said quietly. "If there is anything here to thank—" Her voice cracked. "If you even care whether I give you a riband or take it back, whether I give thanks or spit into your pool!"

But even in her anger Boudica could not bring herself to go that far. This might be no more than water, but it was no less, an element to be respected even now, when they had had so much of it. The Druids would have taken this as the cue for some mystic sermon, but at the moment their wisdom seemed worthless as well. All they had accomplished with their magic was to bring the Romans more quickly to Britannia's shores. In fact, just now she could not think of anything in which she did believe. As if with hope she had also lost the power of motion, she sank down on a piece of log that had been set as a bench nearby.

"I would hate you, if I had the energy," she addressed the pool. "They say your waters are bountiful as the Mother's breasts. *My* breasts are dry. They say your pool is the womb of life. *My* womb is empty!" It was also said that the tears of the Goddess filled the spring. As she leaned over the dark water, her own tears fell into the pool.

When Boudica was here before, she had thought the Lady of the Well spoke to her. She would have resisted any such fancy now. But she could not resist the one thing the waters offered her . . . a place to at last be still. This was neither comfort nor forgiveness nor peace, but a place beyond them all. The sun moved inexorably westward; water continually welled upward and then trickled down the hill; reeds and grass and trees continued to grow. She lived.

For a time she sat without thinking, but presently she became aware of a sound that did not belong to this woodland harmony—an intermittent whimper, coming from a patch of reeds. With the first twitch of curiosity she had felt since the baby died she got up to see. A twist of dirty linen was moving, half in and half out of the water. She peeled the cloth back to reveal what looked like a drowned rat, if there had ever been a rat that was white with one red ear and absurdly large paws.

A puppy—someone had tried to drown a puppy in the sacred spring. Now that was surely a blasphemy! She felt her guts clench as the tiny thing wriggled in her hands.

She wanted to be sick, and she wanted to kill whoever would do such a thing. But already she was stripping away the soggy linen, rubbing at the sodden fur with her shawl. She cradled the shivering creature against her breast and the small head turned and a very pink tongue licked her hand.

Boudica wrapped the puppy in her shawl and took a step down the path. Then she stopped, picked up her rib-and from the ground, and draped it back over a branch of the hazel tree.

When she returned to the shelter the relief on the faces of her servants made her wonder how long she had been gone. If any of them were curious about what she had wrapped so carefully in her shawl none dared to ask.

"Do you wish to stay here tonight, my lady?" asked Calgac. "If we left now we could be back at the dun before darkness falls . . ."

She stared at him. Go back to Eponadunon, where every sight would remind her of what she had lost? She could not do it. She wanted space, and light, and a bed where she had never lain in the deceptive shelter of her husband's arms. There was a farm to the west of here that she had visited once with Prasutagos, when he was introducing her to his people and his land. According to the wedding settlements, it belonged to her.

"I will do neither . . ." she said slowly. "We will pack the wagon and take the road west to Danatobrigos. Go back to Eponadunon." She nodded to the warriors. "You may tell my husband where I have gone, and that it is now safe for him to return to his dun. I will not be there to reproach him"—*or to be reproached in turn* . . .

She did not expect to find happiness, but perhaps in time some healing would come. But first, she thought as the puppy burrowed against her breast, she would have to find some milk for the little dog.

THIRTEEN

$\mathcal{S}$now fountained as the puppy hit the bank, his pale form disappearing and then bursting free like some winter spirit manifesting in canine form. He slid a few feet, then leaped again, leaving a series of splash marks down the hill.

"How he loves the snow!" said Temella. With a shawl wrapped around her head, only the girl's big gray eyes and the tip of a red nose could be seen.

"Bogle loves everything," Boudica replied in amusement. When they had settled into the farmstead at Danatobrigos the previous autumn, bags and baskets and anything else within reach of his tiny teeth had become a plaything. As the puppy grew into the promise of his big paws he had found immense sport in the drifted autumn leaves. From his coloring they guessed him to be part hunting hound, but the other parent must have been something much larger. And now, as high as her knee and still growing, he had discovered snow.

The red mare stamped and snorted as the puppy slid under her hooves, barked, and was off again. But Roud was accustomed to his antics, since riding or walking, where Boudica went, the dog was never more than a whistle away. Temella was almost as constant a companion. The girl was the oldest of the children to whom Boudica had taken the soup the day she gave birth to her baby. She had appeared at the farm about a month after Boudica moved there and attached herself as maid, messenger, and shadow.

Boudica took a deep breath of crisp air. Some snow was to be expected at this season, but a blizzard of the size that had kept them indoors for the past three days was unusual. Field and pasture had been transformed by the snowfall,

all irregularities smoothed to an expanse of pristine white. Even the leafless branches of the ash tree that shaded the ritual hearth were mantled in white, and the ancient trackway that ran toward the coast was no more than a depression in the snow. Beneath that white blanket many things lay sleeping, from the body of her child to the seeds of next year's grain.

In the months since she had come to Danatobrigos, there had been times when she wanted to lie down beneath just such an obliterating coverlet, without thought or movement, until all feeling also disappeared. Even her husband's rare visits had not disturbed her lethargy. It was Bogle, thrusting his shaggy head beneath her palm to be petted, or dropping some amorphous slobbered object in her lap to be thrown, who had kept her connected to the world of the living. Sometimes, she even laughed.

She watched, smiling, as he dashed past a stand of leafless oaks down the road, barking furiously.

"Someone is coming," said Temella as the dog bounced back toward them.

"Bogle! Be still!" Boudica reined in and whistled, and the dog slowed, a low growl vibrating from his throat, plumed tail waving gently. He was uncertain, not alarmed, though at his age, she wondered, how would he tell the difference between what was dangerous and what was merely new? Still, it was unlikely any enemy would be abroad in this weather, especially now, when they were safe beneath the protecting hand of Rome.

On the heels of her thought came the strangers themselves, Romans by their gear, moving in good order past the trees. As they drew closer she recognized Pollio with his escort, all mounted on native ponies whose shaggy coats shrugged off snow.

"Well met, my lady!" he called, his breath making white puffs in the chill air. "But I did not expect to meet you so soon! I was on my way to the ferry—I have a mission to the Brigante lands—and regretted not being able to break my journey at Eponadunon. Are you and your husband visiting hereabouts?" He drew up beside Boudica.

"The king is at Eponadunon," she said flatly. "I live here."

His dark gaze grew more intent. "Truly? Then fortune is with me."

She lifted an eyebrow, wondering what he could possibly wish to say to her rather than to the king. "Temella, ride to the steading and tell them we will have guests." The girl nodded and urged her pony into a trot. Bogle lurched after her, circled her pony, and then skidded back to Boudica.

"Will you ride with me a little up the road?" Pollio asked, moving his mount closer to hers. "Our horses should not stand in this cold."

That was true. She loosened the rein and let Roud fall into step beside his gray.

"Winter agrees with you, lady."

"You do not seem to be suffering, either," she observed. The cold had brought an unaccustomed color to his sallow cheeks and brightened his eyes, though she noticed that even Romans grew out their beards in this cold. "I suppose this is very different from your home."

"Not as much as you might think—I was born in Dacia, and the winters there can be bitter indeed."

"That would explain how you come to be traveling in this weather. I thought you Romans spent Britannic winters stoking the furnaces of your hypocausts and cursing the cold."

This time he laughed out loud, a surprisingly pleasant sound. "No doubt they are doing so in Camulodunum, but even your dog knows there is sport to be had in the wintertime . . ."

Her gaze followed Bogle, who had flushed a hare from the woods and was pursuing it through the snow, barking ecstatically, though it was not clear whether he was trying to hunt or to play.

"My mother was a noblewoman in Dacia." Pollio's eyes flicked to her face and then away. "My father married her when he was stationed there. This is how the new provinces become part of the Empire."

I already have a husband—why is he saying this to me? But she herself had told him that she and Prasutagos were living separately. She had heard that divorce was easy among the Romans. Perhaps he did not consider her married state an impediment. She glanced at him, seeing him for the first time as a not ill-looking man who clearly enjoyed her company. As if he had felt her gaze he turned to her once more, and she looked away.

As they passed through the wood, the horses, sensing their riders' inattention, had slowed. Pollio reached out and took her hand.

"Boudica, you are like a flame, burning in the midst of the snow. I thought so when I first saw you, glowing like a torch in the imperial purple gloom, but you were still a child. You are a woman now, and you are magnificent!"

Since that day she had borne and lost a child. If that was the qualification for womanhood she wondered how the race could survive. And how could she be a flame when she felt frozen inside?

Or was she? Pollio had slid off his glove and now was easing his fingers beneath the woolen mitten that covered her hand. The touch was surprisingly intimate. She felt a sudden rush of heat, as if he had put his hand beneath her gown.

"You are a princess of your people as I am a lord among mine. Together we could do so much for this land . . ."

The horses had stopped. She trembled as he began to trace small circles in the sensitive center of her palm.

"I have dreamed of you, my lady," he said softly. "Sweet and ripe as one of the apples we grow in the southern lands. I dream of tasting that sweetness, as I dream of warming myself at your fire. Blessed Boudica, fairest of women, welcome me to your hearth . . ."

Bogle was barking, but the sound seemed to come from somewhere very far away. Pollio leaned forward, his other arm reaching up to draw her to him. Her lips parted, awaiting his kiss.

And the dog, yipping gleefully, bounded beneath the bellies of the horses. Pollio's mount bucked, kicking, and the red mare shied.

Boudica grabbed a handful of mane and righted herself. The Roman was half off his horse, swearing as he tried to retrieve his reins. Bogle, apparently believing he had at last found a playmate, bounced in and out, dodging the hooves, and then dashed away again, barking in the tone that meant, *"People are coming, come see, come see!"*

She straightened, squinting against the glare of sun on snow as a group of riders approached from the other direction. A big man on a big horse led them. With some sense that went deeper than vision Boudica knew him. She sat back, willing her heartbeat to slow.

By the time Prasutagos reached them, Pollio had also gotten his mount under control. He nodded with a wary courtesy. "Greetings, my lord."

Boudica watched with mingled amusement and consternation. How long had they been in sight before Bogle noticed Prasutagos and started barking? And what, at that distance, could he have seen?

What, indeed, was there to see? Would I really have allowed the Roman to kiss me? She felt nothing for Prasutagos, but next to him the Roman looked—small.

"It is a cold day for riding," the king observed. "We don't often have such a storm." He turned to Boudica. "I was at Coric's steading near the harbor. A roof on one of his outbuildings collapsed from the weight of the snow. I thought I should see if you needed any help here."

It was a reasonable question. The steading had been in some disrepair when she arrived. And she knew that during the past six months Prasutagos had spent most of his time traveling from one steading to another. To strengthen ties between king and people, they said, but it might be that he could not bear living at Eponadunon, either. Surely it was chance that he had happened to be in this part of his lands when the storm struck. But whether it was a happy chance or an ill one she did not know.

"Everything seems to be secure," she answered neutrally.

"That is good news," said Prasutagos. He turned to the Roman. "To lodge your men and mine we will need the second roundhouse, and it would be best to have the horses under shelter as well."

"Oh, there will be no need to crowd your warriors." Pollio's lips stretched in an equally polite smile. "If we push on we should reach the ferry by nightfall. I have messages for the Brigante king that cannot wait, and I must take advantage of the calm to cross before more bad weather rolls in."

Before Prasutagos arrived, thought Boudica, he had seemed quite willing to spend the night with her.

"Perhaps you are wise," the king said thoughtfully. "A ship came in just before the storm, so you will not have to wait long. Greet Venutios and Cartimandua for me."

"I am sorry we will not have the pleasure of your company." Boudica let the Roman take that as he would. "But I understand the claims of duty." *Including,* she wondered warily, *my own?*

Prasutagos had visited from time to time when he was in the neighborhood, staying long enough for a meal, but always off again before dark, checking on her as he would any other possession, she thought bitterly. The first few times she had scarcely noticed whether he was there or not, but lately she found his detachment a little unnerving.

Bogle sat down in the snow, tongue lolling, as Pollio summoned his men and the little troop plodded off down the road.

"They ought to thank us for breaking trail for them," observed Bituitos, the older of the two warriors who were the king's primary guards. As big a man as Prasutagos, but ten years younger, he was some kind of cousin, with the family size and strength and coloring.

"But they had better hurry," added Eoc Mor, equally tall, but with the brown hair and gray eyes of the older race. He had been destined for life as a farmer until someone noticed how deadly quick he was with a sword. "If the Roman cannot read the weather, I can, and clouds are building eastward that will bring more snow before dawn!"

It was true that the wind was beginning to rise, with a damp chill that cut deeper than the crisp cold of the morning.

"Perhaps we, too, should be on our way," she suggested. "When we met the Romans I sent Temella to warn the household we would have guests. It is just as well you arrived—it would have been a pity to waste the food."

*   *   *

$\mathscr{B}$ituitos had read the weather rightly. By sunset the wind was driving the first flurries of snow across the downs. The interlaced framework of beams and withies that supported the thatched roof flexed and groaned with each gust and changing pressure sent smoke from the hearthfire billowing beneath its tall peak. No one suggested that the king and his men should ride anywhere in such a storm, if indeed Prasutagos had ever had such an intention. She was aware of his presence as she had not been before, and did not know whether it was he who had changed, or she. He seemed thinner, she thought, fined down by hard riding to whipcord muscle and bone. Firelight glinted on his mustache and burnished the strong modeling of cheekbones and jaw.

There were two roundhouses at the farmstead, along with other buildings for stabling and storage. When the last of the mutton stew had been eaten, most of the king's men were sent off to the second house where old Kitto and his wife lived with the other men who worked the farm. Even to unlace the hide that covered the doorway long enough to let them out let in a chilly blast that left Boudica shivering. The hides and rugs of heavy wool that hung on the inner side of the house walls caught some of the drafts, but the same permeability that allowed smoke to escape outward through the thatching also allowed cold air to filter in.

Temella found more skins and blankets, and Bituitos and Eoc rolled themselves into them beside the fire where Bogle already lay snoring, his heavy head resting on a bone. Usually, in weather as cold as this, Temella and Boudica would share a bed, but the girl was laying out her own bedding in the partitioned section that was old Nessa's place. That seemed to answer the question of where Prasutagos would be sleeping. Boudica could feel his gaze following her as she banked the fire.

"Lady of the holy fire, ward this flame till morning. Brigantia, blessed one, be you the fire in the hearth as you are the fire in the heart. Against all evil that walks the night be our shield and protection." She drew the Lady's sun-cross in the ash and rose to her feet, dusting her hands.

As she started to turn, the king rose and fell into step beside her. She controlled a flinch—she had forgotten how tall he was. Together they passed through the wool curtains Boudica had woven in her own clan's russet and gold and gray to hang from the houseposts that defined her sleeping place. Swiftly she stripped off her shawl and her outer tunic and shoes and lay down in shift and gown, curling defensively against the cold and away from the man whom she could hear taking off his own outer garments. The straw beneath the sheepskins and linen sheet rustled as Prasutagos got into bed beside her. She did not speak, but surely a turned back made her wishes clear.

Boudica had forgotten that for some things he needed no words at all.

She had been braced to resist his courtship, but this time there were none of the sweet whispers with which he had taken her virginity, only the rasp of his breath in her ear. She stiffened as he pulled up the skirts of shift and gown and curled around her, those strong hands, calloused from sword and bridle, taking possession of all that lay beneath. In silent fury she tried to break free, but legs that could grip a horse's barrel held hers, one muscled arm pinioned her arms while the other hand relearned the shape of her breasts.

"You are my wife . . ." Words escaped set teeth as the same force that gave him the strength to hold her broke through the barriers that had kept him silent. She could feel each tremor that shook his body, pressed so tightly against hers. "You may live without a man . . . but you shall not lie with any . . . man . . . but . . . me!"

That answered the question of whether he had seen Pollio try to kiss her.

Boudica was still trying to think of a response when with a last agile shift he had her, and as once before, when her body was constrained, her outrage exploded inward, driving the thinking self to one side. The Roman had called her a fire, and now she was bursting into flame.

I am the oven that bakes the bread . . . said a voice within. *I am the kiln that fires the cup . . . I am the forge that shapes the blade. Burn!*

When Boudica woke the next morning, the snow had

ceased and Prasutagos was gone. She might have thought his visit all a dream, but by the Turning of Spring, she knew that she was once more with child.

*S*pring came to the Tor bearing a treasure of golden kingcup and yellow flag and heralded by a clamor of returning birds. To Lhiannon, it seemed as if the lengthening days were one long morning, releasing her from the shadows in which she had walked since the fall of the Dun of Stones. The long, slow cycles of winter had accorded with Lhiannon's mood, but with spring, the pace of life grew frenetic, and as she felt that same energy burning in her own veins she realized that so far as she would ever be, she was healed.

Soon, she knew, she would have to leave the Tor, but as the world hovered at the Turning of Spring she found herself as undecided as the season. A year ago at this time she and Ardanos had been preparing to defend the Dun of Stones. Now the dun bore a Roman fort and most of the south and west were in Roman hands. Governor Plautius was driving westward across the midlands. Caratac had gone to ground somewhere in the mountains beyond. Even if Lhiannon had been willing to face more war there was nothing for her to do.

On the first fair day after the equinox an excess of energy drove her up the Tor. This time she did not walk the spiral, but it scarcely mattered. Her awareness of the Otherworld was always with her now. Wind ruffled the new grass. Below, the marshland pools, still full from the spring rains, spread across the levels in a shifting mosaic of silver and blue. But the spring sun was warm on her shoulders, and when she reached the summit she lay down to rest.

Whether what came upon Lhiannon then was sleep or a vision, she was never sure, but it seemed to her that she was in a place of wide skies and open fields where the air had the scent of the sea. Boudica was with her, more beautiful than ever, her breasts full but her face fined down to reveal the lovely curves of cheek and brow. In her eyes Lhiannon saw a grief to match her own.

"Lhiannon..." Across the miles she heard the cry. *"Lhiannon, I am afraid. I need you ... come to me!"*

Boudica knelt at the edge of the offering pit, fingering the ridges that ornamented the curve of the bowl she held. It was a fine piece of cream-colored pottery in the Gallic style her people had brought with them from across the sea, one of a set that had been included in the wedding treasure sent over from Eponadunon when she had taken up residence at Danatobrigos. It was filled with early primroses now, picked as she came through the wood that partly surrounded the Horse Shrine at the foot of the hill. On the other side the ground was open toward the path that ran alongside the stream. In the center of the enclosure the skull of the most recent equine sacrifice contemplated her from its pole.

"You old ones who were here before," she whispered. "Your dust is part of the earth whose fruits feed me and my child. Give us your blessing."

Prasutagos's winter visit had shattered her peace. The quickening of her child roused her to panic and a frantic search for ways to protect the new life within. Once more, she had something to lose.

"The ghosts of this land have taken one life from me," she went on. "Surely you don't need another! Please accept this offering!"

As she stretched to lower the bowl she lost her balance and the smooth ceramic slipped from her hand, hit a stone, and cracked. She collapsed onto hands and knees, staring as the water ran out and soaked into the soil. Like an afterimage came the memory of how the kings had broken the swords and bent the shields before offering them at the Lake of Little Stones. Was this a sign that the ancestors had accepted her offering or an omen that her womb was as useless as the broken bowl?

She was no Druid to interpret it! She had refused to become a priestess, abandoned her duties as wife and queen ... would she ever be a mother? She hunched over her belly, weeping.

"Boudica? Who has hurt you, child? What is wrong?"

For a moment she thought that soft voice a figment of her memory. Then she heard a pony snort and the creak of harness. She turned, vision blurring at the sight of a thin woman in blue with golden hair. Slowly she got to her feet.

"Lhiannon? You're real? I have wanted you so badly! Are you really here?" As the priestess slid down from her pony Boudica ran forward, hugging her in a tumult of mingled laughter and tears.

"You've lost none of your strength, at any rate," Lhiannon said when Boudica released her at last. "And you are blooming. But what are you doing here? They told me I had some days of travel yet to reach Prasutagos's dun. I only took this path to see if I might find a meal at the farm."

"I am sure that Palos and Shanda would make you welcome, but there's no need to trouble them when my home is just up the hill!" exclaimed Boudica. "The farm is busy with preparations for Beltane, but we can slaughter one of the lambs early for a feast of welcome! Follow me!"

As they walked perhaps she could find the words to tell Lhiannon all that had happened to her since they parted at Camulodunon. The gods knew she had rehearsed the story often enough during those sleepless nights when she longed for the other woman to come.

I believe you," said Lhiannon. "When the need is great there is power in such a cry. This time I heard you calling, I think, because I was on the Tor. I am only sorry . . ." She sighed, tugging on the rein by which she was leading the pony as it tried for a particularly juicy clump of new grass.

"That you did not hear me when I was birthing my son?" said Boudica. "I do not blame you now. Even the greatest of priestesses could not have instantly transported herself all the way across Britannia."

In the pastures to either side ewes were taking advantage of the abundance, surrounded by the leaping lambs that had given the farm its name. It seemed to Lhiannon that the fertility of the land and its animals was a good omen for Boudica's pregnancy. Now she understood the young woman's tragic radiance, but it was not yet clear what she should do. A great deal, she thought, depended on whether the king was a violent man or had simply mishandled his young mare.

"How long have you been on the road?"

Lhiannon frowned. "I left soon after the equinox, when the moon was just past the full, and now she is nearly round once more. It was hard going until I struck the old track near Carn Ava, and then I made good progress, except when a Roman detachment crossed my path."

"Were you in danger?"

"Our people are not yet so cowed that they do not honor my Order, and there was always some house where I could find shelter in exchange for a blessing or a spell." Indeed, the journey had reminded her why she was a priestess. As she had told Rianor, the Druids deserved the honor folk gave them because they served. And clearly, she was badly needed here.

The way Boudica was leading them passed through a wood and along the edge of a field. As the sun sank westward its slanting rays filled each leaf and blade of grass with light. It was peaceful here, a good place to seek healing. For both of them, it occurred to her then.

As they reached the hilltop the peace was split by the sound of barking. Lhiannon hung on to the pony's reins as a creature the size of a young calf burst from the gate in the wicker fence that surrounded the farmstead and came bounding toward them.

"Bogle! Down!" Boudica caught the animal in midleap and wrestled him to the ground as he strained to reach the priestess.

"What in the name of An-Dubnion is *that*?"

"He's my puppy." For a moment Boudica's grin reminded her of the girl she had known. "Down, Bogle, be polite! She's a friend!"

It must be a dog, thought Lhiannon as the animal licked her hand, though it was of no breed she had ever seen. Wiry waves of creamy hair covered a lean, long-legged form with a dangerously whipping plumed tail. But the head above the powerful shoulders was broad, with a russet nose and one flopping white ear and one red ear.

"Impressive," said Lhiannon in a neutral tone as the dog gave her a last slurp and bounded off to announce their arrival.

"I think the Goddess sent him to save my reason," Boudica replied.

FOURTEEN

Lhiannon watched Boudica carefully as Beltane month passed and the year began to ripen into June. It was a relief when the weather held fair through July—even without rain, for both of them that month held evil memories. And not for them only, she realized when one morning Bogle's barking announced the arrival of King Prasutagos and his men.

He had come by only twice since the visit in January of which Boudica had told her, and stayed only so long as it took to water his horses and assure himself that his wife was well. Surely that was no surprise, if the encounter had been as—intense—as Boudica had said. But Lhiannon knew very well that her relationship with Ardanos had hardly prepared her to judge a marriage. She was glad of the chance to see for herself what manner of man Boudica's clan had married her to.

"My lady, I salute you," Prasutagos said as Lhiannon emerged from the roundhouse to greet him. For a moment his gaze rested on the doorway, but when it remained empty he turned back to her with a smile. He did not seem surprised to see her, but then word of her arrival would have spread quickly through the countryside. "We are glad to offer you a refuge here."

Clearly, thought Lhiannon, he did not yet realize just *why* the priestess had come. She knew by the increased tension in his shoulders when Boudica appeared, bearing the welcoming horn of ale. She was wearing a linen tunica pinned at the shoulders, and she had tied the belt tightly beneath her breasts so that the new rounding of her belly was clear. For a moment Prasutagos's face was utterly blank. Lhiannon waited for what would come next—joy, or anger? Instead what she saw was fear.

"The blessing of the gods be upon you, my husband," Boudica said evenly.

Prasutagos nodded as he took the horn. But he drank and handed it back to her without saying a word.

The king's silence was covered by the noise made by the other men as they saw to the horses and sat down to the meal the women brought out to them, for on such a fine summer day it would have been a pity to huddle inside. They had set logs for seats around the fire pit, where a cauldron hung above a small flame. Prasutagos sat on a carved stool that had been a wedding present, with Boudica opposite him on the other side of the fire. Lhiannon was glad to be outdoors, where there was light enough for her to continue to observe them both, for she was still not certain just what was going on.

Whatever it was, the past months had been hard on him as well. The prince she had met on Mona had been quiet, but forthcoming enough when speech was needed. The king she had seen at Camulodunon had been so contained he might as well have sent a stone image. If he had married in the same mood, Lhiannon was not surprised Boudica had reacted badly. She had always been a forthright girl. But what the priestess saw in him now went deeper. This was not quiet, it was constriction, as if his silence were a barrier to hold back emotions he did not dare reveal. She could see the tension in the way he held his head, in the abrupt way he moved, and she could see the pain in his eyes when he looked at Boudica.

After the meal, Prasutagos went round the farm with old Kitto, who managed the work for Boudica. Most of his men remained where they could tease little Temella and exchange mock insults with Nessa, but presently Bituitos strode across the yard and came to attention before her, obviously searching for words.

"Is there some way I can help you?" Lhiannon took pity on him.

"Lady," said Bituitos, "it is clear that the queen has great regard for you. Can you speak to her on behalf of my lord? He does not complain, but we know that he is suffering. Another man might have dragged her home by her hair, but he will do nothing, say nothing, until she gives the word."

Lhiannon nodded. "Has he always been so silent?"

Bituitos frowned. "Compared to his brothers he was always the quiet one. But not like this, no. He lost his joy when his first wife died with the child. And then to lose all his brothers—it was hard."

"I would have expected shared sorrow to bring them together after their son died," said Lhiannon.

"I think grief drove them apart," muttered the warrior.

She considered him for a moment in silence. It was worth something to know that the king was a man whom his sworn warriors served not only from duty, but from love.

"I am sorry . . ." she said presently. "I know that you would shed your blood to protect him. But you cannot ward him from the wounds he gives himself. Nor can I so shield the queen. Perhaps things will improve between them when this child is born."

"May the gods grant it is so. I think it will kill him if things go wrong again," Bituitos said in a low voice. "I saw his face when he thought she was dying like the other one."

He straightened, and Lhiannon realized that Prasutagos was coming through the gate, still talking to the old man. His face was quite different when he laughed. But as his men began to ready the horses he came to Lhiannon and his features became impassive once more.

"Priestess, I am glad that you are here. I would never force Boudica back to Eponadunon, but I have feared for her, with no one near who had the authority to rule her and the household if she should take harm. Send to me if there is anything she needs."

Lhiannon might have thought those words only the speech of duty if she had not spoken with his man; if she had not seen how Prasutagos looked when he smiled. As it was, she nodded. But he was no longer looking at her. Boudica had come out once more, with the parting cup in her hands.

"A safe journey to you, my lord," she said clearly.

"The blessing of the Great Mother be on you, my lady," he answered in a low voice, and in a whisper, "and on the child . . ."

When they had gone, the farmstead seemed very silent, and colorless, as if some of the life had gone out of the world. Or perhaps it was only Boudica who seemed suddenly pale.

That evening the queen sought her bed early, but around midnight, Lhiannon woke and heard her weeping. Quietly she parted the curtains and knelt beside the bedstead.

"Hush, my dear one, how is it with you? Are you in pain?"

Boudica stilled, hiccupped, and turned over. "Only in my heart," she whispered. "And I should be used to that by now."

Carefully Lhiannon lay down and put an arm around her, drawing her in so that Boudica could rest against her shoulder.

"It will be all right . . . It will be well, my darling."

Some of the tension left Boudica's body in a long sigh. "I was so happy when I was with child before. But this time when I quickened, I was afraid. What if I lose this one, too?"

It was what Prasutagos had feared as well. Lhiannon stroked the hair that curled with such vigor from Boudica's brow. "Your husband . . ." she began, but Boudica jerked away.

"He came to inspect his mare. Perhaps he'll leave me alone now that he knows I'm breeding again."

The opposite was more likely, thought Lhiannon, but clearly this was no time to say so. "Never mind, then. I will take care of you."

Boudica sighed and settled down beside her. Lhiannon's heart ached with pity for her, and for her husband as well, but it was strangely sweet to hold that strong young body, beginning to ripen now in pregnancy.

And I will love you, silently she swore, *and in Brigantia's name I will stand between you and whatsoever may threaten your life or that of your child!*

It was a golden summer. As the grain ripened in the fields, Boudica felt her own body swell and bloom. And as one month followed the next without incident, her fears began to ease. She could feel Lhiannon's love like a protective shield around her. She blessed the fields as her men brought in the harvest, living model for the image of the Corn Mother they twined from the last sheaves in the field. And as the ninth month of her pregnancy began, she realized that she was looking forward to the birth with joy.

She was crossing the yard with a basket of scraps for the chickens—the heaviest burden they would allow her to bear—when she felt the familiar ache in her lower back begin. She stopped, biting her lip—she had had such pains before and had all the household in a panic around her, only to have them cease. Lhiannon said it was the womb's way of getting ready, practicing like a warrior for the battle to come. They would make her lie down if they knew this was happening, and the compulsion that was on her now was to walk. Not far—she knew better—but if she stayed within earshot she could circle the farmstead. She finished feeding the chickens and went out through the gate into the field.

Boudica had made three circuits, pausing from time to time to let a pain pass, when she realized that Lhiannon was walking beside her.

"Has it begun?" asked the priestess.

Boudica nodded, panting a little as another contraction rolled through her belly. "Please, don't make me go inside . . ."

"I may not have borne a babe, but I have helped at many births," Lhiannon replied tartly. "Lean on my shoulder if you need to, and walk until you tire."

That did help, but when the time came that Boudica could not take two steps without doubling over, she let them lead her within. As Nessa helped her to disrobe, she turned to Lhiannon.

"Send . . . for my husband. He should be here . . . to see what he . . . has done."

"He's just down at the Horse Shrine," said Temella eagerly. "He has been staying with Palos and Shanda at the farm."

"Damn him!" she whispered. "Spying on me!" Then that mighty grip tightened around her belly and she had no breath to say more.

When she bore her son, the pains had been sharp, but she recognized now that they had not lasted long. This labor went on and on. Awareness came and went with the pangs. During one respite she heard Prasutagos's voice and called his name. When the next contraction had passed he was sitting beside her. In the flickering light of the Roman lamp that hung from the crossbeam she could see his face, unmoving as the image of a god.

"You did this to me! You, with your face like stone! Don't you care?" She realized that she was babbling and could not cease, nor could she control the words. She flailed and he gripped her hands. She hung on, panting, and as the pain passed, began to curse him once more. She was vaguely aware of Lhiannon and the others, coming and going in the room, but Prasutagos was the rock to which she clung.

"Why didn't you come? I was cold and it hurt and you didn't come . . ." she whispered in a moment of respite, and saw him close his eyes in pain. But when he looked at her again he had regained his calm.

"I am here . . ." he said quietly. "Boudica, I am here."

"Yes . . ." she said in wonder. "Stay with me . . ." Then she gasped. It still hurt, but this was different. She struggled to sit up.

"It's time," said Nessa, who had seen even more babies come into the world than Lhiannon. But it was the priestess who got into the bed behind her, bracing her back as Prasutagos hauled on her hands.

Boudica grunted, and suddenly mind and body were partnered once more. Again and again she pushed; she was being cleft in two, but it didn't matter. With a scream that was a battle cry, she drove toward her goal. And the child, red-haired, bloody, and already squalling, slid into Nessa's waiting hands.

For a time, the relief was so great that Boudica scarcely cared what happened, as long as she could still hear the baby's lusty cries. But by the time the women had washed and dressed her and changed the bedding, the yells had been replaced by a lullaby.

As she focused, she realized that it was Prasutagos who was singing, sitting beside her with the sleeping baby in his arms. His hands looked scraped and bruised, and there were dark circles beneath his eyes. At least, she thought resentfully, he had suffered, too.

"I would like to name her Rigana," he said thoughtfully. "She looks as my mother did when she was old."

"Who did you expect her to look like, Pollio?"

"I thought it was possible." He kept his eyes fixed on the baby. "I would not blame you."

"Would you not?" she snapped back at him. "That was not what you said the night she was conceived. But the child is yours," she added, "if you care . . ."

Color washed up from his neck to his forehead and then receded again. He looked down at the child.

"How strange that such a miracle should be the fruit of my madness. But perhaps that is why this one is a fighter . . ." His voice sank to a whisper, "and she will live . . ."

"And have you nothing to say to *me*?" *Are you sorry?* her inner voice continued. She wondered that he could not hear.

"I am sorry . . . for many things. I never told you . . ." He closed his eyes, and she suddenly felt she knew what he was going to say. "I was afraid. You know I had a wife who died . . . giving birth to my child. When I saw that you were bearing I armored my heart lest I be hurt again."

"And then the baby died," Boudica said flatly. She could not yet forgive, but she was beginning to understand. *But I have been hurt, too, and I am not yet ready to put down my shield.*

"Silence becomes a habit," he said then. "But I will try."

*C*hortling in triumph, Rigana fixed her chubby fingers in Bogle's fur and pulled herself upright, watched narrowly by Nessa, who was still not quite convinced that the big dog would not turn and eviscerate the child. Only last year Bogle had still been half a puppy himself, but once the baby arrived he seemed to have decided that she was an extension of Boudica, and therefore entitled to boundless patience. As soon as her infant fingers were able to grasp they had closed on Bogle's fur. He had become something to climb on as soon as she could crawl. And now that she was on the verge of walking, the dog was a portable support, with bared teeth to discourage any stranger who came too near.

And today there were many, thought Lhiannon, twisting more wool around her distaff and continuing to spin. Beyond the fence the stubbled field had sprouted a new crop of tents and shelters as the Northern Iceni clans arrived for the autumn council and horse fair. The Romans complained that the Britons were without civilization because they had no cities, but she realized now that these gatherings were the Celtic equivalent, manifesting when and where they were required. Here were traders selling cloth and jewelry and leather shoes, and vessels of copper and Roman glass. Blacksmiths and woodworkers plied their trade. Cattle for meat and milk grazed with the horses that were the reason they had all come.

It was the first time the clan council had been held here. Since Rigana was born Prasutagos had lived at the farm by the Horse Shrine. Not even for the council would he return to Eponadunon while his wife and child were here. They saw him often, and although Boudica had not yet invited him to share her bed, she was still nursing the child, so no one really expected it. They sat together now, listening to the messenger from King Antedios at Dun Garo.

"It is certain, then, that Governor Plautius will be returning to Rome?" asked the king.

"His term is finished, and they do not like to leave men in place too long, lest they begin to think the land belongs to them and not to the Empire."

"This sun is too bright for my old head," said Nessa. "My lady, shall I take the babe inside?" Rigana and her canine servitor had maneuvered themselves halfway across the yard. The child was sitting between his paws, gathering the energy for another attempt to master the balance that enabled the adults to get around so easily.

"She is well enough where she is," said the queen. "We are here to watch her. You should go into the shade."

"Hmph," muttered the old woman as she turned toward the roundhouse. "You named that child after a queen and she is growing up to think she is one. She must learn she can't always do as she wills, or mark my words, you'll have trouble one day!"

That might be so, reflected Lhiannon as the thread spun out between her skillful fingers, but as Nessa prophesied disaster of one sort or another daily, her words were rarely marked at all.

"Who comes after him?" asked Boudica.

"A man called Publius Ostorius Scapuola is being sent, but he cannot arrive much before winter, and that is no time to be starting a campaign, so we may have peace for a while . . ."

"Here, certainly," Prasutagos sighed. "We have paid enough to make them leave us alone . . ."

Indeed, the day was too beautiful to think about war. The heavens always seemed wider up on the shoulders of the chalk hills, an expanse of blue crossed by a few wisps of cloud, as if some of the wool had escaped from her basket into the sky. From beyond the hedge came a thunder of hoofbeats as some of the younger men practiced for the races that would be held the next day. Yesterday they had raced with chariots. Lhiannon had not been there—her memories of the last charge of the Trinovante chariots still held too much pain. She supposed she ought to have watched. The Britons were the only people who still used chariots, and who knew when anyone would see such a spectacle again.

Someone shouted, and the hoofbeats grew abruptly louder. Spindle and distaff flew from Lhiannon's hands as a hysterical horse plunged through the gateway. The animal half-reared as its rider fought for control, sharp hooves striking a pace from the child. The adults were out of their seats and running as the dog leaped for the horse.

The rider went flying into the fence and the horse went down, screaming. Blood splattered as sharp teeth ripped at its throat. Prasutagos scooped up his daughter and passed her to Lhiannon, who ran for the house. Boudica, seeing her child safe, turned to the dog, which was snarling horribly as he tried to reach the jugular.

"Bogle! Leave it! She's safe, lad. Leave it now!"

Lhiannon, hovering in the doorway with Rigana in her

arms, lifted an eyebrow. This was no spindle to be rescued from a puppy's jaws. Could even Boudica's voice penetrate the fury that ruled the animal now? Bogle's leap had been amazing. For him to release his grip and stand trembling, jaws streaming red as Boudica called him again, was a miracle.

Murmuring softly, Boudica waited until the madness left his eyes. Then she got a grip on his collar and led him slowly past a gathering crowd to the horse trough, where she filled his water bowl. The water turned red when he thrust his muzzle in. She filled it again and emptied it over his head, then let him drink until he shook the water from his fur and ambled off toward the roundhouse as if wondering why everyone was fussing.

Prasutagos was speaking to the rider, who had picked himself up and was sputtering excuses to anyone who would listen. The king's voice was low and controlled as always, but Lhiannon had never heard that vibration of fury in it before. The rider slunk off, and Prasutagos knelt by the horse, which lay twitching and bleeding on the ground.

As he laid a hand on the soft muzzle the horse convulsed; a swinging forehoof knocked the king across the yard. Eoc ran toward him. After a few moments he stirred, waving the man away, and moving very carefully, approached the horse once more, this time from behind. The dog had not severed the great artery, but the animal's neck was too torn to repair. Steel flickered as someone handed a knife to the king.

"So, so . . . my beauty," he murmured, kneeling stiffly as Eoc watched with worried eyes. " 'Twas not your fault, even so. Go now to Epona to run in her green fields, where no fool of a rider will do you wrong. Sleep, now, my hero." He laid one hand across the horse's eyes and the beast stilled. The blade struck once, deep beneath the jaw, and then across. The king leaned back as the horse jerked, blood pouring out in a crimson stream, and then subsided into immobility.

By this time Rigana's yells had dwindled into an occasional sniffle. Lhiannon handed her to Boudica and started forward as Eoc put out a hand to help Prasutagos stand.

The king took a step, bit his lip, tried to straighten, and stopped, breathing carefully.

"Come here," said Lhiannon.

"I'm all right," he muttered, not meeting her eye.

"Of course you are," the priestess said genially. "Now come here so I can see." She put a touch of the priestess voice into it, and Prasutagos looked up in surprise. She could see him considering, then, with a sigh, he turned toward her.

"Shall I help him into the house?" asked Eoc.

Lhiannon shook her head. "Bring a blanket out here and lay him down. I will need light."

By the time they had pulled off his tunic and gotten the king on his back on the blanket he was pale and sweating. A fine golden stubble glistened on his chin. Boudica hovered indecisively, Rigana in her arms. On the left side, the skin above the king's lower ribs showed the red mark of a hoof. The flesh around it was already discolored and swelling. He would have a most colorful bruise there before too long.

Closing her eyes, Lhiannon held her palm above the area to identify the point where the energy body was most disturbed. Then, using eyes and fingertips, she began to probe along the ribs.

After a moment she sat back and frowned. "You are a warrior, my lord, and by definition brave. But I can learn little if you insist on hiding your pain. Where does it hurt most? There?" She poked gently. "There?" She nodded as he yelped. "Yes, I thought so . . . You have a broken rib or two, and are lucky your ribs were there to ward what lies within. We will bind them, but you should not be riding horses for a moon or so. Temella"—she turned to the girl—"I'll need my healer's bag, and you should start water boiling for willow bark tea."

By the time Lhiannon had finished strapping Prasutagos's ribs, he was pale once more. Most of the onlookers, seeing that the excitement was over, had drifted away.

"Thank you," he whispered as Eoc helped him to rise. "You have good hands."

"The way you calmed that poor horse was remarkable," she replied. "If you talked to your wife half as much as you talk to your horses, many things would have been different these past two years." His twitch at that was not from physical pain. It was not quite fair to speak so when he lacked the breath to reply, but she had earned the right. It would give him something to think about as he waited for his ribs to heal.

And Lhiannon, too, had something to consider. The messenger from Dun Garo had said that Caratac was in the Ordovice lands with his wife's kin, preparing to take advantage of the governor's absence to punish the Dobunni and Cornovii who had allied with Rome.

She had thought the cause for which she and Ardanos had endured so much was dead. Did she betray his memory by staying here in safety with those whom Caratac would call traitors? She was useful here, but it was work that any village wisewoman could do. Should she return to Mona, or go to Caratac and take up the fight once more?

FIFTEEN

*D*o you think the king will be home soon?" asked
Temella.

Boudica slapped the weaving sword down between the
warp threads and swore as the weft thread wound around
the shuttle broke. It would do no good to scream at the girl
for asking. In truth, Boudica herself was not sure why the
question annoyed her. She ought to have been glad that
Prasutagos was still with Antedios the High King at Dun
Garo. To have him so very much underfoot this last winter
while his broken ribs were healing had driven her half crazy,
though she had tried to hide it for the sake of the child.

It had not helped that where the king was, there came
the messengers, and disturbing news continued to trickle
in. The new governor had apparently never heard that
winter operations were impossible, and attacked with such
vigor that Caratac was forced to retreat northward into
the inaccessible mountains that held the Ordovice strong-
holds. That should have been the end of it, but just after
the feast of Brigantia a rider came galloping from Dun
Garo, calling Prasutagos to an emergency council of the
tribe.

And now a moon had passed. If there had been an accident surely Eoc or Bituitos would have come to tell them.
What could the council have to discuss that would take
so long? And why did she grow more uneasy with each
day her husband was gone? Boudica sighed and began to
separate the broken ends of the yarn so that she could
spit-splice them together again. It would be a little lumpy,
but the weaving could go on.

She was to remember that observation in the days after
Prasutagos came home.

When Bogle's barking brought them all out to greet the returning riders she thought at first that the king must have suffered some wound. Even when his ribs were at their worst he had not looked so gray and grim. Nessa brought him a horn of mead, and poured him another after he drank the first one down. But it was Bituitos who had to tell them the news.

"The Romans have taken our land, our grain, and our gold. Now they are taking our swords!" He saw the confusion in their faces and laughed without humor. "They want us to disarm. This governor fears that if we have weapons we will join Caratac. He has ordered everyone on this side of the border they call the *limes* to give up all weapons of war—the conquered tribes and the allied tribes as well."

"They can't," exclaimed Boudica. "We have a treaty. How can we be their allies if we cannot fight at need?"

"They can . . ." Prasutagos spoke at last. "Cohorts are already going through the Trinovante steadings, commanding men to bring out their weapons, and if they are not convinced by what is put on the pile they tear up the thatching and stab their spears into the stored grain. They will be here before the Turning of Spring."

"The soldiers who are building the fort have conscripted the local farmers as laborers to build their walls. Some of the Trinovantes are already planning rebellion. Many of our southern chieftains and princes want to join them," Eoc said fiercely. "Some are banding together in a secret group to plan resistance—they call it the Society of Ravens."

Boudica shivered, remembering how the Lady of Ravens had spoken through her long ago. If they wanted *her* as their patroness, they must be desperate indeed.

"Are we going to fight?" Temella's eyes had grown very round.

The king looked at her and tried to smile. "Whether to resist or comply is what we were discussing for so long . . ."

"You cannot give up your father's sword," Boudica exclaimed. The sword that had come down to Boudica's father had been lost with her oldest brother at the Tamesa.

With it not only his son, but also the symbol of his family's honor, had gone.

"No . . . but I see no hope in fighting Rome. We will have to give them enough to be convincing, but we will save the weapons that have been blessed by the gods."

"You will give in?" cried Lhiannon. "Don't you see that this is our chance to take back what we have lost?"

Boudica stared at her. They had lived here in peace for so long—these days Lhiannon no longer even wore blue. She had assumed that like the rest of them the priestess had become resigned to living under the yoke of Rome. But even now, Lhiannon would sometimes wake screaming from nightmares of the war in the south.

"This Roman pig is right to fear! While Caratac hits them in the west, the south and east may rise. Only when something that outrages all our people equally happens will they forget old enmities! If we had been able to get all our people fighting on the same side we would not have lost four years ago."

Lhiannon's eyes were white-rimmed; her fair hair stood on end. This was not the beloved friend but some avenging spirit that stood shrieking above the fire. The blood pulsed in Boudica's ears.

"I fear to imagine what further disaster would be required to arouse our spirit if we let this opportunity pass us by," Lhiannon added. "And if that should come to pass, what could we do? We will have no weapons to fight with, no young warriors trained to the use of arms! There will be blood! I see blood and ruin if you do not seize this chance!"

Boudica's gut clenched as she realized that this was not the mask of the invoking priestess, but the Oracle prophesying doom. She had forgotten Lhiannon's training. Perhaps the priestess had forgotten it herself.

"What does the High King say?" she asked.

Prasutagos shook his head. "Antedios is an old man, and ill. We have no war leader to match Caratac. The king is without a son, and your father, who is his tanist, is also old. The High King has ordered that we comply."

"*You* are not old," growled Lhiannon.

"Would you have me rebel against my king and the

Romans, too? We would be as divided as the southern clans."

"Shall I summon Caratac here to lead you?" she spat. "You are all old women, and you will be sorry you did not heed my words!" She stalked out the door.

Boudica stifled a burst of hysterical laughter at the image of Caratac manifesting here by the fire. Lhiannon could probably do it, given the mood she was in just now. Boudica could almost hear the fiery speeches and the fury of the mob's reply.

"Perhaps . . ." murmured Prasutagos, "but I am a king for peace, and what is needed now is a leader of war . . ."

I cannot stay here . . . thought Lhiannon.

She sat by the cauldron in the roundhouse, a veil bound across the betraying sigil on her forehead and a shawl around her shoulders, stirring the soup in the cauldron that hung above the fire. The first of the spring greens had gone into it—tender new nettles and dandelion to eke out the salted beef from their dwindling stores. But it was still winter in her soul.

She could hear the tramp of hobnailed sandals and men's deep voices outside, and the clatter of steel and bronze as swords and shields and spearheads were cast upon the pile.

I came here to get away from warfare, but this is not peace, it is death . . .

Boudica sat across from her, nursing the child. Rigana was mostly weaned, but when she was anxious she still sought her mother's breast. They winced at each clash of metal, but Lhiannon's slow fury boiled beneath a layer of ice. Prasutagos had no choice but to watch the confiscations, if only to control the fury of his men. She hoped that each sword struck him to the heart as it fell.

She started as the heavy hide that hung across the doorway was pulled aside. Light shafted across the center of the roundhouse as the Roman agent Pollio came in, backed by a legionary in a cuirass of overlapping plates like a centipede who held a round helmet with a flared neck-guard under his arm.

"I beg pardon, ladies," he said in surprisingly good British, "but my orders require me to search the house as well—"

Boudica rose to her feet, the sleeping child still in her arms. "I understand," she said sweetly, but there was a dangerous glitter in her eyes. It was just as well they had tied Bogle securely by the horse pen. He was as dangerous as any steel, if the Romans had only known.

Pollio gestured, and the soldier moved hesitantly around the hearth, lifting covers and looking under chests. Lhiannon continued to stir the stew, drawing anonymity around her like a veil.

When he touched the curtains around the bed-place, Boudica stiffened. "Don't forget the mattress! We Celts are such hardy barbarians, we sleep on spears. And why confine yourselves to the furniture?" she added. "Search here in my bosom! I might be hiding a dagger." She pulled down the front of her wrap, still unpinned from nursing, to bare a white breast. The soldier gaped and turned his back, and Pollio colored up to his hairline. "Or perhaps you would like to look in my baby's clouts to see if we have concealed a spearhead inside!"

"No, my lady, I know that you and your husband are friends to Rome," said Pollio. He muttered something to the soldier, who turned, looking relieved.

He would have seen nothing in the bed, thought Lhiannon. Were they really so naïve as to think weapons would be hidden where they could so easily be found? The legionary would not discover Prasutagos's sword unless he could handle coals as she had learned to do on Mona. They had wrapped the heirloom weapons in oiled leather and buried them deep beneath the hearth. Let the goddess who guarded the family fire keep them until the time came to use them once more.

And that day will come. As Pollio and his minion retreated Lhiannon glared at their backs. *Those swords will drink Roman blood as now we drink Roman wine . . .*

She had believed she was done with war. She had thought herself cut off from prophecy. Awareness of both stirred in her now.

I have stayed here too long . . .

* * *

*T*he strangers came limping up the track just as the sun was rising. By the time they reached the gate, Bogle's flurry of barking had awakened the entire steading. Boudica pulled a shawl over her shift and stumbled sleepily to the door, gripping the dog's collar. At her word, his barking modulated to a subliminal growl.

There were three of them, with young bodies and faces prematurely old. One had his arm in a sling. Another had a stained cloth around his head. Together they were supporting the third, whose leg bore bloody bandages from ankle to thigh.

"Lhiannon," she said over her shoulder, "come quickly. We have wounded men."

"Lady . . ." said the one with the hurt arm, "of your mercy, do you have any food, and is there a hidden place we could lie? We would not bring trouble upon you—with sunset we will be on our way—"

"That you will not!" exclaimed Boudica. "You are no more fit to travel than my little girl. Come into the house— none here would betray you, but there's no telling who may be about—you are not the first refugees to come this way." Since the order to disarm had been announced some had chosen to leave their homes rather than give in.

But these were not merely refugees fleeing a Roman advance, she thought with a sinking heart as she helped them inside. These men had seen battle, and that not long ago.

The man with the broken arm was called Mandos. He came from a small farm not far from the dun where Boudica had been born. Of his companions, the one with the knock on the head was Trinovante and the man with the wounded leg from near the coast somewhere. They had not known each other before the battle, he said. They had ended up hiding in the same thicket and had been together since then.

By the time the three were fed and washed, Prasutagos had arrived. Lhiannon was tending the man with the wounded leg, who was fevered, but the others seemed recovered enough to tell their story.

"I am glad you are here, sir," said Mandos. "The gods

know what stories are going around. I know you did not think we could win, and perhaps you were right . . ." With the grime washed off, he looked barely eighteen, two years older than Boudica's younger brother, whom she prayed her father had kept out of the rebellion.

"Perhaps," said Prasutagos quietly. "But it may be that you were right to try. What happened?"

"It should have worked!" his companion put in. "Our war leader was a man of the fens who knew the way to an old earthwork on a islet of raised land there. He figured we could lead the Romans there, where the ground would be no good for their cavalry, and wear them out as they attacked us."

Mandos nodded agreement. "But the Roman commander was a fox, too. He dismounted his men and they rushed us. The ramparts turned into a trap once the Romans were inside. We were trampling over each other, trying to get out. Some of the local people had taken refuge with us. There were old men . . . children . . . they slaughtered them all. That was four days ago." He took another drink of nettle broth. "We could only travel at night. By day the Roman patrols were hunting those who got away."

"You are safe here," said the king. "We will find households where you can stay."

Mandos shook his head, his young face grim beyond its years. "I thank you, lord. Our friend with the bad leg must certainly bide. But this Trinovante fool and I will go on until we reach a land where we are allowed to wear our swords!" He caressed the battered blade at his side. "Perhaps there will be others from the Society of Ravens there."

Boudica saw her husband wince, and this time it was she who could find no words.

Three days after the two young warriors had left, the third man died. At sunset they buried him near the Horse Shrine with his cherished sword in his hand. As they were walking back to the farmstead, a horseman came over the hill. He bore no signs of battle, but his face was grim.

"My lord Prasutagos, you are summoned to Dun Garo."

"Has the king called another council? I thought I had already made my opinion clear!"

"My lord, King Antedios is dead. It is the Roman governor who has summoned you and all the surviving chieftains of the Iceni clans."

"I suppose he died of a broken heart," said Boudica when the messenger had been sent to Palos's farm for food and rest. She started up the track to Danatobrigos and Prasutagos, who had been silent since he heard the news, followed her. "Antedios will have known most of those who fell. I probably played with some of them when I was a child." Despite Lhiannon's tales of the war in the south, it was hard to imagine that young men who should be riding horses and siring children could so easily die.

For a few minutes they walked in silence, but in the king's eyes she glimpsed the glitter of tears. "Well, don't you think so? Say something! Don't you dare turn into a stone again!"

"Don't you think my heart is wounded, too?" Prasutagos burst out suddenly. "Ever since those young men came through our gate, I've been wondering if I should have joined the rebellion, if it might have gone differently with a few wiser heads to lead them, or at least with a few more swords!"

"And it might be you lying dead in the fens if you had gone," she responded. "And then what would we do?"

He stopped in the path, his gaze following a scattering of crows as they winged across the fields. "You got along without me quite well last year and the year before," he said softly, still watching the birds. "I know that you tolerate my presence only for the sake of the child . . ."

"That isn't true!" Boudica exclaimed, and wondered suddenly when her feelings had changed. Prasutagos stood very still, head bowed, and she did not dare to break his silence. She crossed her arms across her breasts, feeling a little cold.

After a few moments, he began to walk again. "I think that if I had been there," he said in a low voice, "I might have helped them to win the battle, but we would still have lost the war. Caratac was right—the time for the tribes to unite was four years ago, before the Roman eagles had sunk their talons into this land. All we can do now is to make the best accommodation we can."

Now he stopped and faced her, a silhouette against the fading sky. "My lady, do you agree with me?"

Boudica looked at him in confusion. Why did it matter what *she* thought about anything? No doubt Lhiannon would say they should keep fighting, but she still remembered the agony in the face of that poor boy as he died. Wasn't peace, even with attendant inconveniences, better than that waste of men?

"Yes, my lord, I do."

"I must go down to Dun Garo," he said soberly. "Your father was Antedios's tanist, but he is old. Of the royal kindred I am next in blood, and I think they will try to make me king of the united tribe. The Romans will allow it only if they trust my commitment to them. I don't want this, but it may be the only way to keep what independence we have."

Isolated on the farm, until the order to disarm, Boudica had been able to pretend that it was possible to live without being troubled by Rome. But Prasutagos had not had that luxury.

"When I leave, will you come with me, Boudica?"

She could not see his eyes. She reached out to reassure herself that the words came not from a shadow but from a living man, and felt the hard muscle of his forearm quiver beneath her hand.

"I will, my husband. I promise you."

Lhiannon untied the roll of bedding and laid it out next to Boudica's. The roundhouse assigned to the queen and her women was barely large enough for them all, and none too clean, but she and Temella had managed to make it habitable. Whoever became High King, they would have to stay at least until Beltane was past.

She looked up as a shadow fell across the open doorway.

"It *is* you!" said a voice she ought to know. "Someone said you had been seen—I can hardly believe it's true!"

As Lhiannon got to her feet she recognized Belina, with the same comfortable figure, though there were new strands of gray in her hair.

"We've counted you lost these three years after Rianor reported that you had disappeared from Avalon," said the priestess. "We set a place for you at Samhain, child. We thought you dead, or gone into Faerie—don't look so surprised—you're not the first to have met the queen of that land."

"I've been serving the queen of this one." Lhiannon found her voice at last.

Belina laughed. "Come out of those shadows and let me see you, darling! Still thin as a wraith—don't they feed you in those fens? But you look healthy, Goddess bless."

Lhiannon blinked as she emerged into the light. Dun Garo buzzed like a hive as the clans continued to come in. Men were dragging in logs to build the great Beltane fire in the meadow. Tents had sprouted in colorful disarray all over the farther pastures. On the other side of the river a palisade enclosed the neat rows of leather tents that housed the Roman governor and his men, a mute but eloquent reminder that although the clan fathers might elect their new High King, they had better not acclaim anyone not approved by Rome.

"But you don't need to wear that band across your brow." Belina plucked at the scarf Lhiannon had tied to cover the crescent of Avalon. "Even if they knew what it means, the Roman pigs don't care what women do. And so far, no one has tried to enforce the ban on the Druid Order here."

Lhiannon wondered if Belina had always chattered so, or did she need the words to cover her emotion at this unexpected reunion?

"We should have expected that you would go to Boudica," the other woman went on. "She was always your pet when she was at the school."

"What are you doing here?" Lhiannon got a word in at last. "Who else has come? Is Helve—"

"Oh no! Surely you don't think our beloved High Priestess would risk herself among the enemy, though she is willing enough to send the rest of us out to foment rebellion here—the other senior priestesses, that is."

Lhiannon laughed. It sounded as if little had changed. "Is that what you are here for? You'll have no luck among the Iceni—their teeth are well and truly drawn, and Prasutagos is not a man to risk what he still has," she added bitterly. The king had not listened when her arguments might still have done some good. Now they did not speak at all.

"Does he cling so to power?" asked Belina.

"Not to power," Lhiannon answered honestly. "To peace. Boudica would make a better war leader than he would, had she been a man."

Belina nodded. "But will she make a queen? There is more to conferring kingship than an election. The transfer of sovereignty is women's business. It is best if the queen can do the rite, but we did not know if Boudica would be able. How much does she remember of what she was taught at the school?"

Lhiannon lowered her eyes. "We have not discussed it."

Of late, Boudica and Prasutagos had seemed easier in one another's company, but she still did not sleep with him, even though the child was weaned. If Boudica did not share his power, could Prasutagos truly reign? Did that matter, now that the true power lay with Rome? And what was left here for Lhiannon, if Boudica did take her place at her husband's side?

"What other commands have you brought from Lys Deru?" she asked.

Belina shrugged. "From Helve, you mean. Lugovalos is failing, and she gives the orders now. I was told to raise what support I might for Caratac. The governor is sending his legions too close to the north and west for comfort."

"Do they threaten Mona?" Lhiannon asked in alarm.

"He knows it is the Druid stronghold," answered Belina. "He knows that Mona has some of the richest land in Britannia, and that with grain or with magic we will support anyone who is willing to fight. He would have to be stupid not to know that while we stand, his hold on Britannia will never be secure."

"The Romans are not stupid," Lhiannon said slowly. "But this is a big island. If we keep worrying at them, they may decide it would be foolish to keep on wasting resources and men . . ."

"You've lost none of your wits." Belina gave her an approving hug. "Whether it is I or Boudica who does the honors, you should leave with me when the inauguration is done." Both women looked up as a sudden commotion rose from the direction of the council fire before the High King's hall.

"After the king-making . . ." Lhiannon said slowly, "I will give you my answer then."

People were beginning to hurry past as the noise grew louder.

"Prasutagos son of the hazel, Prasutagos son of the sun, Prasutagos son of the plow, Prasutagos Ricon, Iceni king!" came the cry.

SIXTEEN

*T*urn, my lady, and lift your arm—"

Boudica complied, controlling a twitch at the feather-touch of the brush with which the old woman was painting a series of spirals along her side. Her breathing was slow and steady. Her pulse throbbed to the vibration beneath her feet, the heartbeat of the Beltane drums.

Rays of setting sun filtered through the roughly woven curtains with which they had walled and roofed the women's enclosure, scattering flickers of ruddy light across the grass. The mask of the White Mare hung from the center post, waiting to play its role in her transformation. Through the cloth walls the noise of the festival came oddly muted, as if this space were separated from the world.

As I am from my former self . . . she thought slowly. *Waiting to learn what I will be . . .* To endure the tedium of the body painting she had drawn on the disciplines she had learned at Mona; she sat as motionless as the image into which the painting was transforming her. Her naked back and belly already bore the running figures of the Hare and the Boar, the Wolf and the Eagle, Ram and Bull and Bear, with a wealth of horses twining among them, totems that the incoming Celts had inherited from the peoples whom they had conquered.

In the Earth-ring, Prasutagos would be receiving the blessings of the Druids who had witnessed the oaths of the chieftains. When Romans were present the priests went disguised. As long as they did not bring themselves to the attention of the conquerors, the current policy seemed to be to ignore them.

But the Horse Queen who blessed the Beltane rites was the priestess of an older magic. The Druids consecrated the king to the tribe. The Goddess linked him to the land on which they lived. Boudica did not yet know if she *could* submit to so overwhelming an energy. Belina was prepared to step in, but if Boudica failed she suspected it would mean the end of her marriage.

A part of her mind lay immobilized within her body, its panicked yammerings suppressed by the same discipline that held her limbs. This time, she thought, she could not ride the red mare to freedom. This time, the White Mare would be riding *her*.

"All done," said the old woman. Slowly she lowered her arm.

"Come back, my darling." Lhiannon's face appeared before her. "You can rule your limbs now. Breathe in and out and in and out again. That is right—you are here with me and soon the ritual will begin. Return!"

Boudica blinked as sensation rippled through her, aware of the stiff paint on her skin, the women's chatter suddenly loud in her ears. The sun had set; she was surrounded by shadows. She shivered. The king's procession would be coming soon.

"No!" Nessa was saying to someone at the entrance. "You may not see her. This space is forbidden to men, especially you! Go away before I call the warriors to throw you in the midden—for that they will need no swords!"

"Who is it?" Boudica called.

"No one you need to care about," muttered the old woman, sighing as she met Boudica's glare. "It's that Pollio . . . he says he must speak with you."

Her first annoyance gave way to alarm. "I'll talk to him," she said in a low voice. "Lhiannon, keep these others out of earshot until I am done." She stepped to the curtain.

"What is it? You must speak quickly," she murmured through the cloth.

"Let me see your face, Boudica," came the familiar Atrebate accent.

"Goddess, no!" She flushed with sudden awareness of her naked body. "In the old days they would have staked you out for the wolves for coming even this close to the women's sanctuary."

"You don't have to do this!" Pollio's words came in a rush. "It's known that you refuse your husband your bed—you don't have to let him lie with you now. It will make no difference. Prasutagos is king because Rome supports him, not because of some barbarous ritual."

"What are you talking about?" Since that day in the snow when he had tried to kiss her she had scarcely seen the man, and never alone. Had he been building up some fantasy in which she loved him all this time?

"Leave your husband! Come away with me!" he hissed. "You are a princess of the royal house—I could make you a ruling queen like Cartimandua!"

"You are mad!" she said with conviction. "And this is sacrilege!"

"I love you, Boudica! I know that you are not indifferent to me!"

"Indeed not," she answered with leashed fury. "A man who would tempt the wife of an ally to betray her marriage can only be despised! Is this the honor they teach in Rome?"

No matter that she had been tempted to flee herself—she would never have gone with this pig of a Roman! And in that moment Boudica realized that her ambivalence had disappeared.

"But my lady—" His words were cut off as the golden blare of the carynx horn reverberated through the evening air.

"They are coming! They will kill you if they find you here. Be gone and be damned to you, Roman! This warning is the last word you will have from me!"

She heard a rustle of retreating footsteps as the horns called again and stepped back, breathing quickly.

"What did he want?" asked Lhiannon.

"Nothing that matters," Boudica muttered, glad that the dim light hid the blush that was warming her cheeks. Lhiannon was the last person to whom she wanted to reveal the shameful proposition the Roman had made.

Outside, drums boomed, commanding attention. The deep voices of the Druids rose and fell, closer and closer, then passing as the king was escorted to his place of honor near the fire. There was more at stake here than a ceremony. If Belina acted as priestess tonight, she would be linked to the king only while the Goddess was present. But for Boudica to take that role would admit Prasutagos as well as Epona into her heart. Boudica felt an anticipatory shiver pebble her skin. Lhiannon brought a white cloak and draped it over her shoulders against the cooling air. The door curtain moved and she saw her mother there.

"Oh, my daughter, you are so beautiful—even more than on your wedding day," Anaveistl said with a tremulous smile. "I just wanted to see you, and now I will be getting back to the house and our darling little girl—"

Boudica patted the older woman's hand. Upon meeting her granddaughter, Anaveistl had become instantly besotted. Rigana could ask for no more devoted guardian.

"What is happening now?" she asked as her mother departed.

"The king has been seated," answered Belina. "I think it is dark enough now to open the curtain a little. If you sit here, you can see—"

One of the Druids knelt to set the fire he had carried from the Earth-ring to the stacked wood in the center; a great shout went up as it burst into flame. The drummers let loose with a thunder of sound as a line of young men came dancing around it, armed with staves.

There should have been more of them, thought Boudica sadly. These were the younger brothers of men who had died at the battle in the fens. But they twirled and struck valiantly. Was Prasutagos thinking the same thing? He looked tired, but his features displayed his usual calm control. As they must, she realized, if he was to rule. Gold rings gleamed from his strong arms, a golden torque circled his neck. They had garbed him in a kilt and cloak in the ancient style. She had never noticed that his legs were as muscular and well shaped as his arms.

Well, when would I have had the chance? she thought with a flush of shame, and something more. A flicker of excitement warmed her at the realization that she was free to look at him all she pleased, and he could not see.

Now some of the girls slipped out of the women's enclosure to join the line of maidens who were tracing sinuous patterns around the fire. They were crowned with haw-thorn, and as they grew heated by the dancing, first one and then another undid the pins that held her garment at the shoulders so that it was held up only by her woven belt, leaving white breasts bare.

Someone brought Boudica a cup of wine; she felt the warmth in her limbs, and in her head a regular pulsing that matched that of the drums.

The young men returned to circle around the maidens, dancing forward until they almost touched, then whirling away once more. Eyes grew bright and faces flushed with more than the heat of the fire. Prasutagos was smiling. Did she imagine that the pulse at the base of his throat was beating more quickly, or was that only the throb she felt in her own?

This festival was not only to honor the new king but to welcome in the summer, and to do all that men might to encourage a bountiful year. Boudica cast a glance toward Lhiannon, remembering how the older woman had hoped to meet Ardanos at the Beltane fires. Child that she was, she had not understood the message of the drums. Her flesh comprehended it now.

They thundered in a final flourish; man and maid joined hands and ran laughing into the darkness. Suddenly the circle was still.

"It is time . . ." said Lhiannon very evenly, as if she, too, were fighting for control.

"It is time indeed—" Belina turned to Boudica. "Are you ready, my dear?"

Boudica could not have found words, but her body was responding for her. She got to her feet. She reached out to take the mask of the White Mare from the priestess' hand. She settled the molded leather over her head, where her hair had been coiled to support it, and Lhiannon reached up to secure the ties. The neck of the mask extended down the back of her head to her shoulders, while the head hid her face, cheekpieces curving down to frame her own while the muzzle projected forward. Real horsehair had been added to form a mane.

"Now . . ." Lhiannon's voice seemed to come from a very long way away. "Now you are a queen . . ."

Boudica scarcely noticed the leather's weight. As the mask enclosed her head, she felt a corresponding pressure within her skull that pushed the self she thought her own into some space from which she could only watch in terror and amazement as her body jerked like a young horse fighting the rein. How many queens had borne this crown? They were all here, whispering, their voices blending into a single Voice.

"Is it time to run?" came the question. *"Is it time to dance?"*

Tremors ran downward along her spine, out her flailing arms, down strong legs to feet that stamped and struck the earth. She reeled, and soft hands pushed her upright again. The mane tossed as she shook her head, breath exploded from her lungs with a sound that was halfway between a laugh and a neigh. She tried to fight, as she had tried to fight the Morrigan. This goddess was both wilder and more benign, but She was just as strong.

"You already know Me, my daughter, why are you afraid? Don't you remember how you rode the red mare?"

And as Boudica recalled that wild ride through the moonlight, past and present, rider and ridden, became one. When she was a little girl she had begged her father for a pony, and ridden her own galloping legs around the dun until he complied. Her body already knew the motions. Letting the cloak fall from Her shoulders, She swept the curtain aside and paced toward the fire.

A whisper of awe swept around the circle, louder than the flutes and rattles that had finally remembered to play. "The goddess is with us . . . Epona has come to us . . . the goddess comes to the king . . ."

The totems of every clan rippled as muscles slid beneath white skin. She turned, arms extended, embracing them all. Women were weeping, men's eyes shone with a hope that had not been there before. She took Her time, for these people had suffered and had need of Her love. Once, twice, thrice, She paced around the circle, blessing Her tribe, and then at last She came to a halt before the king.

Prasutagos's calm had shattered. On his cheeks shone the silver track of tears, in his eyes an astonished joy. The

molded mask bowed before him, lifted with a shake of the
mane. A quiver ran through Her body; She twisted, pre-
senting Herself like a mare. But She was also a woman.
She turned back to him, offering the firm breasts that had
suckled his child, ran Her hands across Boudica's belly,
outlining the womb that had received his seed.

"Come!" came the command in a voice that both was
and was not Boudica's own.

The king stood, fumbling with the golden clasp of his
belt, and let the wrapped kilt fall away. Already his phal-
lus was engorged and rising. Was it the ritual, or was he
really more generously endowed than other men? The
people shouted out their approval as he stepped toward
her. As She was the goddess, he stood before them as the
image of the god.

"Come and serve Me," She whispered. Power jolted
through them both as he took Her hand.

A path was opening through the crowd before them.
Beyond, the plowed field waited to become their bed.

I wish that you were not leaving us," said Boudica, picking up the traveling cloak that Lhiannon had just shaken
out and folding it up again. At Dun Garo the queen and
her women had a sun-house for their own activities, built
in a ring whose center was open to the sky. The light was
welcome, but the company of so many chattering women
grated on Lhiannon's nerves. But there was room here to
pack the many things that the queen had insisted she and
Belina must take on their journey.

"We need you here, Lhiannon. We need your healing
and your wisdom," Boudica continued.

*If you had said, "I need you here, Lhiannon," I might
stay . . .* she thought sadly.

"You are no longer alone on a farmstead," she said
aloud. "You have healers and wise men and warriors in
plenty here in Dun Garo. It is time I became a priestess
once more." She rescued the cloak from the queen's nervous fingers and draped it over one arm.

"Most Druids live at chieftains' duns, not at the school,"
Boudica replied. "If you want to cram wisdom into the

heads of youngsters, stay here and smack some sense into Rigana!" That morning the little girl had managed to elude her keepers. Her short legs had carried her to the blacksmiths' enclave before they heard Bogle barking and found her screaming because the dog would not let her reach the fire.

"For the kind of warding she needs right now Bogle is a better guardian than I could ever be," answered Lhiannon. She bent to strap up her bag. "My dear, this is not forever. I will visit, and when she is older, you may send Rigana to be trained as you were trained . . ." *If there is still a school for her to go to,* came the thought. But wasn't she leaving so that she might do what she could to preserve the life they had known?

"Yes, but . . ." Boudica's words trailed off. Lhiannon looked up and saw that the king had entered. The queen turned toward him as a flower turns toward the sun. Ever since Beltane it had been so. The marriage had at long last been consummated not only in the flesh but in the spirit. The girl was become a woman, priestess to her husband as well as queen.

No, I am leaving because she no longer needs me, Lhiannon admitted to herself as Boudica moved into the circle of Prasutagos's arm. What had she hoped—that having lost the man she loved, she might find a substitute in Boudica, and still retain her virginity? Lhiannon knew quite well that it was not the physical contact but the emotional bond it created that was the distraction for an oracle. By that alone she was disqualified. *I must recover my own sovereignty.*

"Lhiannon, are you ready?" Belina called from the doorway.

She picked up her bag. Prasutagos and Boudica came to embrace her—together. They would always be together now.

"My lady, I thank you for all you have done . . ." murmured the king.

"Lhiannon—" Boudica's voice broke. "Take care! Take care!"

She had no words. She kissed them both and walked out into the blinding light of the sun.

*   *   *

*B*oudica leaned on the rail at the top of the fence around the home meadow of Dun Garo, watching Roud move gracefully across the grass, her chestnut coat shining in the sun. The mare would pause to snatch a mouthful, then flirtatiously switch her tail, looking back to see if the king's gray stallion was following. Boudica had not realized that the red mare was coming into season. She wondered how long it would take the stallion to get her in foal.

And how long will it take Prasutagos to do the same to me? At the thought, she could feel the heat flushing her skin. Her recollections of the Beltane rite were fragmentary, but to recall the authority with which her husband had taken her every night since then left her liquid with longing. And as if the thought had summoned him, senses she had never owned before told Boudica that the king was approaching now.

She turned her head and smiled a welcome, wondering that she could ever have watched that springy walk without wanting his strong body close to hers, or looked into those rugged features without wishing to make him smile.

"Well met, my lady." His lips quirked as he realized what was going on. "The king and queen are expected to bring fertility to the kingdom, but I had not supposed the effect would be quite so immediate."

Laughing, Boudica twitched her hips as the mare was doing now and took a step back so that her buttocks butted against his groin. She felt him hardening against her and moved quickly away again. She had danced naked before all the tribe at the Beltane rite, but she could not do so here.

"That was . . . wise," he said a little breathlessly. "The king should demonstrate self-control as well as virility, and if I touch you, in another moment I'll have you on your knees in the grass . . ."

"Yes . . ." she said in a shaken voice, agreeing to more than desire. He took a deep breath and met her gaze. They were no longer touching, but she felt him as powerfully as if he had been inside her. This was not lust, or not lust only. "What has happened to us?"

Prasutagos swallowed. Whatever it was, he, too, was in its thrall. "Between a king and a queen there should be regard and respect," he said, as if it were a teaching he had memorized. "I never dared to hope . . ."

"For love . . ." she breathed, allowing herself to recognize and accept it at last. She saw his face grow radiant as he realized that for both of them this was forgiveness for what had gone before and a promise for what was to come.

I owe an apology, thought Boudica, *to the spirit of the sacred spring . . .*

Lhiannon bent to fill her waterskin, suppressing an impulse to take off her shoes and soak her feet in the pool. Her horse had gone lame that morning and she had walked, leading it, for the rest of the day. A few rags of cloth fluttered from the birch trees that grew around the water. The local people who had given them milk and cheese called the place Vernemeton, the holy grove. It would not do to offend the spirit of the spring.

She sat back, breathing deeply of the cool, damp air. There was great peace here. She wished that she could stay for a while. She tried to tell herself that it was because she was wearied by travel, but the longer she journeyed in the company of Belina and the other Druids who had joined their party as they made their way across Britannia, the more she remembered why she and Ardanos had been glad to get away.

The moon that had been waning when the little party of Druids left Dun Garo had passed the full and was beginning to shrink once more. In the old days it would have been a somewhat shorter journey, but the Romans were patrolling the territory of their allies in the midlands more closely than expected, in case Caratac and the Ordovice warriors should attack again.

She sighed and got to her feet as Belina called her name. The others had a fire blazing already. Lhiannon poured her water into the cauldron and Belina dropped in the loosely woven bag of dried meat and meal. Two of the Druids were arguing about ways to calculate the dates of the festivals. They were both old men from newly conquered lands, leaving the clans they had served for fear of the Roman ban. What would the people do for spiritual leadership if all the Druids sought sanctuary on Mona? What would the Romans do, she wondered uneasily, when they realized that was where all the Druids had gone?

By the time the food was ready it was quite dark. The overgrown ramparts of the abandoned hillfort above them loomed against the stars. These days it served the region as a site for the seasonal fairs and festivals. Lhiannon hoped that was all it would ever need to be. The last few years had given her a distaste for hillforts—it was too easy for those walls to trap those whom they were supposed to defend.

"And Lugovalos is certain that the Romans will not come to Mona?" asked one of the men.

"Is anything certain, except, possibly, Helve's prophecies?" asked Belina. "But they can only come at us by the coast path, and that will be hard to manage with so many men."

"But if they do," the old man persisted, "can the Arch-Druid defend us? I have heard that his health has been poor."

"The past few years have been hard on him, as they have been on us all," Belina said patiently, serving out the porridge.

"If he does pass, who can succeed him? Cunitor is senior, but he is not very forceful, as I recall."

"I suppose the choice would fall on Ardanos, but we will hope that the need is long delayed."

Lhiannon blinked as the world became a whirl of darkness shot with fire. A burning pain on her thigh brought her back to awareness and she realized that she had dropped her porridge bowl. She swabbed at the mess rather clumsily with her sleeve.

"Lhiannon, are you all right?" Belina was beside her with a cloth.

"I'm sorry," she said numbly. "I didn't mean to waste the food. Ardanos—" She drew a shuddering breath. She would not admit she had thought him dead all this time. "I last saw him when the Dun of Stones fell. I am glad . . . he escaped."

"Oh of course, you have been so out of touch you wouldn't know that. He was wounded and left for dead, it's true, but he is fine now. He'll be glad to see you," she added brightly. "He went around with a face like a sour apple for months, thinking you were lost. I had forgotten that you two worked together when Caratac was leading the Durotriges. I know you were quite close," she chattered on.

Close . . . thought Lhiannon. *As close as blood and breath. He is alive, and I will see him soon!*

As they rounded the granite cliff Lhiannon took a sharp breath, shivering as the cold salt scent for a moment gave way to the sweet verdant breath of the island beyond, a promise of sanctuary in the gray domain of the sea. Past the trees she could see the blue waters of the strait and the island of Mona, a magic island surrounded by magic, glimmering golden in the afternoon sun.

She shivered again as the wind grew stonger. Fits of trembling had seized her at intervals ever since she learned that Ardanos was alive. Belina had dosed her for the ague and Lhiannon did not gainsay her, though she knew this was no illness of the body but a symptom of the turmoil within.

Would Ardanos have changed? Would he look older? Would she? They had lost so much time, wasted so many opportunities. She had seen in the fulfillment that Boudica had finally found what a true marriage could be. She would be the Goddess to Ardanos, and they would renew the world.

As one in a dream she reined her pony after the others down the path. A flat-bottomed boat was drawn up at the landing. Lhiannon went across with the second load. By the time they rode through the gates of Lys Deru the entire community had gathered. There were more than she remembered, priests and priestesses who had fled before the Roman advance. She did not envy the job Helve must have to keep them all fed and occupied.

Still on her horse, Lhiannon searched the crowd for Ardanos's ginger head. The crowd was parting as the High

Priestess herself came out to welcome them, Coventa, taller but otherwise little changed, a half-pace behind. And behind her a gaggle of others, but only one whose face had meaning for Lhiannon. As Helve moved forward he stopped, looked up, and met her searching gaze.

His lips moved, but there was no sound. All the color drained from his face. A woman reached out to hold him as he swayed. But by then, Lhiannon was off the pony and running toward him.

"Lhiannon," came Helve's voice from behind her. "What a miracle to have you among us again! As you can see, our community has acquired many new members. Ardanos—you must introduce your wife and child . . ."

For the first time, Lhiannon looked at the woman who was supporting him. Long, fair hair was knotted underneath a scarf. A green tunic covered a figure that had probably become more matronly with the birth of the towheaded two-year-old who clung to her skirts.

"Nay, my man is too flummoxed to say a word, and he a trained bard!" the woman exclaimed in the accent of the Durotrige tribe. "I am Sciovana, and this here is our daughter, Rheis. He has told me so much about you, my lady—I know it must be a wonder to him to see you alive!"

That speech had saved both of them, thought Lhiannon as she looked from Ardanos, who was fighting to regain his composure, to Helve, who watched with what seemed a malicious smile. She could not scream at this woman who was beaming at her with such welcome, and she would not afford Helve the satisfaction of knowing that her little surprise had wounded Lhiannon as deeply as she could have desired.

Coventa came up beside her. "Lhiannon, you must be exhausted by your journey," she said softly. "Come, we should put your things away—after dinner will be time enough to catch up with old friends . . ."

*I*t was true that it was easier to face most things on a full belly, thought Lhiannon, though she had not expected Coventa to know that.

"I am surprised you are still in plain linen." She indicated the undyed maiden's tunic that the girl wore. "I would have expected to see you in priestess-blue by now."

Coventa shrugged. "I am ready, but Helve has judged the roads too dangerous to make the journey to my homeland after the ceremony at Avalon. Perhaps next year, if things settle down."

Well, that might be the reason. But there could be others. Coventa had always been delicate. Now she looked positively ethereal, as if she would not need to be in trance to visit the Otherworld.

"Have you been well, child?" she asked.

"Oh, safe as I have been here on the island, how could I be otherwise?" Coventa said cheerfully. "It is you who have been having the adventures . . ."

She had made up a bed for Lhiannon in the House of Priestesses and helped her to arrange her few belongings, and she had brought a bowl of barley and greens from the central fire so that she could eat in peace.

"When you are in the midst of the story, the danger is more apparent than the adventure," Lhiannon said wryly. "Such moments are much better experienced secondhand in a bard's tale by the fire."

"Not all the good stories are about terrors," observed Coventa. She sat down cross-legged on the end of Lhiannon's bed. "Tell me all about Boudica. I miss her so much. Is it really true that she ran away from her husband on their wedding night?"

Lhiannon shook her head in wonder that the tale should have traveled this far. "She did, but they are very happy together now—"

She sighed, reminded that for a few short days she had hoped to find a similar joy, and as if the thought had summoned him, she heard Ardanos's voice outside the door.

"Is Lhiannon there? Is she rested enough to come for a walk with me?"

Coventa looked inquiringly at Lhiannon, who got to her feet and reached for a shawl. She had known they would have to have this conversation sometime. Afterward she could forget her dreams, or if that proved impossible, throw herself into the sea.

The sun had set, but so close to midsummer the sky still glowed with no visible source of light. It reminded her of the light in the Faerie world. As they crossed the fire circle Lhiannon saw that more huts had been built around it. The carved gateposts were the same, like the trees that arched over the path to the Sacred Grove. And yet to her they looked strange, as the man who walked beside her was a stranger, limping a little as they moved down the path.

"Your child is very sweet, and your wife seems both good-natured and kind," she said politely.

"Lhiannon, I thought you were dead!" Ardanos answered the question behind her words. "Swords were swinging all around you, and then I was struck down. I thought I was dead myself. The Romans thought so, too, or I would be a slave in Gallia by now. They tossed me on a heap of corpses, and if I had not been found by people from the nearest farmstead looking for some of their own men I would have been food for the ravens."

She said nothing. The Sacred Grove lay before them. By unspoken agreement they paused just outside.

"Sciovana's family took me in," he continued. "I had lost a great deal of blood and taken a fever. She nursed me, and when I lay raving with grief and pain, she held me in her arms."

Not enough pain to keep you from taking advantage of her generosity, thought Lhiannon.

"I didn't know what I was doing, but when I came to myself and realized that I had got the girl with child, I was willing enough to marry her. What did it matter, if you were lost to me?"

Could she blame him, she wondered, remembering how she had sought comfort with Boudica? If Boudica had loved her as Sciovana did Ardanos, she would not have been here at all. But here she was, and her own pain left her with little sympathy for his.

He stared at her, tears in his eyes. "My love is a girl with hair like the yellow flag," he whispered. "Soft as the breast of the swan . . ." He swallowed and took her hand. "You are a priestess, Lhiannon, as Sciovana can never be. In the great rites we can still come together, priest and priestess, raising the power!"

"You have everything figured, I see!" Lhiannon jerked her hand away. "One woman for the altar, and one for the hearth. How very convenient! But I have not stayed virgin so long to become your magical mistress! Go back to your wife, Ardanos! She seems a good woman and deserves better, but it would appear that she loves you . . ."

He tried to hold her, but with a quick twist, she was running back down the path. She did not stop until she reached the House of Priestesses, where she collapsed, weeping, in Coventa's arms.

SEVENTEEN

"Helve asks if you will attend her this afternoon," said Coventa. Spring had come at last to the island, and the soft wind stirred her fair hair.

"My child, you lie." Lhiannon looked up from the quern in which she was grinding grain and smiled. "Helve does not send requests to her inferiors. You were supposed to bring me her *command* ..."

"Well, yes—" Coventa blushed. "But she speaks that way because she thinks her dignity requires it. Truly, she can be very kind."

To you, perhaps, thought Lhiannon. If a belief in Helve's goodness made the young woman feel better about her own position here, it would have been cruel to deprive her of it, especially now, when Helve had transferred her affection to a new girl called Nodona. Except for the fact that her hair was dark, she reminded Lhiannon strongly of what Coventa had been like when she was very young.

"You may tell the High Priestess that I will come."

She scooped another handful of grain into the hole at the top of the upper quern stone, grasped the use-polished stick that served as handle, and began to push it around once more. It was hard work of a kind that she should have delegated to someone like Sciovana, but the repetitive motion had a mind-numbing effect that helped her get through the days.

Before going to Helve, however, Lhiannon took the time to wash and change into a clean tunica. She was glad she had done so when she saw that the High Priestess was not alone. Lugovalos and Belina, Cunitor and Ardanos, and a selection of the more senior Druids who had taken refuge on Mona were also there.

Coventa did not tell me that this was a council—perhaps because Helve feared I might refuse to attend, she thought wryly, though it wasn't true that she avoided Ardanos's company entirely: she only refused to see him alone. She settled into place beside Belina with an armored smile.

"Welcome, my sister—you complete our circle," said Lugovalos kindly. If he was aware of the undercurrents he gave no sign as he went on. "I have called you all here because we have learned that the governor is planning to attack the Deceangli."

"To attack *us*, you mean," put in Divitiac, who had been chief Druid to the Durotriges before the Romans came. He had been spirited away as the legions were marching into Tancoric's dun, and his limbs trembled, though his mind was still strong. "Whatever toleration the Romans had for us is ended. The new governor is killing those of our Order wherever he finds them. We are all that remain, and the Deceangli guard the path around the north coast that any invader must take to come here."

"We must flee!" whispered a priestess who had been with the Belgae, and sometimes woke sobbing in the night from nightmares. "We must take ship for Eriu. The Irish Druids are strong and will welcome us."

"And where will we go after that—the Blessed Isles?" asked Cunitor with grim humor.

"One way or another we will all come there in the end," murmured Belina.

"If we run now we will never stop," objected Cunitor. "Caratac is still fighting, and there are still tribes that have not bent the knee to Rome. If we can stir them up to rebellion, the Romans will leave the Deceangli alone."

For now, thought Lhiannon, but she did not say so aloud.

"My kin among the Brigante clans are not happy with Cartimandua's friendship with the Romans," Cunitor said. "Perhaps I can persuade them that now is the time to make their feelings known . . ."

"Caratac needs to know that we are behind him," said Lugovalos.

"I will go to him," said Ardanos. "I have worked with him before."

"You are still recovering from your wounds, and you have a family," Helve said firmly. "You are needed here."

I can see where this is going, thought Lhiannon. *No doubt she and Lugovalos decided on this course before the rest of us arrived.* But she had no desire to resist their manipulation. She had endured the constriction of winter, but she did not think she could bear to be in the same place as Ardanos when all the world rejoiced at the coming of spring.

"Send me—" She smiled blandly at Helve. "Caratac saved me from death or worse. I owe him what help I can give."

"I will go with her," came another voice. She looked up in surprise as she recognized Brangenos, a shade more gray and thin, but otherwise unchanged. "A wandering bard passes everywhere, and I have training as a healer as well."

Lhiannon frowned. She remembered how he had sung for King Togodumnos before the battle on the Tamesa. And she had heard of him among the Durotriges when Vespasian was laying waste to their lands. A bird of ill omen was this raven son. *What disasters do you expect to celebrate when we are with Caratac, bard?*

"That is settled, then. And we will ask among the younger priests to carry word elsewhere..." rumbled Lugovalos.

As the others rose to take their leave, Helve beckoned to Lhiannon.

"We have never been friends," said the High Priestess when they were alone. "But believe me when I say that I am not sending you on this mission to get rid of you."

No? wondered Lhiannon. *I thought it might be because I threaten your influence on Coventa.* She continued to smile.

"Whatever rivalry divided us in the past, we must work together now," Helve went on. "You have great abilities, and the Goddess knows how badly we need every man and woman of power! I have no choice but to employ whatever tools I have, regardless of the cost. Neither you nor I matter, nor Ardanos, nor Coventa, nor Lugovalos, if by sacrifice we can save our tradition."

Lhiannon opened her awareness a little and was surprised to sense only sincerity. Helve believed what she was saying, and it might even be true. Perhaps she was growing into her job.

"I understand." For the first time she accorded the High Priestess a respectful nod.

"Stay safe, Lhiannon, and come back to us when your task is done."

*B*oudica dreamed that she was walking on a narrow path through thickly forested hills, surrounded by men who carried swords. Their clothing was grimed with mud and blood, a fanatical glint lit their eyes. Before her marched Lhiannon, as dirty as any of the others, but looking fit and hard.

In the valley below lay a farmstead. Silently the warriors surrounded it. She glimpsed Caratac among them. As someone lit a torch his golden torque gleamed. They leaped to the attack, shrilling Silure war cries. Men ran out of the houses. Women screamed as the thatch caught fire. Soon there was more blood, and bodies lying on the ground. And then the attackers were retreating, some carrying livestock or sacks of grain. As they went by, Lhiannon turned and seemed to see Boudica at last.

"So shall we serve all who bend the knee to Rome . . ."

*B*oudica realized she had been weeping when she opened her eyes and saw her husband's worried frown. It must be morning. The door of their house at Teutodunon was open, and sunlight was filtering through the red-and-yellow striped curtains that surrounded the bed place.

"You cried out—are you in pain?"

"A nightmare," she mumbled, wiping her eyes. "It's already going," she lied, for she knew that she would remember this dream. Her youngest brother Braci and Caratac's brother Epilios had joined the rebellion the year before.

But in the dream the Britons seemed to be winning. If Lhiannon had been here she would have asked her for an interpretation. Had the priestess sent the dream, and if so was it a reproof or a warning?

"Come here and kiss the nightmare away." She pulled him back down, fitting her body against his in the way that had become accustomed in the two years since she had truly been his queen. He chuckled and nuzzled her neck, one hand sliding across her breast. She could feel his content, and his desire. Why had it taken her so long to realize that Prasutagos was most eloquent when he was silent?

"Mama, Papa! Bogle's got a hare!"

Prasutagos rolled away as the curtains were jerked back and a redheaded blur bounced onto the bed between them. Boudica blinked and reached out in an attempt to hold her daughter still.

"He caught it out on the heath an' brought it home. The puppies are fighting over it now!"

Boudica exchanged an exasperated look with her husband, who laughed and eased out of the bed, feeling around for the tunic he had stripped off so unceremoniously the night before. What did it mean, she wondered, when your clan totem was hunted down by your dog? It was bound to happen, she supposed, if they allowed Bogle and his numerous offspring to range the heathlands while they were in residence at her father's old dun.

"Rigana! Rigana—is the child there with you?"

Prasutagos hastily pulled his tunic the rest of the way down as Boudica's mother hurried in.

"I'm so sorry, dears, did she wake you?" her mother said. "She runs so fast, you know."

"Yes. It's all right, Mama," said Boudica. "I was getting up anyway."

"I thought you might be," said the older woman. "The smith is here already with the new coins for the king to approve." Since Boudica's father died, Anaveistl had coped fairly well, but sometimes she forgot that she was no longer the queen.

Boudica hugged Rigana, delighting in the firm limbs and the flower scent of her hair. "Is your little sister awake, sprout?" The two girls slept with their grandmother and their nurses in the next roundhouse, close enough so that Boudica could hear if someone cried.

As if the question had been a signal, Nessa came through the door leading Argantilla, who had just begun to toddle, by the hand. Smiling like a sunrise, the smaller girl, as golden and gentle as her sister was fiery and active, clambered into the bed to join Rigana for a morning snuggle before their parents were distracted by the demands of the day.

Breakfast beneath the spreading branches of the oak tree was a time to receive reports and plan the day. This morning they had silver coins with their porridge—the first of the new issue bearing a Roman-style image of the ruler on one side, and the legend *"Subri Esvprasto Esico Fecit,"* with the horse totem of the Iceni, on the other. Esico might have minted them for Prasutagos, but far too many of those coins would have to go to the Romans in taxes. Others might be paid to chieftains who had collected produce from their clans to feed the Romans' never-ending need for supplies.

Esico the coiner, a little dark man with missing teeth and an air of confidence that came from knowing his skills would be needed whoever was in power, also traded in information. His first offering was the news that the governor, finding his resources overstretched, was moving the Twentieth Legion from Camulodunum to a place near the head of the Sabrina estuary where they could keep an eye on the Silures.

"They are withdrawing all their forces from the Trinovante lands?" asked Prasutagos.

"Not exacthly," lisped Esico. "They mean to turn the fort into a Roman-type town and fill it with old tholdierth. 'Victory colony,' they call it." He spat out the words. "Already they levy men to help with the building—an' with harvetht coming on—" He shook his head. "The Trinovante ain't happy, but what can they do?"

What can any of us do, thought Boudica, *but carry on?*

"Romans set great store on impressive buildings . . ." Prasutagos said slowly as Esico departed. "They consider them a mark of civilization." Boudica eyed him suspiciously, recognizing the enthusiastic gleam in his eye.

"The Romans will never allow us to build fortifications. Just what," she added carefully, "did you have in mind?"

"Nothing in stone . . ." he said quickly. "Nothing they'd consider a threat. But I was remembering the way the Romans put a second story on their houses, and I think we could build a roundhouse that way, with two tiers." Boudica blinked. She could not imagine what he was talking about, but it was obvious that Prasutagos could see it clearly. "We'll clear out some of the buildings in the enclosure—move the weaving sheds into an adjacent yard and give the mint its own wall. Make a nice neat bank and ditch around the house here."

"Do you mean to challenge King Cogidubnos?" She laughed. "At Noviomagus he's building a Roman palace."

He shook his head. "This will be purely Celtic, just . . . bigger." He grinned.

Boudica sighed. The rise on which Teutodunon lay was high enough to give her a good view of the river, with the heathland golden in the morning sun beyond. The peace of the scene made the violence of her night visions seem even more unreal—or was this the dream? As she sighed, Bogle lifted his great head from one of her feet to lay it upon the other. She wiggled her toes to restore circulation. The dog, having made his contribution to the community's food supply, clearly felt entitled to a rest.

In another moment, however, Bogle raised his head again, ears pricking, then heaved himself out from under the table and took a few steps toward the gate.

"Are we expecting guests?" inquired Prasutagos. The dog had shown an uncanny ability to distinguish between approaching strangers and the folk who belonged here.

"They are friends, apparently," observed Boudica as the plumed tail began to gently wave.

In a few minutes one of the warriors on guard came trotting through the gate to report three women and a man riding up the road.

"They don't sound too dangerous," said Prasutagos, stroking his mustache to hide a smile. "Why don't you go welcome them in?"

Curiosity gave way to wonder as the three women appeared in the gateway. Boudica had hoped to see Lhiannon, but the curly yellow head of the first figure was nearly as welcome.

"Coventa!" She paused as she recognized Belina and Helve, of all people, behind her, and slowed her progress to something more befitting a queen.

"My lady!" Her nod was carefully calculated to imply equality. "You honor us!" As she gave orders for food and drink she eyed them covertly, seeing Coventa grown tall, and Helve a little more matronly. The High Priestess was still beautiful, but she had some lines in her face that had not been there before. *And that's no wonder,* Boudica thought silently, *the past few years have not been easy on anyone.* She smiled again as their escort proved to be Rianor. Like the others he wore ordinary clothes.

"You'll be wondering what we're doing here," said Belina as they sat down to a plate of bannocks and a flagon of Roman wine. "With the Romans busy building new forts near the Sabrina, the roads seemed safe enough for Coventa's womanhood ceremony at Avalon."

Boudica nodded, remembering her initiation at Lhiannon's hands. She wondered if Helve could bring through the same magic, but then Coventa had enough magic herself for two.

"And now we are going to visit her kinfolk in the Brigante lands before she takes her vows," said Helve. "It has been an interesting journey."

And you have been picking up information everywhere you passed, Boudica observed. It would appear that the kind of thinking required to be a high priestess was not so different from that of a queen.

"I told them it didn't matter," said Coventa. "No one has proposed a great marriage for me, and I would refuse it if they tried—though your little girls are sweet enough to make me think again about motherhood!"

Boudica smiled. "Sweet" was not a term she would have used for Rigana, but the two children had been on their best behavior to meet the priestesses, and she could see how they might be deceived.

"We plan to save some travel time by taking a ship from the north coast of your lands," Helve put in. "We will be staying with Queen Cartimandua in Briga for a while before heading home. I thought that if your husband permits it, you might wish to go with us."

"Oh please do, Boudica!" begged Coventa. "We can only stay here one night, and that is not nearly time enough for all I have to tell you!"

"I don't know," Boudica said uncertainly. The baby was weaned, and the girls surely did not lack for protectors, but she had not slept apart from Prasutagos for more than a night since he became High King, except when she gave birth to Argantilla, and for a week when he had a fever. Without him in the bed beside her she did not sleep well.

*I*n the end it was Prasutagos who counseled her to go, although she could see that he liked the prospect of separation no more than she. But they had not spoken with Cartimandua for some time, and since the western Brigantes had rebelled the year before it had become important to know where she and her husband stood with regard to Rome.

"Cartimandua seemed to have a kindness for you at the wedding," the king observed dryly. Boudica realized for the first time that he was aware that the Brigante queen had encouraged her to ride away. "She is a wily one, but perhaps if you are together for a time she will speak freely."

It was only after they had been on the road for some days that it occurred to Boudica that the reason Helve had invited her was the same.

Three days' journey brought them to the small port on the Wash, on the north coast of the Iceni lands. There they found two wide-bottomed boats that could take the women and their escort four days' sail up the coast and into a great estuary. At the landing they bought rough-coated ponies to carry them upriver until they came to Lys Udra, where Queen Cartimandua made her home.

*O*ne sympathizes with Caratac, of course," said the queen.

She was still the sleek, wry-tongued creature Boudica

remembered, with her black hair shining in the morning sun. Coventa was spending the week with her brother's family, leaving the Brigante queen to entertain her unexpected guests at her hall by the river. The land here was good for farming, but to the west rose moors and mountains where only shepherds could make a living.

"He and his brother were in a fair way to unite most of the south, had the Romans not come." She poured wine into cups of ruddy Samian ware and passed them to her guests. "He is a fine-looking man, too, though depressingly faithful to that Ordovice woman he wed." She smiled.

Boudica raised an eyebrow. *Did you try him, then, and get turned down?* Cartimandua was known to have an eye for a handsome male. Her husband did not object, but then Briga was a wild land, where folk held to older ways than those of the Celts of Gallia who had conquered them. King Venutios was spending the summer at Rigodunon, near the Salmaes firth on the northwestern coast. Clearly his relationship with Cartimandua was very different from the union she and Prasutagos had finally found. Boudica wondered if he had played any role in the rising there.

"They say that Caratac has taken his war band back to the Ordovice lands," said Helve.

"He may take them anywhere he likes, so long as they stay out of Briga," Cartimandua said with sudden venom. "I'll not have him persuading any more of our clans into a rising that could only be put down by bringing the Legions in."

"I, on the other hand, can only be thankful they did. That rebellion saved Mona," observed Helve.

"Do you expect me to say that you're welcome?" Cartimandua answered her unspoken question. "I have no quarrel with your Order, but I like the Romans much better when their tax collectors, annoying as they may be, are the only representatives they need to send into my land."

Helve's lips tightened, but even she could hardly object to the queen's words while she was drinking her wine. It was good for the High Priestess to have to be polite to a fellow sovereign, thought Boudica. She wished that Lhiannon had been here to see.

"They say that Caratac has a priestess of your Order with him, a White Lady with magic powers," added Cartimandua, as if Boudica had spoken her thought aloud. Coventa had told her that Lhiannon had gone to help the rebels. She was glad to have confirmation for her dream.

"Indeed?" Helve said stiffly.

"No doubt the Romans have heard this also. It will not make them more tolerant of your power." Cartimandua sat back and signaled to one of her women to bring more wine.

"If we do not stand up to them we will *have* no power," said Helve with more honesty than Boudica had expected.

"Ah well, we each play the game in a different way," said Cartimandua, smiling. "It will be interesting to see who wins . . ."

The evening before they were to leave Lys Udra, the Brigante queen held Boudica back as the others were seeking their beds after dinner in the great roundhouse that was the royal hall.

"What did she want?" Coventa asked when Boudica returned.

"To warn me against you!" Boudica tried to laugh. "She believes that the Romans will seek to destroy the Druids as soon as they have pacified the tribes."

"I know that you cannot do much to help us, placed as you are," Coventa said seriously, "but it will be a comfort to know that you still hold me in your heart . . ."

"Oh, my dear one, how could I not?" exclaimed Boudica. "But will you not rethink your own decision? I believe you will be safer with me than with Helve."

Coventa shook her head with her usual sweet smile. "I know you do not like her, but indeed she does desire to serve the people and the gods. And she has been kind to me."

She has used you, thought Boudica, but it would do no good to say so aloud.

"This journey has shown me how unhappy I would be if I had to live among people who see and hear only with their ears and eyes. Safe or not, being a priestess on Mona is the only thing I am fit for," said Coventa.

"Then do it, and be happy—" Boudica hugged the thin shoulders. *For as long as you can.* But in truth could she, could anyone, hope for more?

*H*arvest was the most hopeful time of the year. In the old days, warfare ended when it was time to get the crops in. But now, except when it was necessary to pursue an occasional cow that somehow ended up on the other side of a tribal border, they no longer had to worry about fighting— perhaps the only one of Rome's promised benefits that had actually been welcome. When the grain turned golden, everyone, high or low, turned out to help in the fields.

Boudica bent, scooped up the piled stalks before her, and added them to the bunch in the crook of her arm. Ahead, the line of reapers moved in rhythm to the beat of the harvest drum, grasping, cutting, and casting aside the stalks of grain. She squatted down to gather more into her armful, bound what she held with a twist of straw, and started the process all over again.

So much of the Iceni country was pasture or fenland. The places where grain would grow well were doubly precious, and the best were to be found in the high rolling land around Danatobrigos. Boudica had come here after her visit to Cartimandua, and the king had brought the girls up to join her while he traveled around his kingdom. They would all go back to Teutodunon when the harvest was done.

She always looked forward to the season and its festivities, but just at this moment she wished they were over. The sun burned bright, and sweat was running down her back, sticking the linen of the old tunic to her skin and itching where the omnipresent chaff had gotten in. Long sleeves protected her arms from the sun, but by tonight her face would be red and tender despite the oil she had slathered on it before she began and the broad straw hat she wore.

But they could not stop now. Clouds were building over the waters of the Wash, and they would lose most of the wheat if it rained. The families whose farms were near the

Horse Shrine harvested together, moving from one steading to another as the fields ripened. Today they were at Palos and Shanda's place. Earlier in the summer Palos had been ill, but he looked healthy now, his skin darkened and his brown hair bleached by the sun.

Next to him, Prasutagos cut and cast another handful aside. The king had stripped off his tunic. For a moment Boudica paused, appreciating the ripple of muscle across his back as he reached again, then took up the stalks he had cut and tied off another sheaf of grain.

"Here's water, Mother," said Rigana. Boudica stretched to relieve the ache in her back, then took the full skin. It tasted better than Roman wine. At least this was the last field. From the farm came the scent of cooking food—they would be feasting soon.

Very soon, she realized, for the reapers were approaching the end of the field. A ripple of anticipation swept through the onlookers. Sickles flashed as the men raced to finish, then halted, drawing away from Prasutagos, who was reaching for the only clump still standing in the field. Hearing the silence, he stopped, realized he was the last, and looked around him with a rueful laugh.

"The Old Woman!" "The Corn Mother!" "Watch out, she'll get you!" came the cries.

"Palos, this is your field—I'll let you do the honors," the king said hopefully, holding out the sickle to the other man.

"No, my lord." Palos grinned. "It's you she's been waiting for. I'll not stand in your way!" His golden-haired wife took his arm as if to make sure of it.

Prasutagos gave a dramatic sigh. "Well, you've been sick, so I'll take her on—" Drawing himself up, he took a stride forward, grasped the stalks in his left hand, and with a swift slash cut them free. As he stepped back something brown and swift burst from the stubble and went bounding across the field.

"A hare!" whispered someone, making the sign of warding. Boudica felt her arms prickle. Suddenly the king's laughing offer to protect the farmer from the Corn Mother's resentment at being cut down had a deeper meaning. Hares were uncanny beasts, sacred to the Goddess and not to be harmed. His gaze met that of the farmer, who had gone a little pale.

" 'Tis the duty of the king to stand between his folk and danger," Prasutagos said gently, and smiled.

"A neck! A neck! He has the Old Woman!" the others were shouting now.

Prasutagos handed the sheaf to Shanda, who set swiftly to work to tie off sections into limbs and braid the figure a girdle and crown. As soon as she had the grain the other women seized the king, sticking straws through his clothing and into his hair. Then they hustled him down to the river and pushed him in.

When times were truly evil, thought Boudica a little grimly, the ruler, or his substitute, would die for his land in truth and not in play. Would that be required of Caratac? But despite his ambitions, he had never been king for all Britannia. The acceptance must come before the sacrifice.

Now they were pulling Prasutagos out again. Across the tops of their heads his laughing gaze met hers. *They will take him back to the farm for the feasting,* she thought as she managed an answering smile, *and make him dance with the Corn Mother, and eat as much food as Devodaglos, and promise everyone more beer. That's not so great a sacrifice . . .*

"Way-yen, way-yen . . ." As the Corn Mother was borne back to the farm, the call echoed triumphantly across the land.

As Boudica followed the crowd it occurred to her that the rough treatment given to the reaper was only a symbol, but each spring, the Corn Goddess, in the grain that made up last harvest's image, was dismembered and scattered to bless the fields.

EIGHTEEN

*I*t had been a long war. From the doorway of the command tent, Lhiannon watched the campfires flickering in the meadows that edged the river, where the men of the great coalition Caratac had forged had sunk their own past rivalries in hatred of a greater foe. Silures who were veterans of the southern fighting of two years ago and Durotrige survivors from Vespasian's campaign lay by Ordovices and Deceangli who had borne the brunt of the more recent battles, along with a scattering of men from other tribes. The last time so great a British host had been assembled had been on the banks of the Tamesa.

Behind her, Caratac sat with the war leaders, drawing maps in the dirt. Brangenos had settled in the shadows beyond, playing something sweet and meandering that eased the soul without requiring attention.

"They say that the governor was a sick man when he got here, and I don't think his health has been improved by hunting me all around the hills. By all the gods, I am as tired of running as he is of chasing me!"

"So you mean to face him?" asked Tingetorix, an Iceni champion Lhiannon had known when she lived with Boudica.

"I mean to offer battle—at a place of my own choosing." Caratac bared his teeth in a grin. "I doubt he will be able to resist the invitation." Eight years of warfare had transformed the fox of the Cantiaci to an old wolf, the red hair gone brindled roan, his weatherbeaten skin seamed with scars. But the fire in his eyes burned as hot as ever.

Did Lhiannon's? She, too, had left her first youth in these mountains. To the men of Caratac's army, whom she had nursed and comforted through illness and wounds, she was the White Lady. These days she wore undyed homespun. Her robe of priestess-blue had worn out long ago. But her true appearance no longer mattered—although she was not the only Druid with the army, like Caratac she had become a living talisman. And there were times, even here, when the trance of vision came upon her, not as in the ordered ritual of Mona, but as a sudden intuition that left her in a confusion of hope and fear.

"Our scouts report that the governor has brought the Fourteenth Legion down from Viroconium and the Twentieth up from the south," said one of the Ordovice men.

"The Twentieth, which used to be at Camulodunon?" echoed Epilios. "I look forward to seeing them again . . ." His grin was a youthful reflection of his brother's—the last two sons of Cunobelin were together, leading the men of Britannia to war.

"They lie in marching camps down by the fords where the rivers join. Close to twenty thousand men in one camp, and the cavalry in the other."

"We have nearly their numbers, and cavalry won't be much use where I mean to bring them." Caratac gestured to Lhiannon. "Tell them, maiden, the vision you shared with me—"

All eyes turned to Lhiannon as she stepped into the firelight, putting back her veil. "This was a dream—it is for you to interpret it, but this is what I saw. I was like a bird, looking down on the land of Britannia. Below me I saw eagles flying, following Caratac from ocean to river across the pastures and tilled lands. But when he took to the forest they struggled to follow, and when he took to the mountains they grew weary. My vision failed then and I could not see the battle's end. But if you fight on a hill you have a chance. That is what I see."

"The land itself will fight for us, you'll see." Caratac bent to his dirt map and began to point at the hills and rivers modeled there. "The Romans fight like lions on level ground, but our men are like wildcats on their native hills. We will tempt them with a little opposition at the river crossing and then pull back to this hill—" The stick he was using as a pointer stabbed down.

"The old hillfort?" asked a Durotrige warrior who had been with him since Vespasian's campaign. "You'll not be planning to trap us there!"

Lhiannon shuddered. There were still nights when she woke whimpering from memories of the fall of the Dun of Stones.

"No, though it may serve as a last defense if things go ill," Caratac replied. "We'll take up our positions on the slopes leading up to it, where the lie of the land will crowd them, and anywhere the climb is easy we can block with ramparts of stones."

"Stones we have in plenty," said one of the Ordovices, and everyone laughed.

Stones, and cold wind, thought Lhiannon as the breeze that always blew strongest at sunset searched out every imperfection in the weave of her cloak of creamy wool. The sun had gone down behind the western mountains and dusk was drawing a veil of shadow across the lesser hills. The men were arguing over which tribes should stand where on the hill and had forgotten her.

Tomorrow they would be on the move again. Lhiannon made her way through the camp toward the tent she shared with Caratac's wife and daughter and the few other women whose value as potential hostages was too great to leave them where they might risk capture. Now and again a man would look up as she passed his fire. She smiled in return. It cost her nothing to give that comfort. *But who,* she wondered, *will comfort me?*

She thrust the thought away. In her first months with the army the day's march would have left her too tired to think of anything but sleep when night fell. But after more than two years in the field she was as tough as any of the men. Sleep would come hard, with a battle in store. But she would have to try. If she was lucky, she would not dream.

*S*ome men dreamed of wealth or glory. Prasutagos, his wife had come to realize, dreamed of buildings. When Boudica's gaze followed the curling smoke upward she still had to blink in amazement at the added height that the second level of the new roundhouse gave. The area around the hearth was large enough to seat all the chieftains; roomy chambers for the household were created by the partitions that ran from the main supports to the outer wall. There was nothing like the king's two-tiered hall anywhere in the Celtic lands.

They had moved in only a month before. Beneath the scents of woodsmoke and mutton stew there was still a hint of limewash and fresh straw. But for the children, to whom the whole world was made of wonders, their father's new house had become an accustomed miracle. At the moment, putting off the inevitable banishment to their beds was their concern.

"A story, Mama!" Rigana begged. "Tell us one of the stories you learned on the magic island!" Little Tilla clapped her hands.

Boudica smiled to think that her main use for the lore the Druids had taught with such solemnity was as a source of children's tales. And yet these stories were the wellspring of their religion. It was more important than ever that their children learn them now, when so many were turning to the victorious Roman gods.

"Well, now—since it is summer, I should tell you about one of the gods who make things grow. He plays the harp to order the seasons, and in His orchard there is always fruit on the trees. We call Him Dagdevos the Good God, or the Father of All, or the Red One All-Knowing, or the Good Striker, and He can do anything. He is one of the kings of the Shining Ones."

"Like Papa," said Tilla wisely.

"*Just* like Papa," Boudica agreed, keeping her face straight with an effort as her husband blushed. "When the monster-people attacked His land He had to survive the tests they set upon Him. He had to eat a porridge made from four-score gallons of milk, and He did it, though His belly was so full His tunic scarcely covered him."

At this, the look the girls turned on their father was frankly speculative, and Temella and Bituitos both gave way to laughter.

"His belly's not all that was dragging, I've heard," whispered Eoc, and the laughter began once more.

"Oh, do you mean His club?" Boudica asked innocently. "When He strikes, it kills instantly, but if He touches you with the other end you come back to life once more."

"That's the end He uses on the Lady of Ravens," Prasutagos retaliated. "Battle goddess though She may be, He has a weapon to win Her . . ."

"But His best possession is a magic cauldron," said Boudica, though by now she was blushing as well. "Some say it is the same as the one into which you put dead warriors to bring them alive, but others say it can feed an army, and whatever food you like best it will serve."

"Would it serve honey cakes?" asked Rigana.

"An' bilberries in cream?" her sister echoed. "I want to go there!"

"Where you should be going now is your bed," Prasutagos said with a comical frown. "You can feast with Dagdevos in your dreams . . ."

When both girls had been hugged and kissed and handed off to their nurses, he turned to Boudica. "You did not tell them the story of how Dagdevos makes love to the Morrigan each Samhain to still her rage and restore balance to the world," he murmured with a glance that brought the blush back to her skin.

"I think that one can wait until the girls are older," she said primly. "And I have never quite understood how even gods can manage to do it, straddling the stream . . ."

"Do you prefer a bed, then? For if so, I have one . . ."

As he took her hand Boudica smiled, knowing herself blessed by the gods.

*With the other Druids, Lhiannon had made the offerings to Lenos, which was the name they gave the war god here, spilling the blood of a bull upon the ground and hanging the carcass from the branches of an ancient oak tree. Had it been accepted? There had been no roll of thunder, only the ravens, calling as they always did when an army was on the move. It took no Druid to interpret that omen—where humans fought, ravens would feed.

But that night, Lhiannon had dreamed again. Once more she soared above a battlefield, and this time the Romans, like armored insects, were advancing up the hill.

The eagle god strode before them with a tread like thunder and the Britons fell before them, blood splattering the rocks like rain. She had been weeping when she woke, knowing it for a dream of doom. And she had known as well that there was nothing she could do. The Romans were already on their way. Any rumor of defeat would break the British army before they struck a blow. Caratac could have escaped with a small band into the wilderness, but a force so great had no choice but to stand. Even to tell the king what she had seen might deprive him of the hope that could prove her vision wrong. She could only watch, and pray, and hope the gods of Britannia were listening.

Or is it that we are praying for the wrong things? she wondered suddenly.

The hill from which they watched the battle unfolding did not give her quite the vantage of her vision, but neither did she have the same detachment. After slowing the enemy's crossing with slingstones and arrows, the British had retreated in good order to the slope of the hill, pulling in to meet the Roman advance in depth as it grew steeper, shooting and throwing spears from behind the drystone barricades that protected them from the ballista bolts of the enemy.

About midmorning, Caratac's wife and daughter began to cheer, seeing the Roman auxiliaries driven back by the intensity of the defense. But the legions were forming up behind them. And now the blocks of marching men were covered by overlapping shields upon which the British missiles struck in vain. And despite the fury of the defenders, they kept on coming, foot by foot and yard by yard, until they reached the stone walls and threw them down, and then it was sword against sword and shield against shield, and the blood flowed down the hill.

"*Morrigan, goddess of battles, be with them now!*" she prayed. The anguish she heard in the wailing of Caratac's women as they watched the British line break and disappear was the same paean of pain she heard from the ravens that circled the hill. *The goddess* is *with them.* Lhiannon shuddered in appalled understanding. *To death and beyond. But she cannot, or will not, save.*

Someone shouted that soldiers were coming. Too

stunned to move, Lhiannon stood still in the midst of confusion as the others left her alone among the trees.

A darkness like the wings of a thousand ravens had closed around the world. The Roman forces had passed on, pursuing a large band of Silure tribesmen who had managed to get off the hill, leaving the battlefield to those with the courage to seek for anyone left to save. Lhiannon walked like a ghost among them. A pitiful few were able to drink the water she carried. For others, a sure thrust of her dagger was the only possible mercy. Numbed by the horror of the shattered bodies around her, she offered both with equal calm.

And thus, wandering the battlefield in her pale gown, she came upon the king.

It was only by the twisted gold of the torque around his neck that she knew him. Caratac was covered with blood, his clothing mostly torn away. He was sitting with the body of a warrior in his arms. Lhiannon did not recognize the dead man. Perhaps that did not matter. He was all of them.

As she approached, Caratac lifted his head. "The White Lady..." he whispered. "Have you come to take me, too?"

"My lord—" Shock broke through Lhiannon's detachment. "You should not be here!"

"No...I should not. That is very true..." He gazed around him. "Oh, my warriors! See how still they lie...Why am I living? I fought hard...I did not flee...You know that, don't you?" he addressed the dead man. "You will tell them, where they feast with the heroes, that I tried..." His head drooped once more.

"Caratac, get up! The Romans will return and they must not find you here."

"Does it matter?"

It was a question that she had been trying hard not to ask. "It might matter to the ones who escaped this field," she said carefully. "They will be wanting you to lead them again—"

"As I led these?" he asked bitterly. But he seemed at last to recognize that the man he was holding was past all listening. There was a long silence. Then, very gently, he laid the body down. "The Ordovices are broken," he said in a more normal tone. "And the Roman swine will be putting all their attention on the mountains here. Our only hope is to seek support in a direction they will not be looking." Once more he was silent, but he had begun to look like the man she knew. "The Brigantes were willing to rise against them before. What say you, White Lady?"

Lhiannon shook her head. "Don't look to me for answers, my lord. I am empty. When I was at Mona two years ago, the Arch-Druid wanted me to go and study in Eriu. It is said they have knowledge we have lost. But I chose to come to you. I should have gone—I have been little use to you here . . ."

"We are a sad pair indeed," Caratac said softly. "But you are wrong, Lady. You have given me a reason to live. Go west to Eriu and find some wisdom for our future, and I will go east, to Cartimandua."

*Y*ou are going to Cartimandua?" Boudica frowned at the man before her. "Are you certain that is wise?"

She had come upon him at the gates of Teutodunon, sitting hunched in a hooded cloak, anonymous as any other broken man washed up by the wars. When she paused to give him a bannock from the bag she carried for such eventualities, she glimpsed beneath the rag tied around his neck a glint of gold.

He pulled the scarf away. Her face paled as she recognized the torque, and then the fierce gaze of the king.

"My lord Caratac! Be welcome! Come into the dun and let me give you a proper meal!" *And a bath . . . and dressings for those wounds . . .* she added silently.

"No." Strong fingers closed on the hand she held out to him. His glance flicked to the road, where a wagon carrying rolls of woolen cloth from their weaving sheds to Colonia was rumbling by.

"You have too many people here who are friends of Rome. For your sake and mine it is best if no one else knows that I have come."

"But we must talk . . . We heard of the battle. Some said

you were taken, others that you had been slain—" She halted at the pain that darkened his eyes.

"Perhaps I was, and it is only my ghost you see here. I have felt like a ghost these past weeks, making my way unseen across the land. Many—too many—of my men lie dead upon that hill." He hesitated, then looked up at her. "Bracios was one of them. Your brother fell defending mine."

"Thank you for telling me." Boudica replied after a few moments had passed. She had scarcely seen her brother since they were both small; she supposed the pang of grief was more for the death of her childhood than for him. "But you are alive, and I can see that you need feeding . . . If you follow the path to the river you will come to the grove of Andraste. Wait for me there."

And now, with a basket full of food and drink and bandages, she sat facing Caratac in the shadow of the circle of oak trees that surrounded the shrine.

"It has been a long time since I had such a vintage." He took another swallow from the wineskin. "Of late it has been only water, and before that, heather ale. I have rejected all things Roman but this." He sighed. "Our people might be free today if we could have forgone our taste for Roman wine."

"My husband and I will not betray you, but neither can we help you," Boudica said. "I have heard tales of the desert the Romans leave behind when they impose their 'peace' upon a conquered land. And really, I don't think we would be much use to you even if we dared. The Iceni with the fire to fight the Romans did so at the dun in the fens four years ago, and died."

"I wish you well of the peace that the Romans have left you," Caratac said dryly. "I hope that it may last." He nibbled on a piece of bread and set it down. "You have grown into a beautiful woman," he said. "When you bore the mead-cup around the hall at Mona, you were like a young filly, all legs and nervous energy." He took another drink of wine.

"And now I am the Red Mare of the Iceni—I am not supposed to know that the people call me that." She smiled. "But it is the Black Mare of the Brigantes who should concern you."

"I can at least hope that she will listen. Cartimandua had a kindness for me long ago."

She lusted *after you,* corrected Boudica with an inner sigh. These days Prasutagos had grown somewhat substantial around the middle, but she could warm herself at his steady flame. The man before her still had the hard body of a warrior, but the fire that had drawn men to him, and women as well, was burned to ash.

"I must do something," he went on. "The Roman swine captured my brother Epilios, and my wife, and our daughter, my little Eigen, my only remaining child. You have children—surely you can understand how I feel!"

Boudica nodded. "Rigana is six now, and has her first pony. Argantilla is almost four." If she and Prasutagos had no more offspring it was not for lack of trying, but she had not conceived again. Almost the only thing that had the power to wake her fury these days was the thought of danger to the bright, if sometimes exasperating, offspring who looked likely to be the only children she would have.

"If I give myself up now I can do no more than stand in chains beside them. But I may be able to negotiate for their release if the Romans see me as a threat once more," Caratac went on.

Not long ago, thought Boudica, this man swore to defend all Britannia. Now his ambition was limited to the freedom of a man, a woman, and a child. But didn't it always come down to that? No matter what words men used to cloak their ambitions, the abstraction they fought for bore a human face and name.

"All that I can offer you is supplies for the road and my blessing," she began.

"No—there is one thing more you can do for me." He lifted his hands to the torque, gripped the ornate ring-shaped terminals, and began to twist open the spiral rope of gold wires. "This much of your warning I will heed. This torque was made by an Iceni craftsman." Wincing, he dragged it off, leaving a semicircle of white around the base of his neck where it had lain. "Keep it for me, Boudica. If things go well, I will reclaim it. If they go . . . badly, I will not shame the gold by wearing it with Roman chains."

*   *   *

*I*f Mona was called the golden island, wreathed in magic, the lump of rock separated from the rest of it by a tidal strait was said to be more holy still. From this height at the western tip of Mona, one gazed out upon a silver ocean half veiled by mists. Some said it was the last port from which one might set sail for the Isles of the Blessed. Lhiannon was only going to Eriu.

But it felt like death, to be sure, to leave Britannia. She clung to the rail of the tubby little craft as it eased out from the shelter of the harbor and began to roll and dip to the rhythms of the sea. She left behind the limited satisfaction of knowing that the Roman governor Ostorius had died, and sorrow at the news that Queen Cartimandua had sent Caratac to the Romans in chains. By now he, too, must be upon the sea, headed for Rome. To have his wife, daughter, and brother with him was surely no comfort, when all they could hope for was death or captivity.

With the death of the governor, the Silures had resumed a vicious guerrilla warfare. The tribes of the western mountains still stood between Mona and the Romans, but the southern lowlands lay in uneasy peace. There was nothing Lhiannon could do to help Britannia. She told herself she would be glad to be gone.

The uncertainty beneath her feet was all too reflective of her own inner turmoil. All that she had known was disappearing behind her, she had no firm foundation, and the future was shrouded in a mist as gray as the fog that lay upon the sea.

Back on the shore she could still see the blue figure that was Helve. Lhiannon had not expected the High Priestess to see her off. Only when they were on the road did she realize the other woman wanted a chance to talk to her away from the whole Druid community's ears.

"The Romans will try to destroy us," Helve said grimly. "I have seen it and Coventa has seen it as well. Despite our resistance, the new forts they are building are closer every year. They have learned of the gold in the heart of the mountains and the silver in the Deceangli lands. That will draw them, and then they will find the coastal road that leads here. Those mountains will not protect us anymore."

"Then why are you sending me away?" Lhiannon had asked.

"You have proven yourself to be adaptable. I believe that you have the best chance of learning whatever skills the Druids of Eriu can teach. Mearan believed you were the most talented of the younger priestesses—it will be up to you to preserve our tradition if we fall."

The shock of that statement had held Lhiannon speechless. "I thought you despised me," she said at last.

And Helve had looked at her with an expression halfway between exasperation and anger. "You were my rival. But if these ornaments are ever yours"—she touched the gold at her neck—"you will find that the work takes precedence over whatever you may feel. Love and hatred are luxuries I can no longer afford. And if you become High Priestess it will mean that I am dead and beyond all jealousy." She gave a bitter laugh. "So take care of yourself and learn all you can . . ."

NINETEEN

"I want you to keep your eyes open." Boudica addressed her daughters with a warning glare. "The Roman town will be very new and strange. You must always stay in sight of Temella or one of the house guards—do you understand?" The glare fixed on Rigana, who at seven had added to her independence of spirit an uncanny ability to elude her keepers. For a moment the queen wished they had brought Bogle, but the dog was growing old for such a journey, and she winced at the thought of how he might react to the new sounds and smells of the Roman town.

She wondered just how strange Camulodunum, or Colonia Victricensis—the City of Victory—as they were supposed to call it now, would be. She had seen the fort they had built on the hill above the old dun, but she had not been this far south for some years and knew the town only from what she had heard.

"They are confident," observed Prasutagos as they started up the hill.

A straggle of huts and gardens lined the road, and the ditch and bank that had supported the walls were no longer crowned by a palisade. Many of the old legionary buildings had been converted to homes and shops, but there was also a great deal of new construction going on. The retired soldiers had adapted well, but then a legion was like a mobile city, with men trained in every trade. Some had imported wives from their homelands, and others had married girls of the tribes. Boudica wondered how the Trinovantes felt about having so many strangers set down in the midst of their territory. But as a conquered tribe there was little they could do about it. All the more reason, she thought grimly, for the Iceni to maintain their protected status as an ally.

"They have reason to be," she replied. The new governor, Aulus Didius Gallus, had forced the Silures to surrender. With Caratac a prisoner, no British leader with the stature to head a rebellion remained.

"Look, Mama—a big rock with doors!"

Argantilla could be forgiven for not recognizing the gate as a work of man. She had never seen a building made of stone, and this structure with its twin arches and carved pediment had no real purpose except as a statement of Roman pride. Sunlight gave way to shadow as they passed beneath the arch and into the town.

*S*unlight sparkled on the fountain in the midst of Julia Postumia's garden, its subtle tinkle and plash a background to the murmur of women's voices. It reminded Boudica of the waters of the sacred spring. Though this might be more manicured and orderly than the kind of sanctuary her own gods loved, it was still a welcome change from the straight lines and sharp corners of the Roman town. This garden grew nothing so practical as cabbages or beans. It was a shrine to beauty, complete with a stone grotto where the image of a goddess smiled upon the flowers. The gods who had led the Romans to Britannia were Jupiter and Mars. This lovely lady semed a deity of a more gracious kind.

"Who is the goddess?" Boudica asked. Her Latin was still halting, and she spoke with the accent of the Gaulish slave whom they had bought as a teacher and freed, but it served. Postumia had been visibly relieved to find they could speak without needing a translator.

"That is Venus, the lady of love. Do you have such a goddess among the tribes?"

"A goddess for love alone?" Boudica shook her head. "But all of our goddesses are lusty." She smiled a little, remembering some of the tales she had heard about the Morrigan. "Even our goddess of war."

Postumia laughed. "They say that Venus fought in the Trojan War, but not very well. Since then, the bedchamber has been her only battlefield."

"No doubt your men prefer it that way," Boudica replied. "They seem uncomfortable with women in power, even queens." It still rankled that Prasutagos had been invited to the council of chieftains and she had not. Her only consolation was that the prohibition applied to Cartimandua, who sat on the other side of the garden, as well. *At least I trust Prasutagos to tell me what goes on, and ask my counsel,* she thought then. From all accounts, since Cartimandua betrayed Caratac she and Venutios had scarcely exchanged a word.

"It was very kind of you to entertain us while our husbands are otherwise occupied," she said politely. *While your husband is reminding ours who really rules Britannia,* her thought went on.

"Oh I think we have the best of it," answered the governor's wife. "We can sit comfortably in the fresh air while they must sweat in that stuffy hall. But if we follow the emperor's example, that may change. I'm told that when Caratacus and his family were paraded through Rome, Agrippina sat beside her husband on her own throne."

"Do you know more about what happened there?" Boudica asked in a neutral tone.

"He is a brave man, your Caratacus. The others, they say, hung down their heads in despair, but the king wore his chains like royal jewels. He asked why the Romans should want Britannia when they already possessed so magnificent a city. Then he told Claudius that the difficulties he had caused us only magnified our glory in taking him captive, and pointed out that dead, he would be forgotten, while living, he would bear witness to the emperor's magnanimity. Romans always appreciate a good speech, so Claudius let him live, and gave him a house in Rome."

But Caratac will never again see Britannia . . . thought Boudica. *I think that I would rather die than endure even so kind a captivity.*

Postumia looked up as one of her slaves appeared at the gate with Temella close behind.

"Domina—" he began, but Temella pushed past him.

"My lady, the girls are gone!"

But Boudica was already on her feet, muttering an apology to her hostess before Postumia had had a chance to reply. *I should have brought Bogle,* she thought as she hurried away.

It was their Gaulish freedman, Crispus, whose knowledge of Roman towns proved most useful.

"I fear this may have been my fault, mistress," he said as they hastened down the road. "I told the girls about the shops, and they couldn't wait to go see."

Boudica had wanted to visit the shops herself, and had promised to take them. Visions of her children frightened and bleeding alternated with scenarios of what she was going to do to them when she found them safe and sound.

From ahead she could hear shouting. That sounded promising. She exchanged a grimace with Temella and began to run, with Calgac, the warrior who had been assigned as her escort, pounding along behind.

The scene she found brought her up short, tears of relief vying with a strong urge to laugh. Rigana, wearing a ferocious scowl and gripping a pole that had apparently once held up the sunshade that drooped behind her, was standing off a crowd of arguing adults. Apparently the quality of the children's clothing had made the townsfolk think twice about taking stronger action. Behind her sat Argantilla, her arms clasped protectively around a dark-haired boy little older than she who looked equally terrorized by the shouting grown-ups and his small protector. Baskets of beans lay overturned on the ground.

"She is surely your daughter, my lady," murmured Calgac. "Good form with that, um, spear."

Boudica changed her smile for a regal frown, straightened her tunica, and strode forward. Men parted to let her through, as impressed, she hoped, by her air of authority as by the spear in the hand of the man who followed her.

"Mama," cried Rigana as she came into view. "They were going to *kill* the boy!"

"Nay, Lady—noble queen!" said a round little man with a very red face, simultaneously trying to bluster and bow. "I beat the boy because he is stupid and lazy, and the little girls started to yell at me and the red-haired one *hit* me, and look at the mess they have made of my stall!"

Boudica looked more closely and saw the beginnings

of a notable bruise on his cheek. *Good for you, Rigana!*
"I see . . ." she said aloud. Unfortunately, the man was
within his rights, and she had no desire to fight this out in
a Roman court of law. "I suppose the boy is your slave?"

"He is, to my sorrow, and a more stupid, worthless—"

"Then his value is doubtless small," she cut across his
words. "Will this compensate you for the insult to your
honor, the damage to your shop, and this worthless boy?"
She stripped off one of her golden arm rings and held it
out to him.

"Yes, but the boy cost . . ." His protest faded as he got
a good look at the gold. "Yes, great queen, you are most
generous!"

"I am, for that arm ring is worth more than you and
your shop and everything in it." Men straightened and
bowed their heads as she swept the crowd with a regal
glare. "Before all the gods, I call you to witness that compensation has been offered and accepted, and to attest to
that fact if required."

"Yes, Lady," came the murmurs, and from those who
recognized her, "Yes, my queen!"

"Crispus, get a few names in case we need them, while
Calgac and I take these mighty warriors home to face their
own justice," murmured Boudica, moving forward to collect her offspring and their prize.

"Which of you had this idea?" she asked as they entered the Roman-style house that had been assigned to
them during their stay.

Rigana eyed her dubiously, clearly trying to decide
whether claiming leadership would bring her praise or
blame.

"Riga wanted to see the shops," Argantilla said pre-
cisely, "but I saved the boy!"

"Ah yes . . ." For a moment she considered the younger
girl. Rigana had always been more aggressive, but clearly
Tilla also had steel. Then she sighed and turned to the
boy. "Well, let us take a look at you, child." She lifted his
chin and gazed into dark eyes wide with defiance and fear.
"What is your name?"

"*He* called me 'you little bastard,'" muttered the boy,
"but there was a woman who called me Caw." She could

see now that he was desperately thin, and she glimpsed the weals of the whip beneath the tattered tunic he wore.

"Was she your mother?" Boudica asked more gently. He spoke with the accent of the Trinovantes, but that was to be expected. With such hair and eyes, he could be a Roman bastard or the child of a Silure woman taken in war.

"Dunno . . ." Caw looked down.

"Well it's no matter, you belong to us now. We will make your freedom legal once you are grown. And we do not beat our servants, slave or free!" She turned to the warrior. "Calgac, will you take our new child and find him food, a bath, and clothes? When you are recovered, Caw, you will attend my daughters. I expect you to help them, but you must not let them push you around. And you two"—she turned to the girls—"must treat him with courtesy."

"Yes, Mama," they chorused, impressed into good behavior, at least for now.

It was hot in the square. As the line of richly dressed men and women moved sedately forward, Boudica pulled her veil forward to create a little shade. Prasutagos looked at her enviously. His hair was growing thin on top, and he would have a very red pate by the time they were done. The Roman citizens among them had pulled the ends of their togas over their heads. She had always assumed that the voluminous folds of the toga were intended to demonstrate that the wearer was not expected to do anything practical while wearing it, but clearly, in their native land, the garment also served to provide protection to men who had to stand about for hours of official ceremonies in the hot Italian sun. She could feel sweat trickling down her back beneath her linen gown.

Sweet smoke eddied through the air, veiling the tile roofs of the buildings that surrounded the square. This place was the most emphatically Roman part of Colonia. It had been laid out at the eastern edge of the town, where the battlements had been leveled to provide more room. On one side the half-built walls of the new theater gleamed white in the sunlight. Though she saw no image of Jupiter, his brooding presence hung over the place like an invisible cloud. But the figure of Victory on her tall column gazed complacently upon those who had come to the civic altar to offer incense to the *genius* of the emperor. Boudica had no objection to participating, though this rite seemed stiff and perfunctory after the power of the Druid rituals. Anything that increased the virtue of the ruler could only improve the way he dealt with Britannia.

Prasutagos gave a patient sigh as step by step the kings and chieftains moved forward. At least he had been able to amuse himself by looking at the buildings. She had learned to interpret his sighs as she did his silences. This one expressed a number of things he was too politic to say, such as his opinion of the togas some of the Catuvellauni wore. Britons who had come over to the Roman side early had been rewarded by making their tribal center a town, Verulamium, and given the status of citizens. The Peace of Rome required her to be polite to them, as it kept her from speaking her mind to Cartimandua.

Through the smoke she met the Brigante queen's dark eyes. *You despise me as a traitor,* they seemed to say. *Yet here we both are. Caratac came to you in secret, but to me he came openly. Can you swear that faced with my choice you would not have done the same?* And Boudica, recognizing that she might have betrayed Caratac herself if giving him up had been the price of her children's safety, was the first to look away.

Her nostrils flared at the sweet spicy scent as they came to the altar. She bowed her head and cast a pinch of crumbled resin on the fire. Then they were done, and moving toward the chattering group gathered under a sunshade at the edge of the square.

"Do they really think that going through this show will make us love Rome?" she murmured.

"I don't think it matters," Prasutagos replied. "Romans are always most concerned about the forms of things. So long as we go through the motions, they don't seem to care what we really believe. I think they show *their* faith in the things they build . . ." His gaze went back to the square. "Even the walls of their houses are straight and tall, like ramparts, hiding what lies within."

Boudica smiled, wondering what he was dreaming of constructing now, and let him lead her into the shade.

It was cooler beneath the awning. Slaves in green tunics moved among the crowd, bearing trays of spicy tidbits and wine in cups of blue glass.

Boudica's expression of pleasant interest grew a little fixed as she saw Pollio coming toward them.

"A lovely afternoon, is it not? Almost warm enough to make us Romans feel at home." His tone was casual, but she flinched from the intensity of his gaze and drew her veil around her shoulders and across her breast as an additional shield. "It is my honor to present my new assistant—Lucius Cloto from Noviomagus in the Atrebate lands."

Boudica blinked, mentally subtracting fat and facial hair to match this narrow-eyed man to a boy shouting curses as Ardanos dragged him away. Unfortunately Cloto had been right about the power of Rome, and clearly he had been rewarded, though his awkwardly draped toga looked as though it was about to trip him. From the new name, he must have become a client of Pollio when he became a Roman citizen.

"King Prasutagos, of course, you know, but you may not have met his lovely wife, Boudica," Pollio went on.

"Oh I knew Boudica when she was only a gangly girl, long ago," said Cloto. He and Boudica exchanged edged smiles.

"Since then many things have changed," she said blandly. It would probably be neither politic nor dignified to mention that in those days she had outrun him on the hurley field.

Indeed, my lovely wife, said Prasutagos's raised brow, *I sense a tale I have not heard.*

"No doubt we will meet again this fall, when we make the rounds after the harvest," said Cloto. *I was right . . . and now you will pay,* he smiled.

"Did you know that the people here call him by the name of one of the Greek fates, 'Clotho'?" asked Prasutagos when the two tax collectors had gone. "He measures out the amount due."

"He was a student at Mona when I was there," said Boudica, "and just as unpleasant a boy as he is a man. He'll be dangerous—he knows what people are likely to have and what they will be trying to hide . . . Will this affect the building project at Teutodunon?" The double-tiered round-house had not satisfied the king for long. Prasutagos's new plan called for a group of buildings in a vastly expanded enclosure.

"I shouldn't think so," he said thoughtfully. "I'm providing work for people who would otherwise be potential rebels. The Romans ought to thank me for getting them off the roads." He shrugged. "The Romans say that fate is something that no one can evade."

Prasutagos smiled but Boudica did not. Certainly all that the Druids had done to evade the fate foreseen by the seeresses had only helped to bring it to pass. Which of their own efforts to preserve their people would instead bring disaster? Despite the warmth of the day, she felt a chill.

The day had dawned clear but a cold wind was herding clouds across the sky. The Turning of Spring always brought unsettled weather, thought Boudica, picking up a bundle of bedding to transfer from the two-tiered great house to the new roundhouse that had been built for the women beside it. Geese were winging northward, and the royal family was moving out of the two-tiered hall. It would be a relief, she thought wryly, not to have to fall asleep to the sound of men arguing around the central fire.

"Mama! Bogle is gone!"

Boudica turned as Argantilla came running toward her.

"He's an old dog, darling. I am sure he has only lain down somewhere out of the way for a nap." Though it was hard to know where that might be, with the dun a-bustle with men digging the new bank and ditch, now that they had finished the roundhouses that would flank the council hall.

"But I've looked *everywhere*!" At eight, Argantilla was growing into a sturdy, responsible child, red-faced with exertion just now, with her father's thick fair hair. It was a relief to have one daughter who could be depended on to know where she had left her shoes the night before, but Tilla's conviction that she was the only responsible person in the family could sometimes annoy.

"No, you have not," Boudica said tartly, "or you would have found him. These days he is too lame to have gotten far. Ask your sister to help you look, or Caw."

"Rigana is out on her pony, helping the men bring in the cows," Tilla said disapprovingly. "I think Caw is watching the blacksmith."

Raised in the Roman town, Caw did not have the ease on horseback of her girls, who had ridden since before they could walk, but he was clever with his hands. Argantilla still regarded him as her discovery, and the boy revered her as his rescuer. Boudica had no doubt he would drop whatever he might be doing if Tilla asked.

"Go find him, Blossom," she said aloud, "and find the dog, and then you can come back and help *me*."

Prasutagos ought to be helping as well, but he had discovered a convenient errand to Drostac of Ash Hill. Now that the two roundhouses flanking the Council Hall were completed, Boudica and the girls were taking all their things to the one allotted to the queen. Except for a few things he would need at night, the king's gear had to be moved to the Men's House on the other side. The gods alone knew how he and his house guard would organize things over there, but that was not her problem.

What she would have preferred, Boudica thought wryly, was a separate house just big enough for her and him. It was time the king and queen made another journey through the tribal territories, though now that he was High King she supposed they could never be as entirely alone as they had been when she ran away from their wedding feast and woke to find him cooking breakfast over her fire. She smiled reminiscently, then gave herself a mental shake and picked up the bundle of bedding once more.

She had arranged all her own gear and she and Temella were making up the great bed when Caw appeared at the door. It was a new bed, and she was looking forward to testing it when her husband got home.

"My Lady," said Caw with the formality that even after

three years in their household he still used. "We have found the dog." He waited.

"Is he injured?" Boudica asked.

"I believe something is wrong. He lifts his head, but he will not rise. Argantilla is with him down at the end of the new ditch. He is too heavy, Lady, for us to carry home."

"Of course he is." Lately the dog had lost flesh, but he still probably weighed as much as one of the girls. Argantilla would have not hesitated to order the men to help them, but she could understand why the girl had stayed with the dog. She was always the one to whom people would bring a bird with a broken wing.

"If he is hurt he should be moved carefully. Run to the workmen who are building the palisade and have them use some of the poles to make a litter. Tell them it is my order," she added when he looked dubious.

Leaving Temella to finish with the bed, Boudica sniffed the air, then took up her shawl and strode across the yard. The sky was now completely gray, and the air heavy with the promise of rain. She could have wished that Prasutagos had not designed the new rectangular enclosure to be so *big*. He could have fitted an entire Roman fort inside. The original bank and ditch had been filled in, and as each section of the new one was finished the woodworkers were adding the palisade, while the diggers extended the ditch some more.

As she hurried toward the far corner of the enclosure she glimpsed Argantilla's fair head and then the sprawled, creamy limbs of the dog. Bogle lifted his head as she neared, tail twitching in welcome.

"Hello, old friend," she murmured, kneeling beside him and settling the great head in her lap. "How is it with you?"

The dog gave a gusty sigh and closed his eyes as she began to fondle his ears. Boudica's heart twisted in pity, feeling the bone beneath the loose skin. She had known Bogle was aging, but he was a white dog, and there was no graying at his muzzle to warn her just how old he had become.

"Where is the trouble then, my lad?" Gently she worked her hands along his spine, flexed the joints, probed the long muscles of back and thigh. The dog did not wince or move, except for the lazy beat of his tail.

"Mama, what's wrong with him?"

Boudica shrugged helplessly. "I can find no injury, Blossom. I think he is simply old and tired."

"Like Grandma got?" asked the girl.

"Yes, darling." Boudica's mother had died the year before, and in her last days Argantilla had been the one to keep her company. "Bodies wear out, for dogs and humans as well."

"But he is only two years older than Rigana!" Tilla exclaimed.

"Dog years are different," said Boudica. "For a big dog, Bogle is very old . . ." As old as her little son would have been, if he had lived. How strange that a dog's whole life could have passed, when her baby's death still seemed like yesterday.

It was getting cold. Where were the men with the litter?

"But I don't want him to die . . ." muttered the child.

Beyond her, Caw's face had grown very pale. *He has seen death,* thought Boudica, *and knows what it is. Do I?*

When her mother died she had been away from home, and the shell that was left seemed unreal. If she had seen her son's body, perhaps she would not have been haunted for so many years by dreams in which she heard him crying that she had abandoned him, or if she had felt his little life flicker out beneath her hand, as she felt Bogle's life flickering now.

She bent closer, trying to soothe the dog as he twitched and shivered in her arms.

"They will have to be very careful when they lift him," Argantilla was saying as Bogle stiffened, relaxed, and began to tremble once more.

"Oh my poor puppy," Boudica whispered, "be at ease, be at peace. The fields of An-Dubnion are full of hares, they say, and Arimanes loves a good hound . . ."

Death had surrounded her in these years when the Romans had killed her brothers and so many other men, but she had always missed it. She had no choice but to embrace it now.

"You were a good dog, Bogle, a *good* dog . . ." she got out through an aching throat. *Thank you for all your love for me . . .*

The plumed tail slapped the ground. She held him tightly as he convulsed once more, and then was still.

"We have made a litter, Lady. Shall we take the dog to the house?"

Boudica straightened, acknowledging their presence, though at this moment she could not remember their names. She felt as if an age had passed.

"No. We must find a place to bury him," she whispered, and Tilla began to cry. "Have the holes for the gateposts been dug?" When the men nodded, Boudica added, "We will lay him there, where he can continue to guard us, and carve his head upon the pole."

Drops of moisture sparkled on the dog's white coat and she thought it had begun to rain, but it was only her tears.

TWENTY

At Samhain, the doors are open between the old year and the new, between the living and the dead, between the worlds. This year, the new gate of Teutodunon was open as well, with torches set into the ground before the posts where the heads of the cattle sacrificed for the feast had been hung. The inner bank and ditch had been completed, though the palisade was still going in. Now Prasutagos had gotten the idea of adding another outer wall, with a forest of posts between them. Only the Good God knew how long *that* would take to build.

This was the season when the herds were brought in to the home pastures. Next week, when they began to cull those they could not keep through the winter, the scent of blood would hang heavy on the air. But now, as Boudica watched the sun fade into the west, the wind carried the smell of roasting meat and woodsmoke and the promise of more rain.

"Mother, what are you doing? We are waiting for *you!*" Rigana had just turned eleven and with every moon, it seemed, she grew taller. Along with the height came an apparent conviction that her parents were inferior beings who alternately annoyed and amused. Boudica told herself that the girl would grow out of it, but she recalled being much the same.

Well, Mama, you have your revenge, she thought with an inner smile. And perhaps tonight her mother's spirit would hear.

"Yes, dear, I'll come now," she said peaceably, and followed her daughter into the two-tiered hall.

Prasutagos was already seated in his carved chair on the other side of the fire. Her stool was next to his, but then came two seats that would be left empty for her mother and father. The king's guard and the rest of the household were settling into their places. There would be empty seats there as well; one of the warriors had been killed when his horse fell, and the wife of another was dead bearing her child.

An ordinary year, she thought, not like the autumn after her marriage when half the feast had been set aside for Prasutagos's brother and all the men killed at the battle of the Tamesa. If the gods were good, she would never see a Samhain feast like that again.

Prasutagos looked at her with a worried frown and she managed a smile. The feast was sacred, but most years it was not a time of sorrow. The Druids taught that the Otherworld was only a breath away from this one. The dead were not gone, and at Samhain, the veil between the worlds grew thin.

Now the food was coming in on wooden trenchers—bread and honey cakes and steaming barley, dried wild apples and ribs of beef and slices of roast boar. They had been brewing for weeks to get ready, and cups and horns were kept filled.

"I salute my mother, Anaveistl," said Boudica. "Teutodunon has changed a lot since you were lady here, but I hope you are not too disappointed with our housekeeping!" That got a laugh from those who remembered her mother's heroic bouts of spring cleaning. Boudica drained her cup, and the toasting went on.

She bit off the last bit of meat that human teeth could remove from a beef rib, reached down to give it to Bogle, then stopped, tears pricking in her eyes as she remembered why he was not there. But surely the dog had been as valued a member of the household as many of the others they were hailing—with a silent prayer she set the bone on the earth where he had so often lain.

The toasting continued, sometimes with a song or a story as the dead lived again in memory. But as the evening drew on, Boudica saw her daughters beginning to look more often at the open door.

"I think that someone wants to keep watch outside,"

she said, smiling. "Eoc Mor, will you go with them to the gate?"

And because she was listening, even before the girls came running back, Boudica caught the deep vibration of the distant drums.

"The White Mare is coming! The White Mare!"

The whole company poured out into the torchlit night. Overhead a few clouds were playing tag with the moon and a little fog was rising from the moist ground. Beyond the gateposts at the other end of the enclosure she saw a glimmer of light. It was not the great bonfire that burned beyond the gateway, for this light was moving. The misty air lent a quality to that brightness that made the hair prickle on her arms. It pulsed in time to the rattle of pebble-filled bladders and skirling of birch flutes and the throb of the drums. Boudica felt her heartbeat settling to that rhythm and laughed.

And now she could see the beings that bore those torches tumbling into the enclosure, masked and caped to mimic the animals that were the families' totems, or fantastic creatures from the Otherworld. Capes and sleeves fluttered with streamers of colored wool and metal bits and clattering bones. Some had the shape of men, but had painted themselves like the warriors of the old race whose blood they bore. Some had no disguise but chalk paste that turned their faces to skulls from which eyes glittered with unnerving intensity.

And rising from the midst of that screeching, chattering mob was the White Mare Herself, the bleached skull poised with clacking jaw above the drape of the supple white hide. Copper discs had been set into the eyeholes, polished to catch the torchlight with a baleful gleam. This was not the lively, loving horse goddess whose mask Boudica had borne at the kingmaking. At Samhain Epona showed the face of Life beyond life, to which Death was the door.

At Samhain she walks with the Lady of Ravens, thought Boudica, *and that is an aspect no one in her senses would ask to bear . . .*

The invaders formed into a rough semicircle with the White Mare in its center and began to sing—

> *"Behold, here we are,*
> *Come from afar,*
> *Your gates, friends, unbar,*
> *And hear us sing!"*

Each district had its own variation on the festival. Teutodunon had been Boudica's childhood home, so it was for her to step forward with the reply—

> *"Wise ones, tell me true,*
> *How many are you,*
> *And give your names, too*
> *That we may know."*

She probably knew the men who were responding, but through the masks their voices sounded blurred and strange.

> *"You must give us to eat*
> *Both barley and wheat,*
> *As the spirits you treat*
> *So shall you prosper!"*

As the girls ran back to the house for the bannocks and ale, Boudica kept the interchange going. In a few minutes the food and drink were being distributed to the masquers.

> *"The White Mare will sing,*
> *The spirits will bring*
> *New life and blessing*
> *To everyone . . ."*

The massive head dipped. Boudica stepped back, dizzied as if it were she who had drunk the ale, seeing not a horse skull and hide but the entire animal, limned in glimmering skin and bone.

"A gift from you gains a gift from me . . . What would you ask, Iceni Queen?"

Was she hearing that with her ears or with her heart?

"Give me back my little son . . ." she whispered in reply.

"He will return, but not to you. It is not through your children that you will gain immortality. But I will give you back your guardian."

Then the crowd surged between them and the connection was broken. Blinking, Boudica found herself at the edge of the throng.

"My Lady—"

She turned and recognized Brocagnos, a boar-mask dangling from his hand. On his other side something white was moving.

"When you visited my dun last fall my white bitch was in season, and that dog of yours—well you can see the pup is the spit of him. I thought to keep him, Lady, but I think he belongs here . . ."

Boudica scarcely heard. "Bogle . . ." she whispered as a massive white head with a russet nose and one red ear appeared at roughly the level of Brocagnos's hip. "Bogle," she said again, "is it you?"

The silky ears lifted. Then, with a joyful bark, the dog launched himself into her arms.

*T*he ripening grain in the fields around Danatobrigos rippled like an animal's pelt in the cold wind that blew in each day at sunset from the sea. Prasutagos had gone down to Colonia for the annual meeting of the chieftains, but it was five years now since Boudica had accompanied him. She preferred to spend the summer here, on the land she had learned to love, where the girls, now ten and almost thirteen, could run as wild as the ponies they rode.

During the day she was too busy to miss Prasutagos, but when the shadows lengthened and evening began to steal across the world, it had become her custom to whistle up the dogs and walk out to the track across the downs. There were a good half dozen of them now, old Bogle's offspring by bitches all over the Iceni lands. After Brocagnos brought the young dog, others had gifted her with puppies in which his blood ran strong, and now her walks were attended by a frothing of white, red-spotted hounds.

They coursed back and forth, giving chase to a hare that had been hiding in the hedge, barking at the crows that rose in yammering flocks and winged across the fields to their roosting tree. And yet beneath all the surface noise there was a deep quiet in the land that soothed Boudica's soul. Presently she came to the road and gazed southward, hoping to sight the party of men and horses that would herald her husband's return.

Boudica could see nothing on the road, but the dogs had come to a halt, heads lifted, scenting the breeze. She stood waiting, fondling first one and then another furry head as it pushed against her palm, and presently a single figure came into view. It was a man, young by the vigor of his walk, in a worn tunic of undyed wool with a pack on his back and a hat of woven wheatstraw pulled down over his brow.

"Well met, wanderer," she said as he came to a halt before her. "Why it is Rianor!" she exclaimed as he swept off the hat. He was a full priest now, she saw by his beard and shaven brow. "I hope you were coming to see us at Danatobrigos. If not, my hounds and I will carry you off anyhow."

"So long as it's not Arimanes's pack you have there," he said, still smiling. "They look like Faerie hounds, but they seem friendly. But that cannot be your old dog Bogle, unless he's gone to the Land of Youth and returned—"

"Very nearly. This one was born after the first one died, and as you can see, his markings are almost the same." The dog had settled into her life so smoothly that even without the White Mare's prophecy she would have believed him to be the same.

"Somehow Lugovalos's lectures never mentioned the reincarnation of dogs, but I suppose it could be so." Rianor grinned.

"Tell me what you are doing here?" Boudica asked as they started up the path to the farmstead.

"Being among those still young and strong enough to do so, I mostly carry news and messages. And when the soil seems favorable, plant a few seeds that may sprout into rebellion when the stars are right. All that practice in memorizing, you know." He smiled. "Anyhow, that is why I am here."

"Not to persuade me to rebel, I hope—" she began, but he shook his head.

"No. I've a message for you, from Lady Lhiannon."

"Have you seen her? Where is she? Is she well?"

Rianor held up a restraining hand. "I traveled to Eriu, and I hope never to do so again. The ocean and I do not agree. But indeed I did see the lady, and she is well. She is living with a community of Druids in the kingdom of Laigin, and truly they are a wonder, so numerous and powerful they can afford to fight among themselves when they are not using their magic to aid their kings. They are still as we were, I think, before the Romans came."

"And she sent word to me? You had best give it now. The girls are just the age to think you a figure of great romance. Once they catch wind of you the rest of us won't get in a word until you have told them the full tale of your wanderings."

"Very well." They had come to the wood below the farmstead, and Rianor seated himself on a fallen log and closed his eyes. "These are the words of the priestess Lhiannon to Queen Boudica . . ." His voice acquired a lighter timbre, as if Lhiannon had imbued him with her spirit as well as her words.

"My dear, I take this opportunity to send word by one you know well. He will tell you that I am well and happy. It was very hard to leave Britannia, but I am glad to have come. I have learned a great deal that I hope to share with you one day. But the chief news is that I have a daughter—no, not of my body, but a little girl that I found weeping in the marketplace one day, with hair as glossy as a blackbird's wing and eyes the blue of the sea. Her parents had a house full of little ones they could not feed, and were happy enough to sell her to me.

"My little Caillean, which means 'girl' in the tongue of Eriu, does not know when she was born, but I think she must be nearly the age of your younger girl. It is hard to tell, for she was undernourished when I found her, though she is shooting up fast with good food and care. She is a bright little thing, and eager to learn. I understand something of your delight in your daughters as I watch her change from day to day.

"I think of you often, and hope to see you again, though I cannot say when that will be. You may send a message through Rianor, who says you were well and happy—and beautiful—when he saw you seven years ago. If the gods are good, he will be able to bring it to me.

"You have my love always, dear. I remain your Lhiannon."

For a few moments the Druid was silent, then he shook himself and opened his eyes.

"Thank you," said Boudica. "How much of that do you recall?"

"You don't understand—when a message is set in me in trance I don't remember, and it's frustrating when people want more information, and I have no idea what it is that I've said."

"That must be difficult, but I am sure you delivered the message faithfully. It sounded as if she were speaking to me."

"I'm glad." He smiled warmly.

"Come now, our dinner will be ready and I am sure you must be hungry. Did you come from the south? As we walk you can tell me the latest news from Colonia."

Rianor was a good observer, with a gift for describing the things he had seen. They had all wondered what would happen when the emperor Claudius was succeeded by his stepson Nero, but as far as the Druid could see, the major local result seemed to be the temple being built in the dead emperor's name. It was strange that a man who in life had been despised by many should in death be honored as a god, especially since it was widely rumored that his wife had poisoned him. But only the good qualities of the dead were remembered, as if the divine spirit to which they had offered incense was all that remained. The ancient kings whose barrows were all over Britannia were still honored, so perhaps the beliefs of the Celts and the Romans were not so different in that regard. But however benign the emperor's spirit might be, it seemed hard that the Trinovantes, whom Claudius had deprived of king and kingdom, should have to pay for the deification of their conqueror.

"I did not see your husband, but I heard that he was there. He is much respected. They call him 'the prosperous King Prasutagos,' did you know?" Rianor stopped.

They had almost reached the farmstead. Above the hedge the roofs of the roundhouses rose in dark points against the fading sky, but light streamed from the doorways, and there was an enticing scent of cooking beef in the air.

"Before we go in, there is a thing I would say to you. When we were younger," he said with sudden diffidence, "I hoped that you would stay on Mona, and maybe dance with me at the fires."

And then you fancied yourself in love with Lhiannon, thought Boudica.

"But when I was here with the High Priestess and Coventa I saw how your husband looks at you. He is no firebrand, but he has clearly been good for you. Some women only grow old, but you have grown more beautiful."

Was that a declaration or a renunciation? Boudica repressed a temptation to laugh. Now that her daughters were approaching marriagable age it was consoling to know that she herself was still pleasant in men's eyes. "We have been very happy," she said at last. "But I am honored by your regard."

As they came through the gate the dogs came whirling back in a tumult of lolling tongues and wagging tails, followed by her daughters.

"Where *were* you, Mama? We've been back forever, and dinner is *done!*"

*B*oudica swallowed a last spoonful of beef and beans and considered her husband, finishing his own bowl on the other side of the fire. For the first time since she had known him Prasutagos looked old. He and his men had ridden in earlier that afternoon, and for a time they had all been busy unloading the bags and bales of goods and gifts that they had brought with them from Colonia. For Rigana there was a bridle of red leather with fittings of bronze for her pony, and for Argantilla a selection of embroidery yarn in every possible color. The younger girl was already more clever with her needle than her sister, better, really than Boudica herself would ever be.

She wished that Rianor could have stayed with them until the king arrived. It would have been interesting to compare his information with whatever it was Prasutagos had learned at the council . . . the bad news that he was saving until they were alone. It had to be political, she thought unhappily. They would already have heard anything public from the men. The others might think that the king was so quiet because he was tired. Prasutagos did look more fatigued than he ought to, even after such a long ride, but after sixteen years of marriage, his silences said more to her than most people's words.

*B*oudica had always loved the diffuse glow that lit their bed place when the light from the coals on the hearth filtered through the curtains. Neither light nor darkness, it made of their marriage bed a place protected and separate from the world. Now she raised herself on one elbow, looking down at her husband, carefully brushed back a strand of thinning hair, and kissed him on the brow.

"I have missed you," she said softly, and kissed his lips. He pulled her down and the kiss became deeper.

When they came up for air, she snuggled into her accustomed place with her head on his shoulder and her arm across his chest, listening to him breathe.

"And I you," he murmured. "I missed holding you in my arms, and I missed talking to you when the meetings were done."

"Did you? So what is it that you have been so carefully not saying since you got home?" She moved her hand across the muscle of his shoulder, relearning its contours.

"Is it that obvious?"

"It is to me." She tweaked his chest hair and he winced and laughed.

"Money."

Her caressing hand stilled. "What do you mean? The harvest was good this year—"

"To raise the wealth we will need, every grain in every ear would have to be made of gold . . ." He sighed. "All the imperial loans are being called in. You remember, those convenient funds that were offered by Claudius and his patrician friends the year of the floods, and the money we borrowed to build the hall at Teutodunon. The men who rule for young Nero want their money back. They say that Seneca has loaned forty million sesterces to British chieftains. Keeping so large an army here is expensive, and the mines have not proved as rich as they expected. The new procurator, Decianus Catus, seems to have been chosen because he will take a hard line."

"But can't the governor rein him in?" She stared unseeingly at the canopy.

"Varanius is dead. A man called Paulinus is on the way, but we don't know what his policy will be. For the time being, Catus is in charge."

"Catus and Clotho . . ." She shivered, remembering the meaning of the procurator's name. "One to figure out how to cheat us and the other to measure the price. They should deal very well." Mentally she was tallying stock and stores, wondering what could be sold and what they could spare. The curtains around their little world no longer seemed so secure a barrier.

"I suppose Rianor knew better than to talk rebellion here, but elsewhere he has found willing ears," Prasutagos said. "So far everyone still hopes the blow will not fall on them, but once the seizure of property begins, any spark will be enough to set the land aflame. The mood in the council was ugly, there at the end."

"We'll find the money somehow. We have to—rebellion can only bring disaster now . . ." Boudica sat up and set her hands on his shoulders, trying to make out his features. His eyes gleamed in the gloom. "And next year I will go to the council with you. I'll not have you coming home again looking like something Bogle dragged in from the moor." She stroked the strong muscles of his chest and belly as if her touch could make him whole.

"I am reviving already." He tried to laugh but his breathing had grown uneven. She smiled and reached lower, cupping the warm weight of his manhood. As he rose to meet her, she straddled him and welcomed him home.

TWENTY-ONE

*E*ver since the Feast of Brigantia it had been raining, a soft, persistent precipitation that left a pervasive damp behind it, as if earth and sky were both dissolving into primal ooze. If this kept up, thought Boudica, Dun Garo would slide into the river. The sharp cold of winter would have been more welcome.

When she went to the doorway of the weaving shed she could look down the muddy road. But the trees faded into mist beyond it. In such weather she would not be able to see Prasutagos approaching until he was at the gates. Drat the man—he should have been back by now! Drostac from Ash Hill had been waiting for two days for judgment in a boundary dispute, and though he accepted her authority as queen, she wanted her husband's counsel.

This morning a little party had come in from the Trinovante lands, dispossessed from their farmstead by a Roman official who was giving it to one of his underlings. It was a hard thing to be forced from the land where you knew the spirits who lived in each stone and stream by name—harder still to flee to the territory of a different tribe. But they no longer had a king of their own to ward that sacred relationship. Would Prasutagos take them under his cloak? *Could* he, wondered Boudica, when the strain on their own resources was already so great? Between the king's building projects and Roman taxes there was not much left in the coffers.

The greed of the Romans seemed unending. She had already sold a great deal of her jewelry to help her people. Of the major pieces, only the torque of Caratac still lay hidden like a secret defiance at the bottom of the oak chest. The Romans did have a legal right to repayment, though among her own people it would be a poor ruler who would not forgive his people their tribute when times were hard. Even the Romans provided their citizens with bread. That was the difference, she thought bitterly. The Romans fed their own people, but despite all their fine words about the benefits of belonging to the Empire, the Britons were still the enemy.

Boudica let the door flap drop and strode back to her loom. Temella looked up inquiringly but knew better than to ask questions when the queen was in this mood. For a moment she stood staring at the pattern of greens and blues, then turned restlessly away. Weaving required patience and calm, neither of which she currently could claim. She wanted to be out and *doing* something, and until Prasutagos returned, there was nothing she could do.

It was with a sense of profound relief that she heard the sound of horses coming into the yard. As the dogs began to bark she sped to the roundhouse. Crispus had already poured the welcome cup. She took it and stood waiting.

The door was pushed open with a blast of damp wind. Prasutagos was coming in, half supported by Eoc, with Bituitos right behind. Her words of greeting, and the reproof that she had meant to follow them, were forgotten.

"What is it?" she exclaimed as the king shrugged off his helper. "Was there an accident?"

"I am fine! Fussing old women." Prasutagos stood swaying, not seeming to notice that Bituitos had slid a supporting hand under his elbow. Frowning, she handed him the cup. Was that grimace supposed to be an answering smile? He started to drink and went off into a fit of coughing. She handed the cup back to Crispus, then took her husband's head between her hands.

"He's burning with fever!" She looked at his men accusingly. "What were you about to let him travel in this weather. He's ill!"

"Lady, I know it, but he *would* come!" said Eoc desperately. "And he is the king—"

"He said your touch would make him well," added Bituitos.

"My touch will put him in bed where he belongs," she

muttered, easing an arm around her husband. "Help me get him there!"

Once she had Prasutagos out of his wet clothes he did seem easier. She sat by the bed, spooning hot soup into him until he would take no more.

"All right then, if you will not eat, report!"

"Yes, my lady," he said with his old smile, though he was still breathing carefully. "Well . . . I got Morigenos to agree to loan Brocagnos grain for the spring planting . . . They'll share the labor and the harvest."

Boudica nodded. That was one more clan that would survive. "And was there any news from Colonia?"

He nodded. "Paulinus has finished subjugating the Deceangli. Rumor has it"—he paused for breath—"he means to march on Mona and end interference by the Druids once and for all."

"He'll have little luck," she answered, hoping it was true. "Half the Druids in Britannia are there. Mona will be defended by powerful magic. I've heard news as well. Cartimandua has not only broken with Venutios, she's taken his armor bearer Velocatos as her lover."

Prasutagos raised an eyebrow. "Is that intended as a warning? I shall have to keep an eye on Bituitos." His laughter turned into another spate of coughing, and this time when he finished, there were spots of blood on the cloth.

"You will do your watching from this bed, then," she said tartly. "You've been coughing your throat raw." She laid her hand on his forehead and found his fever a little less than it had been.

"Your fingers are cool," he murmured, closing his eyes. "I can rest now. I don't sleep well . . . when you are not by my side . . ."

Nor do I, my love, she bent to kiss his brow. It seemed strange to see him lying there so quietly when it was still day. She'd had to nurse her daughters through various childhood ailments, but Prasutagos had always been aggressively healthy. Strong men were always the most difficult patients. She hoped this illness would not last long.

She wished that Lhiannon were here.

"Sleep, my dear one . . . and heal," she said aloud. "I

must see to the feeding of your men." He would rest, and the fever would break, and he would get well. No other outcome was possible.

*W*hy doesn't Father get better?" Rigana kicked at her pony's sides and brought her up alongside the white mare that had replaced Roud as Boudica's regular mount. The men whom Prasutagos had insisted she bring along trotted behind.

The mare was called Branwen, and she considered herself queen of the road. Boudica saw the white ears flick back and slapped her neck before she could nip the pony. It was a fine day just before the Turning of Spring, and both horses were frisky.

Could she mouth some reassuring platitude when the same question battered at her brain? It had been over a moon since Prasutagos had taken to his bed. He was still coughing, and each time he tried to get up the fever returned. Boudica glanced sidelong at her daughter. Rigana was almost fifteen—more than old enough for her woman-making rite. Boudica had delayed it, dreaming she might take the girl to Avalon to be initiated as she had been. But they could not make so long a journey when Prasutagos was ill. There were other closer shrines that might serve. At this rate, Argantilla would be ready for her own ritual by the time Rigana had hers.

"You are worried about him," Rigana said accusingly. "You don't sleep. There are circles beneath your eyes. If you have to do the king's job"—she indicated the farmstead—"you should let me and Tilla help with yours."

"That is very thoughtful of you darling, but—"

"*Mother!* Don't insult me. I don't need to be protected."

Except, perhaps, from yourself... thought Boudica, uncomfortably reminded of herself at the same age. She had brought Rigana with her from some vague sense that the girl ought to be learning a chieftain's responsibilities, since she would probably marry a ruler someday. The queen did not allow herself to reflect that Rigana was also Prasutagos's heir.

"Perhaps you don't," she said mildly. "But when you have children you will understand why parents feel they have to try . . ."

"It's Father who needs help," Rigana said repressively. "If you cannot heal him, you should find someone who can."

Boudica sighed. "Lhiannon is in Eriu, and the Druids of Mona are hiding behind their wardings, waiting for the Romans to come."

"You can still ask—maybe there's someone who would rather be safe here instead!"

"Very well," answered Boudica. She could tell herself that she was calling for help to please her daughter, not because of the terror that kept her waking in the dark hours when she lay beside her husband, listening to each labored breath. Calgac was a dependable man. She would speak to him about it when they returned to the dun.

Drostac's farmstead lay on a little rise. Cattle and horses grazed in the surrounding fields. As they approached the farm a tide of dogs surged out of the yard, barking furiously. She saw a soldier on guard by some of the horses—apparently the Romans had already arrived.

"There, my lady." Calgac pointed toward a group of men who were arguing in the next field. One of them, she saw with distaste, was Cloto.

Boudica considered jumping Branwen over the wicker fence and arriving on horseback among them, but that would not only have upset Cloto, but spooked the cattle they seemed to be discussing, and besides, it lacked dignity.

"I owe ye three cows," Drostac was exclaiming. "I do not deny it. I've penned them yonder. This beast is a bull, and ye'll not be taking him away!"

The animal in question, a brown bull with heavy shoulders and a suspicious glint in its eye, was standing a few paces away.

"It is I, not you, who will decide which beasts I am taking," said Cloto. "I have selected that one." He smiled, and Boudica was suddenly sure that he knew exactly how much pride Drostac took in that bull.

Heads turned as she came toward them, Rigana a pace

behind. She looked from Cloto to the Roman official who accompanied him, a small man who kept stepping from foot to foot as if afraid he would sink into the mud, and clearly uneasy in the presence of the bull.

"You want the *bull*?" Boudica produced a titter of laughter. "Why, Cloto, have you forgotten everything you ever knew about farming?" She shook her head pityingly and turned to the Roman. "I suppose you will be wanting to tax this man again next year? Where do you suppose the calves will come from if you take the bull away?"

Drostac closed his lips on whatever he'd been about to say as the Roman frowned. Cloto's face had darkened. As he turned to reply, Boudica uttered a small shriek and edged away.

"Rigana dear, I want you to get back behind the fence," she said in a high voice. "And good masters, I think we should do the same. That animal does not look *safe* to me . . ."

Rigana's outrage at being ordered faded as she saw her mother wink. The Roman official needed no more encouragement to follow her. Boudica and Drostac came after him, leaving Cloto to face the bull, which by this time really was disturbed and had begun to paw the ground.

Once through the gate, Boudica took the Roman's arm. "If you did slaughter the beast, he'd not be good for much but sandal leather," she said confidentially. "Your troops will thank you for the meat of three tender heifers, believe me, where they'd curse you for trying to feed them that bull."

In the field they were passing, new lambs played with an energy one could not imagine their mothers had ever had. Now and again one of the ewes would lift its head in an admonitory *baa*. Boudica sympathized. As if her speculations had been a prophecy, just after the Turning of Spring Argantilla had come to her mother to announce that she had begun to bleed "from the woman's place," and when could they have her ceremony? Though Rigana considered her monthly flowering an annoyance, Argantilla had always been much more comfortable with her femininity. To initiate them together seemed the obvious response, and now that they were on the road, the girls were cantering their ponies up and down the line with equal enthusiasm.

"Calm down, you two," she called as her younger daughter bounced by. "If you wear out your mounts before we get there you'll be walking beside them."

Boudica found herself content to hold the white mare to a gentle amble, her anxiety at having left Prasutagos behind at Dun Garo warring with a guilty relief at being free in the open air. Should she have stayed with him? He had insisted that she should take the girls to the sacred spring.

They could have made the journey in two days, but the wagons in which some of the other women were riding moved slowly. Temella was with them, and some chieftains' wives. Her own mother had died long ago, but they had sent someone to bring old Nessa down from Danatobrigos, and Drostac's wife was bringing her own daughter, Aurodil, to share in the ritual.

*W*as the ritual like this for you?" asked Argantilla as they settled into the shelters beneath the trees.

Boudica put an arm around her daughter's shoulders. Tilla had not yet gotten her growth, but her figure was already sweetly rounded. She must have inherited that womanly body and her calm nature from her father's side of the family, thought the queen. It was nothing like the rangy energy she herself shared with Rigana. She would not have been ready for a womanhood ritual at the age of thirteen, but for Argantilla it was time.

"No, for I was with the Druids on Mona. When my courses began we had a celebration, but the ritual was always delayed until a girl was ready to decide whether she wished to become a priestess. So I was much older—" *And in some ways, much younger,* she reflected, giving the girl an extra hug. On Mona the Druids lived in lofty separation from the demands of the world, or at least they had until now, she thought apprehensively. Growing up in the High King's household had given both her daughters a sophistication beyond their years.

That night, however, the giggling that came from the shelter where the three girls were supposed to be sleeping was all too appropriate to their age. Boudica lay wakeful, remembering how Prasutagos had come to her in the darkness, touching herself as he had touched her, imagining he was beside her now. They had not made love since he had fallen ill. She had not realized how much she needed the release she found in his arms.

In the dark hour before the dawning they were awakened, and followed the priestess who tended the sacred spring down the path, rushlights flickering in their hands. When they reached the pool they set their lights around it and stood waiting.

Boudica's hands were tied to those of her daughters. As they approached, the priestess barred the way.

"Who comes to the sacred spring?"

"I am Boudica, daughter of Anaveistl, and these are my daughters, Rigana and Argantilla. Through all the years of their growing I have protected and nourished them. It is my right to stand with them now."

"The children you cherished are no more," said the priestess. "They are women, and their own blood flows red at the call of the moon. On the journey they are beginning they must walk alone."

She turned to the girls. "Rigana, Argantilla, the Goddess has called you to take on the responsibilities of womanhood. Are you willing to separate yourself from your mother and obey?"

"I am," they answered her.

The priestess turned to Boudica. "And are you willing to let them go?"

As she gave her assent her heart was crying *No! They are only children. It is too soon!* But the ritual, like the years that had brought them to this place, had a momentum that carried her along.

"Then I cut the cords that have bound you. From this moment, you shall walk free." With a little sickle-shaped knife the priestess severed the bonds.

As the cord gave way Boudica felt the loss of another connection that she had not consciously realized was there. *I should not have done this for both girls together,* she thought frantically. *I am not ready to lose both my babies at one blow!*

She stood aside as the process was repeated for the other mother and her girl, and followed, unhappily aware that from now on her only function here was to stand as witness. Three of the younger women had stripped off their garments and were helping the girls to disrobe before leading them into the pool. Boudica saw the goose bumps pebble their skin and winced in sympathy. Even at the height of spring the air was chilly at this hour, and the water was always cold.

In the dawn wind ribands fluttered from the branches, some old, some new. She supposed that the one she had left here so many years ago had become dust by now, like the body of her son. But the image of the Goddess was still there—or perhaps it was another one made to the same pattern. Boudica imagined a sequence of such statues, one replacing another as the first decayed, just as new generations of daughters took their mothers' places at the sacred spring.

"Now let the water bear away all stains and soil," chanted the young women, dipping up water and pouring it over the girls. "Let it dissolve all that bound you, let all that hid your true selves be washed away . . . Feel the water caress your bodies, and remember the waters from which you were born."

Red and dark and fair, the girls turned to receive the blessing. In the flickering light their bodies gleamed like ivory, glittering where the water made rivulets across rounded limbs. Boudica's breath caught in wonder at the beauty of budding breasts and the sweet joining of slim thighs. At places like this one and the Blood Spring of Avalon she had sensed a holy power. And there had been times when she had felt it within. But as the three girls embraced each other she saw the Maiden Goddess manifest in all Her infinite variety, radiant with potential, and her tears fell to mingle with the waters of the sacred spring.

"Rigana, Argantilla, Aurodil, clean and shining, revealed in your beauty, arise, O my sisters, and join us now . . ."

The girls got out of the pool with more alacrity than

they had gone in, gasping with cold and laughter as they rubbed each other dry and pulled their tunicas on. Meanwhile, the women faced each other along the path, arms clasped in pairs to make a tunnel through which the girls must pass to reach the feast that waited in the clearing beyond.

"*From the blossom comes the fruit and from the fruit the seed*," the women sang. "*Dying, we are born again, and buried, we are freed . . .*"

Boudica and Aurodil's mother opened their arms to catch Rigana, holding her close.

"With this embrace you are born into the circle of women," whispered Boudica.

"With this embrace you are born into new life," the other woman replied.

Then they were releasing her to the next pair, and opening their arms to Aurodil. Ahead of them the song continued.

"*Birthing and rebirthing, passing, we return,*
Releasing, we are given all, relinquishing, we learn . . ."

As the initiates passed through, the line unraveled behind them and the rest of the women followed. Light from the newly risen sun shafted through the branches in long rays made visible by the steam that rose from the pot boiling over the fire. The girls had been given seats of honor and crowned with wreaths of early primroses and cowslips. Laughing and blushing, they received the wisdom and warning, much of it bawdy, that the women were there to provide.

Boudica sipped the mint tea Nessa gave her in silence. She had felt this mingling of joy and loss after childbirth. And why should she be surprised? She had expected it to hurt when she birthed her daughters' bodies, but this second separation tore at her heart with a new and unexpected pain.

But her children were still with her. The Druids taught that death was another kind of birthing. If her husband made that passage what would she do? After today she would still be able to hold her daughters in her arms even though their relationship had changed. But if Prasutagos died . . .

Goddess! Lady of the Sacred Spring! I will give him your waters to drink, and if he recovers we will build a temple here at your shrine. Lady of Life! Let my husband live!

*P*rasutagos lay in the great bed, utterly still.

Sweet Goddess, is he dead? Boudica stopped short with the curtain half lifted, staring.

Surely, she thought in blind assurance, he would have waited—he could not leave her without saying farewell— and then, more sensibly, surely they would have told her if he had died. She saw his chest rise and fall and her heart began to beat once more. And though she had made no sound, his eyes opened and he greeted her with his old sweet smile.

Boudica forced her lips to respond though her heart was weeping. *He is so thin! I should never have gone away!*

"So, our daughters are women now . . ."

"The rites went well," she said, letting her cloak slide to the floor. The thongs of the bedstead creaked as she sat down beside him.

He sighed. "Surely the years fly fast, when it seems no more than a season since I first held Rigana in my arms . . . You look no older now than you did then, my wife . . . when you began to forgive me for begetting her . . ."

Boudica blinked back tears. "I saw strange horses in the pen," she said with forced briskness. "Do we have visitors?"

"One for you . . . one for me . . ." His lips twitched. "Or I suppose they are both . . . for me, though I only summoned one." His breath caught suddenly and his chest heaved as he struggled for air.

Breathe! Boudica leaned over him, willing him strength, and was rewarded as he drew a shuddering breath. "Shh . . . don't try to talk!"

"It will ease in a moment, my lady," said a new voice. The curtains stirred and a tall thin man in a white robe came in. He took the king's wrist, feeling for the pulse.

Boudica stared at him, memory gradually matching the lean features and graceful hands to those of a Druid she had last seen on Mona more than half her life ago. There was scarcely more silver in his black hair than she had seen there then.

"Brangenos! What are you doing here?"

"Responding to your call, my lady," he replied. "I trained as a healer—I use medicine to heal the body, and song to restore the soul." He looked down at Prasutagos, who seemed to have drifted into sleep, and drew Boudica aside. "I can ease the king's pain, but music is the best treatment I can offer now."

"He is dying?" She closed her eyes against his answering nod.

"Do not blame yourself, my queen. It would have done no good if I had come sooner. This is not the coughing sickness, but some deeper ill. He tells me that a horse kicked him in the chest some years ago. That might be the first cause, or some other evil that we cannot know."

"But he seems so cheerful," she said weakly.

"He knows what comes to him, but he will not show his pain to you. Not yet. But you studied on Mona—soon you will have to remember your training. He will fight—and suffer—until you give him leave. You must be the Goddess for him, my lady, and ease his birth into the Otherworld . . ."

Boudica shook her head. *I don't remember . . . I am not a priestess . . . I can't let him go . . .*

"But not yet," came a whisper from the bed. Boudica and Brangenos both turned. "First . . . we have work to do."

"Yes, my lord." The Druid bowed. "Do you wish the Roman to come in?"

"While you tended our daughters' spirits . . . I have tried to safeguard . . . their inheritance," Prasutagos said as Boudica's brows lifted in surprise.

She resumed her seat beside him as the curtains were drawn aside and Brangenos returned, followed by Bituitos, Crispus, and a bald man in a Roman tunic who eyed her with mingled appreciation and apprehension.

What on earth has he heard about me? She forced her

grimace to something more pleasant. *I won't hurt you, little man, no matter how unwelcome you may be.*

"This is Junius Antonius Calvus, a lawyer from Londinium," said Crispus, in British, and then in Latin, "Sir, this is the queen."

"She speaks our language?" asked Calvus, as if finding it hard to believe.

Boudica bared her teeth in a smile.

"She does, but Bituitos here does not. Therefore I will translate so that he may serve as witness."

The lawyer cleared his throat. "Very well then. Domina, your husband has asked me to draw up a will in our fashion, as he is a client of the emperor and a friend of Rome. Ordinarily, this would have been done long ago and the document sent to Rome to be recorded in the temple of Vesta, but we can keep it in the Office of the Procurator for now." He opened the leather satchel at his side and withdrew a scroll.

Boudica tried to listen as the sonorous Latin rolled forth, its lilting British echo driving the sense of it in. The dower lands already settled on Boudica remained her own, but the king's possessions were divided between his daughters and the emperor. As Calvus read, Prasutagos listened, his features set in the lines of stubborn determination Boudica knew so well.

"In Roman law, it is usual for a woman to inherit from her family, not her husband," the lawyer said apologetically when the reading was done. "A man leaves his wealth to his children. Daughters may inherit when there are no sons."

"But—the emperor?" she asked.

Calvus grew a little pink and looked away. "You may be aware that there are men . . . close to the emperor, who exercise a great deal of power . . ."

Boudica nodded. Seneca and the other old men who controlled the boy emperor had been raping Britannia of her wealth these past few years.

"We think . . . that if Nero is co-heir with your daughters, they will not dare to challenge the will. It was the only legal way I could devise . . ." His voice trailed off. He still looked, thought Boudica, as if he thought she might eat him. She turned to her husband.

"My love, is this indeed what you desire?"

"My *desire* is to live," he breathed. "But if I cannot . . . this is my will. I ask the council to confirm . . . you to rule."

"Until Rigana is grown and chooses a husband," added Bituitos. "The Romans supported Cartimandua because she served them, but they are not comfortable with ruling queens."

Prasutagos's eyes had closed. Brangenos, who for such a tall man had a remarkable ability to fade into the background when he desired, stood up. The Roman jumped, having apparently not realized he was there.

"The king has exhausted his strength—he must sleep now." The Druid's frown was a command.

Calvus hastened to gather his things and was escorted out by Crispus. Bituitos followed. But Boudica remained standing. Her defiant gaze met the compassion in that of the Druid, who bowed. When he had gone, she stood gazing down at Prasutagos's closed features, memorizing the arch of his nose, the line of his brows. There was a little line between them, as if even in sleep he felt pain. His mustache was entirely silver now.

Her vision blurred, and she sank to her knees beside the bed, weeping soundlessly. A long time later, it seemed, she felt a touch upon her hair and jerked upright, trying to dry her eyes.

"Go ahead and cry," he said. "The gods know I have done so. Do you think it is easier for me to go than for you to stay?"

"Yes!" she dashed more tears away. "Was it not worse for you when your first wife died? And you had only lived with her for a year. You and I have been bound for nearly half my life, and you are leaving me alone!"

Prasutagos closed his eyes. Boudica held her breath, appalled at her own words. They had never talked about the first woman to call him husband. What madness had made her mention that now?

"When she died . . . I wept because I could not save her," he whispered at last. "Now . . . because I will not be able to protect *you* . . ."

*   *   *

*B*oudica liked to walk down to the horse pen when Brangenos insisted that she leave Prasutagos to get some air. Now it was only here that she allowed herself the luxury of tears. Bogle and the other dogs trailed her in uncharacteristic silence as they sensed her mood. The afternoon was fading. The white mare came to the fence, butting at her shoulder in hopes of a treat, and Boudica put her arms around the strong neck and buried her face in the mare's white mane. She did not pray. She had not been able to pray since she returned from the sacred spring, but the mare's solid strength was some comfort.

The Beltane celebrations had been a wake instead of a festival, though Prasutagos still lived. The chieftains, shocked at the prospect of losing their king, had been willing enough to agree to all that he asked. Summer was blessing the land with joyous growth, but with each hour the king's strength ebbed as his failing lungs lost their battle to take in air.

With her face pressed against Branwen's coarse mane, Boudica sensed, rather than saw the ebbing of the light. Then the mare stamped and shook her head, and Boudica realized that someone was calling her.

"Mama . . ." Rigana said tightly. "Brangenos says that you should come."

A shudder she could not prevent ran through Boudica's frame, but when she turned, her eyes were dry. She reached out and took her daughter's hand. As they approached the roundhouse she could hear harp notes, sweet as memory. The Druid's potions were no longer of much use, but music seemed to ease the king's pain. As they passed into the entryway she stopped, steeling herself against the smell of sickness.

Rigana joined her sister at the other side of the bed. Bituitos and Eoc were there, and others. Boudica did not see them. Prasutagos's face had grown more gaunt even in the time she had been gone, the flesh shrinking upon his bones. Each uneven breath was a struggle. Was he unconscious, or only so focused on staying alive that he had no attention left for the outside world? Now the tears that blurred her eyes were from pity, not her own sorrow.

What Brangenos had said was suddenly real to her. Her husband could not live. Each hour only prolonged his pain. Was this how Prasutagos had felt when he watched her struggling to give birth to his child? He labored now to release his spirit, and to her fell the task of midwifing his soul.

I cannot do it, she thought.

I must . . .

She took a step forward and her husband's eyes opened. His lips moved, trying to shape her name.

"Prasutagos . . ." She spoke as he had spoken to her so long ago. "Prasutagos, I am here . . ." She knelt and took his hands, willing strength through their linked fingers, and his agony seemed to ease.

His lips moved once more, the words almost without sound. "Watch over my people, Boudica. Guard my girls . . ."

"Yes, my love," she answered steadily. "I will."

With an effort he drew another breath, the body still fighting to live. She leaned forward. Her lips brushed his brow.

"You have done all that you could," she whispered. "No woman ever had a better husband. It is finished now, my beloved. Go onward—go free . . ."

As she sat back his lips curved in their familiar sweet smile. He did not speak again.

Boudica waited, remembering suddenly how it had been when she took ship to go to Avalon, how it had seemed as if it were the shore, not the boat, that was slipping away. A long time later, she became aware that the labored breathing had ceased. His fingers were growing cool against her own. She released them and gently crossed his hands upon his breast.

Then she rose to her feet. If others spoke to her, she did not hear them. Prasutagos was still. In all the years she had railed against his silences, there had been none like this. Plead as she might, he would not answer her.

Boudica turned, brushing aside those who tried to stay her. Her steps led her to the horse pens where the white mare was waiting. What need had she for saddle or bridle? She leaped to the mare's back, and in a moment they were through the open gate and away.

The queen rode the white mare as once she had ridden the red, her wild hounds baying behind her, and men fled inside their houses where she passed. "Epona rides . . ." they whispered. "Epona mourns the king."

But no matter how wildly she galloped, she would never overtake him now.

TWENTY-TWO

Lhiannon gripped the rim of the coracle that had brought her from the larger ship to the shore, and carefully clambered over the side. Sand crunched beneath her feet. She bent and scooped it up with her hand.

"I bind myself to this earth of Britannia," she murmured, "to its soil and stone, stream and spring. To each thing that grows and to all that walks and flies, to the people of this land I pledge myself, not to leave it again."

To her right loomed the gray masses of the holy mount. A few huts clung to the slopes. Fishing boats were drawn up on the shore, where crows squabbled with the seagulls for scraps from the last catch they had brought in.

"Is this Lys Deru?" asked the Irish Druid who had come with her, looking around him dubiously. His elders, responding to rumors of a potential influx of refugees from Britannia, had sent him to see for himself what was going on.

Lhiannon laughed.

"This is but the bare, stormy face Mona shows to the sea. No doubt these good folk will give us some food in exchange for a blessing, and then two days of walking will bring us to the village. But if I have not lost all my magic, someone may meet us sooner with beasts for us to ride."

The prospect did not make the man look much happier, but he asked no more. Lhiannon sighed. *If I have not lost all my magic,* she thought, *and if the Druids of Lys Deru are not too distracted by fear of the Romans to hear my call.* The crew that had brought them from Eriu had carried disquieting rumors of a Roman advance. She had hoped to bring Caillean with her, but with the situation so unsettled it did not seem wise. The girl would be safe with the family Lhiannon had paid to keep her until she sent for her to come.

It was the dream that had awakened Lhiannon just after Beltane that concerned her now. She had heard Boudica weeping, and then she had seen a goddess on horseback who rode wailing across the skies.

*T*he keening of the women cut through the murmur of the crowd. After three days of public mourning, Boudica no longer really heard them. Now that Prasutagos's voice was silent, there was not much that she cared to hear. When the chieftains began to arrive she spoke to them, but a moment later could not remember whom she had seen.

The morning after Prasutagos died, the mare, having run herself out, had brought Boudica home. By then, preparations for the funeral were well under way. Old women had appeared at the dun to wash and lay out the body. Men were already digging a burial pit and gathering wood for the pyre. And by ones and twos and families the Iceni were coming in.

"Mother—it is time to go . . ." Argantilla's warm hand closed on hers.

Blinking, Boudica focused on the scene around her, the somber faces at odds with the splendor of festival clothing—Temella, Crispus, Caw as usual at Argantilla's side. They were all waiting for her to mount the white mare and lead them to the burial ground. Rigana was already on her bay horse, face pale from nights spent weeping. Fragmentary memories told her that it was gentle Argantilla who had held the household together during these past days. A whisper of reviving maternal instinct wondered why that should surprise her. *Rigana is too much like me . . .* she thought numbly. *She is a sword without a sheath.*

Obediently she allowed Calgac to give her a leg up and settled herself. Branwen, too, was on her best behavior, pacing sedately along the road as if she could not imagine galloping wildly across the moors.

A stretch of heathland to the north of Dun Garo bore a series of round barrows raised for ancient kings. Now a new pit lay open beside them. Her eyes avoided the wood-framed burial chamber where the flesh that Prasutagos had left behind rested on sheepskins laid over a bier. During the days he had lain there his people had come to say good-bye. They stood now in a great silent mass, waiting.

There should have been rich grave goods around the body, but much of what would have been offered had been sold. The wealth of "the prosperous King Prasutagos" had gone to help his people. But other items had been added to those she recognized—small things whose value was measured by the heart, not by the scales: a piece of embroidered cloth, a use-smoothed wooden bowl, even a child's toy horse. Such treasure could never be taxed by Roman conquerors.

Brangenos stood by the pyre. Beside him, a burning torch was fixed in the ground. He had found a clean robe somewhere. Its snowy folds billowed in the light wind. He was a Druid of many talents, she thought grimly. Whether you needed music, medicine, or ritual, he was there. She would have liked to hate him for failing to save the king. But that would have required her to feel.

She dismounted and took her place with her daughters before the pyre, where Bituitos and Eoc had kept vigil since their lord was put into his grave. They had stood at the king's shoulder since he and they were boys. Boudica supposed that their loss must bite almost as sharply as her own. Weeping, they jumped down into the grave-chamber and lifted their lord so that others could bear him to the pyre.

"This is the body of a man we loved." The Druid contemplated the bier. "But Prasutagos is not this flesh. This flesh is earth and the food of earth, borrowed for a time. Now we must give it back again. From the waters that are the womb of the Goddess this man came. As blood, those waters flowed through his veins. Now the land is fed by the blood of the king. Through this body passed the breath of life. He has released it to the wind. Breathing that wind we take in his spirit . . . and let it go once more. Within this body burned immortal fire. Let that flame now set him free!"

He pulled the torch from the ground and plunged it into the oil-soaked logs. Instantly the greedy flames raged upward. Boudica felt her daughters' fingers dig sharply into her arms and only then realized that she had started toward the pyre. *Why do you stop me?* she thought resentfully. *If I burn with him I, too, will be free . . .*

Rigana began to sob, and with an instinct that transcended her sorrow Boudica gathered her into her arms while Argantilla tried to hold them both. Boudica was suddenly acutely aware of the warmth of their flesh against her own. *He lives in them . . . so long as I have our children, he is not completely gone . . .* And suddenly that heat melted the ice that had numbed her spirit and the healing tears flowed from her own eyes as well.

As the body burned, people were descending into the burial chamber, taking up each item and ceremonially breaking it, the cloth ripped, the metal snapped in sacrifice, to lie there with the king's ashes once the burning was done. Bituitos brought out the gold-hilted sword that had been hidden when the Roman inspectors came, set the point against a stone, and leaned on it until the iron blade cracked. Eoc bent the bronze-covered shield whose whorled boss glittered with red enamel. The jeweled brilliance blurred through her tears. How could the sun shine so brightly on such a day? Even the skies should have been weeping to lose this man.

Brangenos took up his harp and began to sing—

> *"The king who reigns in peace is the shield of his people—*
> *Their praise is his glory, his wealth is their love,*
> *Until his time is done.*
> *The king who wards his people by the gods is welcomed—*
> *He feasts with the blessed, he walks in the light,*
> *Until he shall come again . . ."*

Smoke billowed blue in the sunlight, the scent of destruction mingling with the pungence of the herbs on the pyre. She would not look, would not bear witness to the withering of hands that had touched her so sweetly, the destruction of his features. Whimpering, Boudica faced the flames, for surely the reality could be no worse than the images her mind was creating now.

"Fire burn!" cried the Druid. "Wind blow! Flesh consume! Spirit go!"

Her vision was dazzled by the blaze. Fire, said the Druids, released the spirit, reducing the flesh that had confined it to its component elements. No wonder the world was rejoicing—Prasutagos was a part of everything now.

Everything . . . For a single eternal moment Boudica was one with the world around her, her daughters, the land, the people who wept for their king. Prasutagos had loved them all. For a moment she felt his presence enfold her once more.

She lifted her head, a sudden tingling awareness shocking through her. Had the heat of the pyre set that shimmer in the air, or was the world only a veil of light that concealed a more enduring reality?

Lys Deru seemed smaller than Lhiannon remembered. Or perhaps it appeared so because so many more people were now crowded within. She should not be surprised—the influx of refugees had begun even before she went to Eriu—but it was strange.

"Thank you for sending out the horses," she said as she followed Coventa down the path to the council hall.

"After my other recent visions, that one was very welcome." Coventa looked back with a sad smile.

It seemed strange to see Coventa in the dark blue robes of a senior priestess, but she must be past thirty by now. *Well,* Lhiannon thought sadly, *we all grow older.*

"Did you return because of Boudica? Her husband has died, they say. Rianor left to see if he could be of service to her. If he had known you were coming perhaps he would have stayed . . ."

Lhiannon stopped short in the path. "I felt . . . that she was in some trouble," she murmured. "Thank you for telling me."

"I'm not surprised. You two were always close. They say he was a good man."

That was true, but after so many years the bond that had been forged between Prasutagos and Boudica at his king-making might have faded to the habitual affection most married couples knew. And yet Lhiannon had felt Boudica's anguish. She would be devastated, but . . . the king was gone. Where now would his queen look for comfort?

From the hall ahead she could hear the mutter of conversation—of argument—she realized as they drew near.

The wicker walls had been removed to let in air, and the benches beneath the thatched roof were full. Helve sat in the great chair at the head of the fire pit, her eyes bright as those of some predatory bird. But her hair was liberally streaked with gray. And the man beside her—Lhiannon missed a step as she realized it was Ardanos.

Even in Eriu she had heard that Ardanos had been chosen Arch-Druid when Lugovalos died. But she had not expected him to *change*. He sat like an image in the white robes, even his hair set in stiff curls. But perhaps his heart was not so armored as it appeared, for it was he who turned first, and as their eyes met, something kindled in his glance.

Whatever she thought she had seen was almost immediately veiled. He bowed his head in greeting and Helve looked around, her expression an odd mixture of exasperation and relief as she saw Lhiannon standing there.

"Our sister Lhiannon has returned from Eriu," she said pleasantly. "I am sure she will have much to tell us when our present deliberations are concluded. In the meantime, let us make her welcome." Her gaze swept the assembled Druids, male and female, and an appropriate murmur rose from among them. Lhiannon recognized Belina and Cunitor and some of the others, and was that stalwart young man with the brown beard little Bendeigid? But many of those sitting there were older priests and priestesses whom she did not know.

She followed Coventa to a seat on one of the back benches.

"This is the situation." Ardanos's voice was even and controlled. "The governor Paulinus has spent the winter in his fortress at Deva, building boats and gathering supplies. The supplies might take him anywhere, but boats—flat-bottomed boats that can run up on mudflats or a sandy shore—can only be intended to bring soldiers here. And now the season of storms is over ..." At the murmur of protest he lifted a hand. "We have long known that it might come to this. We should be grateful that the gods have protected us so long."

"This island is full of Silure and Ordovice and Deceangli warriors who escaped when the Romans conquered their tribes," said Helve. "On the mainland, there is no British king with the force to defend us. We have called you here together to decide whether to disperse, to resist with all our powers, or to surrender to the mercy of Rome."

"The latter is no choice, surely," said someone. "They have none for our kind."

"They hate what they fear—then let us prove them right to do so!" This was an imposing old fellow with a long white beard who had clearly been the chief Druid to some tribal king. "For the warriors who have come here there is nowhere else to run, and when have there ever been so many Druids of our stature gathered in one place? Let us call down the wrath of the gods on Rome!"

Sweet Goddess, thought Lhiannon, *what have I returned to? It will be like the campaign with Caratac all over again.* In nightmares she still wandered across that final battlefield, though the memories had faded while she was in Eriu.

"First, surely, we should seek their favor," said one of the priestesses. "When we fled to this place we brought our treasures. Swords and chariots are not a Druid's weapons. Let us give them to the gods!"

"Better sunk than displayed in a Roman triumph," muttered someone behind her.

"The warrior prepares for battle by practicing his skills," Ardanos said sternly. "You who served in dun and village had more need for the rites of growth and healing than for high magic. And our purpose here at Lys Deru has been to nurture spirits. If we are to stand against the Romans, every one of you must spend the time we have left in prayer and purification, disciplining the mind and preparing the soul."

Lhiannon wondered how much use that would be. She had seen enough warfare to know that the farmer whose hands were more accustomed to wielding a hoe than a spear was useful mostly to fill out the battle line. To use a sword effectively required constant practice. In Eriu, the Druids were often called upon to raise storms or spirits against the armies on whom their kings made war, but only a few of the Druids here—*like Ardanos... and me,* she thought grimly—had actually seen fighting.

Lost in thought, she was taken by surprise when the meeting ended. Before she could protest, Coventa was pulling her into the circle that had formed around Ardanos and Helve.

"Is your family here?" she asked politely as the Arch-Druid turned to her. "I trust that they are well."

Ardanos's features relaxed. "They are indeed, but not here. They are safe, thank the gods, with Sciovana's family in the Durotrige lands. My little Rheis was married to Bendeigid just last year, and is expecting a child."

Lhiannon blinked, mentally tallying the years, for it seemed only yesterday that she had returned to Mona to find Ardanos married with a little child. But the world had not stood still while she was in Eriu. By this time, Boudica's daughters must be husband-high as well.

At the sound of his name Bendeigid looked up. Lhiannon realized that inside that muscular body still lived the lad who used to climb trees to look at birds' nests, just as somewhere within her was a girl who had loved Ardanos. *And despite that shell he has built for protection, there is something in Ardanos that still cares for me...*

She felt no surprise when he came to her after supper was done.

"Walk with me, Lhiannon."

She looked at him dubiously, remembering the last time they had been alone. Reading her expression, Ardanos looked away.

"You need not be afraid," he said in a constricted voice. "I shall say nothing to you that could not be said in full view of the entire Druid community, nothing of a personal nature, that is. But as I also wish to speak frankly of matters that concern the others, I would as soon they did not hear."

"Very well, my lord," she replied. "I will come with you."

This time he led her down the road toward the shore. The cliffs on the other side were thickly wooded. On the height beyond, a point of light marked some shepherd's fire. The dark waters of the strait lay quiet beneath the young moon, belying the strength of the current below, but the tide was coming in and the wavelets, each one a little closer, lapped gently at the sand. It was hard to believe that soon those waters might run with blood.

"You were right to address me as 'lord' a little while ago," Ardanos said presently. "The heart of the man who loves you tells me to send you away while I can, but the Arch-Druid answers to other imperatives. You have seen my 'army,'" he added bitterly. "Good priests and priestesses, most of them, but these are not adepts. Helve, little as you may like her, does have power. So does Coventa, if there is someone to direct it. Most of those who were young enough to remember their training went off to help the warriors and died. But you, Lhiannon, were the most powerful priestess of your generation. We will need you badly. For the sake of our Order, I ask you to stay."

"What chance do we have?" she asked.

Ardanos sighed. "This governor Paulinus worries me. I fear he is another Roman of the breed of Caesar. His gods must love him. He takes risks and wins. He should have died a hundred times when he was in those mountains"—he gestured toward the dark shapes that brooded beyond the water—"but he always came through."

Lhiannon nodded. The fact that Paulinus had been able to finally subdue the Ordovices, who had kept on fighting even after Caratac was gone, bore witness to that.

How could she weigh the need of one woman—even one she loved—against that of the community that guarded the traditions of an entire people? It was the old argument all over again. What good did it do to preserve the body if you lost your soul? And if this enemy was indeed too strong, if all the war gods of the tribes together could not contend against Jupiter and Mars Ultor, could she bear to live in safety with Boudica, knowing that she had not even tried?

*   *   *

We are gathered here to take counsel for the future of the Iceni tribe," Morigenos said with the kind of sober grandeur that he adopted even on less momentous occasions. As the eldest of the clan leaders, he had become the spokesman for the men who were gathered around the great fire before the house of the king.

The cluster of buildings within the palisade had not changed much since she had come here for her wedding, thought Boudica wistfully. Except for the little temple just outside the dun, even in his passion for building, Prasutagos had not ventured to alter the ancient home of his line. Once more the elders of the Iceni clans had assembled at Dun Garo to choose a king.

"We have buried a noble lord, Prasutagos son of Domarotagos, son through many fathers of Brannos, who led us to this land. There is now no male remaining of the blood of our kings." Morigenos pulled at his brindled beard.

Boudica sighed, remembering her lost son. If he had survived he would be nearly the age of the young emperor.

"It was the will of our lord that his daughters inherit with the emperor." Morigenos's lip curled at that, but he said no word that could be reported against him. It was the other chieftains who glared at Cloto, who had arrived the day after the funeral, unheralded, uninvited, and unwelcome.

At least it was only Cloto, thought Boudica. She had feared that Pollio might come to the funeral. She herself was here only for the sake of the living children who sat to either side. Her moment of exaltation at the funeral had gone as swiftly as it came. Without Prasutagos it was a barren world, but for their sakes she must learn to live in it.

"With that we have no quarrel. A man may leave his possessions where he likes—" *and where it is politic,* came the unspoken addendum. "But it is for us to choose who shall lead the tribe."

"On both counts you are wrong." Cloto's voice overrode his. "Prasutagos was a client of the emperor. That relationship dies with him. It is for the emperor to choose another man to rule these lands as client-king or to administer them directly as a conquered territory."

"We were never conquered!"

"We are Rome's allies!"

The meeting erupted in a babble of protest.

"And who are you to speak for the emperor, toad?" roared Bituitos.

"One who is trusted by Nero's procurator. While the governor is in the west it is Decianus Catus whose word you must obey. Neither your will nor that of Prasutagos has any meaning until confirmed by the real rulers of Britannia."

"If they do not do so, they betray that Roman Law they praise so highly!" snapped Drostac, his mustache bristling.

"And they show themselves without honor and unworthy of our obedience," added Morigenos.

Cloto shrugged. "I tell you this for your sake, not for mine."

Boudica surged to her feet. "How dare you say such things while my husband's ashes are still warm? He trusted Rome. Go back to your masters and let them teach you the meaning of honor, if they can!"

"Do you think yourself another Cartimandua?" he sneered. "They do not trust *her*, and they will place even less faith in *you*—"

From the throats of the men around the fire came a deep growl, like that of dogs when they scent an enemy. For the first time, Cloto seemed to realize that he might be in danger. Standing, he draped his cloak over his shoulders with what dignity he could muster.

"On your heads be it," he repeated. "You have been warned."

"We have heard you." Boudica drew herself up. The men laughed as he wilted beneath her glare. "Now be gone!"

When Cloto had departed, she resumed her seat and nodded to Morigenos. "I apologize for interfering. Continue."

"We thank you for ridding us of that cur—" For a moment he considered her, then turned to the others once more. "Not that I believe him. The Romans have been strong in their support of the Brigante queen. Why should they not accept a queen in the Iceni lands? There is no male of the old blood, but Boudica and her daughters are of that line, and she has ruled at her husband's side. I propose that we acclaim her now. When her daughters have husbands it will be time enough to consider the election of a king."

"This is what I hoped for!" Rigana squeezed her hand. "Mother, why do you look so surprised? It was the obvious thing."

Boudica had not expected it. But as the tribesmen began to cheer she heard once more the voice of Prasutagos asking her to guard his people. *For you I will do it* . . . she said silently. *For you* . . .

*B*oudica stood in the Earth-ring where she and Prasutagos had been bound. The body to which the marriage rite had linked her was no more, but he was still a part of her soul. Standing here, with the green fields rolling away on every side, she could almost sense him beside her. He had loved this land, and she had loved him. If she followed in his footsteps perhaps he would walk with her, and she might dare to feel once more.

The Druids who had conducted Prasutagos's rite were long gone, frightened into exile or hiding when the Romans had begun to enforce the ban on their Order. Brangenos, with the surprising assistance of Rianor, who had turned up unexpectedly at their gates a few days after the council, was conducting the ceremony.

"Boudica, daughter of Dubrac, of the line of Brannos, son of the White Mare, will you stand as queen for the people and Lady of the Land?"

"I will."

They had purified and blessed her already with fire and water, with earth and with air. She felt herself suddenly grown heavy, as if she had taken root in the soil.

"And will you swear to be as a mother to the Iceni, nourishing them in time of peace, protecting them in war, upholding the rights of the weak, and punishing the wrongdoing of the strong?"

Suddenly she was acutely aware of the people around her, the chieftains inside the Earth-ring and everyone else outside. The air throbbed with their energy. Her own voice trembled as she replied—

"I so swear."

"And by what will you swear all this, daughter of Dubrac?"

"I swear by the gods of our people." She swallowed as the air around her seemed to thicken. People swore by the gods all the time. She had never before been so certain that They were listening. "I swear by Epona Mistress of Horses, by Brigantia of the Fire, and by Cathubodva Lady of Ravens. I swear by Lugos the Many-Skilled, by Taranis of the Turning Wheel, and by Dagdevos the Good God." She felt the fine hairs prickle up her arms as invisible witnesses crowded around her.

She took a deep breath and continued, "I swear by the spirits of my ancestors, and if I fail in this oath may the sky fall and cover me, may the earth give way beneath me, and may the waters swallow my bones."

The Druid waited, as if to allow time for the oath to reach the Otherworld.

"And what shall bind you, Lady of the Iceni?" he said then.

"My heart's blood I offer in pledge," she answered, drawing her dagger and making a quick slice across the fleshy mound at the base of her thumb. She held out her hand so that the red blood dripped into a slash that had been made in the green turf that covered the ring. She blinked as the opening seemed to shimmer with energy.

"I offer it now to this holy earth, which stands for the whole land, as I have offered my service to you who bear witness, on behalf of the people who here dwell. And if need should require it, I will offer my life as well." *As Corn Mother gives her grain to feed us all* . . . she thought, remembering the harvest ritual.

The Druid turned to the others. "Thus your Lady takes oath to you; will you pledge her your service in return? Your food for her table, your warriors for her defense, your obedience to all lawful commands?"

The answer roared around her. "We will! We will! We will!"

*   *   *

*F*or our faith and our people we make this offering. Look upon us kindly. O ye holy gods." Helve's voice rang out clearly, though her form was barely distinguishable in the misty darkness. It had rained off and on through the night, and though somewhere the sun was rising, the Druids' fire seemed the only light in the world.

Lhiannon huddled into her wool cloak, listening to coughs and sneezes from the people around her. *Pray for the stormy weather to continue, Helve,* she thought with grim amusement. *And perhaps the Romans will not come . . .*

At the ill-fated ritual when the kings made their offering here the dawning had been fair. Today no seagulls swam in the water. Perhaps this grim sky was a good omen.

She wanted to weep, thinking of the treasures that had gone into the pool—swords with gleaming blades and sharp spearheads and bronze shields. There had been a wonderful bronze carynx horn from Eriu, great cauldrons, and the sickles with which they cut the mistletoe. Neck rings and chains of iron once used on prisoners followed the other things into the water. Smaller ornaments had flamed in the firelight before sinking into the dark depths. But she could not feel any difference in the atmosphere.

All those with the strength to make the journey had followed the wagon full of offerings. The very elderly had been sent away by sea, or if they were too frail to travel, taken to crofts and farmsteads elsewhere on the island where they could be passed off as grandmothers and old uncles if the Romans came. The three dozen priests and priestesses who remained stood now with unlit torches in their hands on the shores of the Lake of Little Stones.

From her place on the western side Lhiannon looked across the dark waters at Ardanos. At the south stood Helve, and across from her, Cunitor. *Helve always was fire to my water,* thought Lhiannon. *It is no wonder we have found it hard to get along.*

Ardanos lit his torch and touched it to that of the next man, and he to the priestess beyond him and so from one to another until the pool was circled by flame. Points of fire danced in the water as if the spirits of the pool were joining the ritual. Lhiannon felt a quiver along her spine as the circuit was closed and the Druids set their torches into the ground. Perhaps the gods would hear them after all.

> *"By earth and water, air and fire,*
> *We cast the circle of desire.*
> *Between the darkness and the day,*
> *Between the worlds we find the way!"*

As their voices joined in the chant, Lhiannon sensed the inner dip and expansion of oncoming trance, and knew the magic was beginning.

> *"By sacrifice, the gods are fed,*
> *In offering, our blood we shed—*
> *Cathubodva here we hail,*
> *Make the Roman warriors fail!"*

And one by one, each priest and priestess stepped forward, drew a sharp knife across the soft pad at the base of the thumb, and let the blood drip into the pool. This was the change in the ritual that Helve had decreed—that they should offer neither horse nor bull nor even a hare, but their own blood as a gift of energy.

> *"Their arms grow weak, their weapons break,*
> *Their courage chill, their strength we take!*
> *By the dawning of the day,*
> *They falter, turn, they flee away!"*

Again the chant was repeated, and again. To Lhiannon, it seemed as if a mist were forming over the water. Such a thing might often be seen above chill pools when the air began to warm with the approach of day, but these vapors pulsed with a fire-shot darkness. She reached out to right and left as the power they were raising began to push against the boundaries of the circle, felt Helve's passion and Cunitor's faithful strength, and across the pool, Ardanos's keen intelligence balancing the surge of her love.

The circle held, and the energy, contained, swirled

upward. Around the pool day was breaking, but above it darkness roiled like a cloud of black wings.

"Let fear chill them and fire burn!" cried Helve.

"May they see all they have built destroyed!" echoed Lhiannon.

"Morrigan, Great Queen, send them swiftly away!" called Cunitor.

"Cathubodva, fare eastward, bring death to our foe!" Ardanos opened his arms and the feathered darkness flowed toward him. In the same smooth movement he received it, turned, and released it to wing eastward into the dawn.

As it passed, Lhiannon perceived, with a sense beyond hearing, a sound that was at once a raven's screech and a woman's laugh.

TWENTY-THREE

*H*ow could she have thought she would miss Prasutagos less at Teutodunon?

Boudica blinked back tears as she listened to the last
posts being set into position in their row. Two weeks had
passed since her husband burned on his pyre, and still she
found herself noting things she must tell him, and then
she would remember, and the pain would come. It was
worse here, where she had only known him healthy and
strong. Surely at any moment the king would come striding through the gate, glowing with pride at the completion
of his great achievement and calling to her to come and
admire.

It was a worthy monument. The rectangular enclosure
had been extended to the size of four hurley fields laid side
by side, its bank and ditch enclosing two new roundhouses
that flanked the two-tiered council hall he had built before. It was the posts outside the ditch that made the place
unique. Nine rows of tree trunks and another bank and
ditch surrounded the enclosure, doubling its size. She
wished they could have been living trees, but the heathland soil would not support such a forest. Roman builders
had helped to lay out the site, but the design was her husband's dream.

Oh, my beloved, it is everything you hoped for, she
thought as she started back through the fenced circle that
served as forecourt for the roundhouse in which she and
the girls were living now. And for a moment she felt him
touch her cheek as he always used to do, or perhaps it was
the wind.

But someone *was* calling. She turned again. From between the tall gateposts carved with the totems of the Iceni

clans came a rider on a sweated horse. Her heart sank. Men bearing good news did not ride so desperately. But she had just seen her daughters safe inside the house—for whom else did she have to fear, now that Prasutagos was gone?

The rider pulled up as he saw her coming out to meet him and slid off the horse with a hurried contortion that was not quite a bow. Now others had heard the commotion and were coming out to see.

"My queen!" he forced himself to breathe. "You must do something—the Romans—" He sucked in air again. "The Roman pigs have sent men to seize Brocagnos's farm."

"But his tax is paid," she said in bewilderment. Her mother's gold armband had been sacrificed to pay that debt, she recalled.

"He's not the only one, lady—" the man went on. He began to list names, most of them farmers living near the southern border. "They're driving off stock and taking people as well."

"For the army?" An angry pulse was beginning to throb behind her eyes. Many families had given sons to the military levies. The boys were usually sent to serve in places very far from Britannia. Occasionally a gift from some distant land would arrive, but most of them were as lost as her brother Dubocoveros who had died while a hostage in Rome.

"They are taking slaves, lady—women and men!"

"They can't do that, can they?" asked Argantilla, who had come out of the house. The yard was filling with people as word spread.

"Crispus, I need you," Boudica yelled. "Get your tablets—we must send a message to Colonia. Pollio will know how to sort this out."

"Maybe some Roman official thinks he'll make some quick money while the governor is away," said one of the men.

Boudica hoped it was that. But even as she marshaled words for the message, she was trying not to wonder if Cloto had known what he was talking about after all.

*   *   *

*B*oudica walked with Prasutagos in a hazel wood. From the creamy primroses that starred the ground beneath the trees she judged it must be near Beltane. She rejoiced to see him so strong and healthy—bigger and more solid than he had ever been. Those memories in which she had seen him waste away must be some evil dream. He had a great club balanced on his shoulder, and he was wearing a sleeveless tunic so short she glimpsed his buttocks beneath it. She walked faster, wondering if what she could see from the front would be even more interesting.

"Here is the clearing where I will build the new dun," he said as they came out into the sunlight. He swung the club in a powerful circular stroke that plowed a great ditch in the soil, throwing the earth up beside it in a tumescent pile. He turned to her, his smile radiant, growing bigger as he came to her, the great club in his hand . . .

The scene dissolved around her as the ground heaved, but it was the bed that was shaking as Bogle jumped up, barking. She woke with a gasp, loins throbbing, and began to weep as she realized that Prasutagos had been the dream, and she was alone.

But this was at least a better delusion than the nightmares in which she endlessly pursued his fading form through a barren land. She put her arms around the dog, seeking comfort from his warmth as she rubbed behind his ears. Even in the midst of her tears, the memory of Prasutagos's delight in the prospect of building made her smile.

*I*t was just past noon when the Romans came. Shortly after dawn, clouds had begun to gather, blotting out the sunlight of Boudica's dream. In that gray light the cloaks of the soldiers were the color of old blood; even their armor had a dull sheen. Pollio was leading them. Bogle, who did not like Romans, barked furiously. Boudica told Crispus to tie the dog at the back and bore the beaker of welcome-ale with a grim smile. If Pollio thought her weak because her husband was no longer beside her he was about to learn better. Now they would have an accounting, and the underlings who were responsible for these outrages would suffer for their sins.

"Junius Pollio, *salve*!" she offered him the ale.

The twitch of the lips with which he returned her salutation could hardly be called a smile, but then his long face always seemed shadowed. His dark eyes searched her face as they always did when he encountered her, as if he hoped her feelings for him might have changed. As Pollio reached out for the cup his horse moved suddenly and it slipped through his fingers to smash upon the ground. For a moment Boudica watched the dark liquid soak into the earth. Then she gave herself a mental shake and managed a smile.

"It's no matter—come into the Council Hall and I shall send for more."

"Where are all your warriors?" he asked as he followed her into the central roundhouse.

"Riding the countryside, to gather evidence of Roman crimes . . ." She took her seat upon the great chair before the fire whose warm light cooled as it met the illumination coming in from openings in the upper tier. Pollio glanced about uneasily as he took the lower chair at her side. From fire pit to the apex of the roof the interior was the height of four tall men. Here were no marble columns or statues of bronze, but the images embroidered on the hangings that covered the walls seemed to move in the shifting light of the fire. Roman buildings boasted their owners' might; Prasutagos's hall hid his in mystery.

"Call them back, Boudica," he said in a low voice. "There is nothing you can do."

"What do you mean?" she snapped. "It is my duty to protect my people. I am queen of the Iceni and a client of the emperor."

"No. You are not. Rome makes no treaties with queens."

For a long moment she simply stared at him. "But Cartimandua—"

"—is legitimized by her husband's oath, even though he is in rebellion. Your husband is dead."

The words were like a sword to her heart. Boudica had been learning to live again. For hours at a time, now, she might lose awareness of her grief in dealing with other things until some incautious word, like a dead branch thrust among the coals, would kindle the flame anew.

"Prasutagos was an ally of Rome," she said finally. "Some of that property your men are seizing was left to his daughters by his will. It must be returned."

"The will means nothing. Prasutagos was not a citizen."

Boudica shook her head, unbelieving. "Has Governor Paulinus said this?"

"The procurator says it. Decianus Catus says it," Pollio replied in the same flat voice. "The alliance, and the kingdom, died with Prasutagos. It's over, Boudica."

How odd, she thought numbly. *He sounds as if he is pleading . . .*

"This hall—everything—belongs to Rome . . ."

Without quite knowing how she got there, Boudica found herself on her feet. Pollio rose as well, reaching out to her.

"Boudica!" His voice shook. "I have loved you since I first saw you! Once I offered you my protection and you refused me. I make the same offer now. I know you are not indifferent, Boudica—"

He meant that aborted kiss in the snow, she thought, before she had known what a kiss could mean . . . To her that memory was dim with distance, but to him it was still real. How barren his life must be.

"No." She pulled her arm away, tried to show some pity with a smile.

"You don't understand! I will marry you!" He gripped her again, pulling her against him.

"It is *you* who do not understand—" Her voice was low and dangerous. "I was the wife of a king, a man like the Good God himself! I would not go into your bed, Roman pig, if the alternative were slavery!" She spat in his face.

"It may be!" he hissed, grabbing for her other arm. "You have no choice, bitch—you need a master, and Jupiter witness, if you will not lie in my bed, I will have you on this floor!" Pollio jerked her hard against him, his breath hot on her face.

For a moment shock warred with hysterical laughter. He fumbled for her breast and the pin from one shoulder of her tunica tore loose. Then volition returned, and Boudica wrenched free. *Does he think I am some soft Roman female who cannot piss without permission from a man?* she thought in outrage. *Cloto could tell him differently!*

With an oath Pollio grabbed her again. They swayed dangerously close to the hearth and one of the chairs tipped over with a crash. The blood beat in Boudica's ears; she grabbed his wrists, then brought her knee up with brutal force between his legs and, as he screamed and spasmed, forced him into the fire.

The mingled stinks of burning wool and shit filled the air. Boudica laughed and let him go, recoiling as the space filled with men in armor.

"Take her!" Pollio rolled free of his smoldering cloak, still curled in agony. "Get me out of here!"

More men pushed through the door. These were soldiers, not tax collectors. The ones who dragged Boudica out into the yard had muscles like rope and hands of iron. Others followed, supporting Pollio. His face was the color of whey as he tried to stand.

"If you don't like my cock, I have other weapons," he gasped. "Tie her to that—" He pointed to the fenced forecourt of the Men's House. "Flog her until she bleeds!"

Still struggling, Boudica was forced to the gate, tied spread-eagled to the posts with ropes at wrists and ankles. Someone grabbed the back of her tunica and ripped the other side free, then used a piece of twine to tie up her hair. Bare to the waist, she twisted, watching in disbelief as the decanus who commanded the soldiers walked toward her, a whip with a knotted thong in his hand.

Slaves were flogged. Not free women . . . not queens.

People gathered, whispering with wide eyes. Boudica heard a rattle of hooves as a horse was urged into a gallop. One of the soldiers started toward his own mount but Pollio called him back again. She tugged at her bonds; the rope rasped her wrists but the knots held fast.

Then the first lash burned across her shoulders. Shock surprised her into crying out. She set her teeth against doing it again. The ropes creaked to the strain as the next blow drove her forward.

The decanus was counting slowly in Latin. "Unus, duo, tres . . ."

She tried to focus on the words. *I can bear this . . .* she thought, *and then I will have revenge . . .*

From the corner of her eye she saw Rigana running from the Women's House, brandishing a spear. "Let her go!" she screamed, settling into a crouch with the weapon held ready.

"Look, a gladiatrix!" laughed one of the men, pointing as Argantilla came after her, carrying a shield.

"Back!" Boudica could only grunt. "Get back inside!"

The soldiers were laughing too loudly. The girls could not hear.

"Quattuor, quinque . . ."

Rigana started toward the decanus, jabbing with the spear. Still grinning, one of the legionaries drew his sword and batted it aside. In the next moment another man grabbed her from behind while the first wrested the weapon from her grasp.

"Sir, what shall I do with this lion's cub?" he called.

"Pull her claws—" raged Pollio, his avid gaze still on Boudica. "The lioness is chained! Do what you like with the cub—and with her sister—let all the bitches spread their legs for Rome!"

"No!" Boudica screamed as she had not for her own pain. Argantilla whimpered as a soldier gripped her arm and wrenched away the shield. "Not my daughters, not them, please . . ." The breath was driven out of her as the decanus, who had paused to watch, began his work again.

Prasutagos! her spirit cried. But he had left them. He would not come to save her now.

"Octo . . . undecim . . . tredecim . . ."

Boudica's back and shoulders were webbed with fire.

"Do it!" repeated Pollio as the soldiers hesitated. "Take them now!"

They had torn Rigana's tunica already; she struggled, her young breasts bobbing, and kicked wildly as a soldier pulled the garment the rest of the way off and reached up between her thighs.

Not my daughters not my babies not my little girls . . .

"Sedecim . . . viginti . . ."

Abused flesh recoiled in nauseating waves. Fire and shadow pulsed behind her eyes.

"Please, why are you doing this?" sobbed Argantilla. One of the servants ran forward to help her and was struck down. Now men had gotten both girls on the ground. Someone threw dice to see who should have the first turn.

"Vigintiquinque . . ."

Boudica thrashed, groaning, as her daughters began to scream. She could not protect them . . . she could not break free!

"*Help them! Help me!*" Thwarted, her fury drove inward, shattering the boundaries of identity.

From depths beyond knowledge came a Voice that she had heard once long ago. "*Let Me . . .*"

"Triginta . . ."

The lash came down, dividing self from Self. Boudica slumped in her bonds as ravaged flesh and spirit gave way.

And with a cry like a battlefield of ravens, the Morrigan came in.

She straightened. One by one, She snapped the bonds. Blood splattered from Boudica's ruined back as She turned. Mouths working, men cringed. The soldiers who were holding the girls backed away. The Goddess picked up the man who was pumping atop Rigana and threw him aside, broke the one who had Argantilla as well. The others ran.

Pollio stumbled back as She turned, his face contorted in a rictus of fear. She reached out and drew him into Her embrace.

"Mercy," he croaked. "Let me go . . ."

"As you let them go?" The Morrigan indicated the weeping girls. "But I will be kinder than you were—I will not force you to live . . ."

Pollio struggled as She gripped his head and twisted. There was a sharp *click*. He went limp and She let him fall.

Hoofbeats thundered outside the dun. Bituitos and the warriors were returning. The terrified soldiers tried to outrun them.

They did not get far.

*   *   *

*R*avens were calling, harsh voices echoing back and forth from somewhere very near . . .

Boudica realized that she was lying on something soft; she started to turn over, gasped and groaned as the general ache across her back burst abruptly into a cacophony of individual pains. And there was an odd pressure in her head, as if more than her own brain had been packed into her skull.

"My lady—how do you feel?"

The voice was resonant and calm. Why did she associate it with sorrow?

"As if I had been beaten with—" Her throat closed as memory returned—Latin numbers, and agony, and a mental torment that transcended anything her body might feel. "My girls!" She jerked upright, staring. The curtains of her bed-place contained the dim world around her. Brangenos was sitting beside the bed, his long face lit by the flicker of the little Roman lamp in his hand.

The Druid set the lamp on the table. She flinched as he reached out to take her hands.

"Don't touch me," she said hoarsely. The rope marks around her wrists were still raw. "No one will ever hold me again!" Her gaze sought his face. "Where are my daughters?"

"They are sleeping, lady," he said softly. "Their hurts have been tended. Don't try to go to them—" He halted her involuntary motion. "Sleep is the best medicine for them just now. They were not much damaged—there was not time for more than two or three"—his gaze darkened— "to have at them before you . . . rescued them."

Boudica drew a quick breath at the sudden increase of pressure in her head. "She stopped them, then . . ."

His eyes met hers once more. "How much do you remember?"

"*She* was there, inside my head, and then I . . . was not. I think it was Cathubodva. She spoke through me once before, long ago."

The flicker of expression in the Druid's face was swiftly calmed, but Boudica had recognized a mingling of curiosity, excitement, and fear.

"It would explain . . . much," he said dryly. Suddenly

they were both very aware of the raven voices outside. He looked up at her, his face growing grim. "She killed Pollio and the rapists. Our warriors took care of the rest."

Boudica stared at him in alarm. "The Romans will want revenge!"

"First they have to find the bodies." He sighed. "We might even have been able to pretend they never reached here, but the Goddess wants vengeance, too." He looked up at her once more. "She commanded your warriors to raise the countryside. Already men are beginning to come in."

"I must speak to them—"

"Not yet, lady—please. You are healing well—much faster than one might expect," he added as if to himself. "But you, too, need sleep, and there is no need to face the tribe until everyone has arrived. The ravens are arriving, too," he said reflectively. "The first ones came as we buried the bodies—I was tempted to let them feast—and more keep flying in."

"They are so loud . . . I will never be able to sleep." Torment of mind and body buzzed in her brain.

From his pouch he took a little bottle of Roman glass and poured some of its contents into a spoon. "I will give you tincture of poppy. That will separate you from the pain."

*W*here shall we feed? Where shall we feed?" cried the raven.

With one part of her mind, Boudica knew its clamor had words because she wandered in poppy dreams. She did not care—she had always wanted to know what the birds were saying in their endless conversations among the trees.

"In the wood there's a ripe badger, three days old," cried another bird.

"In the midden there's burned barley," called a third.

"And what shall we eat tomorrow, tomorrow?" the first raven croaked.

Boudica knew that her body lay in the great bed, but her spirit was awake, with senses it did not normally own.

"In the duns the smiths are forging swords and sharpening spears," answered another.

"Soon the Lady will give us man-meat to eat . . ." crowed the third.

In her present state, it seemed to Boudica only right and proper that the ravens should have their food.

"Do you think so, My child?" came another voice, honey sweet, with an undertone of bitter laughter. "That is well, for we have work to do."

This was no raven. Boudica tried to open her eyes and found she could not move. "Where are you?"

"I am as close to you as your own heartbeat," the Other replied.

"Who are you?" Boudica whispered, though her lips were still.

"I am Rage," the Voice resounded through her soul. "I am Destruction, I am the Raven of Battle—"

"You are the Morrigan," Boudica replied. "You avenged my girls!"

"But who will take vengeance for your people?" the Goddess asked, and Boudica could find no answer.

Pollio had been right—the peace of Prasutagos was ended. Their only choice now was between slavery and rebellion. The one would be a living death. The other might lead to death—but there would be glory.

"If you will give Me a form to wear," the Goddess said then, "I will give you power . . ."

"Will You punish the Romans for all they have done to us?" she asked. The men who had attacked her daughters might be dead, but those who had sent them still ruled. If they were not punished, how many more mothers would weep for the lost innocence of their little girls?

"They will wail in terror and call in vain upon their gods . . ."

"And we will have victory?"

"You *are* Victory, and your name will live!"

She had had to make this decision before, when she came to Prasutagos as the White Mare. Then she had assented with joy. She surrendered now in grief, but from an equal need.

"Then I give myself to You as horse to rider," said Boudica. "Use me as You will!"

"A fractious, willful mare you are," came the response, "but strong. Sleep now, My child, and heal." The laughter that Boudica heard was gentle as she slid down into the dark.

*B*oudica sat in the darkened roundhouse with Argantilla in her arms, watching Rigana pace. She would have held her as well, but the girl was strung as tight as a war bow and flinched from any touch. Argantilla simply trembled, her eyes welling with soundless tears. Boudica bit her lip and hugged the younger girl more tightly. The wounds on her back did not hurt her half as much as her children's pain.

Outside the Women's House, the voice of the crowd rose and fell like the wind. "I will have to go out and speak to them soon," she said softly. "Will you come with me?"

Argantilla shuddered and buried her face against her mother's shoulder. Rigana turned, breathing hard.

"How can you ask that of us? They are men! They will look at us and they will *know* . . ."

"They will look at you and see their own daughters," replied Boudica. "They will look at me and see their wives. They will feel the shame I felt when I could not protect you, that you felt when you could not help me, and they will want revenge . . ."

"More than you have already taken?" Rigana's gaze sharpened. "I saw your face when you pulled that animal off me—but it wasn't you, was it, Mother?"

"It was . . . the Morrigan." Boudica's breath caught. Even to speak that name woke awareness of the Presence within.

"Will She come again? Will She lead us against Rome?" Rigana stopped finally, gazing at her mother with avid eyes. Argantilla stiffened and ceased her weeping.

"She will come . . ." Boudica heard her own voice deepen. "She is here . . ." The healing wounds on her back tingled with cool fire as her awareness was pushed gently aside. *Soon*, came the thought, *they will turn into wings . . .*

She felt that prickle of Otherness flow across her skull and down into her body, stretching and twisting as the goddess mastered it. Just so, she thought with inner amusement, she herself would test a new mount until she was certain it would obey. Bogle, who had been lying across the door, stood suddenly, hackles lifting, dark eyes intent.

"Will you come with Me?" She stood up, lifting Argantilla easily, and stretched out Her hand. As Rigana stepped into the shelter of Her other arm, Boudica felt only gratitude that the Goddess could give her girls comfort where she had failed. "You shall be My attendants, and you"—the Goddess snapped Her fingers and Bogle fawned at her feet— "shall be My hound."

Boudica's awareness came and went as they left the Women's House and passed through the forecourt. Night had fallen, and torches flickered around the enclosure. Beyond the bank the lines of tree trunks brooded like a protecting forest, stark against the stars.

Before the Council Hall men had raised a platform flanked by a line of poles. Bogle growled as they passed the first, and she realized that the dark thing at the top was Pollio's head. His legionaries grinned from other poles beside him. Brangenos had not told Boudica that they took the heads before burying them. Perhaps he had not known. Most of them were missing their eyes already—it gave her a grim satisfaction to know that the ravens had gotten their feast after all.

As they mounted the platform the murmuring crowd grew still. Prasutagos had designed the enclosure for just such assemblies, but thank the gods he could never have imagined what its first use would be. In the flickering torchlight familiar faces appeared and disappeared—Brocagnos and Drostac and old Morigenos. She saw Rianor, who had arrived just after the king's funeral, with Brangenos. They had been out tending a sick child when the Romans came. Tingetorix, who had fought under Caratac, was standing with Carvilios and Taximagulos. She recognized with some surprise the faces of Segovax and his sons Beric and Tascio. He was one of the richest of the Iceni, and she would have expected him to support the Romans—but she did recall hearing that his wealth was based on Roman subsidies. Catus must have tried to collect on the loans.

"Men of the Iceni . . ." The voice that rang out through the night was Boudica's, but men stiffened, staring, as they felt its power. "Sons of Epona—you chose me as your queen, as your priestess before the gods, to guide and guard this land!" She had dressed carefully, coiling her red-gold hair high on her head and confining it with golden pins. Gold drops hung from her ears, and from her neck gleamed the great golden torque that Caratac had left in her keeping ten years before. "I swore to uphold the laws the good king Prasutagos made, and to keep the oaths he swore to the Emperor of Rome.

"But see how the Romans have betrayed their honor! Many among you have already suffered from their greed—Drostac, they have taken your livestock—Brocagnos and Taximagulos, they have seized your farms! They have taken away the weapons that marked you as men! Goods and gear they have stolen, they have marched our young men away to die far from their homeland, they have sold our women as slaves. But now they progress from greed to blasphemy!" She turned and pointed to Rigana, who stared defiantly, sheltering her sister in her arms.

"They have defiled the daughters of the king, the flower of this land, and they have treated your queen as if she were a slave." Men flinched as they felt the anger in Her gaze. "Behold!"

She unpinned the great golden brooch that held the cloak and let it fall. She wore a skirt, but no tunica. Boudica would have flinched to bare herself before so many eyes, but Cathubodva displayed Her breasts, still high and full even though Boudica was now thirty-four, with pride. She heard the intake of breath from the men below, and then, as She turned to reveal the ruin of Her back, a whisper of horror that rushed through the crowd like the sighing of trees before the storm.

Boudica felt consciousness receding as the Morrigan turned back to face the tribe. "Too long," She cried, "have the Romans defiled our land! We must cast them forth! Their soldiers we must slay; their cities burn!"

Shouts echoed Her words, but others were objecting

that the Romans had defeated them thirteen years before, and why would they do better against them now?

"If your arms have forgotten the weight of a sword, they can learn once more!" She cried. "Your hearts are strong! If the Iceni are not enough to drive the Romans into the sea we must call on all Britannia!" She touched the torque that gleamed from Her neck. "This is the torque of King Cunobelin that Caratac took from the body of Togodumnos his brother and wore when he raised the tribes!"

"Even for him they would not all come," called Segovax. "Why should they rise for you?"

"Because I am the Great Queen! I am the Raven of Battle, and I shall lead you!" She shook her head and pins flew like sparks as Her hair flamed free. "Because I am Victory!"

"What shall we do? Where shall we go?" came the cries.

"This is the clanhold of the Hare—let Andraste's holy animal show us the way!" She leaped down from the platform.

Men fell back before Her as She strode toward the carved gates, falling in behind in a swirling, shouting mob. Bituitos was close behind Her, holding a bag where something struggled and squirmed. They passed under the lintel and between the fences that lined the way to the road. She waited for the crowd to pour through the opening behind Her, falling silent as they spread out to either side. And when there were sufficient witnesses, She reached into the bag and drew forth the hare, which lay limp and trembling in Her predator hands.

"Fear not, little one," She murmured, stroking the gray pelt. "This is not the night when thou shalt die . . ."

The land lay quiet around them, rolling away beyond the rise that held the dun in long swaths of heathland and pasture, dotted with the huddled shapes of trees. She tipped her head, feeling the tension return to the animal's muscles as its fur bristled with energy.

"Andraste! Andraste! Sister, I call You, Lady of this Land! Show us the way, Lady! Lead us to victory!" She cradled the hare against Her breast and whispered in its long ear: "Run now, and show us our road, run fast and free!"

She bent, placed the hare on the ground, and opened Her hands. For a moment the little beast crouched, quivering. Then with a mighty leap it sped down the road—southward—toward Colonia.

The great cry of the Iceni bore the hare forward on a wave of sound. Men brought up horses, tucking the red-painted war arrows through their belts and grasping torches in their hands. At Her word they sped outward, racing like shooting stars through the night to bear word to the people of every tribe that the Britons were marching to reclaim their native land.

TWENTY-FOUR

"The Great Queen rides a good gray mare,
  Above her, ravens fly.
Where she fares, the eagles fear,
Where she goes, men die!"

The mare shook her head and snorted as Boudica reined her in. Behind her streamed an irregular, relentless tide of people and horses and wagons, beginning to slow and eddy now as they moved off the road to set up camp for the night. Bogle, who had trotted at the mare's heels, lay down with a sigh and the other dogs, footsore with the day's march, settled beside him.

The Iceni had started south on the second day after the gathering, and Brangenos had started the song to cheer their march. The ravens flew with them, black specks circling above the dust, calling in harsh descant to the clatter of hooves and the rumble of wagon wheels.

"Ho—Tingetorix!" she called as a grizzled warrior on a spotted pony came into view. He walked with a limp got in Caratac's wars, but he could still outride most of the younger men. "How many swords did they send us today?"

Back at Teutodunon, the smiths were still hard at work beating out new weapons and repairing the old. Every day a rider would catch up to the column and unload a bag or two more.

"A dozen"—he brought his pony alongside her—"and as many spearheads."

"That's a dozen more lads who can stop using sticks to

practice with, and turn their staffs into spears," she said with satisfaction.

Prasutagos was not the only one to have hidden weapons. Some had come to Teutodunon with supplies and such weapons as had survived the Roman confiscations, but many more had only their bows and slings, or perhaps a hunting spear. The main force was constrained to the pace of the ox-drawn wagons, and there was more than enough time for a horseman to gallop home and retrieve a sword or a shield and helm that his fathers had borne to war, and persuade his neighbors to join him while he was there.

"Brangenos says my back is healed enough to start sword work," Boudica told him. She had always been strong and active, but she had never needed to develop the specific muscles required to use sword and shield. Even men whose upper bodies had been hardened by years of farmwork found themselves aching in unexpected places when they began to train.

"Did he now?" said the warrior. "I shall see you, then, after the evening meal."

Boudica laughed. The flex and sway of riding had left her back sore, but could not sour her spirits. "Then you had better summon the chieftains to meet with me now. We must send someone to the city." She heard her voice deepen and closed her eyes for a moment as she felt the dizzy lurch that meant the Morrigan was moving to the fore. "We need to find out if they know we are coming, what defense they have, and whether they have called for aid."

By the uneasy flicker in his gaze she knew that Tingetorix sensed the presence of her inner advisor. He and the other experienced men had been surprised to find her so knowledgeable about the problems of training and supply. With every hour the partnership between the Iceni queen and the Great Queen was becoming smoother.

When the Morrigan was with her, Boudica did not feel the emptiness Prasutagos had left in her soul.

"Yes, my queen." He bent his head and put his horse into a canter to do her will.

When she turned back to the road, her daughters were there. Like her, in body they had recovered well.

Rigana was surveying her with a frown. "Is he going to

teach you to fight?" she asked abruptly. "I want to learn, too. I don't want to be helpless before a man ever again."

Boudica started to shake her head, but there was something very unchildlike in Rigana's eyes. Among those who had joined the rebellion there were boys who were no older and not much bigger, and who had far less reason to kill Romans than she.

"And what about you?" She looked at Argantilla.

"Caw says I am too small to do anything but carry more arrows to the archers," she said a little tremulously, "but I will do what I can . . ."

The child Tilla had rescued in Colonia had gotten his growth this past year and promised to be a big man. He had become her most devoted protector.

"Don't even *think* about sending us somewhere safer— if there is any such place now!" Rigana said dangerously.

Boudica sighed. That was true enough. If this rebellion failed, there would be no refuge for them anywhere. She looked at her daughters, and felt the Morrigan's fury amplifying her love and her pain.

"Very well . . . we will seek our fate together, whatever it may be . . ."

They had been on the road for three days when a small man in a ragged Roman tunic came limping into camp. Boudica left Rigana struggling to hold her sword steady at arm's length for a count of ten and followed Crispus back to the fire in front of the wagon that carried her gear. A tightly woven woolen cloth had been stretched from the wagon to provide some protection from the thin drizzle, supported in front by spears.

Tingetorix was already questioning him when she arrived.

"My lady—" He turned to her. "This man brings news both good and bad."

The man's eyes widened as she came into the firelight, and she wondered what he had heard. He made an obeisance.

"Great Queen, I was once a freeholder and a notable man among the Trinovantes. Now I am called Tabanus, a debt-slave in Colonia. There are many of us—we will help you however we can."

She nodded. "They've heard we are coming, then?"

"Yes, Lady, and they are afraid. There have been evil omens—the statue of Victory fell from its pedestal, and in the theater and senate house evil cries have been heard. Someone had a vision of a devastated city down by the seashore, and the waters turned red."

"Our gods are stronger than those of the Romans because they belong to this land," she said softly. A slight fuzziness in her awareness told her that the goddess was with her. She was grateful. Cathubodva would know best what to say now.

Tabanus nodded. "A few hundred men are stationed in the fort at the old dun, and in the city there are men who once served in the legions, but they are old now, and Colonia has no walls. They have sent to the procurator in Londinium, and another messenger has gone to the fort north of Durovigutum."

Boudica nodded. The Romans had built an outpost to guard the road they were putting through the fens.

"No one knows what force the procurator may send them, but Petillius Cerealis has part of the Ninth Legion and some cavalry."

"Is he the sort of commander to sit and wait for orders, or will he set out immediately when he gets word?" asked the queen.

"They say he is a hothead. I think that he will come as soon as he can muster his men."

Boudica could feel the goddess considering. "How many experienced warriors are there among us?" she asked. Though the Morrigan might know all things in Her own realm, the part of Her being that was acting through Boudica depended on information available to the queen. "Gather them together, and men who are good hunters as well. Tingetorix, I want you to take our fastest horses and lead them north. Send scouts to learn what road they are taking, and attack them from ambush. This is important— you must not let them catch you in open country. Hit them from cover with javelins and arrows and slings, shoot from trees."

"I understand." His sidelong glance noted the slave's wonder at her expertise and he smiled beneath his grizzled mustache. "You need not fear any surprises from the Ninth Legion, my queen."

*T*he Romans have built a camp on the heights above the strait," said Ardanos. "Paulinus has brought men from two legions. They will take another day to rest, or maybe two, and then they will embark. I have sent runners to every farmstead. Every man who can carry a weapon will be here soon."

"But it would be far better if the soldiers never reached our shore," observed Helve. Someone stifled nervous laughter. "We do not have the powers of the masters from the Drowned Lands who could use sound to move great stones, but here are thirty trained singers. We will raise a barrier of sound against the enemy. Go now and rest while you can . . ."

As the meeting dispersed Lhiannon found her steps lagging. Would the thatch above the meeting hall soon be blazing, or would this place become a healers' shelter where she worked to bind up wounded men? She looked around her with a sigh. The first vision was far more likely. If the Romans managed to cross the strait, she did not think the refugee army the Druids had put together would be able to stand.

What use was the rite they had performed at the Lake of Little Stones? The power had been raised and sent eastward, but at most it had only delayed the enemy. Would their singing do more?

She ought to seek her bed as Helve had commanded, but tension sparked along each nerve. There would be no rest in the House of Priestesses, where she would have to barrier her mind against Coventa's nightmares and old Elin's weeping. Her frown relaxed as she realized that her spirit had already set her on the path to the Sacred Grove.

A soft wind was whispering through the leaves of the oak trees. Even in her moments of greatest anguish Lhiannon had always found peace here. *"Holy Goddess . . . holy Goddess . . ."* The melody sang in her memory, though it was only afternoon. She closed her eyes, opening her awareness to the spirit of the grove.

But it was another spirit, more familiar but infinitely less peaceful, that she found. She blinked, and saw a man in a white robe sitting beside the altar stone. She hesitated, fighting an impulse to flee, but he was holding out his hand. When she first saw him in the robes of the Arch-Druid he had looked like a stranger. Now, for the first time since she had known him, he looked *old*.

"Once more we sit together on the eve of battle," he murmured. "And once more I desire only to know that you are near . . ."

That was just as well, she thought tartly, for if he had asked her to lie with him now she would have slapped him. If in him the fires still burned, he had learned to keep them banked, and as for herself, the armor she had grown around her heart could not be taken off in one afternoon.

"What do you think will happen when they come?" she asked.

"It will be our magic against the spirit of Rome," Ardanos said thoughtfully. "I keep thinking about the stories Brangenos told of Vercingetorix, who could not defeat Caesar though he had all the Druids of Gallia to help him."

"And you are afraid that the will of this commander may bind his men into an entity that can resist the Druids of Britannia?"

"It is possible. And if they make a landing, I fear our warriors will not be able to hold them. Lhiannon, if that happens you must save yourself. You said that becoming Arch-Druid changed me, and it is true. I have to plan for defeat as well as for victory. Coventa has had visions of a house of priestesses on the mainland within a sacred grove, with you as their leader, but for that, you must survive."

Lhiannon shivered, though the wind had ceased. Golden rays of late afternoon sunlight shimmered through the trees. "Mearan saw something of the sort when she lay dying." The old High Priestess had seen Mona drenched in blood as well. "But I hardly dare to believe in this prophecy, since all the others have served us so ill . . ."

"Perhaps . . ." He took her hand. "But Lhiannon, it is the only hope we have!"

"And what about you?" She turned to face him. "Will you flee as well?"

"While our priests stand Helve and I are bound to stand with them," he said with a sigh. "Just now, my dear, my own survival does not seem very likely. But I can face my own end with more peace knowing you are free."

And how will I face life, knowing you are gone? she wondered. Suddenly the shield around her heart did not seem so impervious. From a tree in the grove a raven called, and from somewhere across the fields its mate replied.

*R*avens perched on the gate to the palisaded fortlet that the Romans had built up against the dike that had once defended Camulodunon. It was open, its garrison fled. It had been only five days, thought Boudica, since they had marched out of Teutodunon. Now she watched her haphazard army streaming down the road past the Roman dike that had once sheltered the emperor's encampment and making camp in the remains of Cunobelin's dun. Tents and wagons covered the land halfway around the city whose red roofs glowed from the hilltop two miles away.

She recognized Tabanus pushing through the crowd, and signaled to Eoc to let him approach her.

"I am glad to see you safe." She had been surprised when the Trinovante slave had volunteered to go back to Colonia, and found it amazing that he had been able to leave once more.

The man shrugged. "My master is running about like a chicken destined for the pot, and for certain, no one else is paying attention. Some of the veterans wanted to blockade the main roads, but we started a rumor that this would encourage you to attack the houses on the side streets, and their neighbors stopped them."

"How many have left the city?" asked Morigenos, joining them.

Tabanus shrugged. "A few . . . the others fear they will be picked off more easily if they leave."

"What are they thinking?" asked Boudica, sitting down

on a bag of grain. "Without walls, they must know they cannot resist us."

"*Their leaders were in the legions,*" the Goddess spoke within. "*They think that no barbarian can defeat Rome. They believe that their brother soldiers will rescue them . . .*"

"*And will they?*"

"*Listen—what do the ravens say?*"

Boudica smiled, remembering how she had heard them during her poppy dream. One was calling now from the fort, and from somewhere overhead another answered. As she looked up, it flew over her right shoulder, and she saw a few white feathers in its wing.

"The ravens say that someone brings us good news," she said aloud, and in the next moment they all heard the stuttering hoofbeats of a horse fast ridden coming down the road. Eoc gave her one of those uneasy looks that had become the common response to her pronouncements, then turned to watch with the rest as the rider appeared. A wave of cheering followed him.

"We smashed 'em!" The messenger slid off his horse, still talking. "We did what you said, my lady, and got most of the men on foot. The commander skittered off with his cavalry, didn't stop till they reached their outpost, and doesn't dare stick his nose outside his walls. Tingetorix and the rest are on their way back, but he wanted you to know right away. Attack Colonia whenever you please, my queen—there's no one to stop you now!"

Boudica nodded as the murmur of angry anticipation that spread through the camp found an echo within. As they neared Colonia, ragged men of the Trinovantes had begun to join them, with no arms but their shovels and hoes. They had suffered far more than the Iceni, and far longer, and their eyes burned with a fanatical fire. Secure in her own country, Boudica had not understood the extent to which the Romans had forced the Trinovantes to pay for their own subjugation.

Pollio is dead, but the men who sent him, the men who raped my people, are still in the town. They, too, must die.

More men, and more weapons, arrived every day. Now men of substance were coming in, bringing supplies and workers in wood and leather and iron as well as more food. It would take a day or two more to organize them, but any Roman who changed his mind about fleeing Colonia would not get far now.

> *"The Great Queen's army fills the plain,*
>   *She leads them to the war—*
> *A hundred thousand in her train*
>   *And every day brings more."*

She gazed up at the city with narrowed eyes. *Count our campfires, Romans. Listen to our songs . . . We won't keep you waiting long!*

*W*hat are they waiting for?" murmured Coventa.

Lhiannon squinted across the water as the afternoon sun glanced off Roman helmets. Through dry lips she murmured, "It must take a lot of time to organize so many men." There were certainly a lot of them; the shelving ground on the other side of the strait shimmered with points of reflected light.

The first files had been sighted just after dawn, and by noon the Britons had formed up to meet them where the meadows sloped down to the mudsands, a bare half mile across the water. Veterans from the Durotrige and Silure wars waited with men from all over Mona, and in front of them the Druids, the white robes of the priests mixed with the priestesses' dark blue.

Now and again someone would peer toward the point, where they had stationed a lad with good eyes. Even so, the sound of his horn was a shock after waiting so long. Lhiannon gave herself a mental shake. Eventually all things, good or evil, ended. Had she thought they would sit here like some army out of legend until they all turned to stone?

Now she could make out movement at the far edge of the water. Ardanos was moving down the line of Druids. If there had been clouds, they might have tried to raise a storm against the Romans, but for a week now, Mona had enjoyed blue skies. Lhiannon sipped from her water flask, holding the liquid in her mouth before swallowing.

Ardanos stood with closed eyes, staff outstretched toward the invisible barrier. Against one man, or a few, it would hold, but not against the massed will of thousands. Dark shapes moved on the water as the Romans' landing craft began to put out from shore. The Arch-Druid turned.

"Sweetly, now, my dear ones," he murmured. "Sing now as the Children of Lyr sing beneath the waves, and raise the wall of sound!"

And softly, as he had commanded, the first vibrations rolled from thirty throats. Breathing slowly and easily, Lhiannon let the sound flow, and as the rhythm was established began to shape it with words and will.

It was an ancient spell, so old the words' precise meanings were unclear. Only the sense behind them remained. From voice to water the vibration was passing . . . water shivering, shimmering . . . particles shifting, lifting as they reached the barrier to rise in a sorcerous mist that curled and curdled across the water in shapes of terror.

Lost in sound, Lhiannon sensed the Roman ships lose way and drift helpless on the tide. She noted without comprehension the sun's slow slide toward the west. But beyond the barrier the Druids were raising she could feel the pulsing pressure of another will.

As the day faded the Druids' strength lessened, and that opposition grew stronger. Lhiannon tried to sing louder as first one, then another voice stilled. It was almost dark now. One by one, the remaining Druids fell silent. With a low cry Coventa collapsed against her. Lhiannon's breath caught and abruptly her own voice stopped. A moment later the last male voices cut off. She blinked, and saw one of the warriors catch Ardanos as he swayed.

Red light flared as someone got the piled logs aflame. The glow showed her the slumped forms of the Druids and the warriors with drawn swords behind them. Wavelets caught the light in red glints as if blood already flowed. She heard a drumbeat. Through the thinning mist the prows of the Roman boats were beginning to emerge.

Druids staggered toward the shelter of the trees. Lhiannon gulped water and got her arm around Coventa. She was weary to her marrow, but that did not matter now.

"Coventa, get up, girl! Remember your training! Breathe!" Was she speaking to Coventa or to herself?

She handed her water flask to the other woman and took up two of the torches from the heap by the fire, handed them off to Belina and Brenna, and got more. Of the dozen priestesses, only nine remained standing. They would have to be enough. *The Romans fear our priestesses—let them see us, and be afraid!*

She plunged her torches into the fire and held them high. Helve bared her teeth in a smile and together they led the others forward to stand in front of the warriors in a widely spaced line.

The drumbeat faltered as the men in the first boats caught sight of the dark-robed priestesses. But the pressure of the multitudes behind pushed them forward. Lhiannon could see faces now within the gleaming helms. Behind the priestesses Ardanos had gotten the remaining Druids together and in a hoarse voice was calling down curses upon the enemy. Her own throat was raw, but she no longer needed to sing, only to scream . . .

As the first prows grounded on the mudflats the priestesses rushed forward, ullulating like the furies the Romans feared. The first Romans who jumped out of the boats recoiled, shouting as they sank into the mud. But some canny commander had anticipated the problem and in another moment they were slapping boards on the soft ground. The next men off faced the flurry of Celtic javelins with braced feet and raised shields. In close ranks they began to move forward and as others pressed in behind them the boats in which they had come pushed off and started back across the strait for more.

As the first legionaries reached solid ground the Britons rushed forward to meet them.

"Lhiannon! Helve! Flee!" Ardanos's voice rose above the din. "Now it is work for swords!"

Lhiannon cast her flaming torches at the nearest foes and ran.

*T*he stink of burning buildings lay heavy on the air. Boudica had smelled it once or twice before when the thatching of a roundhouse caught fire—a heavy, acrid smell quite unlike the scent of clean logs. She had ordered the attack at dawn, when the townsfolk, tired of waiting for the Britons to make their move, should be less alert, but they might as well have slept in—there had been little resistance.

She stood now in the atrium of the big building that had housed the city offices and the governor when he was in town. Afternoon light showed her a mass of broken tile, blackened plaster, and smoking beams. The bodies of the servants who had been left to defend them lay among the ruins. Fragments of scorched parchment fluttered in the wind. But the garden where the governor's wife had entertained her was untouched, and the goddess on her plinth still watched with a secret smile.

A warrior put a rope around the statue to pull it down and she waved him away. *As one goddess to another, I thank you...* said the Voice within.

Tascio picked his way through the debris, making an obeisance as he saw her there. "Lady, Bituitos says to come—"

Smoke rose now all over the city. Boudica hoped that the men were remembering to search the buildings for weapons and foodstuffs before setting them afire. They needed no encouragement to pick up any ornaments or jewelry that they found. The streets were littered with abandoned boxes and debris from the burning, with the occasional body, some not quite dead.

She felt little sympathy. As they marched south she had heard a hundred tales of Roman injustice and brutality to rival her own. This was a city of over two thousand. The only surprise was that there were not more bodies on the ground. Of course Celtic slaves and servants had been fleeing ever since the Iceni showed up on their doorstep—many of them had joined the horde, but the Romans and foreign slaves should have been here. She wondered where they had gone.

A pack of grim-faced Trinovantes trotted by. As they passed a building that was still whole, a man in a Roman tunic appeared in the doorway with two scared slaves brandishing clubs behind him. He had a sword, while the

Trinovantes were armed only with hoes and pitchforks, but fear was no match for fury. With a feral cry the Britons were on him, and in moments Roman and slaves alike went down. She could see the attackers' arms rising and falling long after the cries had ceased. When they stopped at last, the Trinovante leader had a sword.

Laughing, the men entered the house, and a few moments later a woman screamed. Boudica suppressed a shudder, but she knew better than to try and stop them. Did she even wish to? Romans had raped her daughters. Let their women suffer now. As she turned away, a flicker of movement in a doorway caught her eye. She shouted, lifting her shield as half a dozen armed men burst into the road between her and her escort.

"Ho, a gladiatrix!" called one, leaping toward her as the other two turned to engage Tascio and the other men.

That was what the Roman soldier had called Rigana.

A surge of fury rent away Boudica's awareness and the Morrigan flowed in, drawing her sword in one smooth sweep that knocked the man's blade from his hand. The laughter hardly had time to change to fear before the sword whirled around and back across and took off his head.

As She leaped forward to fall upon the others, the sound that burst from Her throat was halfway between a shout of rage and a raven's cry. She took one man with a thrust through the back and used Her shield to shove another onto Tascio's blade. By this time his companions had brought the others down.

They stood, breathing hard, listening to distant shouts and a moan as the last of their assailants died. Slowly, as if she were rising up through deep water, Boudica came to herself. Her arm trembled like a bowstring after the arrow has gone. Her blade dripped red. *Thank you . . .* she thought numbly, bending to wipe off the blood on the tunic of one of the men she had killed, and felt the approval of the goddess within. Tascio and the others were staring at her with wide eyes. She did not feel like explaining that the week of training had strengthened her muscles, but it was the goddess who had used them.

"Good work," she said steadily. "Now let us be moving on . . ."

They dodged as burning debris from another house showered down, and came out into a crossroads. Men had gotten ropes around the great bronze statue of the emperor Claudius on a horse that stood there. Having met the emperor, Boudica doubted that he had ever ridden such a horse in his life, certainly not in full parade armor. Everything about this image but the protruding ears was another Roman lie. She smiled in grim satisfaction as men began to heave on the lines. The piece was solidly built, but no match for their rage, especially after they found a smith to knock free the bolts that held it to the pedestal.

Boudica jumped back as the thing crashed down. Screeching triumphantly, someone swung an ax, and in another moment they had gotten the severed head on a pole, still surveying the scene with a gentle frown. As they admired it, Tascio came around a corner, saw her, and grinned.

"We've found them," he cried. "The soldiers and the rest of the people have holed up in the Temple of Claudius. It's going to take a while to winkle them out—the thing is made of stone."

"Secure the rest of the city," she answered him. "Let them sit there and stew for another day, hoping the legions will come to save them . . . and imagining what will happen if no one does," she said, baring her teeth in a smile.

TWENTY-FIVE

Lys Deru was burning. Flames billowed skyward, filling the sky with lurid light, as if the fires had consumed the stars. Below, sparks moved across the meadows as legionaries with torches scoured the land. Their commander had sent several detachments out to form a perimeter and work inward, driving fugitives before them as men might drive game.

Lhiannon lay in a hollow beneath a thorn hedge where a badger's burrow had fallen in. From time to time she heard cries and knew another fugitive had been found. Sometimes it was a woman, and then the screams continued. As long as night lasted her dark robes would hide her—it would be another matter when the sun rose. It was all very well for Ardanos to tell her to save herself, she thought grimly. If he had wanted her to stay safe, he should not have allowed her to stay at all.

But there might be no safety for a Druid priestess anywhere on Mona. The Romans went about their work in an appallingly methodical way. When they had finished scouring the area around Lys Deru, no doubt they would search the island. By now they must know what it meant when a woman bore a blue crescent on her brow. The tattoo would mark her as a priestess even if she got rid of the blue robe.

Sweet Goddess, watch over Caillean, she prayed. *If I cannot return to Eriu to claim her, keep her safe—keep her free!* She would have thrown herself back into the fray and sought a quick ending if it had not been for the child.

She had seen Cunitor struck down as she fled the shore, and glimpsed Brenna being dragged away. It seemed unlikely that Ardanos could have survived. So many men and women she had known were dead, and if she had not liked them all, they still compelled her loyalty. But it would be time enough to feel guilt for having survived them if she lived to see another dawn.

She heard the tramp of hobnailed sandals and a mutter of Latin and grew even more still. *I am night . . . I am shadow . . .* she thought, slowing her breathing, fighting to quiet her soul. *You see nothing here—move on . . .*

She heard two sets of footsteps, and a regular whisper and thump she could not identify. Closer they came. Through the grass stems she glimpsed a metallic gleam and knew it for a spearpoint an instant before it stabbed past her head.

Even Druid training could not prevent a gasp. One of the Romans swore and turned, and in the next moment a hare burst from the hedge and leaped across the grass. The other man laughed, and the pair moved on.

Holy Andraste! thought Lhiannon, remembering the goddess and totem of Boudica's clan. *If I survive this, I owe you an offering!*

It was a long time before she dared to move again. When she raised her head at last, the fires of Lys Deru were burning low. But a little to the east new flames were rising. With a sinking heart she realized that they had set fire to the Sacred Grove. For some reason the sight of the burning trees pierced her heart with a pain she had not yet allowed herself to feel for her fellow men. Weeping silently, she watched the flames and waited for the dawn.

*T*he embers of Colonia were smoldering. From time to time a charred roof-beam would fall in, or a last bit of wicker fencing would burst into flame. It had taken nearly twenty years to turn this Trinovante hilltop into a crude imitation of Rome. The Britons had destroyed it in two days. Colonia Victricensis was victorious no more, except for this final symbol of imperialism, this ultimate hubris, the temple of the deified Claudius, that stood surrounded by devastation, stone columns glowing as men held their torches high.

Boudica felt a flicker of amusement from the goddess within as she reflected that she was the last person to deny that a human could be a vehicle for divinity, or even that each human soul held some spark of the divine. But it was the god that ought to be worshipped, not the man. Even the ancestors at whose barrows her people left offerings took time to grow into their godhood. Let the Romans pay their honors to the Deified Claudius at his own tomb and build him a temple there if their prayers were answered. To worship him here was an insult and a blasphemy.

The building was unscathed except for the scars on the bronze doors where the battering ram had failed. In a detached way Boudica could appreciate the elegance of its proportions. She supposed that Prasutagos would have wept at the thought of destroying it—one more thing she could be glad he was not here to see. She herself had no such compunctions. The only way to get to the meat of an egg was to crack the shell, and this shell still sheltered half the population of Colonia—men, women, children, the soldiers from the fort, and the paltry two hundred the procurator had sent them from Londinium.

"There's no way to burn it from the outside, see," said a gnarled little man with a missing front tooth who had been forced to help build the temple. Boudica turned to look at him, vaguely aware that he had been talking to her for some time. "Outside's all faced with stone, aye? And bronze all over the doors. But the roof, now—" He glowered upward. "Over the roof-beams there's just tiles. I should know, Lady—half broke my back helping to put 'em there. Tear those loose and you've fine stout wooden beams to burn. We can smoke 'em out, just like putting fire down a badger's hole. They'll open the doors themselves and come out when it's a choice between facing us and not breathing!"

The men around them were nodding. Boudica sensed anticipation from Cathubodva. A raven called, settling atop the bronze eagle attached to the peak of the temple's roof as if to show them the way.

"I hear you," she murmured, then turned to the men around her. "Yes—do it now!" As men dragged out the ladders they had been making and swarmed up the side of the building, she told herself there was no work of man that other men, with sufficient motivation, could not destroy. Tiles clinked as men hammered to loosen them and then began to pitch them down, nibbling at the expanse of terra-cotta until the roof began to look like a moth-eaten wool cloak. Soon she saw the long beams laid bare.

Shouts echoed from within as some of the men began to shoot through the openings. But now men were hauling up jars of olive oil and pouring it over the wood, hammering stakes smeared with pitch and flax into the beams and setting them alight. They dropped the remaining jars through holes and followed them with flaming arrows as a promise of what was to come.

The attackers scuttled down the ladders as tendrils of white smoke changed to black, followed by tongues of flame.

"Burn, Claudius," whispered Boudica, "for surely your own people never made you such a noble pyre or gave you so many offerings!" This was a midsummer bonfire such as Britannia had never seen.

Above the mutter of the flames she could hear screaming.

"Not long now," said one of the men.

Inside it would be getting hot and dangerous, as flaming fragments of roof began to shower down. Black smoke billowed through the roof, but as much again must be swirling inside as fire worked its way along the undersides of beams. Those who died from lack of air would be the lucky ones.

A shout brought her attention back to the front of the temple. The bronze doors were opening.

"At last!" exclaimed Bituitos, striding forward. "They will come out to die like men!"

Soldiers appeared in the doorway, each man's shield protecting half his body and the sword arm of his neighbor. Their blades flickered in and out like an adder's tongue. For a few moments they held off the attackers, but the pressure of people behind them was pushing them forward. Now she could see space behind them, and in the next moment the Britons had flowed around to attack them from in back and by sheer weight bore them down. Others tore into the massed bodies behind them. Some tried to retreat, trampling those behind them, only to be thrust out again.

"Pull back," cried someone. "We can't kill them unless we give them room!"

Clouds blazed in the light of the setting sun as if the heavens, too, were aflame. Even at the edge of the square Boudica could feel the heat as the flames rose higher. The attackers began to edge away, leaving a tangle of bodies behind. The blood that covered the temple steps glowed an even more vivid crimson in the light of the fire. A few more Romans emerged from the doorway. For a moment a woman with a child in her arms stood silhouetted against the flames, then turned back again.

After that, no more appeared. Boudica fought to clear her mind of the image—they were Romans! They deserved to die. The shifting wind brought her the reek of the smoke and the choking scent of burnt flesh; she pulled her cloak across her face to filter it, and for one horrible moment she was back at Dun Garo, watching Prasutagos burn on his pyre. The men and women inside the temple were wives and husbands . . . they were Romans . . . anguish seized her, but in the commotion no one heard her moan.

A cheering crowd surrounded her. She could not run away. "Help me," she whispered, but even Eoc, who stood beside her, could not hear.

Only the goddess, rising like a dark tide within her, recognized her agony, and shared it, and absorbed it, drawing a soft veil between Boudica and the world. As one who watches from a far distance she saw slabs of stone crack and pop outward from the walls, leaving a skeleton of burning uprights within. And then even that was gone, and she was in a golden country watching Prasutagos building a wall.

In Colonia, Cathubodva watched the Temple of Claudius burn. Now only the building's facade was still standing. Men began to cheer as it wavered. For another moment the eagle on the rooftree showed stark against the flames, then a gout of smoke swirled around it and it fell.

Celtic horns blared in triumph, but their music was overwhelmed by the shouts of the crowd. Standing in the midst of them, the goddess wept Boudica's tears.

*   *   *

Lhiannon woke with a start. She still lay beneath the thorn hedge. Heart pounding, she tried to identify what new danger had startled her. It was day, but the sun had not yet lifted above the mountains on the mainland. From the direction of Lys Deru she heard shouting, and then the harsh music of a Roman trumpet. Again and again it blew. Wincing as the movement woke a host of pains, she peered through the leaves.

Black smoke still drifted from Lys Deru and the Sacred Grove. On the students' playing field legionaries were gathering, more and more of them as the trumpets continued to call. Lhiannon shrank back into her hole as a pair of soldiers jingled by at a swift march, perhaps the same two who had nearly found her the night before. They were not hunting now. From the sound of their muttering they were as puzzled as she.

There was a disturbing beauty in the speed with which the confusion of men settled into orderly ranks. You would never see Britons bracing to attention like so many images as an officer came by. As she watched, men continued to arrive. They must be pulling in the perimeter guards as well. But why? Surely they would want to do another sweep for fugitives in the light of day.

Lhiannon watched throughout the morning, but no more soldiers came near. A little before noon the trumpets blew once more, and still in their precise formations, the Romans marched back to the shore. As the last of them disappeared, Lhiannon began to weep, releasing all the tears that through that long and terrible night she had locked within. And when she was done, she wriggled out of her refuge and started across the fields toward what remained of the Druids' sanctuary.

The reek of charred thatch lay heavy on the air. Lhiannon tied her veil across her face, but it did little good. As she got closer she could smell a sickening hint of burned flesh and the iron tang of blood. The timbers of the gatepost lay charred, but before they burned, someone had hacked at the swirling sigils that had given them magic. The devastation beyond made a mockery of the bright day.

Sweet Goddess have mercy, she thought numbly, *am I the only one who survived?* She stiffened as something moved, but it was only a raven lifting from the corpse of one of the community's dogs with a flick of black wings.

As she let out her breath, something stirred in what she had taken for a pile of rags. It was Belina. Slowly the older priestess focused on Lhiannon, and humanity came back into her eyes. There was a bruise on her cheek and the livid marks of fingers on her arms.

"Lhiannon . . . you are alive . . ." Her lips twisted in what was intended to be a smile.

"How is it with you?" Lhiannon knelt at her side.

"No worse than one might expect, save for a knock on the head." Belina winced as Lhiannon helped her to stand. "Help me to wash their filth away. Thank the Goddess I was no virgin."

And what of those who had been? wondered Lhiannon. Was a quick death the best fate she could hope for them?

A dead cow lay half in and half out of the stream, but the water above it ran cold and clear. Both women felt better when they had washed and drunk. Lhiannon was even beginning to wonder if any food had been left unfouled. They returned to the houses and began the grim work of identifying the dead. Some of the older Druids had chosen to burn in the houses. Elin had died beside the hut where she kept her herbs. Mandua seemed to have found a knife and killed herself after the Romans were done.

And astonishingly, some were still alive.

Lhiannon was binding up a long gash in the leg of one of the younger Druids when a new sound brought her around. The blood left her head as she looked up and saw Ardanos, leaning on Bendeigid's arm. Or perhaps it was his spirit, for she had never seen such grief in the eyes of a living man.

He had bruises and scrapes, but otherwise seemed unharmed. His lips opened, but no words came.

"Sit down, my lord," said Bendeigid gently, leading him to a bench that had somehow escaped destruction. "You see, you are not the only one to survive . . ." His bleak gaze met the women's stares. "And it is a wonder he did," he said. "He would have thrown himself on the Roman swords. I hauled him away from the fighting—we spent most of last night in the water. He was cursing me, but I made him live. We will need him to lead us when we fight again . . ."

"No . . ." Ardanos whispered. "Never again. We cannot fight Rome."

"When you are recovered, sir, you'll feel differently," Bendeigid replied, but Ardanos continued to shake his head.

"The soldiers are all gone?" asked Lhiannon. "I saw them forming up and marching away—"

Bendeigid nodded. "Just past dawn another boat crossed the strait with a courier clinging to the rail. He went haring up the road as soon as it touched sand, and soon after we heard the trumpets. They are gone, though the Goddess knows why."

"Something has happened . . ." said Belina in a still voice. "Our magic worked. Only not . . . in time . . ."

"In time for us to save something!" said Lhiannon as briskly as she could. "They would have found the rest of us by the end of the day."

"Where *are* the others?" Bendeigid's face grew grim as he saw the row of bodies. "Where is the High Priestess? The Roman scum took no prisoners with them—they cannot all have died . . ."

They found Coventa behind a screen of willow branches at a bend in the stream where the girls had made a shrine to Brigantia. She was naked, curled against the altar, shivering. At the sight of the blood on those white limbs Lhiannon put out a hand to stop Bendeigid.

"Go back and find something to cover her—"

Softly she knelt at Coventa's side.

"It is all right, my dear one, you are safe—we are here . . ."

Coventa's eyes opened, and somehow she managed a smile. Belina held the water flask to her lips. She drank eagerly, then lay back with a sigh.

"Why did they do it?" she whispered. "I never wanted a lover, but I saw how eagerly women went to the Beltane fires . . . I thought that when men and women came together there was joy. This was like being attacked by *animals!*"

"Coventa, that's what they were—"

"When they hurt my body, I willed myself not to feel— but I couldn't close my mind to their rage and their fear. And all the time they were shouting—animals don't curse, Lhiannon!" she exclaimed. "It is not true, what they say about the ability to see visions depending on virginity . . ." she went on. "Since then I cannot stop seeing images, but they are all evil—blood and a burning city, bodies everywhere . . ."

Lhiannon winced. Was this why they said the Oracle must be virgin, not because of the intimacy of the body, but because for an adept, intercourse must also bring intimacy of the mind?

"Those images were in the minds of the men who raped you," said Belina. "Let them go."

"They couldn't be—" Coventa shook her head. "The men I saw were of our people, and Boudica was with them, waving a bloody sword."

"Desire shapes her dreams," murmured Belina. "Boudica protected her when they were young, so she summons her image again."

Lhiannon was not so sure, but she could do nothing for Boudica, and there were those who needed her help desperately here and now.

"It was Boudica, but it was not—" Coventa babbled on. "I saw the shape of a great raven rising up behind her, with blood on its beak and claws . . ."

The Lady of Ravens stalked through the ruins of Colonia, directing the storage of looted supplies, the distribution of captured arms, the assignment of camping space to the men who continued to arrive. Queen, icon, no one questioned Her right to lead them, though Boudica's household had begun suggesting She take time to eat and sleep as the night passed and the next day drew on.

It was nearly sunset when Brangenos came to Her, Rianor at his side. Behind them, Rigana and Argantilla watched warily.

"My Lady, how is it with You?" the elder Druid said carefully.

It was clear that he knew Whom he was speaking to. Why did he not say what he meant?

"*I* am very well—how could I be otherwise, after such a feast?" She laughed. "Or did you mean to ask after My horse?"

Some of the others looked at them in confusion, as the queen had been on foot all day, but Brangenos answered.

"Yes, my Lady, as You know full well, and You are too good a horsewoman to ride a willing mount to exhaustion."

"I suppose that is true." She sent awareness inward, noting sore feet and an aching back. They had kept Her supplied with beer, but what the ravens ate put nothing in Boudica's belly. A glance around the camp showed things in as good an order as it was possible for these people to achieve. She could see that in another moment he was going to pass from request to command, and with the body so tired, She might not be able to retain control.

"Would you like Me to leave her now?" She grinned.

"Please, Lady, come back to your tent—" Brangenos cast a wary glance at the interested faces around him.

Perhaps he had a point. Amusing as it might be to drop Her mount right here, it was probably best to let the Britons believe that it was Boudica who was leading them.

"Mother—we need you, too," Argantilla said then, and at the sound of that voice, Boudica began to wake within.

"Yes . . . it is time . . ." The goddess leaned on the older Druid and allowed the younger to take her other arm, withdrawing a little more with each step, so that by the time they reached Boudica's camp, the Druids were supporting her.

"Is this what you desired?" She laughed softly. Then Her eyes closed and She was gone.

*W*hen they had gotten Coventa back to the shelter of the Council Hall and she was sleeping peacefully, they left Belina to watch her and went out again to look for Helve. They found the High Priestess at the Sacred Grove.

The outer ring of trees had burned, but in the center the trunks of the great oaks were only scorched and their leaves baked brown. Helve sat with her back against the altar stone, a Roman javelin lodged in her side. She still wore the torque and armrings of her office. Dark blood soaked the blue robes.

"They were afraid to touch her," Bendeigid said softly. "She made her stand here, and I'll warrant she cursed them. That's why her body was not defiled."

He stepped back, fingers flickering in a sign of warding as the dark draperies stirred. But Lhiannon stiffened, pointing—

"Look—that blood is still red—she is alive!"

Bendeigid went to her side, calling her name, but there was no response.

Ardanos straightened, with an effort putting on the authority of the Arch-Druid once more. He knelt at Helve's side.

"Helve—I call you. From the place where your spirit wanders I call you back. Open your eyes, my lady, and answer me . . ."

A quiver ran through the still form as the priestess opened her eyes. New blood welled from the wound. Slowly her gaze fixed on Ardanos.

"My lord . . ." It was only a breath of sound, but she winced as if even that much movement caused her pain. "Knew you . . . would come."

Even now, thought Lhiannon, Helve's voice held not gratitude but pride.

"Helve, you are wounded. We must remove this blade."

The priestess raised one eyebrow. "Dying," she corrected. "Let me . . . speak, then . . . pull the spear." She fell silent, breathing carefully. "I gave Nodona the kiss of blessing . . . she shall be High Priestess . . ." She plucked at the torque. "Until Lhiannon comes back . . . from Eriu." She drew a shuddering breath and her eyes closed.

"Helve, I am here!" Lhiannon took the woman's cold hand.

"She thinks I hate . . . her," the pale lips twisted. "She was too . . . good. I was afraid."

"No—I understood," Lhiannon said, trying to stop herself from babbling. "You did well."

This was wrong. A high priestess should pass with all her women around her. Save for Belina, not one of them was in any condition to come to the Sacred Grove, even Nodona, who was still hysterical, though aside from rape her body seemed to have taken little harm.

"I saved . . . the sacred stone . . ."

Did Helve even realize that Lhiannon was there? Behind them Bendeigid had begun to murmur the chant that eased the passage of an adept to the Otherworld.

Helve's eyes opened, and with an effort she focused on Ardanos. "My lord . . . I am ready. Pull . . . out the damned . . . spear!"

Ardanos was shivering, but when he sang his voice was firm. "You are not this pain . . . you are not this body . . . From all oaths that bound you, be free. You are Light, you are Joy that cannot die. Rise, holy one, on the wings of the morning. Speed westward until you come to the Isles of the Blessed. There you shall rest until it is time to take a body once more. It is the Arch-Druid of Britannia who releases you. Be at peace, Helve. You have leave to go . . ."

Helve's eyes were closed. Ardanos's face had gone white, but his hand was steady as he grasped the shaft of the javelin just behind the head and slowly eased it from the wound. A gush of bright blood followed. Helve's body jerked, struggling, then went slack. For a moment Lhiannon seemed to see a mist of brightness above the still form, but perhaps it was a haze of sunlight passing through the trees. Then it was gone.

"I should be lying beside her," Ardanos breathed. "What use was all our wisdom and our magic? Lys Deru is gone. We failed." And then, at last, he began to weep.

*O*f Colonia, only rubble and a few wisps of smoke remained where some stubborn flame still burned. Most of the inhabitants were ashes, but a few had been nailed to the charred beams of their houses as a warning, and at the little fort, heads now adorned the gateposts. For four days the Britons had been celebrating their victory, as drunk on the Roman blood they had spilled as they were on Roman wine.

Boudica sat before her tent in a Roman curule chair set with ivory and gold, listening to the chieftains who lounged on a variety of seats around her fire. It was a surprisingly comfortable chair—a good thing, considering how many of her muscles were still sore.

"The City of Victory, they called it!" exclaimed Segovax. "It's the City of Victims now!"

"This is the oldest Roman settlement in Britannia," said King Corio. "Well, it *was* . . ." he said, grinning. The Dobunni lord had arrived while she was sleeping, along with several chieftains from the Catuvellauni lands. "The others won't stand a chance!"

"If all the people rise in rebellion," said Boudica, "no conqueror can hold a land. But *all* of us must attack the Romans—and we must take the forts as well as the towns."

When Boudica had awakened after a night and part of the following day, she had found half a dozen chieftains from the Cantiaci and Catuvellauni waiting. They listened with a respect that surprised her. Whatever the goddess had been doing during the day after the Temple of Claudius had burned had apparently done her reputation no harm.

She signaled to Rigana to carry the wine pitcher around, suppressing an impulse to ask for beer instead. Her head still had that feeling of having been swept clean, like the shore after high tide—the pressure she had felt from the goddess was almost gone, but Boudica had the feeling that certain things, like beer, or blood, would bring Her back again. That day of absence had frightened her daughters. She must not give in to the temptation to lose herself in the goddess without need. At least Cathubodva seemed to have left some of Her wisdom behind.

"We have enough war arrows to send to all the tribes, and these have been reddened in Roman blood. We need four more hosts the size of this one to pin down the legions, to convince the Romans that Britannia is a pit into which they may cast their gold and their men for a century and still it will not be filled."

"An offering pit," murmured Brangenos, "a gift for the gods . . ."

At the words, Boudica felt a flutter of raven wings within. *She is still hungry . . .* At the thought, the scent of carrion grew stronger, carried on the wind.

*W*hen the wind blew through the Sacred Grove one could smell the burning, though four days had now passed, but the scent of burned wood was clean compared to the reek that still hung over what had been Lys Deru. Of the Druids who had remained at the sanctuary, barely half had suvived to chant the funeral hymn while the others burned. Of those, some might recover in body, thought Lhiannon as she watched Coventa gaze vaguely at the play of the light in the leaves; she was less sure about their minds.

"Lys Deru is no more," said Ardanos. "The magic is departed." He had made sure of it, ordering them to pull down the remains of the buildings to fuel the funeral pyre. "We will leave nothing for the Romans to triumph over when they return, as they surely will . . ."

He blinked twice, a facial twitch that had appeared the day after the attack. Despite the energy with which Ardanos had supervised the demolition and funeral, Lhiannon wondered if he ought to be counted among the wounded as well.

"And where do you wish us to go?" she asked gently. She looked around the circle. The day after the Romans departed, some of their neighbors had appeared bringing supplies, so at least they were clothed and fed, though it was strange to see Druids in the natural colors of wool and flax instead of white and dark blue.

"For a time we must disperse. We come from many tribes—we must seek those of our Order who remain in the clanholds to arrange for shelter in remote farmsteads where those who are injured can heal."

And our priestesses can wait to learn if the seed the Romans planted will take root in their wombs, Lhiannon thought grimly. Belina was already talking of raising any sons to take vengeance, and of all the raped women she was the closest to sane. *We are all broken in one way or another . . . it remains to be seen if we will be able to mend.*

One by one the survivors began to speak of places they might find refuge.

"I have no family left in the Cornovii lands," said Lhiannon when it came to her turn, "but there are those in the Summer Country who will shelter me. I will take Coventa and go to Avalon."

"And we may be able to return here one day," said Belina. "One of the fisherfolk heard talk among the soldiers as they moved out. There is a rebellion in the east—in the Iceni and Trinovante lands. That is why the legion left so suddenly. Maybe this is the revolt for which we have waited, when all the tribes of Britannia will rise as one."

Lhiannon stiffened, understanding flooding her. Boudica was caught up in this somehow. She twitched with sudden exasperation at all these wounded people. Ardanos was right—Lys Deru was gone, and with it the Druid power. Perhaps she belonged now with those who had not yet given up the fight . . .

"Is it possible that our sacrifice bought time for a rebellion to begin?" asked old Brigomaglos. "To believe that it achieved *something* would ease my soul."

"I will not deny the possibility of a miracle," Ardanos said in a dry voice. "But we dare not assume that this will be the time our people achieve a unity they were never able to manage before." He shook his head. "No—we will go into hiding, and we will do whatever we must to survive. Let the Romans think us broken until we can find a way to live with them in safety."

"Will we cease to be Druids?" asked Belina. "Our High Priestess is dead." Her gaze moved to the bloodstain that still marked the sacred stone.

"She said that Nodona should succeed her," said Brigomaglos.

"But will she be able to serve?" Belina asked.

Lhiannon kept silent. Too many here knew of the tension between her and Helve. Anything she said would be suspect now. And she could not forget how like manacles the golden rings had seemed as they weighted Helve's arms.

She had dreamed of being High Priestess for so many years, and never realized how much she liked being free.

"Until we have a place in which to perform the ceremonies once more, does it matter?" Brigomaglos asked. "By the time we do, the girl will have recovered. If she survives the ordeal and is able to bear the power of the Goddess, then Helve's will may be done. If not—we shall choose again."

Some of the other men were agreeing. Ardanos looked at Lhiannon as if about to speak, but she shook her head. In time she might regret allowing the priests to claim so much power, but just now she found it hard to care. Could they not see that everything depended on the Iceni rebellion? She understood Coventa's vision now. Boudica bore the power of the Morrigan. If she succeeded, no one would question the power of the priestesses. And there might be no hope for any of them if she failed.

TWENTY-SIX

*B*oudica laughed and grabbed for the rail as the chariot bounced beneath her, the javelin swinging wildly in her other hand. It was ancient, one of several that had been brought in after the attack on Colonia. Its leather fittings were much in need of repair, but an inspiring reminder of the glories of the past.

Tascio, her driver, ducked with an oath, wrenching the ponies' heads around to avoid Rigana's chariot and throwing Boudica to the other side. Footing was tricky—with Tascio seated on the platform before her and her shield and spears attached to the wicker sides, there was scarcely room left to stand.

As they cantered around again the people cheered. The sight of a war cart evoked ancient glories—reason enough to shrink new iron rims to wooden wheels and replace the leather fittings. For Boudica to appear in a chariot confirmed her role as leader. She had given one of the restored vehicles to her older daughter on the understanding that Calgac, who was driving it, would get her away at the first sign of real danger. But unless they could learn to use them properly, no one was going to take the chariots into battle at all.

Boudica had a moment to envy Rigana's resilience as they sped by. Constant walking and riding had kept her fit, but she could not match a fifteen-year-old's flexibility.

"Balance! Don't hold on!" called Tingetorix. His bad leg kept him on horseback, but if he could not set an example, he could certainly tell the rest of them what they were doing wrong.

The leather straps that suspended the bouncing wooden platform creaked as the wheels skittered over the rough ground. Boudica had thought the heaving deck of a ship unsteady; this was like trying to stand on a quaking bog. As another turn flung her against the rail she could feel Cathubodva laughing. The goddess danced on chaos as Her ravens danced on the wind. For humans, the stability of the ground was the only certainty. But tempting as it was to let the goddess take over, Boudica had schooled enough horses to know that the more reflexes she trained into her muscles, the less her rider would have to do.

As a tiny girl she had loved watching her older brothers practicing with the chariots. Dubi had been able to run out along the shaft to the yoke that linked the two ponies, fling a javelin, and get back again. He usually hit the target as well. That would not be a problem in battle—as long as you launched a projectile in the right direction it was bound to hit somebody.

Tascio brought the chariot around and for a moment she had it, balancing on the balls of her feet to keep the same relationship to the earth no matter which way the platform was jumping. Then the ache in her leg became a sudden cramp.

"Whoa . . ." she gasped as she slid the javelin into its rest and bent to massage the limb.

When she could stand again, she saw Rigana's chariot thundering toward her. As they passed, the girl let out a skull-splitting screech and flourished her javelin with a grin that had been absent for far too long. Boudica waved back, then turned as someone called.

"That will be enough for now, Tascio—bring us in." She straightened as he turned the ponies toward the knot of people who had gathered at the edge of the crowd, doing her best to support the image of a bold warrior queen without revealing how grateful she was for an excuse to stand still.

From the chariot Boudica could see much of the camp, which since the fall of Colonia had come to resemble a gathering of clans for the Lughnasa fair. Warriors were still arriving, but now they were bringing their families, and bards and merchants were arriving as well. Anywhere you walked you might hear singing, or find some impromptu contest of strength or skill. A giddy, holiday atmosphere filled the air.

But the men who awaited her were not in a festive mood.

"Have the scouts returned?" she asked, looking down at them. After the defeat of the Ninth Legion she had sent men to watch all the Roman forts, especially in the east, where the governor had posted the Twentieth and Fourth, and the southeast, where he'd placed the Second Legion. A host the size of her impromptu army could not move unnoticed—she was surprised that there had been no other response from the Romans by now.

The group parted to let a weary man step forward. "I rode east, my lady, as you ordered. Didn't have to go farther than that new fort they call Letocetum, on the Great Road. There was plenty of news in the wineshop there."

"Is the Twentieth coming?"

"Aye, with the Fourth right behind them, but they'll be on the road awhile. They were on Mona, my lady! They burned the sanctuary to the ground and killed every Druid they could find!"

"Sacrilege!" came the cry. "The gods will strike them—"

Boudica closed her eyes, clutching at the rail of the chariot as a murmur of horror spread through the crowd. She had just seen the devastation fire could wreak on a city. Her imagination pictured only too vividly flames rising from the house circle at Lys Deru and the Sacred Grove. What had happened to Belina and Coventa, and the others whom she had loved? She prayed to the gods that Lhiannon was still safe in Eriu.

"The gods will strike them indeed," she echoed, dashing tears from her eyes. She jerked her javelin from its rest and held it high. "My arm is their weapon! And yours—" She swung the spear above the crowd. "Every fist that can hold a blade is the hand of the gods. And we will avenge!" She felt her face flush at the roar of fury that answered her.

"The Twentieth will be some weeks on the road," the messenger went on. "My news is from the cavalry troop that rode in with Governor Paulinus three days ago. They barely took time to eat and sleep before they were on fresh horses heading south to Londinium."

"Will he try to hold the city? What will he do for men?" came the questions.

Boudica had been undecided which way to lead her forces. This was the news she had needed.

"I don't know what *he'll* do," she said viciously, "but what *we* must do is clear! Cry the word through the camp, all of you! Give your beasts a good feed and pack up your wagons. Tomorrow we march on Londinium, and if we are very lucky, we'll catch the butcher of Mona there!"

*T*he ship rolled and lifted and dipped once more as a fair wind drove her toward the Summer Country. Since the funerals, three days had passed, and it was not until they got out into the strait that the brisk sea wind drove the last taint of burning from the air. Only then did Lhiannon realize how accustomed to that reek she had become. Even Coventa, though she had been sick that morning, seemed to be reviving.

But was she herself any better off? The piled purple mountains beyond the shoreline slid by like a dream. The sea glittered in the bright air, and the sky was a beneficent blue. In the old days, Lhiannon would have said that the sea gods had blessed their journey, but just now she found it hard to believe that they cared.

"I wish that we could stay forever on the sea," murmured Coventa, "between the worlds." She was still quiet and pale, but the visions only came at night now, as dreams. "No one knows where we are . . . no one can tell us what to do. I thought you were an exile, and was sorry that you could not stay safe with us. But I begin to see why you spent so much time away."

"It was not all a holiday," Lhiannon observed reminiscently. "When I was with Caratac I was often hungry or cold or in danger, but it is true that I did not have the Druids telling me what to do every time I turned around."

"I have been very naïve," Coventa said quietly. "I am like some wild bird that has been bred up captive in a cage, and when the door to freedom is opened I do not know how to fly. I am not fit for this new world we have been forced into. But you are, Lhiannon. I hope you will not let Ardanos put you into a cage. He is so afraid—and perhaps he is right—the world is more terrible than I could have imagined. If there is ever a place where our priestesses can live all together again, I think he will try to make it a fortress."

Ardanos would never . . . the thought faltered. The Ardanos she had loved would not have tried to rule with so heavy a hand, but the Romans had done something to his soul.

"The world goes as it will, not as we would have it," Coventa continued, "and all we can do is to try to serve the gods."

"The gods! If I believed that all this was their will I would curse them—" Lhiannon stopped short, realizing only now how long she had been refusing to face her despair. "As it is, either they hate us, or they have no power. Everything we have done to propitiate them has only made things worse, so far as I can see . . ."

She had spoken softly, but Coventa was looking at her in shocked surprise. *I am a priestess,* she told herself. *For her sake I should pretend to believe* . . . That was what she had done ever since the crescent of the Goddess was placed between her brows.

"What do you want me to say?" she burst out suddenly. "Do you want me to tell you that everything will be all right? It won't! It's *not* . . ."

Her throat ached too fiercely to say more. Through war and disaster she had been kept too busy dealing with crises to consider their implications . . . but on this sunlit, smiling sea she had let down her defenses and now she was lost. She held her hands over her face, shaking with sobs.

After what seemed a long time she felt soft arms around her. Coventa was holding her, rocking her as the ship was rocked by the sea. And presently she came to the end of her tears.

"Thank you," she whispered. "I've stopped now." She hugged Coventa back and saw the younger woman relax, but for her the brightness had gone out of the day.

Lhiannon understood now why some Druids retreated

to the wilderness to live out their days in a cave by a sacred spring. Though the changing seasons held their own disasters, in nature there was an underlying order in which one might find some certainty. But she could see no such hope in the world of humankind.

*F*rom the next street over Boudica could hear a howling that sounded more like beasts than men. The white mare danced beneath her, ears flicking nervously, and Bogle growled a warning as another band trotted by. Two men were carrying Roman heads on their spears. The others bore bags of loot and supplies. The tangle of homes and shops and warehouses that had sprung up on the north bank of the Tamesa seemed to huddle beneath a lowering sky. One could trace the progress of the attacking Britons by the ravens that followed them through the town.

Londinium, like Colonia, was undefended. Decianus Catus had fled to Gallia when Colonia fell, and his staff, including Cloto, had gone with him. They had missed the governor by two days. Paulinus had at least made an attempt to evacuate the city, but those inhabitants who were stubbornly determined to protect their property or too old or infirm to flee remained, and were dying in the place of those more deserving of killing as the Britons swept from one street to the next.

Boudica had given orders that the city not be burned until they had stripped it of everything of value. Most of those who had joined her had brought food, but they could not risk running short before they caught up with the governor. And much of what these warehouses held had been taken as Roman taxes. She found a grim satisfaction in the symmetry of taking it back again.

As they turned a corner the shouting grew louder. Boudica's escort drew in protectively as they sighted a knot of struggling men. A woman's scream pierced the babble like a blade to the heart. Unthinking, Boudica urged the mare forward. She saw blades flash as the attackers scrambled out of the way. Their features were those of men she knew, but in this moment their faces were stamped with a single identity.

A Roman stood behind the splintered door of his house, holding up a table as a shield. A Briton with an ax hewed at it, making chunks fly like kindling, while others jabbed with spears. Boudica recognized the ax man. He had been a small farmer who got into debt and fought back when the Romans came to seize his land. In the struggle he had escaped, but his wife had been captured and sold into slavery.

The man lurched as one of the spears pierced his leg; the next blow of the ax sent the battered table spinning. Many hands pulled him out into the street and the red blades rose and fell. With a rending of wood others knocked the remains of the door away and pushed inside. The woman began to scream once more.

A little boy burst through the doorway, his thin wail abruptly silenced as someone clubbed him and tossed the body aside. Then men were dragging his mother into the street, tearing at her tunica and forcing her down. Boudica saw her desperate eyes white-rimmed above a muffling hand.

"If you try to stop them they will turn on you," came the voice of the goddess within as she opened her lips to protest. The white limbs thrashing before her merged with the image of Argantilla's body as the Roman had dragged her down.

Are we no better than they? her spirit cried.

"This is not about lust, but about power—"

Help her! Vision blurred as the conflict drove awareness inward. Boudica felt the horse move beneath her as she grabbed a spear from one of her men, but the unerring aim was Cathubodva's, like the power that drove the spear past the rapist's shoulder and into his victim's heart.

This is your work, Lady, she thought despairingly. *If it must be done, I don't want to see.* This time she willingly abandoned consciousness, and the mercy of the Morrigan folded dark wings between her and the pain.

Even the queen's escort left a distance between them and the One they followed through the streets where blood flowed in the gutters, for the calm, clear voice that directed them where to search for valuables held a resonance that was more than human, and the mind that directed it had a deadly patience that they did not understand.

But Boudica found herself walking through an oak wood drifted with autumn leaves and scattered with what she took to be acorns. As she drew closer she could see that they were human heads. Their faces were contorted, but she could not tell if it was in exaltation or rage.

"This is My harvest . . . their blood will feed the land," came a harsh voice from above.

She looked up. Balancing on one of the branches was a Raven with red eyes.

"Men are no different from any other creature," said the Raven. "When one group is stronger they conquer, and when they weaken, another comes and feeds on them in turn. Conflict and competition are necessary. The fury passes through like a great fire, burning weakness away, and in its light the essence is revealed. The strongest in both groups survive. Blood and spirit are blended and what grows from them is stronger still."

"Is this the only way?" Boudica cried.

"This is the way you must follow now," came the reply. "Britannia is a mingling of many bloods already, from peoples that strove against each other as they came to these shores. In time more will come and today's victor will fail, leaving his own strength in the land."

"That is a hard teaching," Boudica said.

"It is my truth—the Raven's Way. One way or another the cycle must continue. The balance must be maintained. And there is more than one kind of victory . . ."

When Boudica came to herself once more, she was back in their camp, dismounting from the mare. Brangenos caught her as her knees buckled and Eos took the rein to lead Branwen away. Red smeared and splattered the mare's white hide. The stink of blood was all around her. Boudica looked down and saw her legs splashed with clotting red to the knee. Bogle whined and sat down. He was blood-smeared as well.

"It is a red woman on a white horse that leads us . . ." ran the whispers, "and with her the hunters of the Otherworld, the white, red-eared hounds . . ."

"Is my horse all right?" Her voice seemed to come from a distance.

"She needs to be cleansed, like you, but she is Branwen, the white raven. What better mount for the Lady of Ravens to ride?"

But I was the horse, thought Boudica dizzily. She wondered what had happened after the goddess severed her from her own identity.

The faces around her were warmed by a sunset glow, but the horizon was dark. Slowly she realized that the light was reflecting off the clouds over the burning city. It was over, then—for now—and the dead had their pyre.

"Come," said Brangenos. As she steadied, he set his hand beneath her elbow. "You need water. You need rest."

"Yes, but not to drink. First I must get clean."

They had made their camp by one of the streams that ran into the Tamesa. Ignoring the startled exclamations of her household, Boudica plunged through the reeds and into the water, Bogle bounding after her. The cold shocked her fully into her body as it washed the blood away. When she struggled back ashore she was shivering with reaction. The dog pushed through the reeds and shook himself, sending out arcs of spray.

Temella hurried toward her with a blanket. When she was dry and had a bowl of hot soup in her hands Brangenos settled beside her. Beyond the tent poles men bowed as they passed.

"I saw that man in the city," she said as a burly figure with an ax stuck through his belt went by. "He was killing a Roman who was defending his home. But he looked different—" She gestured toward the crowd. "They all did. Now they look like themselves again. Was it my imagination? What did I see?"

The Druid sighed. "Another spirit can possess men who are joined by great emotion. I do not know if it is a curse or a mercy."

"The mercy of the Morrigan," she said bitterly. "Is it like the thing that happens to me?"

"Somewhat, except that this is a shared ecstasy, created when many souls under pressure become one."

"Will they remember what they did?"

"In such a state men are capable of great feats of valor—or of cruelty." His lean face was somber. "To be unable to remember the former relieves them of the yearning to reach a level they will never again be able to attain. To forget the latter . . . do you think they could face their own wives and children if they had full memory of what they had done?"

"But if they do not remember, they will do it again," she said, knowing she had no right to judge, having given up her own will to a force equally implacable. "And if the Battle Raven rides me again, so will I . . ." She swallowed. "Is there no way to make war with honor?"

"With perfect warriors—with perfect discipline," he replied. "In the old days the champions would go out to fight between the armies, and the will of each side rode with its defender, and all were ennobled by their strife. The Romans will not allow us that kind of war. What we have here is not an army, my queen. It is a mob, a creature composed of outrage and pain that burns its way across the land."

"*She* said something like that," murmured Boudica, and saw his gaze sharpen. "While She was doing battle She was also talking to me in an oak wood where men's heads lay on the ground." Haltingly she recounted Cathubodva's words.

"It is a harsh teaching indeed," the Druid agreed when she was done. "But it is all we have. If this fire you have started can kindle the valor of all the tribes we may yet drive the Romans from this land. If not, our own blood will feed the ground. You cannot stop it now, my queen, you can only fan the flames and hope they burn quick and clean."

Boudica gulped soup, but its heat could not warm her. Now, more than ever, she understood why Prasutagos had sought peace so earnestly. Suddenly she ached with the need to feel his arms around her, to make life in this wasteland. Would he turn from her in horror if he saw what she was doing now? But the peace the Romans would have given them was a living death, destruction with no hope of renewal.

"My lady, if you wish I can mix you something to make you sleep," said Brangenos.

She looked up, seeing him suddenly as a man, still strong, despite the white in his hair. If she asked, would he lie with her? Their eyes met, and she knew his answer.

"No—" She shook her head, denying him, denying herself the respite that she craved. "If those who died today could bear their pain, the least I can do is endure my dreams . . ."

*T*he journey by sea had gone by like a dream, but the Summer Country seemed scarcely closer to the world of death and battle Lhiannon had left behind. As the boatman poled the long, flat craft through the marshes, reed and willow closed around them, and their only enemies were the midges that rose in humming clouds as they passed.

Each morning the mist rose from the water to veil the marshes in mystery. Lhiannon found herself half hoping that when it cleared she would find herself in the Otherworld, but the long shafts of afternoon sunlight showed the same landscape as before. But with each day the pointed tip of the Tor appeared more clearly above the tangled trees, until they came with the last light of sunset to the shores of Avalon.

The little house in which Lhiannon had lived had lost some of its thatching—the Druids had not had much time for initiations in recent years, and only one old priestess, a woman called Nan, remained—but everything else seemed unchanged. The slender, dark-haired folk of the marshes provided them with food and brought their sick for healing. As the Summer Country drowsed through the long days, Lhiannon found her heart easing. If Avalon held no answers, at least here she could sometimes forget the questions.

Her only anxiety was Coventa, who continued to be sick during the day, and troubled at night by evil dreams. A week after they had arrived on the isle Coventa awoke one morning weeping. With a sigh, Lhiannon rose and held her until the sobs began to ease.

"Nan, will you make up the fire and fill the hanging pot with water so we can have some chamomile tea?"

"Thank you," said Coventa when the old woman brought her the cup. "I am sorry to be such a bother to you all."

"Was it another bad dream?" Lhiannon asked the girl.

Coventa sighed. "I dreamed that I gave birth to a son, who grew up tall and strong with golden hair. But when he was grown, he turned into a raven and flew away."

"Is that why you were crying?"

Coventa shook her head. "He was a beautiful boy. It made me happy to see him. I wept because when he is grown he will become a warrior."

"In your dream," said Lhiannon, frowning.

"In this world." Coventa looked up at her with an odd smile. "I never expected to have to know such things, but living among women one cannot help learning something. My breasts are tender and I have missed my courses and I am sick in the mornings. I think I am with child."

"By the Romans . . ." breathed Lhiannon.

"By one of them," Coventa corrected, "even among the Romans I believe there is only one father for each child."

"I know of herbs you can take to cast the abomination from you," said Lhiannon. "I will ask the marsh folk to show me where they grow."

"No. What I carry is not yet a child, but I cannot deny him life. I believe that in the future he will have some part to play."

Lhiannon stared at her, uncomprehending. *I would tear out my womb rather than bear a Roman's child! Coventa will not be the only one burdened this way,* she thought then. *Perhaps the other women will be more sensible, and if they cannot kill the babes before they are born, they will destroy them after.* But she did not say so aloud.

Coventa looked better than she had for many days, and Lhiannon was unwilling to jeopardize any belief that led to happiness.

*C*learly our next objective should be Verlamion," said Vordilic. "Or rather, Verulam*ium*," he said, adding the Latin ending with a vicious snarl. Grizzled as a badger, he was a man of the Catuvellauni, some kind of relation to Caratac. "The royal enclosure on the banks of the Ver was the sacred center for my tribe. The town that squats there now is a Roman blasphemy."

From the circle of chieftains and kings who had gathered around Boudica's fire came a mutter of agreement. The stretched cloths that kept off the evening dew were costly fabrics that had once curtained Roman doorways. The discussion had been lubricated by an amphora of Roman wine.

"But they are Britons," someone objected.

"They are traitors," Vordilic spat. "They were once Catuvellauni, but they have abandoned their name and race to wear the toga and boast of being Roman citizens."

"That makes them worse than honest enemies," another man replied. "They show us what will become of us if we do not win. We must make them an example for all Britannia."

"That great road the Romans carved across our holy earth at least makes it easy to travel. If we set off tomorrow, we could be in Verlamion in two days!" Vordilic had joined them when they reached Londinium. His skin hung loose on his bones and the good cloth of his tunic was worn threadbare. Everything about him spoke of a vanished prosperity.

Boudica drew back. Vordilic's tattered clothing was only a visible representation of the hatred that was eating away at his soul. Being near him was like standing by some noxious bog. The problem with calling on all the tribes was that the people most motivated to fight the Romans were the most damaged, in body or in mind, and the least willing to conduct an intelligent campaign.

"We could be," she said mildly, "but should we take the time to attack? Unlike an army, a town cannot run away. The legions are on the move, and we should be getting ready to meet them."

"We obliterated the Ninth with half the men we have now," boasted Drostac. "Why should the men of the Twentieth and the Fourth give us more trouble?"

"The Second Legion will not reinforce them," said someone else to general laughter. "The word we hear from the Durotriges is that their camp prefect thinks the situation 'too uncertain for secure operations.' They're staying in Isca."

"Whereas we gain more warriors every day!" said King Corio. "We don't need a fancy strategy—we can crush them by sheer numbers!"

Numbers they certainly had. Campfires dotted the rolling country north of what had been Londinium like poppies in a wheatfield. They had captured enough wine and meat for everyone to make merry. The night wind was musical with laughter and song.

Boudica traded glances with Tingetorix. He was the best commander they had, and he had done his best to make her understand how men made war.

"Numbers are not enough. We defeated the foot soldiers of the Ninth Legion because we made the land fight for us," the old warrior said reprovingly. "If we can catch Governor Paulinus on the march, we have a good chance of whittling away his strength. But we dare not let him force us into a pitched battle."

"And that means we must march northward, and quickly," said Boudica, "even if some of the wagons, especially the ones with the women and children, are left behind." Perhaps she could persuade her daughters, as representatives of the royal house, to stay with them.

"We'll move out in the morning," she continued. "Tingetorix, I want you to take your best horsemen and scout ahead. Morigenos, will you work with the men who have just joined us? Show them where they should march, make sure they have weapons. Drostac, you are in charge of the supply wagons. We must take some care with the food—we do not know how long it will have to last."

Cities had warehouses. Gathering supplies for the horde had been another reason to attack Londinium.

"There is food in Verlamion," muttered Vordilic.

"And it will still be there when we have the time to deal with the town as it deserves." Boudica frowned, and the Catuvellaunian looked away.

In the golden days of the heroes it had all been much simpler, she reflected as the chieftains finished their wine and made ready to go. When they celebrated ancient battles, did the bards simply skip over the challenges of strategy and supply? Her young men had grown up denied the experience that would have taught them the realities of war, and the old men seemed to have selective memories. The responsibilities she shouldered now had little to do with the glory of which the poets sang, but though they might be far greater in scale, they were not so different from the planning any woman who ran a large household must do every day.

But fighting Romans was not like killing rats in a store shed. These were wolves. As if he had sensed her thought, Bogle lifted his great head with a soft growl.

TWENTY-SEVEN

*T*he ravens were dancing, black wings scattering shadows across the Roman road. Boudica watched them lift and dive, rolling over and under in an ecstasy of flight, her own body flexing easily as the war cart swayed.

From somewhere down the line she heard singing—

> *"The Great Queen sows the land with flame*
> *The black smoke rises high*
> *Where dying warriors call her name*
> *And ravens soar the sky."*

"And is it a celebration or a war dance they are performing up there?" she wondered aloud.

"A dance of anticipation, perhaps. We fed the ravens well at Londinium," said Tascio, following her gaze. "They will be hoping for another battle soon."

Londinium was not a battle, it was a massacre, thought Boudica, but she doubted Tascio would understand her lack of enthusiasm for slaughter. Yet even the Morrigan did not love blood for its own sake, only for what it could buy.

"Perhaps they are entertaining themselves while they wait for us to catch up with them," she said aloud.

"They would have to wait longer if we were traveling over hill and dale," said Tascio. "The Romans build good roads . . ."

Boudica nodded. The Great Road cut straight as a sword slash through the country north of Londinium, where a Celtic trail would have followed the contours of the land.

"The Great Queen tramples down the grain,
    She treads upon the vine,
    Her meal is ground with heroes' pain,
    Their blood she turns to wine."

Behind her they were still singing. In two days the horde had come farther than she would have believed possible. But a Roman legion could march more swiftly still. As the riders and chariots moved north with the vast, untidy mob of men and wagons streaming out behind them, Boudica seemed to hear like an echo the steady tramp of hobnailed sandals on stone.

The Romans were coming. The last scout to arrive said that Paulinus had rejoined his army. Would he keep them at the fort at Letocetum or would they continue southward? The Roman road was a channel through which Britons and Romans were being forced toward an unavoidable confrontation. Boudica thought of the turbulence at the seashore when the waters rushing down from a mountain stream collided with the incoming tide—two unquenchable currents, each obeying the law of its own nature. Where they met they created a chaos in which neither could win.

The road is a trap . . . she thought, eyeing the ribbon of stone that drew her toward the horizon. *Before we meet the Romans we will have to get off it into country where we have some cover.* But in the meantime, horses and wagons were rolling forward at a steady walking pace.

Already the sun was dipping toward the western hills. In the distance she glimpsed the gleam of water through a line of trees. That might make a good place to camp. Tonight she would gather the chieftains and make them agree on a route that would take them around Verulamium.

The ponies tossed their heads, snorting, and Tascio reined in as they heard a clatter of hoofbeats from the other side of those trees. In another moment a horseman clattered into view, coming fast.

"Verulamium!" he cried. "It's just beyond the river, and undefended!"

Men cheered as the news was passed down the line. In moments, horsemen were galloping forward. Boudica glimpsed Tingetorix, but the tumult was already too loud for her to make out his words. She closed her lips on the order she had been about to give. The old warrior had told her himself that a command that could not, or would not, be obeyed was worse than useless. The road had already trapped her. Men and horses were following the ravens toward the town, eyes alight at the prospect of more slaughter. Whether she wished it or not, they were going to attack Verulamium.

*S*unset light slanted through the trees, intensifying the ruddy color that stained the stones around the pool. The day had been a warm one, but there was always a cool breath of air beside the Blood Spring. Lhiannon dipped up another mouthful of the iron-rich water and sat back with a sigh.

"I feel stronger already," said Coventa, gazing into the pool as the dark waters stilled.

Iron to nourish a Roman child . . . thought Lhiannon, the liquid turning bitter on her tongue, and tried to will the thought away. She would not allow the Romans to steal the Tor from her as well. To show Coventa her favorite places on the isle had given her joy. As the younger woman pointed out, when you traveled with Helve you did not have much time to listen to the land.

This afternoon they had bathed in the Blood Spring, and Lhiannon observed with mingled pain and wonder the new glow that pregnancy imparted to her friend. Since she had learned she was with child Coventa had not wept in the night. Was it possible that such a horror could leave a blessing behind it? Lhiannon did not want to believe it, but she was not so cruel as to question any happiness Coventa might find.

She shut her eyes, striving to lose herself in the musical murmur the water made as it passed through the channel from the spring and trickled into the pool.

"Blood . . ." whispered Coventa.

For a moment, Lhiannon thought she was commenting on the spring. She opened her eyes, alarm bringing her upright as she saw the other woman crouched and rigid, staring into the water. Mearan had told them that the waters of the Blood Spring could be used for scrying—she should have warned Coventa not to look into the pool.

"Coventa." She steadied her own voice to a soothing murmur. "What do you see?"

"A river in a valley . . . blood in the water . . . red sunset, red flames, red everywhere . . ." Coventa's tone was detached, and Lhiannon thanked the Goddess for giving her this knowledge as an oracle's vision instead of a dream.

"Where is it?" Lhiannon asked. Clearly virginity was not required for vision, although there might be side effects she could not foresee. But the damage was done now, and they might as well take advantage of it.

"The land is gentle. I see scattered roundhouses and others that are straight-sided with strange red roofs like scales. There are buildings beside a road. As the men attack, one collapses and scatters pieces of ice across the road—no they are pieces of glass."

Roman buildings, thought Lhiannon, beginning to suspect what, if not exactly where, this must be.

"There is a strange square enclosure with some long houses in it. They are built of wood and they burn well."

"Who is doing the burning?" asked Lhiannon.

"Our people . . ." came the answer. "They drag men out of the buildings and strike them down."

Lhiannon had been taught that a Druid should respond to both joy and sorrow with equal detachment, but she could not repress a spurt of vicious satisfaction.

"Men . . . and women, too . . ." Coventa faltered. "Women with fair hair. They are our people, too—" She shook her head. "I don't want to see this anymore . . ."

"It's all right, Coventa—let it go, let it fade away," Lhiannon said quickly. She recalled now that the people of Verlamion had adopted Roman ways, and understood only too clearly what must be happening there. "Do you see the road that goes through the town? Follow it, my dear. Leave the fighting behind."

"The road is before me . . ." Coventa gave a grateful sigh. "Night is falling and the land is at peace. What would you have me see?"

"Follow the road northward and tell me if anyone else

is on it. Fare northward, seeress, and look for Roman soldiers," Lhiannon said grimly.

For several moments Coventa said nothing, her fair hair falling forward as she bent over the pool. Lhiannon watched her closely, waiting for the moment when she stiffened and began to tremble.

"They can't see you, they can't touch you," she murmured. "Rise into the heavens and look down and tell me what you see—"

"The road runs across a plain. To the west the ground rises. There is a small fort, but the Romans are not in it. I see many campfires and those leather tents they use. They are camped on a rise at the entrance to a fold in the hills, with woods behind them. Between them and the road there is a river, edged with reeds."

"Go higher, Coventa," murmured Lhiannon, but she was thinking hard. If the Romans were not marching, Paulinus must have chosen a battlefield. "You've seen enough, my dear—speed back to us now, eastward across the land until you come to the Tor. All that you've seen you leave behind you . . . you will not remember, you will not care . . . come back now, your body is waiting—" She reached out as Coventa collapsed into her arms.

"Will she be all right?" asked Nan, her wrinkled brow furrowed, as Lhiannon laid the younger priestess down.

"In a little while she will wake, and very likely remember nothing at all." With a gentle hand Lhiannon smoothed back the curling hair.

"Do you think that what she saw was true?" the other priestess asked.

"I am afraid so," answered Lhiannon. "I think that Queen Boudica is attacking Verlamion now."

"But the Romans are waiting for her," said Nessa.

Lhiannon sighed. "Yes," she said grimly. "And she does not know."

"But there is no way we can tell her . . ." Nan looked at her in sudden alarm. "Is there?"

"I must try to warn her," said Lhiannon, decision crystallizing as she spoke. "They will give me a horse and food in Camadunon, and I can ride quickly at need."

"But it will be dangerous!"

"No Briton would harm me, and all the Romans are hiding in their forts or waiting for Boudica. You and Coventa will be safe here on Avalon. Hush now, she is waking," she said as the other woman began to stir. "Boudica needs me, but I promise I will come back to you!"

*B*oudica rode into Verulamium in her chariot like a Roman general at his Triumph, but her heart held no joy. These had been Britons, however traitorous, and they were not the only ones who had succumbed to the temptation to ape the conqueror's ways. How would she win back her people if all she could offer was revenge? She had at least been able to stop her warriors from attacking the nearby farmsteads, but the palisade that surrounded the civic buildings was burning merrily.

Vordilic stood before its gate, to which a man had been bound in mockery of a Roman crucifixion. A pile of white cloth that might have been a toga lay on the ground. His well-fed flesh was bruised and scored, but he was still alive. Blood matted his gray hair and ran from his mouth where they had severed his tongue.

Vordilic looked around as Boudica neared. It was not only the hatred in their eyes that stamped the crucified man and his tormentor as kin.

"Behold Claudius Nectovelius filius Bracius—" There was venom in each syllable. "Magistrate of Verulamium. I have taken the tongue with which he denied his people and his gods. Next, perhaps, it will be his eyes—his testicles have been no use to him for many a day."

"Was he of your family?" she asked softly. A sob came from the gatepost where a woman and two children had been tied.

"My ancestors deny him!" spat Vordilic. "Let him go to Hades with his Roman friends!"

Then it shall be so! The words vibrated without and within. Vordilic blanched as the goddess seized Boudica's body. In a single sure move She grasped a javelin and thrust it through flesh, heart, and the wood on which they had crucified the man.

The gathering crowd hooted and cheered as the pudgy

body jerked and twitched and then with a last convulsion went still, but that part of Boudica that watched from within understood that this had been mercy.

"Give the carrion to the birds and purify this place by fire," the voice, at once more harsh and more resonant than her own, penetrated the babble of the crowd.

"Have we done well, Lady?" a dozen voices asked.

"You have done what you must," came the reply. "You are My fire, you are My sword, you are My fury . . . But understand this," She said, Her gaze sweeping the upturned faces that then grew still. "The fire that burns your enemy burns you as well, and the blood and fire will not cease until they have run their course throughout Britannia."

The Morrigan gestured toward the slack body on the gate. From the gash in Nectovelius's chest a trail of red blood twined across the pale flesh to drip to the dirt below. "Your blood or theirs—it all feeds the ground."

"Then let all of it flow!" snarled Vordilic, frustrated bloodlust hurling him toward the woman by the gate. A shout rose from a hundred throats and clubs and swords blurred through the air. In moments Nectovelius's family had gone to join him.

Is this, too, Your mercy? gibbered Boudica within.

"Would you not have welcomed it, after you lost your king?" came the reply. The resulting surge of anguish plunged Boudica back into her body with a shaken sob.

She took a deep breath, staring around her. A fire-haired goddess red with blood was turning away from the battered bodies at the gate. A jolt of recognition sent fire through Boudica's veins. *This is how they see Me, before they die . . .* said the goddess within. Boudica closed her eyes, dizzied at the doubling of vision.

When she opened them she was fully herself once more. With a mother's appalled certainty she recognized the figure before her as Rigana.

"What are you doing? Get away—" She bit back the words, observing the lingering battle fury in her daughter's eyes, and knew herself for a hypocrite for wishing to deny her daughter the same release she craved. "Rigana . . ." Her voice sounded strange in her own ears. "Rigana, it's over . . . come back to me, my child . . ."

The thought was her own, but it was the goddess who put power in the words. She continued to murmur as the fire died in Rigana's eyes, until she was only a girl again, her eyes widening in disquiet as she realized who and where she was. But this final sacrifice seemed to have satiated the bloodlust of the mob as well, which was now focusing more on loot than on vengeance.

That night the Ver ran red below the town.

"Rigana, I must talk to you." Boudica took her daughter by the arm and made her sit down with Argantilla beside their fire. The Britons had settled in a loose cluster of tents and wagons just beyond the embers of Verulamium. Now they were gorging themselves on the looted food and getting drunk on captured wine. "We will be fighting the Romans soon."

"And what have we been doing for the past moon?" Rigana jerked free and looked around her with a laugh.

"Slaughter," Boudica said grimly. "We have destroyed three towns, none of which were defended by soldiers. The legions will be another matter. When we fight them, I don't want you in the battle. You and Argantilla will stay with the wagons."

"*You* want?" Rigana's eyes flashed. "And what gives you the right to deny us the choice that's free to everyone else here?"

"You are children—" Boudica began.

"The Romans didn't think so . . ." muttered Argantilla.

"We are *women*! Remember, the umbilical cord was cut at the sacred spring!" Rigana exclaimed. "If we are old enough to risk death in childbed, we are old enough to risk it in battle!"

"What do you mean?" Boudica scanned them in alarm. "Did those vermin leave you with child?"

Rigana fixed her mother with a bright, bitter gaze. "No, Mother. Our moon blood still flows, and mine will continue to do so, for I see no reason to ever want a man. But if you do not know that for the past two weeks your little Tilla has been sharing her blankets with Caw, you are blind indeed!"

The flush staining Argantilla's fair skin as she glared at her sister told Boudica all she needed to know.

"You take life," the girl protested, turning to her mother again. "I'd rather give it. I have loved Caw since we were children, and when I was weeping because the Roman pigs had defiled me he comforted me. When his arms are around me, I am perfect and whole."

Boudica gazed at her helplessly, shaken by a surge of longing as she remembered how she had been completed in Prasutagos's arms. If Argantilla had found such a love, should she forbid it? *Could* she?

"You are royal women of the Iceni," she said weakly. "We do not marry at our own whim . . ."

But Rigana was laughing. "Are those only the Iceni I hear out there? When we have fought the Romans you will be the mistress of Britannia or of nothing. If we win, the chieftains will not cross your will. If we lose, what you want will not matter at all."

"I am your daughter." Argantilla straightened and wiped away her tears. "If you can lead an army, I can at least choose my own man. And I swear to you that I will have no other, so if you wish the line of Prasutagos to continue, you will accept my will!"

"After we have fought the Romans we'll speak of this again," said Boudica repressively. But her daughters were smiling.

TWENTY-EIGHT

To look at the fields, one would have thought the land at peace. The swelling heads of wheat and barley hung heavy on the stalk as they waited for harvest. In the fields with a southern exposure the reapers were already at work, scythe blades flickering in the summer sun. Just so the swords would flash when the time came for the Morrigan to begin her harvest, Lhiannon thought grimly as she passed. Now and again a worker would look up, then bend to his task with steady patience, as his fathers had served these fields before ever the Druids came into the land.

And as they will when we are only a memory, she reflected, urging her horse forward.

Rumor held that the soldiers of the Second Legion were still hiding behind their walls at Isca. The road they should have taken to reinforce the governor carried Lhiannon north more swiftly than she could have imagined, though her heart sped faster still. As she moved into the midlands of Britannia, the farmsteads where she stopped were full of rumors of the destruction of Verulamium.

Farther north, though, the talk grew more guarded. Lhiannon had been traveling for just over a week when the farmer whose fields she blessed in exchange for a bed and a meal told her that she was nearing the point where the Isca road crossed the road from Londinium. A day or two's journey farther north lay the new Roman fort at Letocetum, though the legionaries had marched out of it a week or so before.

But they had not passed the crossroads. They were waiting, thought Lhiannon, on that hillside where Coventa had seen them. Did Boudica know?

"The Great Queen is coming up the other road to the east of here with all the warriors in Britannia in her train," the farmer said with mingled pride and fear. "If you wish to join her, my son Kitto will go with you. He has been begging my leave to join the army, and I take your coming as a sign that he is meant to go . . ."

The Great Queen . . . With an effort, Lhiannon kept her face serene. That title could have more than one meaning. Not for the first time, she wondered who was really leading that army, and to what end.

> "The Great Queen gathers all the brave
> To muster in their might,
> To strike with spear and sword and stave
> And put the foe to flight!"

The people in one of the nearer wagons were singing. That song had been a frequent accompaniment to the rebellion, but this evening it came constantly, now from one direction and now from another as a new group took up the refrain. Boudica had heard birds do that in a wood, the song shifting and swelling from one tree to another as a migrating flock settled there.

Since the destruction of Verulamium a little more than a week had passed. The Britons had come to the plain beside the little river as the sun was going down, catching the glitter of Roman armor on the hill above it, where the governor had taken up position to wait for them. Boudica had hoped to catch them on the march. Attacking them uphill would be difficult, but if the Romans wanted to stay safe they would have taken refuge in their fortress. This evening the Celts feasted on the oxen the Druids had sacrificed to the gods who govern war. When they faced the legions tomorrow the Romans would have to come down the hill, and one way or another, the song would have an end.

> "She is the Raven and she is the Dove,
> The ecstasy of battle and of love . . ."

The chorus followed. Brangenos had begun it, but not all the verses men were singing now were his own. *The song has escaped him,* thought Boudica, *as the army escapes me. I am not their leader, but their icon ... their talisman.* That much had been clear to her for some time. A Roman general might be able to command from the rear, but as they journeyed north, Boudica had been thinking. Her only hope of directing what her warriors did tomorrow was to be the point of their spear.

And if she must be in the forefront of the battle, what were the chances that when it was over she would still be alive? The question came with a cold clarity that surprised her, but no fear. Her life would be a small price to pay for victory. Given their numbers, she found it hard to doubt the confidence of her men. And if they were defeated? The world the Romans would make then was one in which she would not want to survive. But it would be hard to part from those she loved.

Boudica considered them as they passed the wineskin, their faces warmed by the light of the fire. Some belonged to her life with Prasutagos. She had grown close to others on this journey. Argantilla sat with Caw, her bright head close to his dark one as they whispered. Rigana was at Tingetorix's feet, listening to the war stories of which he had an endless store. Brangenos was speaking calmly to Rianor.

The old storm crow had seen so many battles. This one would just be another verse for his song. But even as the thought came to her she suppressed it as unworthy. During the past weeks the older Druid had been a welcome source of counsel. As if he had felt her thought, Brangenos looked up. Before that calm gaze, her own slid away to rest on Eoc and Bituitos, who would stand by her to the end, whatever that might be.

She missed Prasutagos and Lhiannon most of those she had loved. But if her husband had still been alive none of them would be here. She tried not to think about him. The king walked now on the Isles of the Blessed. Would he even recognize the person she was becoming now?

Lhiannon, she devoutly hoped, was still on the Isle of Eriu. Once, Boudica's anguish had drawn her friend all the way from Avalon. But too much time had passed, and their bond had surely weakened. She tried to be glad the priestess lived now in a peace and safety that Boudica would never know again, and even as she did so felt her heart twist with longing to see her friend's luminous eyes smiling at her across the fire.

They all looked up as a young man appeared at the edge of the firelight and bent to whisper in Tingetorix's ear. It was Drostac's son, who had been on patrol. Boudica got to her feet.

"What is the news?"

"The Romans appear to have no more than ten thousand men, to judge by the number of their fires."

"It's kind of them to make it so easy for us to count them," Bituitos laughed.

"They don't have to send scouts to guess *our* numbers," observed Eoc. "They can see us from that hill!"

Boudica smiled. On their march yet more men had come in. She herself had no real idea how many Britons had camped on the plain, but surely they outnumbered the Romans at least ten to one.

"See us, and tremble," Bituitos replied.

"We've no need to draw sword against them," said Drostac with a grin. "We can stampede across them and trample them into the dust."

Boudica exchanged glances with Tingetorix. Numbers could be a handicap if they were not well used, but she was not about to tell any of these people to go home.

"Get some rest, lad," she said to the scout. "Whether you use your sword or your feet, tomorrow you will need your strength."

"We should all sleep," said Argantilla seriously, "including you, Mother." Drostac had taken his son's arm. Others began to rise.

"I know." Boudica gave her younger daughter a hug. "But my legs are too restless to lie still. I will walk for a little, and then I promise that I will lie down."

Argantilla looked dubious, but Caw had taken her hand. *She will be loved*, thought Boudica, picking up her dark cloak, *whatever happens to me*. From nearby she heard more singing and smiled.

> *"The horn blares and the carynx sounds*
> *When the Great Queen rides,*

White with red ears, her seven hounds
Run baying at her side."

As if the song had summoned him, Bogle rose from his place by the fire and thrust his great head beneath her hand. The other dogs were leashed for the night, but they had learned the futility of trying to keep Bogle from following.

"You see, I will not be alone."

Boudica moved among the wagons, stopping now and again to exchange a word with one of the men she had come to know on their journey. From the fires she heard song and laughter, or the rhythmic scrape and screech where someone was putting a better edge on his sword. From the shadows beneath some of the wagons came the soft sounds of people making love. Some of the women were wives, but men would lie with anyone willing when on campaign. It was natural enough—when people faced death there was a powerful urge to affirm life.

Even the Morrigan, on the day before a battle, made love to Dagodevos, thought Boudica, suppressing an unwelcome tremor of arousal. But She had no mate here to balance Her destructive powers with love. From somewhere close by a woman cried out at the moment of fulfillment. The queen stopped, touching her own breast. But that was no solution— she had tried, in the long nights when she slept alone. It was not only her husband's body that she missed beside her, but his spirit, enfolding her own.

Lovers raise the power and offer it to each other, she told herself grimly. *I can only offer my need to the gods.* She forced herself to move on.

In the center of the camp the people had built a votive shrine, surrounded by torches and poles on which hung the heads and hides of the animals that had been offered to the gods while the meat was boiled in a thousand cauldrons and roasted on a thousand fires. The scent of blood lay heavy on the air.

The altar itself was a construction of poles and logs covered with rich fabrics looted from Londinium. Among their folds the people had placed silver plates and kraters and dishes of Samian ware, carved wooden stools, amphorae of wine and statuary and clothing with embroidery. At the top were the heads of two Roman scouts who had been caught by the Celtic vanguard, and above them, a hurdle of poles from which three crows dangled, blood from their death wounds red on their black breasts.

"You, I recognize," Boudica said softly. "You are the three of ill-boding, always slaughtered and always receiving the sacrifice . . ."

"Some die that others may live . . ." said the goddess within, *"and their blood feeds the ground."*

"I know . . ." the queen replied. It was not a man she needed, but answers, and whether they came from the goddess or her own heart, to hear them she must be alone.

She turned away from the wagons and made her way across the field toward the reedy banks of the stream.

*W*ater gleamed where the brook flowed across the pale ribbon of the road. Lhiannon's pony pulled at the rein and she loosened it to let him drink.

"Lady, it grows late," said the farmer's boy. "Should we not make camp for the night? There's water here, and we could shelter by those trees."

Lhiannon straightened her legs, trying to ease the ache of muscles cramped by a ride that had begun early that morning. His suggestion was tempting, but the urgency that drove her was, if anything, greater than it had been the day before.

"How far is the Roman fort from here?" she asked.

"It might be five miles to Manduessedum, but we won't want to camp near there."

"No, Kitto, where I *want* to camp is with the queen's army. The signs of their passage are so recent, they cannot be far." Even by night the traces where so many men and animals had passed were clear.

In the stillness when the pony lifted his head it seemed to her that she could hear a faint murmur, like the distant sea.

"We will continue until midnight, but I think that before then we will find them." She shortened her reins, set heels to the pony's sides, and they went on.

"Yes, Lady," said the boy, clearly assuming her certainty came from Druid magic. Lhiannon did not tell him that what drove her was fear that the battle would be fought before they got there, and she would never see Boudica again.

But at last the gods seemed to be smiling. Before they had gone a mile she realized that ahead the stars were dimmed by an orange glow, and presently, on the hill to the left of the road, she saw the regular lines of Roman fires.

"The Great Queen's folk lie ahead of us on the plain." She pointed up the road. "We can afford to push the horses now, for they will have rest soon."

Shortly thereafter a man rose up like a spirit from the side of the road and barred their way with a spear.

"It is Carvilios, is it not?" Lhiannon peered through the gloom. "Where will I find the queen?"

"In the center of the camp, Lady, to the right of the road." He grinned. "She will be glad of your coming."

But it was Crispus and the rest of the household who made her welcome.

"She went off a little while ago to walk through the camp," said Temella. "She often does so before she sleeps, but I thought she would be back by now."

"Perhaps I should look for her," said the priestess. "My legs are cramping from too many hours in the saddle, and I need to walk the kinks out of them."

"We would be grateful." Crispus looked relieved. "She said she was too tight-wound to sleep. Well, so are we all, but not all of us will be fighting a battle tomorrow. She must rest, my lady. She will listen when *you* tell her to come in."

$\mathcal{I}$t was very quiet here in the no-man's-land between friend and foe. The ducks that paddled in the water by day were asleep in the reeds, but an owl slid past on silent wing. Above the murmur of the current Boudica could hear a familiar splash and slap. She glanced at the dog, but Bogle's tail was wagging. She followed the path along the banks toward the ford, and halted as she saw a figure kneeling at the water's edge.

What she had heard was the sound of someone beating laundry. But why in the middle of the night before a battle would someone—her thought stopped as the woman turned. Pale in the starlight, the face before her was her own.

"What are you doing?" Did the question come from without or within?

"I cleanse the clothing of the slain . . . Ravens gnaw the necks of men, blood spurts in the furious fray, flesh is hewn in battle fury, and blades bite bodies in red war. Heroes in their battle-heat harry the foe with hacking blows. War is waged, each trampling each . . ." On the smooth cheeks gleamed the silver track of tears. "Do not fight tomorrow. It will be your doom."

"I have no choice but to pay that price," Boudica replied. "To do otherwise would be to betray my people—" She gestured toward the scattered fires. "You wear my face, but I know You, Strife-Stirrer, Gore-Crow, Raven of Battle. You delight in conflict. Why do You pretend to weep? You led these people here."

The woman shook her head. "They would say they followed Boudica."

"But You are the one with the power!"

"My heart is your heart. My rage is your rage. You are the goddess—"

Boudica realized that as the woman spoke she was saying the words as well. She shook her head in desperation. Was this a delusion, or had she been deluding herself all along?

"And are my hands *Your* hands?" she cried.

The woman got to her feet and Boudica saw herself reflected in the Other's eyes.

"Only when you allow Me to use them," came the soft reply. "You shape the gods as We shape you. But the forms in which you see Us have been honed through many lives of men. Through Us you pass from mortality to eternity. Through Us, the Divine becomes manifest in you."

Boudica realized that she was trembling, and did not know whether what she felt was terror or ecstasy.

"Then will You use my hands tomorrow?" Boudica retreated to a fear she did understand. "Will You lead us to victory?"

"It will end as it must for the greater good," came the reply. "To give everything in the cause of life is one path to growth, but conflict is another. In war, you are tested to destruction. Winners and losers alike can fail, giving way to greed or fear. And winners and losers alike can transcend mortality. But only those who fall fighting bravely tap the last reserves of valor. Only those who give everything win the glory that lives in song and feeds generations to come. That is a prize that the winners cannot claim."

"And to gain that victory, will many die?" Boudica asked then.

"Death is only a doorway, but how you go through that door will change what you see on the other side . . ."

Lhiannon stopped, skin prickling at the presence of power, as she saw the figure standing by the stream. The great dog sat at her side.

When Crispus asked her to look for the queen Lhiannon had wondered if power had made Boudica willful. But if so, she thought now, the power, and the will, were not the queen's. The figure before her stood tall beyond the height of mortals, with a light around her that did not come from the stars. Leached of color by the night, her hair flowed down in waves of shadow. From beneath the closed eyelids came a steady stream of tears.

The priestess took a deep breath, forcing her voice to calm. "Great Queen—the night is passing, and the body You wear must rest."

The goddess turned, opening eyes that held a sorrow older than the world.

"You have so little time, and so much to learn . . ."

Lhiannon fought the temptation to use this opportunity to ask a few questions of her own.

"No time," she agreed, "if the woman is to sleep at all. In the name of Dagdevos, Lady, let her go."

After a thoughtful moment, the still features were transformed by a smile. "In the name of He who loves the one Boudica loved, I will . . ."

Once more the eyes closed, but now the face was chang-

ing as the energy ebbed away. Lhiannon reached as Boudica's limbs gave way, and staggering a little, for since she
had seen her last the queen had gained mass and muscle,
lowered her to the grass.

"Lhiannon . . ." Boudica struggled to sit up. "I dreamed
you had come." She looked around her in confusion as Bogle
whined and nosed at her hand. "Or is this the dream?"

"This," said the priestess with a tartness born of relief,
"is the eve of battle, and we all belong in our beds."

"There was a woman washing bloody clothes."

"I know Who you met here," Lhiannon said grimly and
sighed. "Do you think you can walk now, or do I summon
men to carry you?"

"In the morning we will fight," Boudica continued as if
she had not heard. "Watch over my daughters, Lhiannon.
Keep them safe for me!"

"Yes, Boudica—" *If I can . . .*

Boudica caught her breath and focused fully on the
priestess for the first time. "Oh, Lhiannon, thank the gods
you are here! I have needed you so badly, for so long!"
She turned, weeping, and Lhiannon gathered her into her
arms.

TWENTY-NINE

The gods had given them a beautiful morning. The sun filled a transparent sky with light, and the poppies glowed like spots of blood upon the bright gold of the ripening fields. On the plain between the stream and the slope the Britons were assembled by tribe and clan. In that clear light, their striped and checkered garments and their painted shields were a riot of fierce hues. Some had stripped to the waist, the swirls and spirals of war paint showing bright against fair skin. Others wore mail shirts whose links shimmered in the sun. Sunlight glanced from shield boss and gleamed on bright blade. The same light glared from the armor of the Romans who waited on the hill.

Holding the high ground gave the enemy an advantage, but they were facing into the sun, thought Boudica as she jumped into the chariot behind Tascio. She worked her shoulders back and forth to distribute the weight of her mail. The shirt had been made for a large man and except across the bosom hung loosely. The added weight seemed to give her more stability in the chariot, though after the miles she had journeyed standing in the thing, balance was no longer a problem. As Tascio reined the ponies toward the line the ruddy plaid of her own cloak streamed out behind her. She could feel the raven wings attached to her cone-shaped helmet flutter in the wind. A second chariot, bearing Rigana and Argantilla, followed. When the fighting began, Calgac would drive them back to the wagons drawn up in a semicircle at the other end of the field. Argantilla, at least, could be trusted to stay there.

As the chariot bore her along the line the men began to cheer. "Boud! Victory! Boud-ee-cah!" Ravens flew up from a cluster of trees, cawing exultantly.

Lady, I hear You . . . Boudica's heart answered. *Do You hear me? You brought us here—help us now! Help* me*!*

She flinched as the first wave of sound vibrated through flesh and bone. She could see faces now. She lifted her sword in salute to Brocagnos and his boys. Segovax and his older son Beric and their men made a group near the clan of Morigenos. Farther down the line Drostac of Ash Hill and his household shook their spears.

"Boud-i-ca!" came the shout, and with it a surge of energy that was like the power when Cathubodva came in. Other faces emerged from the blur before her—Mandos, who had returned from his exile in the Brigante lands when he heard about the rebellion, bearing the sword he had refused to yield; Tabanus, who had been a slave in Colonia; Vordilic and his grim band of Catuvellauni; Corio of the Dobunni with the men of his tribe. She saw Iceni and Trinovantes, Durotriges and Dobunni, and smaller groups from a dozen other tribes. There were even a few Silures who had fought with Caratac, who saluted as they recognized the torque she wore. At the far end of the line Tingetorix led a mixed group of mounted warriors. They were all cheering, waves of sound rolling through the bright air.

"Boud-i-ca! Victory!"

If this was not the whole might of Britannia, there were men from more tribes than even Caratac had ever gathered assembled here. Last night Boudica had wept because so many would be slain, but today, with all the host before her, it seemed to her that they could lose half their men and still have the numbers to crush the enemy who huddled up there on the hill.

Tascio halted the chariot on a little rise.

As the multitude grew still, Boudica fought to contain the energy that sparked through every vein. At her neck Caratac's torque was warm to the touch, as if it were absorbing power. She had wondered where she would find the strength to reach these warriors, but the power was theirs—their spirit, their fierce joy at finally coming to grips with their foe—all she had to do was to find the words. She did not know if this was the Morrigan's answer, but it would serve.

"Men—no, *warriors* of Britannia!" she corrected, meeting Rigana's glare. "The Romans despise you because you follow a woman, but I am not the first queen to have led Britons to victory. Ask the men of Colonia and Londinium if a woman knows how to avenge her injuries!" She paused to let the cries of invective rise and fall.

"At long last, we face our foe with sword in hand. You whose sons have been carried off to die in other lands, defend your own earth now. You who have been driven from your homes, reclaim them! You whose wives and daughters have been outraged, as I and mine were defiled"—she pointed to the other chariot and a new roar shook the skies—"restore our honor!"

With each word, the power the warriors had given her flowed back to them, inchoate rage transmuted into purpose and focused on the enemy. When she drew breath, she could hear a tinny gabble from the slope and knew the Roman general must be addressing his troops as well.

"Look at them, cowering on their hill!" She swept her sword toward the enemy. "We destroyed one legion with only a tithe of the force we have now. Lift your voices and Taranis the thunderer will crush them with sound!" A new cry shook the heavens as she stabbed at the air. "They cannot even stand against our shouting, much less resist our swords and spears!" As she drew breath the curses changed to grim laughter.

From the trees the ravens echoed them. Boudica felt the hairs lifting along her arms and sensed that the Morrigan was near.

"See what a fair day the gods have given us!" she cried. She could hear her own voice becoming more resonant and knew that the glamour of the goddess was being added to the power raised by men. "Roman blood will be a worthy offering! See how the glory of the Otherworld shines through the surface of things—I see that same glory blazing in your eyes. Go forth to battle and may the gods go with you, as they are within you."

And in me . . . the silent thought came as her last fears faded away.

"Those who live will have honor unending; those who fall will feast with the blessed gods. In this battle I will conquer or I will fall—that is a woman's resolve! And as for you—fight as men or live as slaves!"

Her arms rose as if to embrace them all. No longer patient oxen beneath the yoke of Rome, they pawed the ground like stallions. In that moment Boudica loved her people as she had never known how to love them before.

"Be My sword, Boudica . . ." came the voice of the goddess within, *"and I will be your shield."*

"Boudica! Victory!" shouted the host. "Great Queen! Boudica!"

*T*he ground trembled as the warriors of Britannia stamped. Their battle cry shook the air. At the other end of the field, Lhiannon could feel the vibration in her bones. The fine hairs on her arms stiffened with energy. Even when Caratac addressed his troops she had never felt such power, but Caratac had only had a White Lady to ward him. Today, the Battle Raven Herself would lead Britannia. Lhiannon had watched her people fight at Durovernon, on the banks of the Tamesa, in the Ordovice hills. But for the first time since she had arrived at Manduessedum, Lhiannon began to believe that this time they might win.

She stood up in the wagon, shading her eyes with her hand, as the chariot bearing Argantilla and Rigana made its way through the gaps between the groups of warriors, splashed across the stream, and rumbled toward the semi-circle of wagons. Caw, who had been expressly ordered by the queen to stay and guard them, moved restlessly beside her, and Bogle tugged at his rope and whined. Lhiannon understood their frustration. The power Boudica had invoked thrummed in her veins; she, too, wanted a sword in her hand.

The rest of the host was beginning to move toward the foe. Now and again an individual champion would dart forward, shaking his spear and shouting invective. What must it be like for the Romans, forced to stand sweating in their armor as they waited for this horde of humanity to roll over them? It would be like trying to stand against the sea.

The chariot drew to a halt, and Argantilla jumped down

and ran into Caw's arms. Rigana remained where she was, watching with a superior smile. Then she picked up her helmet, unadorned and rising to a rounded point, and settled it over her russet braids. She was already wearing a sleeveless shirt of mail.

Well, that answered the question of whether Boudica's older daughter was going to stay with the wagons. Lhiannon tried to summon the resolve to plead with her, but it was taking all her self-discipline not to join her. Instead, she lifted her hands in blessing.

"May the strength of Sucellos shield you, may the skill of Lugos guide your arm, and may the wrath of Cathubodva carry you to victory!"

Rigana answered with a flashing grin so like her mother's that Lhiannon's heart twisted. She and Boudica had parted with few words that morning, the queen's mind already focused on the demands of the day, that of the priestess too full for words. And surely they had said everything that was needful the night before. Only now, seeing the child whom she had swaddled as a squalling infant armed and ready to face the foe, did Lhiannon understand that even if she had stayed with Boudica all those years, there would not have been time for all she might wish to say.

Rigana grabbed one of the javelins from its slot on the rim of the chariot and brandished it. Then Calgac shook the reins on the ponies' necks and they sped away.

*B*oudica braced as the chariot rocked into motion, the other five war carts that the Britons had been able to repair rattling along behind her. For this, she had no need to seek oblivion in the Morrigan's embrace. Their lust for this battle was the same. A swift glance back showed her Rigana's helm at the end of the line. She had no time for regret, or even surprise. As they neared, the blur of men in the Roman formation was swiftly resolving into a series of matched shields and helmets, each man with his pilum in his hand. But any hope she might have had that the chariot charge would panic the enemy faded as the slope grew steeper and the ponies began to slow.

The Roman general had disposed his men in three blocks. In the center she could see the hated legionaries standing in cohorts eight ranks deep, spaced a little over a man's width apart with twice that much room between the lines. More lightly armed auxiliary troops stood in blocks to either side. The cavalry must be hidden in the woods behind.

"Turn," she said to Tascio. "Bring us along the line—"

With an invocation to Cathubodva, she plucked a javelin free, drew back her arm, and threw. Her first missile fell short, but the second arced past the front line and pierced the neck of a man in the second row.

"First blood to me!" She gave them a snarling smile.

A quiver ran through the enemy ranks, but a clipped Latin order steadied them. Again and again Boudica threw. Some of the javelins were caught on shields, but several more got through. Then she ran out of missiles and Tascio reined the ponies back down the hill. The other chariots followed her, but the Romans refused to advance after them.

As she approached her own lines she drew her sword, and at the signal, Celtic arrows filled the sky in a whickering cloud. Perhaps that would sting the Romans into action. The Britons' numbers would be of little use unless they could draw the enemy away from the wooded slopes that protected their flanks.

The warriors drew aside to let the chariots back through. Near the edge of the field men were waiting to hold the horses. As Boudica took up her shield and started back toward the front, Bituitos and Eoc fell in behind her in the traditional triad formation. To have these men who had guarded her husband at her back was almost like having Prasutagos himself there.

As she reached the end of the Britons' line one of the carynx players caught sight of her and let out a triumphant blare. In the next moment they were all blowing, the wooden clappers in the mouths of the bronze dragon heads buzzing like maddened bees. Tascio ran past her to join his father and brother. She felt the battle rage of her warriors lift her as the host of Britons surged forward, screaming.

*   *   *

*W*hen Lhiannon was in the mountains with Caratac she had once heard the roar of a distant avalanche. The sound that rose from the battlefield now carried the same explosive sense of releasing tension. Light shattered on the points of myriad spears.

Boudica's wagon had been parked where the ground rose on the northern side of the field so it could serve as a healer's station for the wounded. Beyond the bright surging mass of the Britons Lhiannon could see the strongest warriors surging up the slope toward the silent line of steel. Closer and closer—in another moment the enemy must be swept away.

At forty yards movement shivered through the Roman ranks. As each man cast his pilum, a glittering blur filled the air. Five thousand flung spears scythed down the leading Britons; a moment later a second volley felled those behind. Suddenly the slope was a tangle of writhing bodies. Above the battle cries she could hear a dreadful descant of screams.

Exultation changed to horror as the Celtic charge faltered. Lhiannon forced herself to breathe. She had seen the chariots driven to the sidelines. Had Boudica had time to get back to the center of the line? Was hers one of the bodies lying there?

Roman trumpets blatted their own defiance. With a deep shout, the center of the legionary line extended and the block of troops became a wicked wedge that stabbed into the confused mass below. And yet the Britons still outnumbered their enemies by the thousands. Now that the Romans were moving, they could surround them.

Lhiannon realized she had dug her fingernails into her palm. She forced her hands to open and check the bandages she had laid ready. Brangenos and Rianor would be bringing them wounded soon.

Lady of Ravens! her heart cried. *Watch over Boudica!*

*B*oudica flinched as the Roman spears darkened the sky and a wave of shadow rippled down the slope. Linked to her warriors, the shock as the missiles struck rocked her back against Eoc's shield.

"Lady, are you hit?"

Only in spirit, she thought, pulling herself upright. They had to attack now, before the Romans could use their momentary advantage.

"Charge them!" she screamed. "Kill!" She drew her sword and ran toward the heaving mass of men. As she neared, the Celts surged forward, then recoiled. She saw men struggling to keep their feet or go down as they were pushed aside. Where were the Romans? She wanted blood on her blade.

A high keening shriek burst from her throat and men recoiled. Through the momentary gap she glimpsed Roman helms above red shields and the flicker of stabbing swords. She and her companions began to work their way into the mass as the Roman line rolled forward. Longer Celtic swords were flashing, but crammed together, the Britons had no room to put power in their blows. She saw Morigenos's face contort as a Roman sword went into his chest.

"Give way and surround them," Boudica cried, but even the Morrigan's shriek could not be heard above the din. More and more Britons flung themselves forward, tripping on the bodies of their fallen companions, and with an inevitable deliberation the Roman wedge pushed into them, a thousand gladii stabbing into a thousand unarmored Celtic bodies with each foot of gained ground.

Boudica saw an opening and stabbed, braced by Eoc and Bituitos, their swords batting away the Roman blades. She struck again, aiming below a shield; the Roman lurched and for a moment there was a gap in the line. Moving as one, the three attacked, long blades whirling. More Romans went down, then their companions moved to restore the line and Boudica fell back again, her shield groaning beneath a flurry of blows.

Shield arm aching, she stood a moment to catch her breath and glimpsed Rigana with Calgac behind her, near Drostac and Brocagnos and their men. She started to edge toward them. More Britons were coalescing into groups, hurling themselves against the legionary line, but still the Roman meat-grinder inched on.

Once more the Roman trumpets blared. A tumult behind her brought her around. The auxiliaries were forming a wedge and beginning their own advance. *Good,* thought Boudica, *maybe these will come in range of my sword!*

Beyond them she glimpsed men on horseback. The Roman cavalry had emerged from hiding and were skirmishing along the edges of the mob, lances striking those who tried to flee. With a shrill cry, Tingetorix led his riders up the hill to engage them.

"Lady," shouted Bituitos, "they'll catch us between them. We must get back."

She looked at him without understanding. The Romans were in front of her. With an exchange of glances, the two big men moved closer, easing her back down the hill.

Corio and his Dobunni were attacking the auxiliaries furiously, but presently he, too, fell. Then Boudica was caught once more in the surge of warriors throwing themselves against the Roman line.

It went on like that, in an endless struggle that moved as slowly as the sun crossed the sky. Boudica saw the ex-slave Tabanus go down, and Carvilios, and others she knew, but there was no time for mourning. Her focus had narrowed to the line of swords that were chewing their way through her men as the battle flowed down the slope and onto the plain.

The fight slowed when they reached the stream. As the field broadened, new trumpet calls formed the three wedges with which the Romans had started into a dozen, widening the battle line, savaging the Celtic horde. Soon bodies choked the channel, and the Romans began to advance once more.

The enemy still maintained its formations, but the smaller wedges could sometimes be broken. With Eoc and Bituitos behind her, Boudica had the weight to drive forward, and her thirsty blade drank deep as she traded blows. She had received several slashes, but no serious wound. She moved now in a state beyond exhaustion, in which all she knew was the need to kill.

Life ebbed from the wounded man's face as his blood welled through the bandages with which Lhiannon had tried to stanch the wound in his side. She touched his neck, felt the pulse flutter and fade, and sat back with a sigh. At her nod, Caw carried the body to lie with the others they had not been able to save.

The only good thing about caring for the wounded was that it kept her too busy to worry about what was happening on the battlefield. Lhiannon allowed herself to look up, and realized with a little shock that the fighting was now mostly on this side of the stream. Bodies lay heaped upon the slope beyond it like grain when the reapers have passed. Already the ravens were gleaning among them. It was a mighty harvest of heroes, mostly Britons, though here and there Roman armor gleamed. How many of those bodies still had life in them? Until the battle was over, they could not search and see.

On the other side of the wagons those few who might recover lay in the shade of the trees. Argantilla and some of the other young women moved among them, offering water or a little of the precious syrup of poppy to those in the greatest pain. For some, the sight of a girl's sweet face was sufficient medicine. For so many, there was nothing to be done—and the men they had tended were only the ones who had managed to crawl to the edge of the battlefield, where Brangenos and Rianor and some of the stronger women could reach them.

"The fighting is getting closer," said Caw. His tunic was smeared with other men's blood. He was, at most, sixteen, but just now a much older soul looked out of his dark eyes.

"Yes," replied Lhiannon. The battle had already covered more ground than she had expected, and had lasted longer. The fighting was almost close enough to make out individuals. She scanned the struggling mass, but could not find Boudica's raven-winged helmet or bright hair.

"We're still retreating."

"They've been pushing us back all day," she answered tartly. "But our men are still resisting." Yet of the mass of men who had surged up that hill scarcely half remained.

"The queen said that if it looked like we were losing we should get Argantilla away . . ."

While the Britons who still faced the enemy refused to

admit that they were beaten, it was hard to abandon them, though the Goddess knew she had seen enough lost battles to be able to recognize the signs by now. Lhiannon had told herself that if the fighting crossed the water she would start getting ready, or when it passed the end of the semicircle of wagons. It was clear to her now that if the fight reached the wagons at the end of the field anyone who remained on his feet would be trapped. It would be a slaughter.

It was a slaughter now.

"Get your things together," she said through stiff lips. Boudica had insisted that they all make up packs with journey supplies. "Take Argantilla up into the under-growth beyond the trees, and take the dog."

"But that's the direction of the fort," he said.

Lhiannon nodded. "If there's pursuit, they won't expect anyone to run that way."

"And what about you?"

She looked back at the battlefield. "I must wait a little longer. Until the Druids come back—" *Until I know what has happened to Boudica . . .*

*B*oudica staggered as a legionary's gladius struck her shield and stuck fast. For a moment the man stared, eyes widening as he realized who she must be. He was still holding on as she swung, her sword blurring into the gap between helmet and the shoulder plate of his lorica. The shock as it sliced muscle and shattered bone vibrated up her arm. Blood sprayed as she wrenched the sword free.

As the slain man fell his weight dragged the split shield from her arm. Eoc Mor stepped forward to cover her with his own. She heard a grunt, turned, and saw him folding as another legionary jerked back his blade. Her instinctive response took off the man's hand.

"Pick up his shield!" came Bituitos's voice at her ear. She looked down and saw Eoc curled in agony as blood poured from a great wound in his armpit. But he was still holding up the shield. As she took it, his fingers released the grip and he fell back with a fierce smile.

Boudica drew a shuddering breath, aware for the first

time that she was growing tired. The Roman line rippled as men at the front stepped back to let others, less wearied, take their places there.

Across the nearest warriors she glimpsed Rigana at the end of the wedge, near the angle where the next began. Helm and shield were both gone, though Calgac was still by her side. But even as she recognized them, she saw the tall warrior begin to fall. She started toward her daughter, stumbled on a body, lurched over it, and trod on another.

Had Rigana even noticed that her protector was gone? Screeching, she gripped her sword two-handed and brought it around in a whirling stroke that took a legionary down. Boudica was an arm's-length away when a Roman from the edge of the next wedge thrust past the edge of the girl's mail from behind. Rigana continued to turn, her bloody sword flying from nerveless fingers in a glittering arc into the mass of enemies beyond.

"You cannot help her!" cried Bituitos as Rigana crumpled. "We'll be surrounded! Come away!"

But he stayed with her as Boudica shoved past another Briton and over a body to straddle the convulsing form of her child. Romans drew in to either side of them as the two wedges ground forward. Black wings thundered in Boudica's ears, but her vision was all red, red as her daughter's blood soaking into the ground.

Her lips curled back and the Morrigan screamed.

*T*he scream held all the world's anguish, and fury, and loss. Men on both sides dropped their weapons, hearing that cry. Lhiannon felt her heart stop. For the space of a long breath nothing moved on the battlefield.

Then, slowly, the Roman wedges began to push forward once more. Only at one point was there a knot of resistance, where the flanks of two wedges joined. The massed men swayed and swirled; even from here she could hear their cries, but presently the struggle eased and she knew that whatever valiant warriors were fighting there had been overcome.

And with that, the Celtic resistance began to unravel

like a knot of yarn when one pulls the central strand. As the Roman advance resumed, the remaining Britons scattered, throwing down their shields. And now at last the Romans broke ranks to pursue.

"It's over—" Brangenos took her arm. "We must go."

"But the wounded," she said distractedly. "We cannot leave—"

"They are safe," his harsh response silenced her. "The Romans will not touch them now."

And looking beyond him she saw the blood where each man had received the mercy stroke. She felt as if he had struck her to the heart as well.

"May the Goddess in Her mercy receive them," she murmured. "If She has any mercy . . . If She cares . . ."

As Brangenos dragged her up the slope Lhiannon heard screaming. Those Britons who had managed to get beyond the line of wagons were streaming across the fields, pursued by Roman cavalry. But the great mass of men were trapped, trampled by their fellows or falling to Roman swords. And not content with killing warriors, the legionaries were pulling women and children from the wagons and slaughtering them as well.

Lhiannon was glad of Brangenos's firm grasp, for by the time they reached the trees she was weeping too fiercely to see anything at all. As she sank down Argantilla came to her, and though Lhiannon knew that she ought to find some words of comfort, it was the girl who cradled the priestess in her arms. She could hear the Druids chanting as they wove a spell of concealment. Was that why the wood was growing so dark around them, or had the death of their hopes taken all light from the world?

THIRTY

*T*he ravens had departed at sunset. As night fell over Manduessedum it was the turn of the wolves. The four-legged kind skulked down from the forest as a waning moon rose above the plain. The Roman wolves prowled the battlefield with torches, dispatching any Britons who still lived and stripping the bodies of gear and gold.

No one had yet searched the woods above the battlefield, but if the fugitives were to reach safety by morning they must leave soon.

"Not until I know what happened to my mother and my sister!" said Argantilla stubbornly.

"They are dead, Tilla." Caw's voice cracked with pain. "You can see what it's like down there!"

"Not all of them, or who are the Romans killing now? But even if you are right, do you want those monsters to defile their bodies? If no one else will search, I will."

At that, Lhiannon roused from her despair. "I promised the queen that I would see you safe, and with Brangenos and Caw you will be. Rianor and I will go—we have been trained to pass unseen."

"Take the dog," said Argantilla. "Bogle would track his mistress to the gates of An-Dubnion."

"He may have to," muttered Rianor, but he took the rope from her hand.

"Where'er I bide, my shape I hide." The Druid began to murmur the spell. Lhiannon's blue gown faded into the shadows, and Rianor had covered his white robe with a cloak of checkered browns and greens that blended with the terrain. As they whispered Lhiannon could feel herself becoming one with the night, until there were only two shadows following the pale shape of the great dog.

"No need to fear . . . no one is here . . ."

Only the dead, thought Lhiannon. Of those, there was an abundance, lying with staring eyes and tangled limbs to either side of the line along which the Romans had advanced. The chariot in which Boudica had ridden so triumphantly still stood at the edge of the field, though the ponies were long gone.

She knelt beside the dog. "Find Boudica, Bogle—find her. Find Boudica now—"

The dog gave an anxious whimper, looking around him as if he expected the queen to appear, then began to sniff along the ground. For the first time, Lhiannon felt a flicker of hope.

With the dog for a guide, they did not have to identify each body, though they could not help finding some they knew—Mandos, still holding his beloved sword, and Tingetorix, crushed beneath his horse; Brocagnos and Drostac, neighbors in death as they had been in life. Astonishingly, some still lived. Kitto, the farmer's son, had been felled by a blow to the head and was just regaining consciousness when they found him. Lhiannon kept him with her as they went on.

She found it hard to believe that Bogle could make out any scent above the pervasive reek of blood, but the dog continued to move among the bodies, and when Lhiannon recognized Eoc she knew that Bogle was leading them well.

"The gods reward you—I know you defended her," murmured the priestess, bending to close the staring eyes. Holding Bogle's leash in one hand and Kitto's arm with the other, she went on.

"Here," she said softly as the dog paused, whining. Before them the dead were piled high, Romans mixed with Britons. She tied the dog to a dead man's leg and she and Kitto began to drag the cold bodies to either side.

They found Bituitos first, his mail hacked and a great wound in his chest, and just beyond him, Boudica, crumpled over the body of her daughter in the center of a ring of slain. Rigana was quite dead, but as Lhiannon gently took Boudica in her arms, Bogle surged forward with a muffled bark and began to lick the blood from her face.

"Hush, Bogle, get back, get down!" Lhiannon whispered with a frantic glance toward the Roman torches. The dog crouched, tail wagging. For a moment Lhiannon stared, then pressed her finger to the pulse point in the queen's neck. She could not tell if what she felt was a heartbeat or her own trembling. But she had touched enough dead flesh tonight to realize that Boudica was not quite cold.

"Blessed Goddess, she's alive! Quickly, Rianor, help me lift her."

Kitto took up Rigana's body, and moving with infinite care they started toward the hill. Twice they had to drop flat when Roman searchers came too near, but the very magnitude of the disaster was in their favor. Even the greediest legionary needed time to search all the slain.

As they reached the shelter of the first trees Lhiannon looked back. Beyond the flicker of Roman torches, another figure moved among the dead. Tall and graceful, a glimmer of light followed where it passed. She touched Rianor's shoulder.

"Is that one of our women, walking down there?"

He followed her gaze, swallowed, and then, very softly, whispered the final verse of Brangenos's song—

> *"The Great Queen walks the battlefield*
> *And weeps for all the slain,*
> *To Her embrace their souls they yield,*
> *She takes away their pain."*

The Morrigan weeps . . . thought Lhiannon, and found a bitter comfort in knowing that they did not mourn alone.

*S*he has lost a great deal of blood," said Brangenos as they laid the queen down on the hill.

"Yes—" The fitful moonlight that shafted through the trees showed them the gashes on Boudica's long limbs. Those had mostly stopped bleeding, but there was a deep slash in her side that looked bad. All they could do was to bind the wounds and lay her, wrapped warmly, on a litter of branches. Lhiannon looked up as Caw came back through the trees.

"The Romans are searching the east and south, along the road. We cannot go that way."

"I have hunted all through these hills." Kitto spoke from the shadows where he and Argantilla had been scraping a shallow grave for Rigana. "I can lead you past the Roman fort and around to the west of this ridge. From there we can make our way to my father's farm."

It would appear that the Goddess had not abandoned them entirely. For the first time Lhiannon dared to hope they might escape. To what, was a question for another day.

For Boudica, consciousness returned on a wave of agony. She was lying on something that jerked and swayed; each movement sending agony jolting through every limb. She drew a shuddering breath, felt below her ribs a pain so profound that she could not even scream. The motion stopped and something sweet was forced between her lips. She recognized the taste of poppy seed in honey and presently knew no more.

When again she found herself aware, she thought she was on the ship that had carried her to Avalon. But Prasutagos was beside her, his skin bronzed and his hair burnished to pale gold by the sun.

"I saw you on your pyre. Am I dead, too?" Her heart leaped as he smiled.

"Not yet, my love. You have a way to go." His face began to dim as the motion beneath her increased. She clung to the vision, trying to ignore the persistent gnawing agony.

"Don't leave me again!" her spirit cried.

Darkness swirled between them, but she heard his voice, as through her pain she had heard it long ago—*"Boudica, I am here . . ."*

The next time she woke she was lying in shadow on something soft that did not move. Familiar voices murmured nearby. She must have made some sound, for Argantilla's face swam into view above her.

"Mother! You're awake! How do you feel?"

As if I would rather be whipped again, and weak as a day-old pup, she thought, realizing in just how many places she was hurting now. "The better for seeing you," she said aloud. "Where are we?" she added as Tilla managed a watery smile.

"At Kitto's farm. They have been kind." The girl stopped, swallowed. "Rigana—"

"—is dead. I saw her fall. It was what she wanted." *It is what I wanted, too . . .* Boudica did not let that knowledge alter her smile. It would have been better if she had died on the battlefield. She was a danger to them all. But Lhiannon would never grant her the mercy stroke now.

She found that she could remember the battle quite clearly, and wondered if the trauma to her flesh had somehow insulated her from its terror, or whether the magnitude of the disaster helped her to bear her body's pain.

Argantilla moved aside and she saw Lhiannon, her face gaunt and her eyes shadowed by fatigue. With gentle efficiency the priestess took her pulse and tested the temperature of her brow.

"You have a little fever, but we were able to clean and stitch your wounds while you were unconscious, and they seem to be doing well. Rest while you can. The Romans are searching. We cannot stay here long."

"Are there horses?" Boudica asked.

"We can get them. We could make a horse litter, I suppose . . ." Lhiannon said doubtfully.

"Tie me into the saddle. If I fall, tie me over it. If I die, bury me as you did Rigana," she said baldly. "If you are in danger of being caught, slit my throat and run. I will not be dragged in chains through the streets of Rome."

Lhiannon's lips set, and she touched Boudica's brow once more. "I will not allow you to die. We are making soup. You must drink as much as you are able to build up your blood. We will stay here as long as we can."

The Roman road was closed to them now. Kitto guided them by winding tracks and cowpaths to the farm of his uncle, who in turn passed them on to a foster-brother and so, guided from one friend to the next, they made their way through the lands of the Cornovii and Dobunni toward Avalon.

The countryside was full of rumors. It was said that the commander of the legion in Isca, hearing of the great victory that his fear had kept his troops from sharing, fell on his sword. If so, thought Lhiannon bitterly, that was one Roman officer whom they had managed to kill. The rest of them were vigorously alive, slaughtering anyone they suspected of sympathy for the Killer Queen.

But the Romans had not yet begun to look westward. Most of Boudica's army had come from the south and east, and it was they who were the targets of the legions' wrath. Those Iceni who made it back to their homes might soon wish that they had died on the battlefield.

The fugitives rode slowly by hidden paths, and they encountered no patrols. As they moved on, Boudica seemed to grow stronger. Her wounds were beginning to close. But though she never complained, when they stopped each night she fell immediately into an exhausted sleep, and her color alternated between flushed and pale.

When we get to Avalon, she can rest, thought Lhiannon. *I will make her well.*

The old moon had worn away and was swelling to the full once more by the time they descended the southern slopes of the Lead Hills and saw across the marshes the pointed tip of the Tor.

And so, after everything, I am back at Avalon, thought Boudica.

They had brought her to the apple orchard to bask in the dreaming peace of the afternoon. She wished that she could believe that everything that had happened since she and Lhiannon left this place had been a nightmare. But that would have been to lose Prasutagos. She did not tell Lhiannon, who was working so hard to make her live, that he came to her in her dreams.

Sunlight spangled the grass beneath the apple trees that grew below the Blood Spring. In Avalon the world seemed very fair. But in her homeland things might be otherwise. Was it cowardice to flee what the Romans would do to the Iceni now? At the thought, Boudica started to raise herself, and a wave of anguish felled her once more.

The wounds on her arms and legs were healing, but there was something very wrong within. Perhaps the decision to live would not be hers. And why was she surprised, she wondered when the darkness receded and she was able to focus once more on the leaves. Some fates could not be fought—losing her son, losing Prasutagos, losing the battle for Britannia . . .

Goddess, why did You betray me? Her eyes stung with angry tears. *You promised me victory . . .* But since Manduessedum, the place in Boudica's mind where the Morrigan had been was empty. Perhaps what she thought was the Lady of Ravens had been no more than a delusion born of her own rage, and it was she herself who had betrayed them all . . .

*B*ituitos, look out!" Boudica's cry jerked Lhiannon awake, heart pounding. "So many, damn them—I can't get past their shields!"

Since Manduessedum the priestess had learned to sleep lightly, alert for the first muttering that meant Boudica's fever was rising once more. Brangenos helped to dress her wound, and Coventa or Argantilla could keep watch during the day, but through the nights Lhiannon fought for Boudica's life as fiercely as the queen had battled Rome.

The light of the oil lamp showed her Boudica flailing as if she held a sword. In the hut they shared, two steps took her to her patient's side. She soaked a cloth in cold water and laid it on the queen's burning brow. Bogle, who had risen when she did, rested his head on the pillow.

"Hush, be easy, my dear one. The battle's over. You're safe with me now . . ." Lhiannon judged the time to be near midnight—she could safely let her patient have more willow-bark tea. "Wake now—open your eyes and I will give you something to make it easier." She held the cup to Boudica's lips and the queen swallowed. Her eyelids fluttered and she drank again.

"Damn all Romans . . ." she whispered as Lhiannon eased her back down. "I fought them a whole day. I should not have to do it all over again." She laid her hand on the dog's head.

"Never mind, darling. Eventually the memories will fade. It takes time for the dead to leave us," said Lhiannon. "At first we see them everywhere. But as time passes and the world is changed they withdraw, and we go on."

"Not always," Boudica replied. "And it is not all nightmares. Prasutagos is with me all the time." She stopped. "I'm sorry. I know you don't like to hear me speak of him."

"He was a good man," answered Lhiannon briskly. "But he is dead, and you must think about getting well."

"Perhaps." Boudica sighed. "When we were here before, you found the way to Faerie, and I could not follow you. But I think that where I am going now, one day you will follow me."

Boudica had always been a strong woman with good muscle on her tall frame. With time and childbearing she had even grown matronly, until she lost that softness during the campaign. But now, stark in the lamplight, the good bones of her face stood clear. Lhiannon's belly clenched as she recognized how fever was wearing the flesh away.

"You could still go there," Lhiannon said desperately, trying to deny what she had just seen. "The Faerie queen could heal you, or keep you living until—"

"Until nothing," Boudica cut in. "Life eternal and unchanging, never meeting the ones you loved, never growing wiser, never returning to this world to live anew?"

Lhiannon winced, hearing from Boudica the argument she herself had offered the Faerie queen.

"Would you wish that for yourself, Lhiannon? Why would you want it for me?"

"Never seeing Prasutagos again, you mean?" Lhiannon asked bitterly. "But when he was dying, would you not have taken him anywhere he might live a little longer if you had the chance?"

"Prasutagos was my—" Boudica fell silent, eyes widening as she met Lhiannon's gaze.

Now do you understand? thought the priestess. *Now do you understand that I love you?*

"He was your husband," she said aloud. "Nor did I ever try to part you while he lived. But I will not let him drag you down to death if there is any way you may be saved.

Curse it, Boudica," she added suddenly, "do you *want* to die?"

"Not just at the moment, no," the other woman said honestly. "I didn't want to go into battle, either, but when the time came, I did it. I admit it is easier when a thousand warriors are baying for blood all around you. It is hard to go through that door alone. Prasutagos had to do it, and I had to help him. But you won't help me . . . It hurts, Lhiannon," Boudica said then. "Would you condemn me to live in agony?"

"I daresay it does," the priestess said tartly. "You have always had the constitution of one of your own ponies. Except when you lay in childbed, have you ever known pain? You lived soft for seventeen years and then spent three months in one campaign. What do you know of the long struggle that exhausts the soul?"

Boudica recoiled as each barbed word struck home. Bogle unfolded his long limbs and stood looking from one woman to the other with anxious eyes. A lifetime of anguish the priestess had not known she held was flooding forth, and she could not stem the flow until she was done.

"You lost one battle—I have had to spend all my strength in fruitless magic and see our warriors slain again and again. To fail and die is hard, but it's harder still to fail and fight on, knowing you will probably lose!"

Boudica was weeping silently. Lhiannon felt suddenly sick and old. The hatred she felt for the Romans was a bright, clean thing, a justified rage. What she and Boudica were doing to each other now was the shadow side of love.

But weak as she was, the queen was not yet beaten. After a few moments she took a deep breath and fixed the priestess with the gaze that had commanded an army.

"And what about the things *you* have not dared?" she asked. "When I first came to Mona, your deepest desire was to sit as Oracle—at least"—her lips quirked—"when you were not dreaming of lying in Ardanos's arms. Helve is dead, and you are our High Priestess here. Why haven't you seized the chance to ride the spirit road?"

It was not fair, thought Lhiannon, to use what they had shared against her, but they were both desperate now. What hurt so badly was the truth in Boudica's words. In

Eriu she had learned how to seek illumination through depriving the senses in a darkened room, how to divine by touch, and how poetry might drive the mind past reason to the intuitive leap that brings truth. But since she rode with Caratac she had not used magic to ask any question about whose answer she cared.

I have cut myself off from the ecstasy of the flesh and the spirit both, she realized.

"And if I do . . ." she said slowly, "if I go out and seek the answers I fear, will you fight to live?"

This time, she noted sourly, Boudica's wince did not come from physical pain.

"I will fight," the queen said with a sudden grim resolve, "if, when you stand between the worlds, you will let me question you." There was a long silence. Bogle, sensing that the quarrel was done, gave a gusty sigh and stretched himself on the floor.

"I am sorry, Lhiannon, sorry for everything," Boudica said presently. "I wish you had never returned from Eriu."

"I am not." In the emptiness her fury had left behind Lhiannon glimpsed something that might be peace. This, too, she thought numbly, was the gift of the Morrigan. "I would regret forever not having shared this final battle with you."

"Then you had better give me some more of your magic potion . . ." Suddenly Boudica was very pale.

As the queen's eyes closed, Lhiannon bent over her in sudden fright, but Boudica was still breathing. Why had they wasted this time in hurting each other, the priestess thought despairingly, when this might be all they had?

Lhiannon observed Boudica warily as they settled her litter beside the fire, too anxious for her friend to fear for herself. The queen's fever had risen. She watched with eyes that were far too bright as Lhiannon took her place on the tripod stool Caw had fashioned for the ritual.

You have compelled me to sit here, Lhiannon said silently. *What dreadful answer will you require of me?* For a long moment their eyes held, and Boudica lifted her hand as a warrior salutes one who rides out to face the foe.

The sacred drink burned in Lhiannon's belly, the garland bound her brows. Her finger ached where she had pricked it to add her blood to the water in the blessing bowl. Answers always came most easily when need impelled the questions, and the gods knew they needed wisdom here.

They had gathered for the rite at the foot of the Tor, between the Blood Spring and the Milk Spring. Even here she could feel the energy that spiraled up the hill, and knew it would carry her far and fast. As she drew down her veil, Lhiannon could feel her awareness beginning to shift, and suppressed a tremor of fear.

> *"Soft, how soft the evening air,*
> *Sunset leaves the world more fair,*
> *Peace a blessing everywhere . . ."*

Dusk had left the world in cool shadow beneath a scattering of stars. Despite her anxiety, that peace eased her as Brangenos sang the familiar words.

> *"Now, at the dying of the day,*
> *Our road, a final shining ray,*
> *Between the worlds we find the way . . ."*

Lhiannon felt herself falling, though her body remained poised upon the stool. As from a great distance, she heard Brangenos call.

"Children of Don, why have you come here?"

"We seek the blessing of the Goddess," the others replied.

"Then call Her!"

The many names by which the tribes had called their goddesses rang through the still air, myriad parts building toward a greater whole. Lhiannon felt her identity tremble as if she stood in a strong wind. And then Boudica's voice rose above the others—

"Cathubodva, I call You! Lady of Ravens, You have brought us to this pass. Give us Your counsel now!"

Lhiannon tried to shake her head in denial. Of all the faces the Goddess might wear, this was surely not the one they needed now! But already black wings were beating at her consciousness and bearing it away.

From a great distance she was aware that she was straightening, working her shoulders back and forth, stretching out her arms with a low laugh as the Morrigan came in.

"This horse is not so strong as the other was, but she will serve your need. What would you ask of Me?"

There was an uncomfortable silence, as if the onlookers, having summoned the goddess, were now regretting it. The first to pull himself together was Caw.

"Lady, when will the Roman reprisals be over? When can I take Argantilla home?"

There was another silence. Lhiannon trembled, feeling the Morrigan's amusement ebb away. What replaced it was pain.

"I shall not see a world that will be dear to me," the goddess keened. "A spring without sowing, an autumn without harvest, women slaughtered in their houses and men in their fields. Danatobrigos burns, and the walls of Teutodunon are cast down. Mars Ultor stalks the land, avenging those who burned in the Roman towns."

Brangenos cleared his throat. "Is there no hope for us, Great Queen? How shall we survive?"

"Even the gods cannot combat necessity," the goddess replied. "Blood feeds the earth, flesh feeds the ravens, and you feed the people, O raven-son, with your songs—" The Druid flinched at the Morrigan's harsh laugh.

"Today you Britons fall, but one day it will be Rome's turn, and when the legions are gone, your stories and your blood will still be here. Again and again you will fall, but something always survives. You were not wrong to make war—you have forced your conquerors to respect you. Now you must bend to the blast, using your wits to scavenge what you can."

It was what Ardanos had said, and Lhiannon did not like it any better knowing that the Morrigan agreed.

"The blood of my thousands has already fed Manduessedum's field," Boudica cried. "What can I offer to save those who remain?"

"Your own . . ." The answer fell into the silence like a

stone. In that hidden place in which her spirit sheltered, Lhiannon began to wail as the goddess used her lips to pronounce Boudica's doom. "Your own oath binds you. The blood of the ruler is the final sacrifice."

Argantilla voiced the protest that Lhiannon's heart was screaming, but the Morrigan's cry was louder.

"Do you not, even now, understand? I am the moan of the dying warrior and the shout of the one who slays him; I am the scream of the woman in childbed and her baby's first cry. Fear my fury, for without balance, it will destroy the world. Only from the Cauldron of Dagdevos can your people be reborn!"

The Cauldron was the Blood Spring.

Lhiannon could not deny the words that had come from her own mouth, though she would rather have sewn her lips shut than speak them. This time it had been given to her to remember not only what the Morrigan had said, but the emotion behind it, the terrible outpouring of love and pain. But in giving the goddess a voice she had done all she could bear. And so it was Brangenos's disciplined calm that ruled them as they prepared for the ritual.

In frozen silence, Lhiannon followed Boudica's litter as Caw and Rianor bore it to the pool. There was too much light, she thought as they set it down. The sparkle of sunlight on water hurt her eyes. Boudica's hair flamed upon the pillow, her face seemed lit from within.

She seems so peaceful, thought the priestess despairingly. The queen looked as she had before the battle, all her forces focused toward one goal. *Perhaps,* thought the priestess, *it is I who bears her fear*... But whether that was the Morrigan's punishment or her mercy, she did not know.

Coventa took her arm and helped her to sit down. Caw had moved to his usual place beside Argantilla, and the two Druids stood together nearby.

"Tilla," the queen said softly. "Come here, darling, and listen to me. I wish so much that I could stay with you. I think that you and Caw will have beautiful children. You cannot go back to Danatobrigos just yet, but if the gods accept my offering it may be safe one day.

"You must take the torque with you." She bent her head so that her daughter could twist the woven golden wires that formed the neck ring. They did not want to give, and in the end Brangenos had to ease his dagger under one of the terminals and cut it free.

"Perhaps it is as well," said the queen as Argantilla sat back with the two pieces in her hand. "I think it will be a very long time before a prince of our people wears such a torque again. But it should go home. Bury it in Iceni earth, and my spirit will go with it to watch over you."

"We will build a mound above it and our people will bring offerings to honor you!" the girl said passionately.

"No!" cried the queen. "If you do, the Romans will find it, and you! The place and manner of my death must remain a mystery. Hide the torque in some secret spot that no one knows . . . But make my pyre atop the Tor, and the wind will carry my ashes throughout the land. I took oath to the Iceni, but I fought for all Britannia."

So had Caratac, thought Lhiannon, but he had refused the final sacrifice. If he had offered his blood in that last battle would Boudica have to do so now?

For a long moment the queen cradled the girl's fair head against her breast. Then her hand fell. Argantilla straightened, weeping, and Caw took her in his arms.

"Lhiannon," Boudica whispered then, and the priestess forced her limbs to bear her to the queen's side. "We had an agreement. You fulfilled your part. I ask you now to release me from mine."

"The goddess has absolved you," Lhiannon said stiffly. "You need no permission from me."

Boudica shook her head with a little smile. "No—only forgiveness. My dear one, you have been better to me than I deserved. I leave you my love . . ."

But still, you leave me . . . Lhiannon thought as their eyes met. "We do what we must," she said aloud. *I must let you go, but I will not assent to it, and it will be long before I forgive the gods.*

Boudica reached up, and for the last time Lhiannon took her in her arms, heart wrenched anew as she felt how thin the frame beneath the white gown had grown. As she released her, Boudica sighed deeply and her eyes closed.

"Lady, how is it with you?" Brangenos asked after a few moments had passed.

"I feel very light." Boudica's voice held wonder. "And there is no pain. I think that we had best act quickly or I will go with my work undone."

"The ritual requirements are clear," Brangenos said softly. "The ruler's blood must be shed. It must be a willing offering. The water that comes from the spring will carry it into the land."

"Then let it be so . . ." The queen held out first one arm, then the other, and with a swift stroke he drew the sharp knife lengthwise along the veins. Blood sprang crimson upon the white skin, spiraling downward to drip onto the stones.

"Now, put me into the pool . . ."

*B*ehold the Cauldron of the Mighty Ones." The Druid's voice seemed to come from very far away.

Boudica winced as the litter was picked up and maneuvered down the steps into the pool. Her arms stung where the knife had cut, but by comparison with what she had borne for so long, she scarcely recognized the sensation as pain. She was bleeding freely, lightheaded already as the strength left her limbs. Her blood bloomed in a crimson cloud through the iron-tanged water, flowing onward through the channel where it left the pool, spreading like a mist of light.

She had hoped to hear the voice of the goddess within once more, but at least She had spoken through Lhiannon. *If it is permitted*, Boudica sent a last thought toward her friend, *I will come to you as Prasutagos came to me . . .*

"Let the waters receive you . . ." Brangenos's voice shook. "This is the Cauldron of Dagdevos, in which you shall be reborn."

Lady of Ravens, the queen added silently. *I am Your sacrifice.*

"Boudica," came the answer, "*you are My victory.*"

The cool waters closed over her and carried her away.

*   *   *

... And she was Elsewhere, standing naked in a flowing stream, whole, strong, and not the self she knew.

With a shock of recognition Boudica understood that she was one with the Morrigan. In sheer relief, She threw back Her head and laughed, and like an echo, heard deeper laughter answering. *He* was standing on the shore, blond and burly, leaning on His club, His other weapon making a tent of the absurdly short tunic he wore.

"Dagdevos," She challenged Him. And the part of Her that was Boudica recognized Prasutagos smiling through the god's eyes.

She scooped up water and splashed it between her thighs, the touch sending a tingle of sensation across Her skin. She looked at Him again. He had stripped off his tunic and laid his club aside. Erect and ready He strode into the water, planted His feet in the streambed, and drew Her into His arms.

"Now is the hour of our coming together." His deep voice rumbled against Her hair. "Let Your rage be satisfied. Release the raven and become the dove, and let the destruction end. Accept the woman's offering."

He lifted Her and She swung up Her leg to hold Him, giving and taking, Her passion arousing His power, His peace transmuting Her anger to love, until they shuddered at last to equilibrium.

And as the waters of the sacred spring bore the queen's blood to the earth of Britannia, the power that flowed from Avalon began its healing.

EPILOGUE

Lhiannon Speaks

*D*arkness has fallen, and the wind whines in bare branches like Boudica's hounds. At this season the Morrigan rides, but I do not welcome Her. Since our community was established at Vernemeton the Goddess has spoken through me many times, but never again have I opened my soul to the Lady of Ravens.

And yet She spoke truly. After Boudica died, I sent to bring Caillean from Eriu. We lived for a time in a stone tower on the northern coast, but even in that lonely place I heard rumors of the terror that followed the battle at Manduessedum. Governor Paulinus sought to restore his lost honor with fire and sword, and by the next summer scarcely a farmstead was left standing in the Iceni lands. But the procurator who replaced Decianus Catus understood that Roman crimes had driven the people to desperation, and he stopped the governor before he destroyed Britannia. And gradually, peace began to return.

Even now, much of Boudica's kingdom lies desolate. But Argantilla and Caw went back eventually and built a house near where Danatobrigos once stood, where they scratch a living from the soil. The Romans have rebuilt their ravaged cities. Camulodunum and Londinium and Verulamium are bigger than ever, and as Caratac feared, the children of our chieftains are learning Latin and becoming citizens.

The following spring, the priestesses left pregnant by Roman rape bore their bastards. Some of the girl-children were drowned, but the boys were claimed by the Society of Ravens. Coventa gave birth to a son as she had dreamed, and died in the bearing. Bendeigid has raised him as his own.

In the years after the attack on Mona, Ardanos traveled

Britannia ceaselessly, visiting those of our Order who survived, and in time revealing himself to a few of the more liberal Romans and becoming their ally. I wonder if they have ever realized what a rebel he was when he was young. The Goddess knows he is a model for what the priest of a conquered people should be today.

I suppose his submission has been justified. Four years after the burning of Lys Deru, he got permission to establish a community at Vernemeton, where our priestesses might live secluded from the world. The Romans seem to have quite forgotten the dark-robed furies who terrified them on the shore of Mona, and think us kin to their Vestals.

The priests chose as Ardanos bade them, and made me High Priestess as Lady Mearan once foretold. Some days I myself find it hard to remember exactly how it came about. But I suppose the Goddess approves, for I have grown old in office. Caillean has become as fine a priestess as any we ever had on Mona, though I do not think the Council of Druids will accept her as my successor. She thinks for herself, and that is never popular with men.

I have never gone back to Avalon, and now I do not have the strength for the journey even if I should wish to go. Though Caillean loves me too well to admit it, I think that soon I will find the way to follow Boudica. I trust she has forgiven me for trying to hold her, as I have forgiven her for leaving me. I have done what I could to preserve the faith of our people, though there were times when I myself had none. Our ways will not be lost.

The procession that escorts the White Mare is coming, but louder than their voices is the song of the wind. That wind carried Boudica's ashes throughout Britannia. Our people do not speak her name where Romans can hear, but she is remembered.

Rome will not give our women even so much freedom as our men are allowed. But once, a woman stood against the might of Rome, and for one shining, terrible summer, had the victory.

AFTERWORD

*W*hen Marion Zimmer Bradley's health began to fail during the writing of *The Forest House*, she asked me to help her finish the book. Marion's invention of the Society of Ravens, a secret society of the sons of the Druid priestesses raped by Roman soldiers during the attack on the Isle of Mona, placed the novel firmly at the end of the first century. But the backstory of *The Forest House* offered even more enticing possibilities, including the Roman conquest of Britannia and the rebellion led by Queen Boudica, and Marion and I promised each other to tackle that story one day.

In this book, I have had the opportunity to do so at last. In the process, I struggled with a number of problems that the writer of fantasy is usually free to ignore. No matter how bravely Boudica fought, or how powerfully the Druids worked their magic, history tells us that they failed, as other brave and good people have failed throughout the centuries, or worse still, in the process of resisting commited the same kinds of crimes as their enemies.

Why do the gods allow such injustice? Can destiny overwhelm both virtue and free will? I do not pretend to have solved problems with which humans have struggled throughout history. I can only hope that the book will cause you, as it did me, to spend some time thinking about the questions.

The events in the novel are based on historical and archaeological evidence, where known. The Claudian invasion of Britain took place in 43 CE. Boudica's rebellion and the Roman attack on the Druids occured simultaneously sometime in 60 CE. For photos of some of the sites, a timeline, and further background information on how

I worked it all out, and information on the other Avalon novels, see my Web site—www.avalonbooks.net.

We are currently experiencing a revival of interest in Boudica. Recent biographies include those by M. J. Trow, Graham Webster, and Vanessa Collingridge. For a different view of the Roman conquest, try *The Heirs of King Verica*, by Martin Henig. In researching the book I also made use of the many Web sites devoted to British antiquities on the Internet. In particular, for the site and sequence of Caratac's last battle, I drew on the work of Graham J. Morris: www.battlefieldanomalies.com/caradoc/index.htm.

I am grateful to the staff at the Sedgeford Historical and Archaeological Research Project (SHARP), especially Dr. Neil Faulkner, for taking the time from their work to talk to me when I visited the sites I call the "Horse Shrine" and "Danatobrigos." For information on finds in the area, see the BBC production *Boudica's Treasure*; the book *The Sedgeford Hoard*, by Dennis Megan and Neil Faulkner; and the SHARP Web site, www.sharp.org.uk. The details of Prasutagos's building projects are based on East Anglian Archaeology Publications Reports EAA 30 and 53, describing excavations in Norfolk. Any mistakes in interpretation are my own.

If you should wish to visit the (most probable) site of Boudica's last battle, just outside of Mancetter, I recommend the Old House B&B (www.theoldhousebandb.co.uk). The battlefield is on the other side of the A-5 from the B&B.

—Samhain 2006

Read on for an exciting excerpt
from the next novel in the Avalon saga,

MARION ZIMMER BRADLEY'S
SWORD OF AVALON

by Diana L. Paxson

Coming from Roc in December 2009

Morgaine speaks:

They say that the old sleep little, as if they have no need of rest with the body's last sleep so near. Whether it is age or the weight of memory that keeps me restless, at night my sleep is broken, and I rise early. This morning I left my bed without waking my maidens, to walk by the Lake just at that misty hour between the dark and the dawning, when the birds sing forth their promise that the light will return. As the first rays of the sun glimmered through the clouds, a gleam of light pierced the waters, and for a moment I saw the blazing length of the Sword.

Time converged around me, and once more I was in the Sacred Barge of Avalon, and Arthur lay dying in my arms. Lancelet cast Excalibur into the Lake and saw it received by the Lady. My breath stopped as I waited to see if Her hand would reappear, returning the Sword from the depths to choose a new king to save Britannia.

Vision followed vision, but what I saw was fire—the metal first forged in the fires of heaven, hailed as a thing of power by the folk who dwelled on the chalk before ever a Druid or Adept from the drowned islands came to these shores. I saw the fires of the forge in which a master smith, fleeing his people's doom, had made it into a sword to fit the hand of a king. Hidden and renewed, broken and re-forged, in the time of Britannia's greatest need it had returned to bring victory.

I stared, and clearing vision showed me the surface of the Lake, gray and still once more. Then I wept, and even that image blurred. The dark people of the hills who had been the Sword's keepers were gone. Water, not fire, hid the blade Arthur wielded, and there was no king of the an-

cient line to call it forth again. The gleam that I had seen had been the leap of a fish, no more.

And yet as I began to walk again I realized that the tears in my eyes were not from despair. When Excalibur went into the Lake, I knew it for the end of an age, the loss of all that I had loved. And yet behind its shield of mist, Avalon endures. The star-steel was only metal until the skill of a smith and the passion of a priestess ensouled it. What they did in those days, when the world they knew seemed doomed, may be done again if the Lady of the Forge takes up her hammer once more.

The Sword is gone, but hope does not die.

Fire.

The acrid reek of burning thatch catches in her throat; then smoke sets her coughing, panic flaring along her limbs as red light flickers across the floor. She snatches up the wailing child. The hide across the door is wrenched away. Beyond, she glimpses figures and the gleam of blades.

A woman screams with a shrill intensity that cuts across the clash of bronze weapons and battle cries. The scream is her own, and yet the self that knows this is somehow detached from the hot breath of the flames. The baby coughs and struggles, strong limbs, strong spirit fighting to survive. A roof beam crashes across the doorway and she whimpers, racked by an anguish beyond her body's pain. She stares through the flames, seeking an escape, and enemy faces leer back at her. She recoils and sinks to the floor, smoke stealing her breath as a cry severs soul from sense—"So dies the Son of a Hundred Kings!"

And awareness whirls outward—she sees the thatched roofs of the royal enclosure collapsing as the fire spreads; the bullhorns mounted above the great gate crash down. The bodies of warriors, startled naked from sleep, lie scattered on the bloody ground as enemies pile up the looted cauldrons of bronze, the fine weavings, the cups and ornaments of gold.

Time speeds, and the charred timbers of Azan-Ylir become sodden lumps that are soon covered by green. But the flames spread, and the Ai-Giru, the Ai-Ilf, the Ai-Utu, and then the Ai-Akhsi and the Ai-Ushen and even the Ai-

Siwanet far to the north are engulfed in turn. The tribes of the Island of the Mighty tear at one another's throats as if starving dogs as generations pass. And when ships with painted sails approach the white cliffs of the island, there is no one to face the fair-haired warriors who leap onto the sand, their striped and checkered garments swirling about their knees. They rampage across the countryside, burning whatever the earlier wars have left, and the songs, the arts, the wisdom of the Seven Tribes are as if they had never been.

"Goddess, what can save us?" her spirit cries.

And in answer she hears a call. "From the stars will come the Sword of the King!"

The bed was too soft. In the house of the Lady of Avalon, even the high priestess slept on a pallet of straw on the floor. At Azan, the bed place reserved for honored guests was of a different order entirely—a yielding mattress of goose down laid atop one of straw, supported by a web of rope strung across a frame. Each time Anderle or Ellet turned, it creaked and swung. Anderle had expected to fall asleep quickly. The younger priestess had nodded off as soon as they retired, but Anderle lay wakeful, listening to the snorts and whistles coming from the other sections. The partitions of wicker or woven wool between the posts and the wall did little to muffle the sound.

Even the disciplines that were a part of the training of a priestess had brought her no more than a few hours of rest. True sleep eluded her, and at length she sighed and carefully levered herself upright. Ellet stirred with a mumbled query.

"Sleep, child," she whispered. "I am only going to relieve myself. There's no need for you to get up, too." It was true enough that with the baby sitting on her bladder it had been months since she had been able to sleep the night through, but whether the reason was discomfort or anxiety, Anderle could no longer bear to lie still.

She parted the hangings that defined their sleeping place and carefully stepped over Durrin, who snored on a straw pallet just outside. The dim glow of the coals gave enough light for her to thread her way between the warriors who lay by the fire, and eased out past the hide that curtained the main door.

It was the still hour just before dawn, dank and chill. Fog curled among the buildings. Anderle took a deep breath as she emerged from behind the wicker screen and coughed as an acrid reek caught in her lungs. Shock pebbled the skin of her arms. This was no fog! This was smoke, illuminated by the first faint glow of a fire. The thatch of one of the smaller roundhouses was burning. For a moment despair paralyzed her limbs. It was the scene of her vision. But in her vision *she* had not been here.

She swallowed a shout as she lumbered back across the yard. What good was a warning if she could not use it to change the outcome? Swiftly she slipped through the door, bending to shake the shoulder of the first sleeping warrior.

"Up, man! There are foes within the ward. But quietly, and you may take them by surprise before they know you are warned."

She felt rather than saw the ripple of motion as the word was passed. Men leaped to their feet, scrambling to snatch swords from their pegs on the posts and shields from the wall. Anderle clung to one of the uprights. Indoors, she risked being trapped in a burning building, but would she be safer outside? No man of the tribes would knowingly harm the Lady of Avalon, but even if she had been wearing the blue robes of her calling instead of a shift and a shawl, they might not have recognized her in the dark. She tried to convince herself that she was safest here.

Metal clanked and someone swore. She heard Uldan's voice, low but firm, and felt her galloping heartbeat slow. The lack of imagination that had made him ignore her warning kept him from panic now. Tall forms shoved past her, gathering in front of the doorway. Then a curt command sent them pounding forward. There was a cry, a clash of bronze. "Ai-Zir!'Ware the horns of the bull!" came the full-throated roar.

"Fear the fang! Ai-Ushen!" was drawn out in a wolf's shrill howl in reply.

She should have expected it. The tribe to the north was under constant pressure from mountain dwellers who had suffered worse still. No doubt the heifers of which Irnana had boasted were already on their way to the Ai-Ushen fields. Productive land was the greatest treasure, but gold and bronze could buy food from those who could still get grain to grow.

Someone stirred up the hearthfire and she met Ellet's horrified gaze. Durrin was struggling to his feet, blinking at the commotion around him. "Get our cloaks! Irnana, are you here?"

But the king's wife was already pushing toward her. Red hair streaming wildly, she clutched at Anderle's arm. Outside the shouting was louder, the scent of smoke stronger now.

"Help me get to Mikantor!"

For a heartbeat the priestess stared. Then she remembered that the child slept with his nurse in one of the other roundhouses. Anderle quailed at the turmoil she could hear outside. Her spirit, if not her body, had been weakened by Kiri's cosseting. No use to protest that she was unable to help—Uldan's men were fighting; Ellet and Durrin looked to her for direction. Pregnant or not, she would have to use whatever power she had. *And if the Lady of Avalon cannot find a few spells for protection*, she thought then, *our line deserves to fail.*

"We will go together. Be still and remember your training!" she said aloud. "Take a deep breath; blur the air around you. If we rush out in a panic, they will cut us down!" She hoped Zamara had the sense to stay inside. Her house was in the center of the enclosure, marked by the standard on its pole. Even the Ai-Ushen wolves would not dare to kill a queen.

We must be shadows . . . She drew power from the earth and wrapped it around them, extending her inner awareness to sense the flow of energies outside. There was no one near. She squeezed Irnana's arm and drew her through the door.

The body of one of the house guards lay before it and other forms littered the ground nearby, but near the main gate bronze flared as struggling figures moved in and out of the fitful glow. A woman screamed as a warrior forced her down, tearing at her clothes. Anderle's gut twisted as a child's wail went on and on.

"Which house?" she whispered as they edged forward, and Irnana pointed toward a small building behind the house of the queen.

Behind them light flared as someone set a torch to the thatch of Uldan's feasting hall. Men were running in and out of the building, bundling goods and gear into the woolen hangings that had insulated the walls. If Irnana had not begged her for help, she would have been inside. Could either rank or magic have protected her against men maddened by battle lust and greed?

They had nearly reached the house where Mikantor slept with the other children. Anderle recoiled, hands flashing a gesture of warding as a slight figure darted toward them, then recognized her as one of the maids who had served in the hall.

"My lady, you're safe—" She clutched at Irnana's arm.

"Be quiet, you fool," hissed Anderle. But it was already too late. The girl's movement had caught the attention of one of the warriors as the scurry of a mouse will bring an owl. As the man leaped toward them Anderle tensed, then recognized the bulky figure as the chieftain from Oakhill who had been in the feasting hall.

"Galid!" cried Irnana. "Guard us—I must get to my son!"

The man shook his head, lips curling in a mirthless grin. "Let Uldan's spawn die as my sons died. Uldan has lost the favor of the gods!"

For a moment Irnana stood, staring. "Was it you? Are you the traitor who let in the wolves?"

Galid's gaze kindled as he looked her up and down, firelight glinting on the bands that confined the many braids of his hair. "Indeed, and you are a bleating ewe, but a pretty one. I'll spare you to warm my bed if you behave."

Fury blazed in her face—no, Anderle could see it so clearly because the Children's House was on fire. As Galid reached for her, Irnana ducked under his arm and dove through the doorway.

As the man turned back Anderle drew herself up, rage and terror beating in her veins. "Do you dare to oppose the power of Avalon!"

His eyes widened. What was he seeing? This was the

first time Anderle had put on the glamour of the Dark Mother in earnest. She had not known whether she could, especially now. It was need that had unleashed the power, observed that part of her mind that was not gibbering, need channeled by the disciplines of Avalon. She had never truly *needed* that power before.

"You will stand aside," she said in a compelling voice. "We are not your enemies."

Her heart leaped as she realized that the cruel triumph in his face was giving way to fear. She turned to follow Irnana through the door.

"Anderle, it's too late!" Durrin grabbed her arm. Heat seared her face, and she realized that not only the thatching but the walls were aflame. Had smoke already overwhelmed those within? She reached out with her spirit and heard a child's wailing cry.

So dies the Son of a Hundred Kings!

"No!" Anderle denied the words that reverberated in memory. The smoldering hide that curtained the door was pulled aside. Through a swirl of smoke she glimpsed Irnana with her son clasped to her breast.

"Save him!"

**COMING SOON
IN HARDCOVER**

MARION ZIMMER BRADLEY'S
SWORD OF AVALON

DIANA L. PAXSON

Marion Zimmer Bradley's legendary saga of
Avalon's extraordinary women continues
with a tale of fiery visions, a lost king,
and a forthcoming destiny...

A boy raised in secret after traitors kill his
parents will return to Avalon—and when he
does, he'll be faced with a formidable task:
to prove his worth as a son of the kings
and priestesses of his land and lead his
followers to victory, wielding the newly-
forged sword Excalibur.

**Available wherever books are sold or at
penguin.com**